HE WILL GET YOU

An absolutely gripping crime thriller with a massive twist

CHARLIE GALLAGHER

Detective Maddie Ives Book 5

D0514127

JOFFE BOOKS

First published in Great Britain 2020
Joffe Books, London

**Please join our mailing list for free Kindle
books and new releases.**

www.joffebooks.com

ISBN 978-1-78931-398-7

AUTHOR'S NOTE

I am inspired by what I do and see in my day job as a front-line police detective, though my books are entirely fictional. I am aware that the police officers in my novels are not always shown positively. They are human and they make mistakes. This is sometimes the case in real life too, but the vast majority of officers are honest and do a good job in trying circumstances. From what I see on a daily basis, the men and women who wear the uniform are among the very finest, and I am proud to be part of one of the best police forces in the world.

Charlie Gallagher

CHAPTER 1

'I see the world. I see the people in it, but from a distance. I am detached, part of nothing. Invisible.' He had been pacing. He stepped close to her now, to linger on her soft skin. He breathed in deeply.

'I saw two people embrace while I walked here, true love blooming beside the canal — the rest of their lives starting, maybe. Who knows? But they didn't see me. No one sees me. You didn't see me . . .' He raised the blade, revelling as she flinched away from it as much as her constraints would allow. The coarse material that served as a gag pinched her cheeks to a shocking white against the deep red smudge that was left of her lipstick. A tear had been building and it leaked now, bursting onto her cheek at first, but it slowed. He let out a rushed sigh in excitement and moved to lick it from her face. He closed his eyes to savour the taste. When he opened them again, he focused on the tip of the blade. He rested it against her throat.

'But you see me now,' he said. She stared back, unblinking, and their eyes locked in a moment of utter perfection. Her eyes were big and beautiful. They studied every part of him. He not only existed to her but he held her life in his hands. He was *everything* to her.

He jerked the blade forward, shifting his weight as he did to give the blow extra strength. He broke her stare by closing his eyes. He could feel the blade finding its way and his hands were instantly slick with hot fluid. His step forward into her was like an embrace. She was bound at the wrists, her hands tugged upwards, her whole form presented to him on tiptoe.

He waited for the noises to stop. He kept his eyes closed. The hot fluid still came. He could feel it cascade down his front while her knees twitched against his groin as much as her tied ankles would allow. Her final dance lasted just a few seconds and he inhaled the whole time, absorbing her life, her beauty . . . her fear.

She slumped into him.

'Okay . . . It's okay. Let's get you right, shall we?' He unwrapped the binding from around her hands. She was heavy as she rocked forward. He was desperate not to drop her — she didn't deserve that — as he lowered her to the floor. She was close enough to the back wall of the apartment that he could use it to take some of the weight. He left her in a seated position against the wall. The binding that had been around her wrists he now put over her head to pull up under her chin. It did the job of holding her head up in a more natural stance against the pristine paint of the walls. The paint might have even been fresh, a few weeks old at most. The whole place smacked of newly done, like a show home. He cut the restraint around her ankles and splayed them out to a wider base so she wouldn't fall. He arranged her hands so they sat in her lap, one holding the other, then cut the gag from her mouth.

He moved back almost as far as the door. He was pleased with himself. She looked just like she was sitting, waiting. Now her head was slightly raised, the wound to her neck was visible, but it might not be the first thing you saw. She hadn't lost all of her beauty, her natural grace. There was something of her spirit left, perhaps. It had been strong. She was a powerful woman. It was the reason she had been chosen.

He suddenly felt hot — it happened when he was excited. He needed to take a moment, to get back control. There was work to be done. He couldn't lose concentration.

He held his breath and used the moment of stillness to savour what he had done. The seated woman peered right back with eyes that were still open, one more so than the other. But the focus had gone. Everything had gone.

He was invisible again.

CHAPTER 2

The patrol car passed under the barrier to be absorbed by the shadows of the multi-storey car park beyond. PC Vince Arnold had his window down. The acoustics changed instantly as the throb of the diesel engine bounced off the concrete walls and ceiling and the squeal from the tyres was shrill as he turned for the first ramp. Vince's patrol sergeant, Tim Betts, cussed as the smartphone slipped from his lap, where he was trying to pinch and zoom to read the tiny text. The details of the call to which they were responding had been sent to his screen. He scooped it back up and sighed at the content.

'From what we have here, it could be anything from someone trying car doors to a suicide risk. A member of the public has seen a sus male ducking down between cars, leaning out over the edge and generally running about.'

'Sounds perfectly normal behaviour for in here,' Vince said. 'You get a lot of skags and drinkers using the stairwells. They all move like that . . . feral!'

Tim gave up with the phone. He muttered a profanity and threw it onto the dash in front of him.

'I see the exercise is helping with the stress!' Vince said.

'What?'

'Exercise. I told you it would help. I can see you have ignored me completely.'

'Who's got time for exercise?' Tim snapped.

'All of the calm people you see.' Vince winced at the sound of a plastic bumper scraping concrete.

'You'll see how calm I am if I have to write up another damage report for a car *you* were driving.'

Vince waved him away. 'What is it they say about making an omelette? You have to break some eggs, right?'

'You're not making an omelette, Vince. You're just driving through a car park.'

'Where the ramps don't need to be this steep.'

The car fell silent for a few moments as both men tried to pick out their suspicious male from the shadows. Vince's starting pace had been just above a walk, but his speed was increasing the higher they went. He had been bored with this call long before they had entered the car park. Skags trying door handles for a bit of loose change was an everyday occurrence and this was the perfect place. There was a concentration of cars parked in the shadows of a poorly designed structure with an elevated view out onto the approach. A marked police car would have been seen in plenty of time and the way out on foot was in the opposite corner to the vehicle entrance. Vince had once written a business case himself to the council lamenting the poor lighting and lack of CCTV cameras. Of course, it had been ignored. He was younger in service and keener then. He wouldn't waste his time now.

The engine chugged as they turned towards daylight and Vince had to change down the gears. The final ramp seemed steeper, the emergence into daylight also brought with it a deluge of raindrops that woke the windscreen wipers and removed all visibility. Vince put his window back up.

'Well, if he's up here, we know it's a suicide risk.' There were only three cars on this level, hardly worth it for the opportunist thief. Two of the cars were close to a covered door that led out into the stairwell. The third was in the far corner. Vince rolled towards that one.

'Over there!' Tim pointed across Vince, who squinted out into the deluge. He brought the car to a stop, rolling his window back down for a better view. The two cars parked over to his right were both facing out over the town. The rain seemed heavier still, the individual drops visible as they thundered against the tarmac, filling the cabin with white noise. The door to the stairwell was between the two cars. It was a double door and the left one was falling shut.

'What did you see?'

'I don't know. Something moved.'

'They're messing with us. They'll be long gone. It's a lot quicker to the bottom down those stairs than it would be in this.'

'Drop me over there. I'll take a walk through and meet you at the bottom. Get the registrations of the cars we have up here and we'll run them through — just in case there's a high-risk misper who's out in his car. You never know. And check if any of the cars are insecure.'

Now it was Vince's turn to sigh. 'Yeah, okay. I'll meet you at the bottom. Make sure you hold your breath though, I can smell those piss-soaked steps from here!'

Tim scowled as he swung his door out into the rain. The door was soaked instantly and Vince felt freezing water ricochet onto his bare arm. Tim's rain jacket was on the back seat, its owner bent forward by the rain as he tugged open the back door to get to it. Vince couldn't resist. He lifted the clutch to roll the patrol car forward a few paces. He watched in his mirror as the sergeant jogged to catch up. Vince moved the car further to stay out of his reach, then dropped the passenger window. 'There's no time to be getting your rain-coat on, sarge! There's police work to be done!' He was still booming laughter when his sergeant reached into the open door and pulled out his coat.

'I love being crewed up with you, Vince,' he muttered.

'You remember that when you do my PDR!' Vince replied.

'Oh, I'll remember this, don't you worry about that.' The door thudded shut and Vince watched his sergeant walk towards the double doors. He was pulling on his jacket and struggling with his hood to protect his bald head from the torrent. He was wasting his time — it was already running with water. Vince's chuckles were interrupted by a request over the radio for an update.

'Well, we've been here more than a minute,' he grumbled before reaching for the dash-mounted radio button. 'Yeah control, this is Yankee Four Zero. We are at scene and carrying out an area search. I have sent the sergeant out in the rain to make sure it's a thorough one. We should be updating away shortly.'

'All received!' Vince detected laughter in the operator's voice. He had a laugh himself when he saw Tim Betts, still walking away, extend his arm and middle finger skywards. He would have heard the exchange on the radio clinging to his chest.

Vince moved over to the car that was parked out on its own. He noted the registration number then pulled alongside as close as he could to get a look inside. The windows were misted enough to suggest it had been occupied recently. He couldn't see in. He was going to have to get out of his car. *Dammit!*

He rolled the car back and wrenched up the handbrake. His windscreen became an opaque slither of water the moment the wipers stopped. He pushed the door and the rain forced itself upon him, soaking the side of his face as he stood up.

'Dammit!' he said out loud. The radio on his chest made a noise. He had a direct call. He dropped back into the shelter of his seat and pressed the button to take it.

'Yeah?'

'Vince, there's someone moving down here, but I can't get near them. I'm near the bottom but he's headed back up the stairs, I think. Can you head down from the top on foot, see if we can head him off?' Tim sounded harassed.

Vince peered into the grey torrent. He turned the key and the wipers cleared a distant view of the doors.

'Can do. He better not make me run. I get upset when people make me run.'

'Just block the door. No thinking required. Finally something you're good for.' The radio beeped to confirm the talk-through was over. The voices from the network started back up almost immediately. Vince turned them down.

He parked as close as he could to the stairwell. The door was heavy to open and slow to close. He stopped at the top to wipe the water that was slick on his face and arms. He listened. Any movement in the stairwell would be obvious — there was nothing to deaden sound. All he could hear was the constant rain outside and an irregular dripping pattern where water was finding somewhere to come in. He was standing in a puddle that covered the entrance area and could see smudged but fresh footprints towards the top of the stairs. At least two different people had used them recently. He followed the trail.

Just a few steps down, he froze. A loud *crack* reverberated up the stairwell. It sounded like a car hitting a wall. Then came the sound of a door being flung open and bouncing solidly off the wall. It seemed to have come from the next level down. The footfalls followed immediately, moving up the stairs directly towards him. Vince peered around. There was only time to step into the shadows. The footfalls came closer — someone was taking two steps at a time. There was breathing, too, heavy and panicked. Vince pushed off the wall, timing it so he met the running figure as he reached the top step.

The man shouted in surprise. Vince grabbed the man's right arm with both hands, his grip either side of the elbow to wrap the arm round behind the man's back. He used the man's momentum to force him into the wall. The man's eyes bulged. He was out of breath and wearing just a shirt and trousers. His back was soaked, his shirt stuck to it in a pattern that was more like sweat than rain water. He felt warm, too.

'Get off me! We have to go!'

'What are you up to? Why are you running?' Vince felt him try to snatch his arm away and increased the angle of the hold, knowing it would get him the pain compliance he needed. The man grimaced and pushed himself flatter against the wall.

'They're trying to kill me! You don't understand, they'll kill us both!'

'What are you talking about? Who?'

'Your mate down there! They shot him! I saw it. They want me, they're going to kill me!'

Vince was able to shift his hold so he could keep the tension with one hand. With the other he tore his handcuffs from the holder on the outside of his load vest. He snapped them over the wrist of the arm he had locked in the small of the man's back. He dragged the man a few paces to where he could fix the other end of the cuffs to thick railings. The man's eyes widened.

'What are you *doing*? They're looking for me! They'll find me here! We have to go, you have to get me out of here!'

Vince ignored him. He lifted his hand to his radio to call Tim.

'I wouldn't do that.' A different voice, the tone firm and determined, it came from behind him. Something solid was pushed into the back of Vince's neck, restricting his movement. 'Don't look at me. Right now, I don't have to kill you.'

'Who are you? What's going on?' Vince said. The man he had cuffed was still facing him, his eyes wide with fear. They locked on to Vince's.

'Like I said, right now, I don't have to kill you. Do as I say and that doesn't change. Your mate didn't.'

Vince twitched. There was instant additional pressure on the back of his neck. He bent forward to ease the pain.

'Don't!' the voice warned.

'What did you do to him?'

'He doesn't have to bleed out. But he will if you keep asking questions.'

Vince heard more scuffed steps to his right. Someone stopped short on the steps below, just out of his sight. Vince had to assume they were with the man behind him.

'Put your hands out. Any sudden movements and I pull this trigger.'

Vince hesitated. The initial shock had passed and he was starting to bubble with rage. He told himself that he was in no position to react, that he would get himself killed. His arms were tense as he lifted them away from his body. He felt someone move closer to him and a hand reach round to snap the radio from the clip on his chest, twisting it and pulling it away in one smooth movement like he knew what he was doing. Next, his pockets were patted down and his phones and car keys were removed. He was aware of items being dropped down the stairwell. There was a short delay before he heard them clatter to the ground.

'When I tell you, turn to the left and walk to the wall. As close as you can get. Face it. Wait for me to tell you to move again. Then you can go to your mate. If you turn — if I think you're going to turn — I will shoot you in the head. Do you understand?'

'Where is he?' Vince felt the pressure release from the back of his neck. He straightened up. His lower back ached from the tension. He was still looking at the man he had cuffed to the railings, whose lips bumped together until he managed to make them form words.

'You can't leave me! You're the fucking police! He's going to kill me!'

'Shut up!' the voice was louder behind him. Vince saw a black blur in his peripheral vision. The man recoiled, leaning back and raising the one arm that was free. 'Now, turn slowly to your left and stand against the wall. Do not make me kill you. I will not hesitate.'

The instruction was for Vince, spoken directly in his ear. Vince turned, breaking away from the pleading look of the stricken man. He took two steps until he was close enough to breathe on bricks that were polished smooth.

'You move when I tell you. Your mate's on the next floor down. Between the first two cars. Take a right out the doors.'

Vince heard more scuffs on the stairs and at least two sets of footsteps came up past him. He heard the door open behind him, the sound of the rain forced itself in to dominate the moment. The door fell shut and it was gone. Seconds ticked by. They felt like an age.

'Can I go?' Vince growled. There was no answer, then the sound of the rain again. He could hear an engine outside, and sloshing water as it pulled up and then revved to pull away. Vince waited, his whole body rigid with tension.

'Look down the stairs. Do not look at me. Go down one floor and out through the door. If you come back into the stairwell, you will be shot. If you so much as look in the direction of the stairs, you will be shot. Go now.'

Vince hesitated. He turned slowly, keeping his gaze towards the stairs. He heard the metallic scrape on the railings but avoided eye contact with the man he had cuffed. When Vince reached the top of the stairs, his hesitancy was gone. He flew down the stairs, jumping down the last few steps onto a landing where he had to turn sharply. He kept his head down, looking only for the doors that led out of the stairwell. He slammed through them, turning hard right as he had been instructed, past the first car on his right.

Tim was instantly visible and lying on his side. The next car along was supposed to be white, but its side ran with enough red spatter to stop Vince momentarily. Then he crashed to his knees beside his fallen colleague to tug him onto his back. His face was an unnatural white, his lips a shade of scarlet and his eyes open and unmoving.

'Tim! Tim, can you hear me?' He shook him by his shoulders. There was no reply, no movement. He leaned down so his cheek almost rested against Tim's lips — no breath either.

Vince scrabbled over his colleague's rain jacket, which hung open. He pulled it apart to unzip his load vest, looking desperately around. Tim's black T shirt beneath was sodden, but it wasn't water. It was sticky. Vince's bloody hand darted to his own load vest — to where his radio had been stripped and thrown down the stairs.

'*Help!*' he bawled. '*Help!*'

He untucked Tim's shirt to assess for wounds. There was a mass of blood. It had pooled under Tim's top and now it was released, slapping on the floor.

Vince heard another *crack*. It was the same sound as before. Vince knew it was a gunshot. He froze for a moment, his eyes searching for someone passing with a phone. Anyone. He heard heavy footsteps running down the stairwell behind him. They came right past his level. He didn't turn around. They didn't stop. Vince had started chest compressions. He knew it was already too late.

CHAPTER 3

Alexander Mason instantly looked different from when Robbie Holt had seen him previously. His usual demeanour was strutting, cocksure. He typically walked with his chest out, his face a confident sneer, while the room and its occupants would bend and flex around him. It was exactly the sort of presence and exterior he needed. Among other business ventures, Mason ran illicit poker games and, despite the pot often containing more money than Robbie had seen in his whole lifetime, the behaviour around those tables was generally impeccable. He had seen a man lose the equivalent of a house and just stand up and walk away.

You didn't cause trouble in Alexander Mason's place.

Robbie could recall only one exception. Mason had dealt with it personally, ushering the man out, his arm round his shoulders, offering condolences for his sudden financial concerns and assuring him they would go somewhere quieter to talk about it. Robbie hadn't seen the final exchange or even been in the room where it had happened, but he had seen Mason walk back out onto the floor ten minutes later, fiddling with the cuffs on his changed shirt, his chest rising and falling with exertion. A drink had been waiting for him.

The interior of the club had already fallen back to a hushed and respectful murmur.

Robbie was just trying to keep his head down. He was only there as part of his schooling. He was on the outside of Alexander Mason and his activities, being moved around the crew to see if he could be trusted. He had only managed to get that close because his half-brother was already part of Mason's inner circle and he was still being chaperoned at all times by Mikey. Mikey was someone Robbie didn't know much about, but he seemed to have the boss's ear and his half-brother's respect.

But today, the man who was always sharply dressed and sharper tongued was different: his shirt was open, his tie hung down in two creased lines as if it had been pulled undone and forgotten about. A curved glass decanter held a deep orange liquid in its belly in front of him. Mason drained the matching glass with a smooth movement. Its base sounded thick and heavy as he slammed it on the table.

'Mikey!' Mason lifted glazed eyes and leaned forward to pour another drink. He glanced at Robbie, then leaned back to swallow again. He bared his teeth as the glass thudded back down.

'Boss?' Mikey said.

'I sent you out for a solution.'

'I know that.'

'And you come back with?'

'There will be a solution.'

'*Will* be?' Mason laughed — there was an edge. There always was with him. His unpredictable nature added to his facade. Robbie had been told to keep his mouth shut before they had stepped into his office and right now, he was thankful.

'My boy is dead. Shackled to a railing in a *shithole car park*!' Mason's eyes didn't seem so glazed anymore as they focused on Mikey. He stepped out from behind his desk to circle him. Robbie took a step back to stay out of his path.

'Left to die! Chained up like some lame dog and shot two hundred miles from home. Do you think this what I wanted for my son? Do you think I should *outlive* my son? That I should be the head of the family still on the day he dies?'

'No, of course—'

'*No!*'

'We need patience.' Mikey spoke facing forward. He seemed to swallow hard. Mason didn't reply straight away. Robbie held his breath, once again thanking his lucky stars that he wasn't the one stood in the circle that Mason was marking out with his slow footsteps.

'Patience?' Mason uttered. He stopped as he passed his desk to top up his glass, keeping hold of it to continue his pacing.

'The police will be expecting a reaction. They'll come for you the moment anything goes down. No one wants the job — not right now. I'm only trying to protect you, boss. I know you want retribution and you'll—'

'Retribution!' Mason gave a grin that barely contained that edge. 'Is that what I want? I just want a man dead. Time was, that was a simple thing. But you come here and you tell me you can't get it done? What's happened to you Mikey? Do I need to be looking elsewhere, asking elsewhere? What about you?' Mason spun to fix his stare on Robbie, his eyes cutting into him like he was reading his thoughts. Robbie was transfixed. He couldn't break away. The pressure to speak was unbearable.

'Mikey's right. We only got one taker and he's not an option . . .' Robbie stammered. He still couldn't break away from Mason. He could feel Mikey's stare. He realised what he had said and shut his mouth so hard, it made his teeth clang. Mason held his gaze until he mumbled on. 'I mean, we dismissed it. Mikey don't like him. He's messy . . . bad.' Robbie stumbled to a finish. Finally Mason broke off, releasing him.

'So there *is* someone?'

Mikey faced his boss, who had stopped to lean on the edge of his desk. 'He's not an option.'

'You making the decisions now, Mikey? No one told me you had taken over?'

'He's not right.'

'He wants the job?'

'He . . . He will do it, but he's not right.'

'I thought I had sent you out to get me options. Turns out I sent you out to make decisions, is that right?'

'I'm just trying to protect you—'

'So you said!' Mason snapped. 'Like some *fucking* child!' He pushed off the table. 'So . . . Tell me about him, then?'

Mikey exhaled.

'Not *you!* I was talking to the boy, here. Seems he understands a simple request. So then, kid, tell me about this option?'

Robbie felt his throat tighten. He could barely speak. He had been told not to and now there was nothing he could say that wouldn't undermine Mikey.

'We met a guy. He used to be someone Mikey worked with. I don't really know much about him — I was only there to listen. Mikey was doing the talking. He made a call. Said this guy ain't right anymore. Not for this.'

'And what about you?'

'Me?'

'So Mikey here made a call that he ain't right. He decides that he ain't right, he makes that decision for me and he walks away. Do you think he can do the job?'

Mikey hadn't moved. Robbie could only see the back of his head. Robbie shrugged. 'He said he could.'

'So who is he then, Mikey? Because a moment ago you were telling me I got no options and yet the kid here is telling me that you have someone. Who is he?'

'There's a guy I have used before. He was a pro — quick and clever with it, but he's not right. Not now.'

'Not now?'

'He's in it for the wrong reasons, for the thrill. It's all a game to him. He likes to make a mess and I hear he's getting worse. He gets off on it, see. It's only a matter of time before he goes too far.'

'A mess? What does that mean, *a mess?*'

'He was proposing to take out a load of random people around your target. He would take them out in a way that was similar enough so the cops would think they've got some serial killer psycho on the go. The target gets taken out in the middle of it all.'

Mason swilled his drink. He lifted it to his nose and inhaled. His eyes peered over the rim of the glass and they seemed to have lost their focus again, as if he was lost in his thoughts.

'That's a solution! That's a good solution!' Mason snapped upright. 'So we have a killer who gets his rocks off by taking an ear as a trophy or stealing their panties or whatever his thing is, and it just so happens that the copper who fed my son to the dogs is caught up in it all. The cops go looking for some serial killer doing what he does and there's no comeback on me at all — no reason to even speak to me! And this all goes down two hundred miles from here? It's perfect!'

'Except he *is* some serial killer psycho, boss. And he's getting worse — he's escalating. He used to be good — the go-to guy — but not anymore. Not for someone like you. Just taking people out isn't enough for him no more. He likes to make a big scene. The cops will be all over him and if they get him, who knows what he'll say in an interview room.'

'You think he would talk about *me?* Has he done that before? Talked to the cops, I mean?'

'Well, no. But he's not been caught before.'

'Not been caught? You're not doing a good job of talking me out of this!'

'We can't control him.'

'I don't want to *control* him! I want to let him off the leash, let him go and be the psycho killer he wants to be! Why wouldn't I? He does what I want and at the same time gives the rest of them a living nightmare with the mess he makes all around him. They'll be chasing their own arses, but they won't be chasing mine.'

'Think on it . . . It's an option, but take some time, I'm asking you. You've just lost your son. This is not the time to be putting your head up. This guy makes a big mess and he's expensi—'

'You think this is about *money?*' Mason's mood switched back to furious. He spat his last word, the phlegm still visible on his lips as he stomped away from his desk to a silver cabinet. One of the doors hung open. He yanked them both so they clattered off the wall. He dragged out two big bags that had been stacked on their ends and threw them on the floor. He scooped one up and pushed it firmly enough into Mikey's midriff that he had to take two steps back. He threw the other one at Robbie's feet. The phlegm played between his lips as he hissed, 'Thinking about it, maybe I should give all the money to the kid. He seems to have the balls in this setup. Or can you go out and make this happen?'

'I'll get in touch. But he said he wanted to speak to you direct before he took the job. It's another reason I wasn't keen.'

Mason's reaction surprised Robbie. His mood changed again and his face lit up. 'I'd like to meet him! We *should* talk. He's doing something for me. Something important. We should talk about what that looks like. I'm liking this bloke more and more, Mikey. Set up the meeting.'

'That's not a good idea, boss. We need to keep you as far aw—'

'*Mikey!*' Mason brought his fist down on the table. His back rose as he breathed hard, his weight on his palms. 'I'm done with you telling me whether you think my ideas are good or not. I'm tired of you second-guessing me and telling me you're protecting me. I've been in this game a long time now — I know how it works. I know how to protect myself. How about you just do as you're told? How does that sound?'

Mikey didn't respond. It was probably wise.

Mason's back was turned. 'Set up the meeting,' he snarled. 'Don't come back here until it is done, you understand me? I want to talk to him. I want him to know that this is personal. He can take out half the whole *world* if he wants to, but I'm only paying him for one name: *PC Vince Arnold*. The one the press are calling a "*hero cop.*" I already paid enough to find him, now I want him to know how we treat hero cops. Now, can I still trust you to deliver messages for me?'

'I'll set up the meet.' He stared at Robbie, who got the hint and picked up the bag at his feet. Mikey was furious — Robbie could tell that without a word being said. He knew he would have to take the brunt of that. Robbie cast a look over to where Alexander Mason was pouring himself another drink. He was back in his chair, his feet up on his desk.

The bag was heavy. Robbie grunted as he threw it over his shoulder and headed for the door.

* * *

The vibrating phone made him jump.

Vince Arnold still lay where he had collapsed on the soft carpet of his living room. His legs had given out the moment he had crossed the threshold, and he had barely made it over that. His back was against his front door. The energy needed to keep him standing had left him the moment he had shut out the outside world and the questions that had come constantly since that day in the car park. He had given a lengthy statement, then had rewritten it with a member of PSD hovering over him, prompting him to ensure his account covered everything. Then there was a meeting with the senior management team — the same account given time and time again. The questions didn't matter, his account didn't matter, the outcome was always the same: Tim Betts lying in a pool of blood while Vince pumped his chest, knowing it was futile, his pleading yells for help bouncing back from a cold, empty space.

It had been three days and the need to constantly relive it was taking its toll. The demand was always for him to remember *more* detail when all he wanted to do was blur the edges, to remember less. Just long enough to get some rest would be a start.

He hadn't been allowed the space to even start coming to terms with it yet and the magnitude of what had happened kept catching him out. It would come all at once the moment he was alone, like a wave overwhelming him, bringing him to his knees, taking the last of him. He could only wait for it to pass.

He struggled to tug the ringing phone from his pocket. He discarded it, throwing it onto the carpet in front of him. The lit screen was harsh in a room which had been held in shadow for the last three days, its curtains firmly drawn. At least its ring was silenced. The phone stayed lit and then a tinny voice broke the silence of his house. He must have answered it with his thumb when he threw it away.

'*Vince! Vince? You there?*' He recognised the voice: Maddie Ives. He knew she was off on leave, but he didn't know where. She would have heard — he had no doubt about that. He didn't have the energy to go over it again, not with her, but if he didn't answer, she might turn up. That would be just like her.

He reached out. It took the last of the energy to tap the screen and put her on speaker. He slumped to lie on his side next to it.

'Mads.' His voice was a tired croak.

'Oh, you *are* there!' She waited for him to answer.

'I can't talk. Not right now.'

'You're okay though?'

'Always.' He managed to make his voice sound brighter. The delay in Maddie's reply told him she was far from convinced.

'I'm back tomorrow. I wanted to come and see you. Is that going to be okay?'

'Sure. Not straight away, though, Mads. Not tomorrow. I got stuff to do, you know?'

Another pause. 'Okay then. I'll call you when I'm back and we'll sort something out. That okay?'

'Sure.'

'You know where I am. If you want to talk, I mean.'

'Sure.' Vince said again. The weak light leaking in around the curtains flickered as his eyelids became heavy, each blink longer than the next.

'I'll be offline for an hour or so from now but then I'm available any time. You can call me . . . any time, yeah?' Maddie's voice was more insistent but also getting quieter, like it was moving further away. She said something else but he didn't pick it up. It was just the background to the darkness as his eyes fell closed and stayed that way.

Three feet from his front door, on the floor of his living room, Vince Arnold finally succumbed to his exhaustion.

CHAPTER 4

'So, here I am.' Alexander Mason threw his arms out, his nose twitching with a sniff. His hands came to a rest in his trouser pockets, trapping his suit jacket tight to his body, his gold watch visible. He scuffed his foot, the sound amplified by the solid concrete surrounds of the multi-storey car park. His hair was pushed over to one side, disturbed by a cool breeze. Robbie was by the car, observing the conversation that was playing out two parking bays over. Mikey and a man he knew only as 'Pete' were just off the boss's shoulder. He had been told to hang back again and keep his mouth shut. This time, his instructions had been accompanied by a threat. It wasn't needed. Once again, he was delighted to be hanging in the background.

'Here you are . . . *the* Alex Mason. I'm so glad you came.' The man had appeared from nowhere it seemed, like he had unmerged himself from the shadows having been there all along. Robbie considered that his ability was not stealth but rather being so unassuming, he was practically invisible. He hadn't been expecting that. Mikey had called him 'Lance' but he had also heard others talking about him by his street name: 'The Tax Man.'

'Seems there might have been a bit of a misunderstanding. I came to make myself clear.' Mason said. Robbie watched him closely. He could see him looking Lance up and down with an expression that seemed to suggest he'd been expecting someone with a different look, too — more physically impressive, perhaps.

'I appreciate that.'

'I didn't realise such a trip would be required, though.' Mason's anger had been building steadily all morning. Overall, his mood was very different from when the idea of a meeting had first been put to him. Then, he had been excited — animated even — but he had quickly realised that he was now bending to the will of another. This was not something he was used to. Mikey had wisely resisted the urge to say, '*I told you so.*'

The drive from Bristol to Canterbury had taken over four hours as they had picked up heavy traffic on the outskirts of London. They had come down in two cars. Robbie was glad not to have been in the one transporting the boss. His mood had clearly darkened further.

'I had to know you were serious. I don't like being messed around. I don't normally work with people who change their minds. I wanted to see you were committed.'

'I assume I passed your test?'

'You did. I also wanted you to see this place. I think it's rather fitting. You see that stain, over there on the floor?' Lance pointed out into the middle of an empty parking bay where the concrete was slick with a brown stain. Alex Mason didn't deviate. He held his stare on the grinning Lance.

'That's your boy's brains.' The movement from Robbie's two colleagues was instant. Both men either side of Mason took a step forward and the one called Pete lifted his arm to point a stubby pistol. Robbie straightened from where he had been leaning on the car. Mason himself didn't move. He gave no reaction at all. Lance lifted his hands as if he was backing down, but he was grinning. 'I don't mean to cause a scene. Like I said, I don't work with people that change their minds. I just needed to see that you're still angry. That's a good sign for me. It started here . . . I will end it for you.'

Pete kept his gun levelled. Mason had his hands in his pockets and he sniffed again. It was one of his tells when he was upset. It gave him a moment to think, to be a little more measured when he came back with a reply.

'The "Tax Man," right? That's what they call you?'

'So I've heard.'

'Two certainties in life and one of them is taxes. So once you have a name, a target, the outcome is certain — is that it? That's quite a claim.'

'Not mine — or my choice of name, for that matter. Seems I've picked up a nickname based on reputation.'

Mason sniffed again. 'And what *end* did you have in mind?'

'I have some ideas. I like to have the freedom to choose, to take my time. It needs to be done right. But fear will be part of it — he will know what's coming. If you want someone to shoot him in the back then you're talking to the wrong man. Where's the fun in that?'

Mason signalled to Pete. He finally lowered his weapon but it stayed in his hand. Mason then tipped his head towards Mikey. 'My friend here says you make a scene.'

'Me and Mikey are old friends! But he doesn't get that a scene is exactly what you want right now. The fact you came all the way down here to speak with me tells me that you know that too, Mr Mason. Otherwise you could get your man here to walk up behind him when he was getting into his car or coming out of his front door and put a bullet in him, just like that. A quick pop and everyone gets on with their lives. Except they don't. The cops don't. Their lives all stop and their heads all turn to stare right at you, at your business, every inch of it. He's one of their own, Mr Mason. They would be all over you like you were pig food in a trough!'

'So hiring the Tax Man is my solution?'

'You drove two hundred miles today because you know that already. And so do I. Now I'll be staying until the job is done. I need to get to know the area. I can't say I've been here before. I always wanted a job where I could travel!'

'So, how does this work?'

'It's really very simple. I'll spend some time in the cathedral city of Canterbury. Over time, I'll find some locals that are worthy of taking part. My games will be in and around our ultimate target but, yes, I will be making a *scene*. And each *scene* will have its similarities to the last and then to the next. The local police force will fear they have a series of murders on their hands. PC Vince Arnold lives nearby. When the time is right, he will simply become one of the unfortunate souls — seemingly chosen at random — who'll fit the pattern of their serial killer. It'll be seamless. There'll be no reason for the police to question your involvement.' Lance suddenly took a step towards Mason. Mason didn't flinch, but Pete and Mikey started forward. Lance leaned in, his face contorting into a snarl. 'But know this, Mr Mason . . . They will suffer. All of them.'

Mason broke off the stare first and seemed to edge back a little. Robbie thought he even looked a little rattled. There was something decidedly unnerving about Lance that he couldn't quite put his finger on. Perhaps it was just his reputation? Mikey had talked him up as a psychotic killer who knew no bounds and Robbie had built an image in his mind prior to their first meeting. This was now the second time Robbie had seen him and he looked like an old, almost frail man who had sauntered out of the shadows and seemed far from capable of the worst types of violence. He had a build so slight that his trousers were sucked in at the waist with enough of his belt left over to hang downward. He had long, greying hair that was untidy and fell over small, dark eyes in wisps. Even his voice was an octave higher than the average, something that hardly added to an overall impression of a capable killer. But there was something about him, something that seemed to surround him — a presence. It made him appear bigger. And behind those sunken eyes there seemed to be nothing at all but darkness. His reaction to Pete pointing his pistol directly at him had been a mischievous grin. He was a long way from intimidated. Instead he seemed to have sized up the armed group standing in front of him and been left unimpressed.

'*Robbie!*' Mikey's voice cut through his musing, his tone suggesting this wasn't the first time his name had been called. Robbie snatched to attention. 'The money!' Mikey hissed.

It was Robbie's only job. He fumbled with the boot latch. It rose on a motor that whirred. The two holdalls were in a false floor activated by a button tucked under the sill. It popped open and he dragged out the bags. When he straightened up, Mikey was already coming back for the second. They dropped both bags at Lance's feet.

'How long?' Mason growled.

Lance didn't reply. Instead his expression was pensive. He licked his lips. 'This deals with the man who trussed your son up, left him to die. What of the men that pulled the trigger? Is that anything that you might need my assistance with?'

'No.' Mason's answer was strong and instant. Lance smiled.

'I see. That's a little more personal, is it?'

'This is all personal. You're only here because it seems I may need a little more separation for this particular job. I deal with my own issues.'

'Of course you do.'

'So again, how does this work?'

'I'll get started straight away, but these things take time.'

'What does that mean?'

'That it will take time. You want it done right . . . And me? Well . . . I have a whole new city to play with!'

Mason spun away and, just like that, the meeting was over. Mikey was ahead of him to tug the rear door open so he didn't need to break stride. Pete moved to the driver's door. Mikey's and Robbie's car was a few bays over. Robbie was almost jogging to keep up as Mikey made for it. Robbie lingered by his door. The car was quick to start, but he was drawn to peering back over the roof at the man they had just hired.

His fee was still where it had been dropped casually on the ground. He was paying it no attention. He was walking away from it and away from Robbie. His pace was slow, his steps deliberate, as if he was savouring every one of them, and his head was tilted back. He stopped when he reached the edge. Here his hands lifted to the back of his head and his fingers interlocked. The sunlight was low and bright enough to make him a dark silhouette, as if he was merging back into the shadows. Even now, from a distance, with his skinny figure a dark form and the wind playing with wisps of his hair, there was something about him. Robbie's shudder was involuntary. Lance's last words ran through his mind.

A whole new city to play with.

Robbie was glad to be leaving it.

CHAPTER 5

Maddie Ives lifted the cup to her lips. Her attention was drawn to the shadow of an HGV that lumbered by, rattling a few of the loose items in the living room as it went. Once it had passed, the sound dipped back to the steady stream of traffic. The house was on a busy tributary of Sittingbourne's high street. A woman with a pushchair was visible through the net curtain, accompanied by the sound of a screaming baby. She passed so close, her shoulder brushed against the glass.

Maddie didn't know what to say. She hadn't from the moment she had stepped in. Her mother seemed just as awkward. Maddie was on her last day of a period of leave she had set aside to sort some personal affairs. A visit to her mother was the last item on the itinerary and it was perhaps telling that she couldn't have left it any longer. She didn't like having time away from work at the best of times, but it had been even harder with news of a fallen colleague filtering through and all the fallout that had inevitably come with it. She was distracted — how could she not be? Her desire to be elsewhere was even stronger than it might have been.

'You still a hotshot secret agent, I take it?' Her mum's voice was harsh, her words rushed, like she was relieved to find something to say — anything to break through the silence.

'I was never a hotshot or a secret agent, Mum.'

'Oh? I thought that was what you said last time.'

'I worked undercover. I don't do that anymore.'

'Still police, though?'

'Still *in* the police, yes. And you still don't approve.'

'Not something I can approve of, love. When you've had the life I've had, you learn to know what to like.'

'Does that include me? Have you learned to like me yet?'

Her mother rolled her eyes. 'That's why you agreed to visit? To carry this on? We've been through all this before. You know I love you. You know the police made me give you up, too. All that bitterness you've got inside you when it comes to me? Your precious police caused that.'

'And what about the bitterness you've got? Did the police cause that, too?'

'You know they did.'

'I know the police don't take children away.'

'They did. I remember that night, so don't go telling me what I did or didn't see.'

'*Social Services* take kids away. They just need police powers to help them sometimes. And they don't do it lightly. It's pretty much got to be life or d—'

'Life or death?' Her mother snorted. Her coffee cup slopped back down on the coaster and she reached for her packet of cigarettes. Just a few minutes earlier, she had gestured at the packet and asked if Maddie minded. She had said she did and her mother had sat back, leaving the packet on the arm of the chair to glance at it intermittently. The room was tiny. Adding second-hand smoke to the environment could only make it even more oppressive, though Maddie hadn't given that as a reason.

Now her mother hastily pulled out a cigarette. Maddie had known this whole situation was going to go downhill at some point. The only surprise was that they had managed to make a drink and sit down first.

'He could have killed you. When he was at his worst, I mean.' Maddie didn't see the point in dancing around the elephant in the room anymore. There no longer seemed to be enough space.

'He went to prison instead, though, didn't he?'

'I sometimes think that wasn't your preference. You'd still have him here, wouldn't you?'

'He's always welcome here.'

'And that was the problem and why I wasn't.'

'I don't even recall you asking to come back here. Broke my heart it did, all of this.' Her cigarette played between her lips, bobbing with every word, affecting her pronunciation. Maddie found it infuriating.

'I was nine years old. I guess I thought that the mother comes for the child, not the other way around. I should have known better.' Maddie regretted the words the instant they fell from her mouth, not because she didn't mean them, but because she knew there would be an escalation. She waited for her mother's inevitable explosion, to be thrown out and to reset the clock to another four years of silence.

But she was calm. 'I called you here today, didn't I?' her mother said.

Maddie hid her surprise well. 'You did. I'm not sure why.'

'He's dying.' Her mum finally lit the cigarette. She leaned back and blew the smoke from her mouth.

'Who?'

'Your dad.' Despite the context, Maddie still cringed at him being called that. Normally she would protest. She didn't this time.

'Okay.'

'Okay? Like, *that's okay?* Maybe it isn't. I just thought you should know and for some reason, I thought I should be the one to tell you.'

'I don't know what else to say. I don't think it's okay — of course that's not what I'm saying.'

'I don't expect you to shed no tears, but you should know. That's it. I've told you. I wanted you to know before . . . before it was too late.'

'How?'

'What? You want to know if he's suffering?'

'Jesus, Mum! You've told me this much — that's a standard follow-up question, isn't it?'

'You've always wanted him dead, so you get your way. Bone cancer. Nothing they can do for him besides managing his pain. He's waiting to die in his prison cell. The cell your police put him in.'

Maddie shook her head. She had sworn never to have this argument again, but even if she hadn't, this was not the time. Her mother continued.

'He's given up, too. You hear these stories about people beating it, about being told they've got a few months or whatever and going on to live for years, to die of something else. Not him . . . Your dad's given up, and I know why. It's being in there. He's got nothing to live for. Whenever he goes back in that joint, we always talk about getting out, that's what we focus on. But just recently, he's got himself convinced your lot are never going to leave him alone. Not never. He gets out and then he's back in before you know it . . . Some jumped-up fraud charge this time.' She took another long drag.

Maddie sipped her tea, trying to contain any reaction. Her upbringing may have been terrifying and confusing in equal measure, but she had always been certain of one thing: her dad was going to kill someone. And her mother was the most likely candidate by far. Maddie knew he had been in and out of prison most of his life, she didn't know the specifics, but assumed it to be mainly violent offences of some sort. Even without those details, she knew that he shouldn't be left alone by the authorities — not for a moment. He was a dangerous man, incapable of being anything else — and angry, too. Certainly, he was incapable of loving his daughter.

'I'm sorry,' Maddie said eventually. She couldn't think of anything else. It seemed like the right thing to say.

'No, you're not!' her mother snapped back.

'I am for you. I know you loved him.' She did, too. Maddie had almost torn herself apart trying to understand why. That had been a big reason for her staying away for so long. Her mother had always taken his side, no matter what he did to her, what he did to them both. She could always make excuses.

'*Loved?* He ain't even gone yet, and you're telling me, "*loved!*"'

'You know what I mean.'

'Oh, I know what you mean, alright. Anyway, it doesn't matter now, does it?'

Maddie gulped her tea. It was far too hot, but finishing it would give her the excuse she needed to leave. Her mother must have noticed.

'You in a rush? What's it been? Three years or more, and now you can't wait to get out.'

'Four years. And I appreciate you've gone out of your way to make me feel welcome.'

Her mother sucked on her cigarette, narrowing her eyes as she did. This time when she breathed it out, she squashed it into an ashtray on the same arm as the packet. 'This wasn't how I wanted this to go. I wanted to tell you, but I wanted to know about you, too. I'm just on edge. This has been a difficult time.'

'Don't worry about it.'

'So . . . Are you seeing anyone? Is there any love in your life yet, Maddie?'

Maddie smiled. She ignored the edge to her mother's voice. If the tension in the room was going to decrease, it was going to have to be her stepping it down.

'I'm seeing someone, sure. It's a bit off and on, you know . . . Complicated.'

'Nothing's complicated if you love each other.'

Again, Maddie held back her first reaction. She wanted to point out the complications in her mother's relationship, like having her jaw broken twice, a busted rib, being beaten unconscious more times than Maddie could remember and the police turning up to cut her down where her dad had trussed her up by her neck. She was pretty sure *love* wasn't massively involved in anything that man did. But it wasn't the time to make her point.

'It's just distance, mainly. I met him when I was working up north. Now it's a five-hour trip . . .'

'He didn't follow you down, then?'

Maddie didn't want to go into it anymore. She didn't have the time or the inclination to explain herself. She shrugged. The silence returned. Maddie abandoned the tea. She was done trying to protect her mother's feelings. She stood up.

'Right then . . . I'd better be going. I do appreciate you talking to me, keeping me up to date. You will tell me . . . when . . .'

'He wants to see you.' Her mother pushed another cigarette between her lips the instant she finished her sentence. She lit it in one smooth movement. She didn't look up.

'See me?'

'Your dad. He wants to see you. One last time, that's what he said. I think he wants to make his peace, Maddie.' Her mother looked up, her eyes welling with emotion. She snatched away to balance her cigarette on the ashtray that was looking more and more precarious balancing on the arm of her chair.

'Make his peace . . .' Maddie ran the expression back over in her mind.

'You can't blame a dying man for wanting to tie up loose ends.'

'Loose ends?' Maddie clapped her hands — it was entirely reactive. She felt a rush of emotion that she didn't think was anger. Surely it wasn't sadness? 'I don't owe that man anything. He's had a whole lifetime to sort out his loose ends.'

'I told him you wouldn't, that I was wasting my time. But he made me promise I would ask, at least. He's got a couple of months — six at a push. For most of that, he might not be too with it . . . They're already upping his pain meds. I don't want no arguing . . . I don't want no falling out. I don't have the energy anymore.'

'It's just—'

'Two choices, my Maddie.' She stood to her feet with renewed vigour to stare Maddie in the eye. 'You come with me and talk with your dad. For a minute or two, just so he gets to say what he has to say. You just have to listen. Or you tell me now you don't want to, and that's it. We don't argue about it . . . You just leave this house and you don't come back.'

'Don't . . . What do you mean, "Don't come back?"'

'If you walk away from that man now, in his darkest hour, in his *last* hour, I'll only ever see that when I see you. I'll see what you done. We couldn't have a chat like this . . . about the time of day, about complications with your love life. No chit-chat like all is well. You come see your dad, or you lose us both.'

'I see.' It was all Maddie could manage. There was so much she wanted to say, but nothing that didn't mean the instant loss of the only family she had.

'And I know that might not be much of a threat to you. Maybe that's what you want. So you just let me know. I don't mean you no ill, Maddie, that ain't what I'm saying. I do love you as my daughter, but just know that I can't be doing this if you walk.'

'Fine, I'll come.' It was almost blurted and she flushed with anger instantly. Her mother had backed her into a corner and she had reacted. It wasn't even as if it had made her mother happy.

'Okay, then.' Her mother said. She stepped past Maddie to open the door that led out of the cramped living room and directly onto the noisy street. 'I go once a month at least. I'll get something sorted.'

CHAPTER 6

Three weeks later, Maddie was rubbing her hands together and shifting her weight from one foot to the other in the middle of a line of her colleagues, directly facing a similar line-up of figures on the other side of the road approaching the crematorium. The officers all blended into one long strip of navy blue with only individual medals marking out individual chests. Each had their boots bulled like glass, their white gloves pristine, brand new out of the packet that morning but seemingly just for show. The freezing mist penetrated them easily. The frost crunched under Maddie's shuffling feet.

To her right was a different block of colour: a sombre black where Sergeant Tim Betts's family and friends huddled together, gawping at the lines of police that stretched half way back to the main road. The hearse carrying their fallen colleague was due any minute.

Everywhere, everyone was silent. A marked police van provided the only colour vibrant enough to stand out in the grey mist. Tim's force number was stuck over the crest on the bonnet as a makeshift tribute. Maddie turned to a tapping sound. Other heads turned, too. The funeral director had come through the gate. He cut a solitary figure, out on foot and in top hat and tails with his cane clipping the frozen concrete.

From somewhere came the call: '*ATTEN-SHUN!*' and Maddie heard a hundred sets of heels knock together.

The hearse turned in. It was as polished as any of their boots, its engine smooth and quiet as it skulked past, the coffin visible through the long window down the side. Maddie caught her own reflection as she peered in to see Tim's hat lying on top with the Union Jack. The next vehicle to pass her was a matching stretched limousine. Tim's fiancée was on the back seat, her face largely covered by a black veil. Maddie was glad. She wouldn't know how to handle eye contact.

The service was short. A nod perhaps to the weather conditions outside where most of Tim's colleagues remained. There was no room inside. The readings and tales of Tim's life were piped out through hardy speakers to mingle with the mist that picked at the two lines of blue that held the road. No one seemed to know what else to do, just that it didn't feel right to stand down. Not yet.

Maddie studied some of their faces. The sadness was clear and to be expected, but as with any funeral for an officer killed on duty, anger and fear were prominent, too.

The sounds of car doors and engines were quick to follow the closing words of the service. The family requested a private few moments out in the grounds before they made their way to the wake. The gardens were extensive and beautifully tended, sloping downhill to give a view over graves and memorials as far as the mist would allow. Maddie stood there long enough for most of the cars to leave, for silence to return. In the distance, on the left side of the gardens, a solitary figure sat on a bench. His broad back was to her. The mist seemed to thicken as she watched, threatening to swallow him whole. There was no sign of him moving any time soon. She was going to have to.

'I think it's actually colder down here, somehow,' Maddie said when she finally made it to the bench. She hung a few paces behind, waiting to see what sort of reaction she might get. Vince Arnold was rubbing his gloved hands together. He chose this moment to peel the gloves off, putting them next to him, one on top of the other. They looked almost odd, something pure, white and gentle being tugged from Vince's big, rough hands. The position of the gloves next to him was not lost on her. It was where she might have sat.

'Did you want to be left alone?' she said.

'Yeah, Mads. Yeah. Just for a bit, I guess.'

'You're not cold, then?'

'It's a bit parky. But it's nice here.'

'It is. What are your plans, Vince? I think all of our lot have gone on to the wake. Just the family left now.'

'The family . . .' Vince said. He didn't turn. Maddie fixed back on his gloves.

'I tried calling you a few times. I was hoping to have popped round, just to see how you were. It's been nearly a month. This could have done with being a while ago. I think everyone needs this . . . the closure . . .' Maddie had the feeling she was rambling. It was the fourth time she had said that sentence so far. It had become her small talk of choice — that and how four weeks from Tim falling to getting to this point was too long. She knew the process, though. A full autopsy took a while. They hadn't even moved the body for the first couple of days. This was being done properly.

'I've not really had my phone on me,' Vince said. 'I saw you called, though. I'm not much company at the moment. At least today I don't have to be.'

'You're okay, though?'

'I'll be good. Time, right? That's what people keep telling me.'

'Sounds like good advice to me.' Maddie looked out over the view. When she turned to the right, she could see Tim's family shoulder-to-shoulder, a still smudge of black. She wasn't close enough to make out faces, but there was a sudden eruption of hugging and shoulder slapping. Then the group stretched out as they started to move back up the hill. She recognised the fiancée hanging back by the gravestone that had been the focus of this part of the ceremony. In the order of service, it had been described as a member of Tim's family. It was somewhere to visit, to feel closer, maybe to take comfort from the fact that he was not to be alone in the afterlife.

'Looks like they're finishing up down there. We should head to the wake. Get a beer in, yeah?'

'Not for me, Mads. I'm gonna head home in a bit.'

'You want to make me a cup of tea at your place? Not sure I fancy it either, to be honest. I'll give you some time down here, you can come find me—'

'You should go. To the wake, I mean. I'm not much company for now.'

'You beating yourself up, Vince?' Maddie paused for a response but didn't get one. 'I read the report, spoke to the first on the scene . . . There was nothing you could have done any different. These things can happen, we all know it, but the piece of shit who pulled the trigger needs to suffer for what he did, not you.'

Vince turned towards her. His eyes were glazed, the skin surrounding them flushed and stretched. He looked exhausted. 'I should have been standing next to him. I sent him out on his own. And you know why? I didn't want to get wet. I thought the call was nothing — some skag trying door handles — but it wasn't, was it?'

'It wasn't. No way you could have known that.'

'But I'd decided that before I drove the car into that car park. Ten years ago I would have been first out of that car and down those stairs. Skag or not, I would have been looking for the man we were sent there to find. I think it's time to jack it in, Mads. I'm not the copper I was. It's not a job you can do half-arsed. Someone got killed.'

'Someone would still have got killed. I'd have been standing at your funeral instead is all. I might have been warmer, though. No way you could fill that building!'

'I should have been next to him. When he . . .' Vince might not have heard her at all. He hadn't reacted to her teasing at least.

'Then you'd both be dead,' she said.

'But that's what you're supposed to do! Me and Tim . . . We were crewed together. You stand together. You stand up to whatever's out there — that's what we do. That's what we're here for.'

'Tim went out to search on foot, you went to get car details and you were going to meet him at the bottom of the stairs. And for a job that looked like nothing. That's common sense. Everyone who was lined up back there in their number ones would have made that same decision. Yes, it went wrong. But not because of you. Not because of any decision you made, but because someone turned up with a gun.'

'I could have done more. The bloke who shot him, the man responsible . . . He was right there. And I left another man to die.'

'You mean Daniel Mason? He had it coming. The man executed in that stairwell was a lead player in one of the biggest suppliers of class A drugs in the country, among other things. He was the epitome of *living by the sword*. We think he was only in the county en route to Europe to flee from people he'd upset.'

'He never stood a chance. I cuffed him to a handrail to die. We serve and protect — and we don't get to choose *who*.'

'You had the best of intentions. You were on your own. You secured him so you could find your crewmate whom you knew to be injured. You didn't know what was going on, so you thought on your feet. Your suspension is standard practice. The force has to be seen to be doing something but, from what I hear, no one's gunning for you. No one's blaming you, either. This is a freak circumstance. You reacted to what you saw in front of you. And — Jesus, Vince — they were carrying guns! And they were shooting them! The only thing you *could* do was stay alive!'

'And I am. I don't really understand why. If you're gonna shoot one of us, shoot us both. Makes no sense.'

'You were clever — for once! Maybe Tim had a go. Someone with a gun is always going to win. You need to be sensible, live to fight another day. The next time we meet him, we can be sure the tables are turned.'

'I've never been so helpless. Not like that. And *scared*, Mads, terrified.'

'Of course you were. And that's okay. You're only human.'

Vince's attention seemed to be fixed on Tim's family where they were moving up the hill with more purpose.

'Let's go find somewhere warm for a drink. It doesn't have to be the wake, but it does have to be a drink!' Maddie rubbed her hands to emphasise her discomfort.

Vince's face flickered something like a smile. 'All this time trying to get you out for a drink and all I had to do was get the skipper shot. If I'd known that I would have pushed the old bastard out in front of a gangster ages ago!' His smile dropped away as quickly as it had formed. Maddie moved her hand to his shoulder.

'Beautiful words, Vince. With thoughts like that, maybe we *should* go and see the family.'

Vince's laughter came out all at once and in a tight ball of mist. He raised his hand to stop it. It was only when she felt his shoulders shake that she knew he had moved on to weeping. Ignoring the gloves, she sat beside him. She noticed how cold he was when she took hold of his arm.

CHAPTER 7

Tuesday

He had been watching Alice Oxley at the Westgate Café, Canterbury intently. She was almost graceful in her movements as she crossed the vinyl flooring that clung to its faint smell of lemons and bleach despite the approach of mid-morning. She was self-assured too — it was her café, after all — and she moved around it like someone who had been doing this a while, someone who had a routine, someone who reckoned they already knew roughly how this day might play out.

Only, today, she could have no idea.

It was quiet. It always was at this time. The passing office workers snatching caffeine to fuel them the last half-mile into their grey blocks to sit behind their grey desks had come and gone, their tinny headphones and just-to-get-me-through-the-day grimaces gone with them. Then had come the casual breakfasts. That morning, there had been a couple with a day off without the kids, who had seemed to have lost all sense of direction as a result.

Now there was only one other occupant. It was a shame, as he liked to watch people, to observe their behaviour, to read them. He was good at it, too. He'd had a lifetime of sizing people up, of noticing the small details everyone pinned to their exteriors as if the rest of the world might be interested.

It seemed everyone wanted to be *interesting*. Not him.

He'd sized up the only other occupant already, sitting at the very next table. A retired pensioner, living alone — divorced rather than widowed — he was sure of that. He tutted constantly over the complimentary newspaper, the more enthusiastic tuts reserved for any story involving politicians. His bitterness at the life that may have passed him by was worn as a permanent scowl directed outwards at the world. But inside, he was lonely, desperate for the human interaction his exterior repelled. There had been plenty of tables free and he had chosen to sit right next to the only other one occupied. His tuts and sighs, his head shaking and the occasional glance to try and catch the eye were all signs of someone desperate for a conversation, for someone to interact with him, for a witness that he had existed in the world, that today he was *interesting*. When he continued to be ignored, he gave up and moved to a sofa-style seat against the window.

Good. He hadn't come for idle conversation, nor to be anyone's witness. He liked to watch people around him, not interact. You learned the truth about people by watching them, not listening to what they had to say. The bitter divorcee, the childless couple, the beaten-down workers . . . He knew them all instinctively from a myriad of tiny observations of which he was only half aware, but he had learned to trust himself by now.

'Hey, can I get you a top-up?' Alice Oxley's first name was pinned on her lapel. He had seen her fuss over the name tag to make sure it was level above her left breast. He liked that. He knew her story in more detail than most, but very little of that was conjecture, not now at least. He had taken the time to get to know her for real.

'Actually, I think I will have the breakfast.' His voice was rougher than normal, and she seemed to react, maybe even back away a little. He coughed to clear it. He didn't talk much. That was the consequence of a high, almost squeaky voice as a child. He had been teased. His reaction had been to shut up entirely. He soon realised that staying quiet and observing could put you at a real advantage.

'The breakfast? That might be the first time you've eaten in here, sir. Is this a special occasion that you need to tell me about?' She had a pretty chuckle that was instantly carefree. It seemed to come naturally to her and she stepped back in closer. He suppressed his first reaction. He wanted to tell her what he knew about her: how she should be more careful with what she told people who were just popping in for a cup of coffee, how she didn't know who might be listening and what they might do with what they learned. But these days, people didn't care. They were happy for you to know about their lives. What they didn't tell you to your face, they wrote on their social media posts.

Alice Oxley was thirty years old and single. Her ex caused her far more stress than he should over their child. She had a young son. She had a lot of male friends, too. Most of them were trying to sleep with her and some brought their attempts into the café during the day. She was more comfortable in the company of men than women. She'd had a few short flings, but these were mainly from dating apps on her phone and she was frustrated that she seemed to meet men who were only after one thing. She wanted more. She blamed the men, but she should have blamed herself. The messages she gave out were easily misinterpreted.

'It is, actually,' he said. 'Today's my birthday.'

Alice's hand rose to her chest. She sucked in air in a gasp of fake excitement and her smile was as wide as he had ever seen.

'Well, happy birthday! Do you want me to sing? I can sing if you want!'

'No. There won't be any need, thank you.' His smile lingered while hers faded. It just about turned awkward. He didn't feel it himself, but he had trained himself to be more aware of social cues. You needed to master that if you wanted to get close to someone. 'You know, I saw a place that was offering a free breakfast for people on their birthday. I nearly went there instead.' He added.

'Oh, really? What a lovely thing, where was that?'

'Up town. I don't suppose you do that here?'

She was flustered. He watched her lips closely as they fidgeted while she tried to find a response. Her cheeks flushed a little, too. He had put her on the spot.

'I'm joking!' he said, and her smile returned. She reached out with her right hand to push him lightly on the shoulder. She was wearing a white polo shirt, the buttons undone just enough for him to catch a sight of her cleavage as she rocked forward.

'You really had me going then! Is it even your birthday?'

'Of course!'

'Okay, then. How about I shout you a free coffee? That's like meeting half way, right?'

'Very kind.'

She gave a final smile and the hint of a wink as she swept up his empty mug from the table and walked away, her hips giving an extra swing while she knew he would be watching. She wore a tight pair of leggings into shoes with a low heel, just enough to make a pleasing *click* with each step. She was good at this, flirting with customers, making them feel like they were special when she would never cast them a second glance in any other situation. But he knew her. He knew women *like* her. He had known them all his life and for a few years they'd had him fooled. But not anymore. Not for some time now.

She re-emerged quickly, walking towards him with his fresh coffee on a small tray next to some cutlery. Someone else came in, another couple. She flicked them a smile and told them to take a seat — she would be right over. She talked to the fat husband. Of course she did. She called him *'darling'* and he loved it. His eyes fell to her tight leggings the moment she looked away.

She was back, fixed on him now with another smile, then another wink.

'For the birthday boy!' she said. The door pushed open firmly and her attention was again dragged towards it. She was placing his coffee at the same time and, with the distraction, the liquid shook and dribbled over the side. A few drips pooled on the tabletop.

'Hey!' She called over to the three teenage lads who were all trying to bundle through the door at the same time. 'Easy, lads! I'll be with you in a second!' She turned back to him — to where he was gripping the table so hard he could feel the pain in his knuckles.

'Your breakfast will be right out. Any sauces with it, hon?'

'Hon' — how he hated that! Such a throwaway expression! Just like her attention — throwaway, nondescript, utterly *fucking* insincere. *'I'll be with you in a minute,'* she had said while stood with him, already moving her attention away to her next target. The man had probably got a wink, too, maybe when his wife wasn't looking. She was no better than a cheap whore, and now she was so desperate to serve anyone other than him that she was slopping coffee all over his space. He still gripped the table. It was stopping him getting up.

'No. And I get a free coffee just for saying it's my birthday?' His voice sounded rough again. He swallowed to try and line his throat. This wasn't for lack of talking now. His throat always went dry when he was excited, when he was building up to something. He couldn't wait any longer. He let go of the table. This was almost his favourite part. *Almost.*

He bit his lip. He was watching her closer, enough to make her feel uncomfortable. It didn't matter anymore. In fact, it was all part of it. He liked to see every flinch, every facial movement, every nervous dart of the eyes. She was normally so comfortable here. This was her place, her second home. She could have no idea. It was perfect.

'Sure, why not,' she said. 'What is this world without trust?' She smiled again, but it was weaker. No wink, either.

She was holding herself differently, too, and she had tipped the empty tray on its side to hold it across her front like a shield.

'But I like to show that I'm *trustworthy*.' He leaned forward to reach for the wallet that he could feel as a bulge in his back pocket. He opened it and slipped out his ID. He held it up, leaning forwards to push it closer and to get closer, to be able to savour her face. He could smell her this close: cheap perfume mingled with washing-up liquid.

Her eyes chased over the card, her lips making the shape of some of the words. Her eyes flicked back to read it again. Double-checking. Then, in a moment that sucked the air from his lungs in its perfection, her attention moved beyond the card, her pupils restricted to focus and it was all on *him*. Suddenly, no one else mattered. Her mouth hung open a little, her carefully shaped eyebrows bent inwards to show a moment of confusion.

'Did you see something you recognise?' he said. She still looked confused. Now she was out of her comfort zone, where everything was so familiar. She was scared. She looked like she wanted to break away, but he knew she wouldn't. She wanted answers.

'This ID states that I'm Thomas Wright, born on the thirteenth of June, 2013. That would make me six years old! It shows an address of 19 Princes Way, Canterbury. It's a fake ID.' He stood up. Their eyes were locked. She stepped back. She had pushed the tray firmer into her midriff and it pushed her breasts out against the material of the polo shirt. 'Those are the details for your son, aren't they? That's *your* address?'

She managed to break away from his gaze long enough to flick back to where he was holding the ID at eye level. She nodded. 'Why?' she uttered.

'He's dead.' He leaned in. This was the bit he liked the best . . . the moment of realisation. Outwardly, she would deny it — to him, to herself. She would shake her head, tell him he was wrong, that it *couldn't be*. But people had a sixth sense in moments like this. They could tell when someone

46

was telling them the truth. Her head was already shaking. It started slowly, then her eyes glazed. Her mind would be processing his words, trying to make sense of them. It was time to add in some detail. To confirm what she already knew.

'I killed him.'

Her eyes snatched back to him.

'You left him with your ex. He always has him on a Tuesday. He told you he was taking him to the zoo. Last Tuesday, he said he was taking him to the soft play park. He didn't take him. He wasn't going to take him to the zoo today, either. But you know he lies. He always has. That doesn't really matter to you, as long as you can work. You should know, Justin is dead, too. Your ex-boyfriend is no longer your problem. I left them on the stairs at your house. Under the picture on the wall, the one you took at that tree-top adventure place. The one where you're both smiling so wide!'

Her eyes broke away again and he stepped closer to inhale through his nose. The *fear*! He could smell it! He could barely control himself. He inhaled again, deeper, saturating his nostrils, savouring the essence of her fear, letting it fill his lungs and course through his veins. He could *feel her!* Suddenly he flushed hot, too. So hot that he had a sudden urge to shed his layers.

She locked back on to him, her face drained of all colour, a mask of shock, as if all her beauty had leaked away for him to inhale. He lingered for one more moment. He knew what she was waiting for.

'Go!' he hissed, demonstrating his power. Released from her trance, she spun away from him as if he had struck her. She collided with a chair and it scraped loudly. The couple looked over. She sprinted to the kitchen, clipping another chair as she went. There were more noises from the kitchen. The wife from the fat couple got to her feet, she was looking over at him with a questioning scowl. Her focus snatched back to the waitress who reappeared to flash across the floor to the exit.

'You okay?' the woman called after her. Next to her, her husband also got slowly to his feet. He took hold of her arm gently, holding her back, telling her not to get involved. People didn't like to. They watched her leave.

He ignored the questioning looks from the couple to reach down into his bag. They quickly looked away. He produced a packet of antiseptic wipes and tugged some out. He wiped down the table. Despite being aware the whole time he was there, he had forgotten to only grab the edges, at least. His fresh coffee sat in the middle. He left it to walk towards the kitchen, sticking his head around to where a couple of coffee cups littered a preparation table in the middle of the kitchen. It was Tuesday, the only day of the week Alice Oxley didn't have help in the kitchen. She had to run the place all on her own. But she had a system. He reached for the cups, using a wipe to cover his hands first. The second one he picked up had the tiny slash of yellow pen he had made on the base. He dropped it into the sink that was overflowing with bubbles.

He made it back to his table and gave it one last wipe. The couple were now back to watching him. He stared over. He still flushed hot — it was centred on his back and his head felt light. *He was giddy!* He smiled.

'Kills ninety-nine percent of bacteria!' he said, then dropped the wipes back into his bag.

'She okay?' The woman called back over, stopping him as he reached the door. He leaned into it, opening it with his shoulder, a wipe covering his hand — just in case.

'*She* is,' he said, then walked out, letting the door close before the woman could bother him with anything else. He cast a quick glance back through the window. The woman shrugged, already going back to her day. Her fat husband checked his watch. The three teenage lads had all gathered around one mobile phone and erupted in silent laughter, all pointing at the tiny screen.

No one knew him. No one would remember him. People were like that. He merged back into the bustling crowd of shoppers and he was gone.

CHAPTER 8

Her lungs felt like they were about to burst. Every breath was tinged with scorching heat. Her mouth gulped wide but it seemed like there was no oxygen coming in. She had to slow down. She couldn't maintain her pace. Her house was still a couple of streets away. She gripped her phone in her hand and she flicked it up to see the screen. The display shook angrily to reject her thumbprint. She cussed and wiped her clammy hand on her jeans. She stumbled, the sole of her bare right foot coming down hard on something sharp as she powered forwards, her low heels abandoned a long time since. Her phone clattered to the ground in her stumble. She cussed again.

'No, no, no!' She scooped her phone up to reveal a new crack, a bad one, the display now distorted around it. She pushed her thumb back over the sensor, praying for it to work, having to come to a full stop for just a moment. It felt like a lifetime. The phone unlocked, she pressed to redial Justin and it rang out again. She limped the next few paces until the phone cut to his recorded voice, calmly asking her to leave a message. She cut the call and started her sprint again. Her chest burned instantly.

The movement of the high-visibility jacket was the first thing she saw, then the flat hat. She tried to shout but could only manage a breathy moan. She was too far away, anyway. Her house was in the distance. A police officer stood on her front step. He turned as if he could see her coming, the peak of his hat towards her. He walked a couple of steps down, lingering just above street level.

'My *son!*' It came out as a shriek, the strength returning to her voice from somewhere. It was just the other side of the street, now. She ran across blindly, aware of a blue strobe in her peripheral vision. The officer's face changed. He already knew who she was, why she was there. His hands lifted, his palms towards her. She could see police tape tied off either side of him, tight knots around the black metal of her railings.

Now she knew for sure.

She tried to speak, but there were no words. Her legs gave out, the strength from every part of her body seemed to go at once and she crashed to the pavement. She felt the impact in her arms, her shins, her chin. She twisted her head to one side, her eyes focused on her right hand where her palm was flat against the concrete. She tried to push down on it, to get back to her feet. There was nothing left. A black boot appeared in front of her eyes, it blurred with her tears. She felt a hand under her arm. There were two voices at the same time, one directed at her, the other tinny and distant through his radio.

'He's dead! My son . . . He's dead!' she wailed, trying to push herself off the floor. She felt herself hoisted up. Her head was like a dead weight. She was pulled up, but her legs wouldn't keep her up. She was lowered back to rest on her knees.

'He killed him!' she sobbed. 'Didn't he?'

* * *

Detective Inspector Harry Blaker saw the source of the noise immediately. A sobbing woman was kneeling at the bottom of the steps, just outside of his scene. A uniform officer was kneeling over her, trying to pull her to her feet. She was giving him problems, shrieking and squealing into the pavement. There was no way the officer was getting her up and, judging by the expression on his face, he knew it, too. Harry made his way down the steps.

'Alice . . .' he said, his tone as warm as he could muster. 'Alice, your son . . . He's okay.' The reaction was instant. She lifted her head, swept her hair out of her eyes and got shakily to her feet. 'We put him in a car, just over there.'

Her head snatched in the direction the inspector was pointing. At the same time, the back door of a pulsing police car cracked open. The officer standing next to it stepped out of the way for a boy to emerge. Even from this distance, his face was flushed red from crying. He ran down the closed-off street and the woman sprung towards him. As they met in the road, she swept him off his feet and wrapped him up in a tight hug. The next moment, she put him back on his feet and pushed him away far enough for her to check him over, her hands and eyes running all over his body, through his hair and demanding he speak, that he tell her he was okay. He nodded. Harry walked out into the road and stopped a few metres short to wait for the inevitable. It was another couple of seconds before Alice turned to him, scooping up the boy in the same movement.

'What's going on?' she breathed.

'I was hoping you could help us with that,' Harry said. 'He's fine. I've had an ambulance check him over. We need to monitor him for shock. He's had quite a morning.'

'What . . . I don't understand . . . Justin?'

'He's in the house. I'm sorry, Alice . . .' Harry hesitated, aware that the boy was staring up at him.

'He's dead, isn't he?' Alice said. The boy turned his face to bury it in her shoulder. 'The man . . . He told me they both were. I ran . . .'

'*Who* told you, Alice?' Harry moved closer.

'I don't know! I don't know him. He said they were both . . .'

'Where, Alice? Where is he?'

'At my café. He was there. He's been there a lot! The last month, maybe . . .' The boy was sobbing. Alice placed her hand on the back of his head.

'Where's your café? Is he still there?'

'The Westgate Café. I don't know, I just left . . . When he said it, I just ran!'

'Your radio?' Harry snapped at the officer in the high-visibility jacket. He twisted it from his chest and handed it over.

'What did he look like, Alice? This is important . . . Think, if you can. I need to get patrols out looking for him.'

Alice's head was shaking before Harry even finished her sentence. 'I don't know! I just ran!'

'You said he's been in there a lot . . . Tell me what you remember. Is he white?'

'White, yeah. Old. I don't know, sixty?'

'Okay, good. What else?'

'Fat, just like a pot belly, really. And he's got long hair. He ties it back in a ponytail, dark with grey and thinning out on top. And glasses!'

'Okay. Do you remember what he was wearing today?'

'Dark colours. I don't know!' She was starting to panic. Harry backed away.

'That's okay. That's enough for now.' He lifted the radio to broadcast the description. Instantly, there was confirmation from the control room and then at least four other patrols confirmed they were either in the area or making their way. He tasked one specifically to go into the café and hold. The rest were to cover the area. He had no expectation their offender would still be there, but it would be a scene now. He needed to get control of it.

Alice looked up at him. 'Why are you here? And how do you know my name?'

'I bet you have a lot of questions. I do, too. Let's go back to the police station and get this all sorted out.'

* * *

The sound of the door opening echoed in the sparse toilet. It was large, marked up as a disabled toilet. Lance pushed the door shut and lingered on the lock mechanism, feeling the sensation of the cold metal through thin gloves and using it as something to focus on, to slow himself down. He needed to relax, to be less hasty, less noisy. Now more than ever was the time to blend back in. He knew his excitement could make him stand out — or worse, make mistakes.

He dropped his bag against the door and turned to the mirror. His eyes had a visible sparkle — to him, at least. To him, he was standing out. He was concerned that he looked like he felt: charged with excitement through his whole body. He inhaled long and deep, in through his nose and out through his mouth. He knew his high would last for the rest of the day at least, but he needed to contain it. He needed to walk out of there.

He stood straighter. His breathing was back under control and now his focus was on being deliberate and thorough for what was to come. He was still burning up, too. He always flushed hot when he was excited. He was relieved then to tug away his wig. He liked using the ponytail. Not only was it one of the more effective looks, but it was easier to get off than some. Despite cropping his own hair short, he could feel it being pulled as he got hold of it for a final tug. He checked in the mirror. It had left red lines on his forehead and behind his ears. He pulled a beaten-up old beanie hat from his bag that would cover it until the lines faded away. Next, he unbuttoned his shirt. He was always relieved to take the padding out from underneath. It was hot and oppressive, a fake belly that pushed upwards when he sat down and made any sort of movement uncomfortable. He often wondered how close it must be to being overweight in real life. That wasn't something that he was ever going to know — he despised fat people. It was an outward sign of laziness and no one would ever convince him any differently. He dropped his shirt and the padding into his bag. He pulled out a crumpled green suit jacket in the same movement and slipped it over his shoulders. He pulled it tight, watching in the mirror as he did, trying to pull out the creases.

'It'll do,' he said. He slipped his glasses off and folded them up to push them into the inside pocket. He opened his eyes wide, then blinked away a moment of blurred vision. Even though the glasses had no prescription, they could still mess with his eyes.

He zipped up his bag then backed away from the full-length mirror to take in his reflection. He knew people. He knew what they would see when they looked at him — or at least, he knew what they wouldn't look beyond: the long hair tied up, the cheap-looking glasses, and the protruding gut. Now those things were missing, he could step back into the blur of the crowd, maybe even enjoy the aftermath, but he needed to be careful. He couldn't forget himself. He was so close to perfection.

He pushed open the toilet door to emerge into the tight corridor of a hotel. A group of giggling teenage girls came the other way. They were in a school uniform of sorts and obviously getting away with it. They didn't hold the door. It swung shut to snuff out the square of bright daylight burning behind them. He pushed his way out into it, emerging almost directly opposite the Westgate Café. The police were there already. He could see two officers standing inside. One was close to the entrance door that was now pushed closed and he was talking to the fat couple. A third officer emerged from the kitchen area. Outside the café, he could see two more police officers, one each side of the road, standing firm in the blur of passing people like rocks in a flowing river. The officer closest to him stopped an elderly man with a stick. The man had an awkward posture and had to lean forward on the stick to look up through thick-framed glasses. His hair was almost to his collar and wispy like it was thinning out on top, while his belly had a small overhang from trousers held up by braces. The officer took out a notebook and wrote something down. He looked to be doing most of the talking. The elderly man struggled to find his wallet in his back pocket and the officer took a card off him to look at. The officer wrote something down, then handed the card back and the man was on his way, even more unsteadily on his stick. The officer watched him for a few paces before turning back into the torrent of movement.

On the other side of the road, the police were stopping people, too. He could just make the officer out over the line of cars that were at crawling speed and bumper to bumper in both directions on the road between them.

Lance took a step away from the hotel. It wasn't the main entrance — that was pristine glass and fancier. He had pushed out of a fire exit. It was a door you wouldn't know was there unless you had spent the last three weeks mapping the area carefully. He had to take a rushed breath, caught out by a sudden surge of excitement that seemed to make his heart beat harder and faster and his back flared again with heat. His mind flashed with a bad idea. He should be walking away and the police presence was quicker than he had anticipated — but he couldn't resist.

He moved to the right, directly towards an ancient stone tower that loomed over the passing traffic. It was a hundred metres ahead of him. He walked half that distance until he came to a mini roundabout where traffic merged from three directions. He stepped out in front of a car. Its brakes squealed and its horn tooted. Everyone looked at him, just like he had hoped. He revelled in the attention. It was gone as soon as it had come. If they had known who he was and what he had just done, they would all have held their gaze for longer, maybe even gathered up their children and pushed them out of sight until he passed. They would have been terrified. It would have been the respect he deserved.

He made it across and turned left, back the way he had come. Ahead, and through the bobbing shoulders and heads of the bustling pavement, he could see the stationary police officer on this side with his eyes flicking over people as they approached. He walked straight at him, watching as the officer's eyes ran over the people in front. Then they rested on him.

'Morning.' His voice was strained again, higher even than normal, his throat tight with the excitement. His grip tightened on the bag in his hand.

'Morning, sir.'

And then he was past! He couldn't stop his grin. He had to fight the urge to cross back over and pass the officer on the other side — who also hunted for somebody. For him.

Instead he stayed with the stream, maintaining the direction that took him away until the buildings closed in a little on both sides. They seemed to get taller, too, enough for the sunlight to vanish. He chanced a look back. The officers on both sides were facing away, one of them had stopped a couple — the man looked to be at least twenty years his senior. He slid his glasses off to rub them, his expression incredulous that he would be stopped for such a thing. Beyond him was the entrance to the café. A police officer stepped out of it and ran a hand through his hair to smooth it down before replacing a hat. He thought he detected a gentle shake of the head as he did so.

A marked police car arrived. It pushed through the choked traffic as best it could with its blue lights flickering. More officers got out. Lance could feel his temperature rising again, his heart beating against his chest, and there was a feeling so joyous and so sudden that it forced a little whine. It was chaos. It was hopeless. It was beautiful.

CHAPTER 9

Wednesday

'So, Harry, what you're saying is that I take a couple of days off and everything goes to hell down here?' Maddie chuckled.

Harry didn't. 'So it would seem,' he said. He sipped at the coffee she had just made. They were in a meeting room accessed off the Major Crime office. A whiteboard was propped up in the corner on spindly legs with the beginnings of a VOWS assessment marked up on it. These were used to keep early investigations in some sort of order. Any known facts would be categorised quickly under the headings of *Victim*, *Offender*, *Witness* and *Scene*. It was a mess of hurried handwriting that smacked of a room full of people calling out what they knew. This sort of method was becoming a less common sight with investigations led increasingly by computer systems but Harry was sticking with what he knew.

Harry was hunched over a laptop. The screen was towards him so Maddie couldn't see what he was tutting over. He kept looking up at the big television mounted on the wall as if he was expecting something to appear.

'Did you want me to come around there and have a look?' Maddie said, trying to hide the humour in her voice. 'Technology and you, Harry . . . I swear you've never met.'

'No.' Harry was gruff.

Maddie sat back to leave him to his frustration. She peered back into the office through the smoked windows. You could tell a charged office, even with no sound. It was always a busy place, but today it had the look and feel of an office with a major job on the go. Maddie didn't like being the one coming into it late and not knowing anything. This was why she didn't take leave. She focused on sipping at her drink to stop her shooting questions at Harry, or worse, hurrying him up. 'Speaking of technology, is that a smartwatch I can see back on your wrist?'

Harry stopped his fiddling to stare at his watch.

'Yes,' he growled.

'You sound delighted!'

'No.'

'That's the one your daughter gave you, right? I thought you had a plan . . . You were going to wear it when your daughter was around and pretend to wear it when she wasn't.'

'I was. She caught me.'

Maddie laughed. 'When did it all change round? When did she become the parent and you the scolded child?'

'Round about the time we taught her to speak,' Harry grumbled.

'So now you have to wear it all the time?'

'She's back. Home I mean. For now.' Harry paused again. Maddie picked up on his expression.

'Everything okay?'

'For now,' he said again. 'She split up with her boyfriend. She seems to have taken it okay, actually, but I was worried. I didn't want it to be a trigger . . .' He petered out and his attention went back to fiddling with the electronics. Maddie knew what he meant. His daughter had suffered with her mental health in the past. It sounded like severe depression and she had self-harmed, too, seriously enough to be hospitalised. Losing her mother had made it worse — of course it had — but they had worked through it. Maddie could see how this might be another trigger.

'There!' Harry exclaimed. The mounted television came on all at once. It flashed white then settled to show an image.

'Shit!' Maddie exclaimed then met eyes with Harry, knowing him to dislike profanities immensely. 'Sorry . . . But a little warning might've helped.'

'I know you, Maddie. I know you would have been out there digging around already. What do you know? Save me wasting my time.'

'I really haven't! We have a murder.'

'That's all you've been told?'

'I've not been told anything. I asked anyone I could see what was going on, but they just pointed me towards you and this briefing.' She gestured back at the screen. 'He didn't do that to himself, did he?' Maddie referenced the high-definition digital photo that filled the large television and had prompted her profanity. It was a photo taken by CSI. Nobody seemed to be able to capture horror in a still image like they could. The background was a carpeted staircase, the foreground a man's body that looked to be suspended by a thin rope or cable that was light in colour and looped around his neck. The man was stripped naked and clearly dead. This was obvious by the washed-out pallor of his skin with a darker tone around his feet and ankles where the blood was obeying the laws of gravity rather than being circulated round the body by a beating heart. The man's head was slumped, his arms more forward than by his side. It looked unnatural and made him look smaller overall, but Maddie could see that he was actually well-built, with sturdy shoulders and muscular thighs. His abdomen was well-defined, too. His eyes were open. The captured angle had him almost looking right down the lens but with sad eyes that had lost all their focus. His face was the whitest part, made to look more so, perhaps, by the purple skin on his lips, the lobes of his ears and the end of his nose. Even the stubble on his chin stood starkly against his wax-like complexion. Maddie stood up and took a couple of steps towards the large television.

'Someone really had the hump with him to . . .' She counted under her breath. 'Thirteen stab wounds?'

'Seventeen. A small, sharp implement. The bruising is interesting.'

'How so?'

'Early word from CSI is that the stab wounds were delivered from behind. The post mortem will confirm that, of course.'

'From behind? You mean like someone reaching round?'

'Exactly.'

'Why would they do that?'

Harry shrugged. 'It might make sense if you were forensically aware. It would be messy to be standing in front of him.'

'It would . . .'

'But?' Harry prompted.

Maddie stepped back and her hands found her hips. 'To me, that is someone trying to make a statement. I mean, pick how you want to die! You don't hang someone and stab them multiple times unless you're trying to make a statement.'

'Okay?'

'I dunno. This is very personal. If you're that upset with someone, you look them right in the eyes when you do it, don't you?'

'I think you're right,' Harry conceded. 'That could be an important point.'

'Or it could be nothing at all,' Maddie said. 'It's okay, I know. It just doesn't fit for me.'

'I wasn't going to say that. I agree.'

'What else do we know, then?'

Harry flicked back to a piece of paper he had in his hand. 'He was killed where you see him. He was left clothed, CSI have stripped him here. The actual cause of death is likely to be a combination so we know it was all done at the same time.'

'Combination?'

'Asphyxiation and blood loss.'

Maddie moved back closer to the image. The wounds were mainly in his abdomen, but some reached up to his chest. Each one looked like two raised, white lips with a dash of exposed pink between them. There would have been a lot of blood at the time, but the wounds were cleaner in this photo following the CSI work. They would take photos as he was found and then, when all their swabs and body mapping was complete, they would take another to show the wounds clearer while he was still in situ. The body would be swabbed and washed properly and the wounds studied more fully on the autopsy table, but it was important to do as much as they could at the scene.

'So he was strung up first and then stabbed?' She scowled at the ligature round the man's neck and considered it was a piece of white wire rather than rope. His head was slumped forward to cover any marking on the neck.

'The autopsy results will give us more idea. As you see him, he can stand on his tiptoes, enough to prevent asphyxiation for sure. Death has constricted his limbs, but if his legs were pushed out fully, they would hold him up. CSI reckon he was strung up and stabbed where you see him. From there, he bled out and would have got to the point where he was too weak to hold his weight and the rope would then have taken his breath.'

'Not a nice way to go, is it?'

'No. I'm not sure there is a *nice* way to be murdered, however.'

'This wouldn't feature in your top ten, though, would it?'

'You have a top ten? In fact, don't answer that. It's a lot of paperwork to request a psych test on a colleague.'

Maddie smiled but was still studying the picture. 'So this . . . As a method of killing, it's like he's making him fight for his life. That's a visual thing, something you're going to want to watch, isn't it? If you go to all that trouble, you want to see that fight. So, again, why deliver the stab wounds from behind?'

'Just because the wounds were from behind, doesn't mean our killer stayed there.'

'Maybe not. But think about it . . . You're strung up by the neck, pulled up on your tiptoes and struggling to keep your airwaves open. That's a pretty bad situation, but it's about to get worse when you start getting stabbed. And you would know that straight away, if you were the victim. So, again, the killer would want to *see* that surely?'

'Maybe that psych test is worth the paperwork.'

'One offender?' Maddie said.

'We don't know.'

'No defensive wounds on his hands that I saw?'

'No.'

'So were his hands bound?'

'Not when he was found.'

'But he didn't defend himself?'

'No. So it's possible they were bound when he was killed.'

'Marks on the wrist?'

'It looks like it to me, but nothing official from the experts yet. There are more photos. I'll run through them so you get to see everything I have.'

Harry did as promised, but it was a whistle-stop tour of the CSI's photographic work. The screen changed quickly. There were a number of pictures of the hands, including a distant shot of each, then a close-up of the palms with and without labels. Any lacerations or marks were individually photographed with a ruler held beside the mark to show the size. Maddie stood back a little as Harry's scrolling picked up speed. He rattled through more images, quite a few more of the hands, then blood stains, including the smallest of drops, so small that the photos needed arrow stickers on the carpet or wall to point them out to the viewer. Harry's scrolling stopped at the image of an internal door. A chest of drawers looked out of place in the photo. It was pulled across at an angle with a piece of rope that was tied off and hung limp from one of the drawer handles. She held off on questions as Harry looked like he was building up to an explanation.

'This is a bedroom door. When the first patrol gained entry, that chest of drawers was against the door and the rope you can see was tied to the handle to prevent the door being opened. This is the son's bedroom. He was in there at the time. He is six years old.'

'He was there!' Maddie gasped.

'He was. We lifted fresh prints from the chest of drawers, their placement would suggest they were left by whoever pushed the drawers across the landing. We got DNA from the rope, too — where the knot was tied around the handle. They're both from the same person.'

'We have a forensic hit!' Maddie could feel her excitement building.

'Both matched the victim.'

'The victim?'

'Justin Wright. At some point before he was murdered, he barricaded his six-year-old son inside his own bedroom. Another lift of prints tells us that he also screwed the loop into the ceiling that he would later hang from.'

Maddie's hand lifted to her mouth. Her voice came out distorted behind it. 'Jesus, Harry. What the hell happened here?'

'That's about where we are.'

'Shit . . .' Maddie muttered.

Harry didn't respond, he let her have that one. She took a moment to look back through the window, out to where the office was still as busy. At least now, she had a better idea why.

'Did he see anything? This boy?'

'No. And he's six years old and just been through an incredible trauma, so his evidence is as you would expect.'

She glanced back over at the whiteboard, her eyes scanning the 'O' for *Offender* category. *'Old man, white-skinned, white beard, long hair in a ponytail,'* she read. 'So where did we get that from, then?' She read the 'W' category to try and answer her own question. 'Alice Wright?'

'The boy's mother, the victim's ex-partner.'

'She was there, too?' She turned back to face Harry now, bracing herself for the image of a seriously injured young woman.

'She was at a café. It's her business. Walking distance from where this happened. The man with that description was in her café. He suddenly produced an ID with all her son's details on it. Like he was trying to freak her out. There was no way he should even have known she had a child. Then he told her that her son's dead, Justin too, that he had killed them. Alice ran home to find us already at the house.'

'How did you beat her there?'

'The Force Control Room received a timed email to its Crimestoppers account. It told us we would find two bodies at a residential address in Canterbury. We didn't know it was her address at the time. The patrol turned up to see the victim through the letterbox and they forced entry. Half an hour later, Alice ran to the door. I was doing what I could to try and find her when she just turned up.'

'No coincidence that he could be seen through the letterbox.' Maddie was thinking out loud.

'I think you're right.'

'So the stabbing could have been for us, so we would see a lot of blood and force entry?'

Harry shrugged. 'I hadn't thought of that, but it's a theory. We would have forced entry anyway, but someone might have wanted to be sure.'

'And there was only one body?'

'There was.'

'So why say two?'

'I don't know. Maybe he was disturbed or it didn't go to plan.'

'Or the killer was able to achieve whatever he wanted with just our friend there? The email? You said we received an email?'

'We did. We're not getting anything from that. The address was made up of seemingly random numbers and letters put through something clever that shows it was sent from India. The IT boys explained it much better. Feel free to ask again, but it's a dead end. We're not tracing anything from it.'

Maddie let out a lungful of air. 'What the hell is going on here, Harry?'

'A fair question. Remind me to refuse any annual leave requests you may make in the future. Like you said, you go away for a day and it all goes to hell. Nice time?'

Maddie's mind was reeling. She turned away from the screen and took a few steps away to gather her thoughts.

'What? Oh . . . No, not really. Tim's funeral was Monday, of course, but the rest was just bits and bobs, really. Mostly stuff I'd been putting off because I didn't want to do it.'

'I didn't see you at the wake?'

'I didn't make it. I tried to take Vince out for a beer, but he was having none of it. I didn't much fancy it myself.'

'I didn't see him, either.'

'He went home. That's what he said, anyway. I'm worried about him.'

'Me too. I need to go out and see him, actually. I'm not sure anyone from here has yet.'

'It's been a month, Harry,' Maddie snapped.

'I know. It's not good enough. This is going to keep us busy, but I'll make sure I get out there.'

'This will certainly keep us busy.' Maddie was still turned away from the image on the screen, trying to silence her mind, to make sense of what she had been told and to juggle thoughts of Vince. She couldn't do it all at once. It was too much. 'I should come with you — to see Vince, I mean. I need to see he's okay. Then I can make a start on all this.'

'We'll see how it goes. So that was it? You book annual leave and end up at a funeral?' Harry being non-committal wasn't lost on Maddie.

'I booked it to go and see my mum, actually. I won't be making that mistake again.'

'Your mum?'

'Yeah, she had something she wanted to talk to me about. I kept putting it off, but I finally made the time.'

'Good news?'

'Yes, actually. My dad's dying.'

Harry couldn't stifle his reaction. 'I see,' he said.

'Long story, Harry. He wasn't a dad to me. That's one of the few times I've called him that, come to think of it.'

'You're okay, then?'

'I'm fine. It might even have cheered me up a little.' Harry eyed her as if he was waiting for a punchline. She shrugged.

'Well, I'm glad you had a nice time overall.'

'So where are we with this?'

'All over the place. We've got a lot of detectives and a lot of tasks, but there's one I kept back for us to do. We're meeting the informant back at her café. CSI are there already. I want her to walk through where he was and what happened exactly, just in case we've missed any opportunities. I want to do a walkabout for CCTV, too.'

'Is it Charley Mace on CSI?'

'I asked for her. Why's that?'

'If it is Charley, just don't mention the part about being sure CSI haven't missed anything. She tends to take that sort of thing personally.'

Harry leaked a grin. 'Good point.'

'What do you need from me? Do you want me to start the CCTV enquiries while you do the café walk? I know Charley won't want any more people than necessary inside that scene.'

'No.' Harry rushed his answer. He came back softer, 'I need you to be there. Our informant is very shaken up. I couldn't get too much out of her. I was hoping she might open up a little more to you . . . You have that way about you.'

'A compliment?' Maddie said.

'Take it as you will. We need to get going.'

'That's it?' Maddie gestured at the image still on the screen. 'I have a lot of questions, Harry!'

'Don't you always. You can ask them on the way.'

* * *

The Westgate Café was situated at the top end of the city limits, just a hundred metres or less from a pair of medieval drum towers that made up the Westgate, from which the café had rather ambitiously borrowed its name. The towers and the steel gate below had originally been built as part of the city's defences, acting as a lookout point, where visitors could be stopped and screened at a safe distance from the hugely significant cathedral and its resident Archbishop. They rose up twenty metres in height, still dwarfing the buildings around them, but their watch was now over roads and pavements, their ancient cells now a tourist attraction and the solid gates fixed permanently open. The steady stream of traffic passing through them was incessant. Maddie had really come to love this city, but she feared for it. Medieval Canterbury seemed to be on a collision course with the modern day and the scars and scrapes taken out of the grey stone walls were a literal example of this.

Despite the high street ending on the other side of the Westgate, the foot traffic was still heavy. This part of the town was largely pubs and restaurants. There was a luxury hotel, too, with a modern glass front juxtaposed to the ancient brick of the surroundings. The café stood out for different reasons: its front was low-key and cheery with '*Come on in and try me!*' across its window. It was out of place among the modern-fronted businesses that seemed to make up the rest of the street. Rent would be high here. Canterbury was expensive in general, but this area felt prime.

Looking beyond the hopeful slogan etched into the window, Maddie could see a suited Charley Mace straighten up from where she had been crouched on the floor.

'She should be here any minute.' Harry was just off her shoulder, his growl cut through the throng of the traffic. The café was attracting attention, or at least the police and forensic activity were. People slowed as they passed, some holding camera phones up to the glass.

Charley seemed oblivious to the outside interest as she moved out of sight. Maddie was watching through the window when Charley reappeared with a coffee pot in her gloved hand. She gestured at them with it, then patted her stomach like it was delicious. She was looking at Harry and so Maddie glanced at him, too. He didn't look impressed. Charley looked to be laughing hard. Maddie couldn't help but join in. Then Charley snatched the pot away, the smile dropping off her face at the same time.

'Inspector Blaker?' It was a woman's voice, meek and monotone behind them. Maddie turned to the source. The woman looked to be a few years younger than Maddie. She was attractive, slim and with a good shape. She looked beyond both officers to the interior of the café. Her café.

'You must be Alice.' Maddie held out her hand.

Harry shook her hand, too. 'Call me Harry. I told you that already.'

'Sorry. I guess I'm not used to talking to the police.'

'I appreciate that. Thank you for coming down. I know this isn't easy. I know it's all a bit soon, but you must understand how important this could be.'

'I guess I do. We talked about this though, about what he did in the café, about how he always sat at the same table if he could. I told you what I remember. I don't see what coming down here does differently.'

'Maybe nothing.' Harry shrugged. The woman eyed him and her expression seemed to harden.

'But maybe it tips something out of your mind that you didn't even know you had forgotten,' Maddie interjected. 'We do this a lot. For serious incidents like this, it can be really useful. How long have you worked here?'

Alice turned to Maddie. Her eyes were prettier when they were engaged and looking right at you. 'I've had the café six years now. I used to be based a little further out. It was always a bit of a dream to move up here. I never thought I would . . .'

'It's a lovely area.'

'It is.'

'And you do okay?'

'I can meet the rent and take a salary. Most days I could do with more help. I was at the stage where I was thinking about taking someone else on full time. I only get help a couple of days a week. It's getting too much.'

'You *were* considering it?'

The woman sighed. 'I don't know what happens. Not now.' She bit her lip. Maddie turned to where Charley was fiddling with the door to let Harry in. Her greeting was muted. She glanced at Alice and nodded.

'Come in.'

Right off, Charley took to making sure everybody knew how to conduct themselves at her crime scene. Maddie smiled to herself, aware as to just how uncomfortable this would be for Charley. She didn't even like the trained professionals in her crime scenes and here they were with a member of the public.

'Alice, I know this is your place, but we are working in here and what we do today is essential to these two finding out who this man is. I have some simple instructions that need to be followed while you are in here so you don't cause any issues with evidence. Does that make sense?'

Alice nodded.

Charley now directed her message to Alice, but Maddie knew it was for all of them.

'Okay, then. We are largely done in here. We've completed the first sweep. That means we have swabs, a few part-footprints and all the internal photos are done. Places like this are a bit of a problem for us, see? Members of the public come and go with their grubby hands and feet and they don't care about making my life more difficult. They don't care about much at all, in fact. So . . .' Charley surveyed the interior as she gathered her thoughts. 'So, I'm going to ask you to show me the table the suspect was sitting at, then talk me through what he did while he was here and what was brought to his table and taken away. We're going to try and isolate those items. That gives me something to focus my energy on. Does that make sense?'

'Yes,' Alice muttered.

'Good stuff. The first rule is the only rule. No touching! I know this is your place and there is probably a trace of you on every surface, but what we don't want are traces of other people rubbed off. So point at things, tell me things . . . Do not pick things up! Is that okay?'

'Yes.'

'Thank you, Alice. Harry, do you have a moment?' Charley gestured and withdrew. Harry followed her and they both turned away. When Maddie looked over at Alice, she looked like she had moved further into a corner.

'You okay?' Maddie said.

'Sure.'

'Of course you're not! Silly question really. I can't imagine what you're going through with all this.'

'It's just strange being back here. I've always wanted to do this . . . this place . . . this location. I was getting there.'

'That doesn't have to change.'

'It feels like it has already. It feels like everything's changed . . . Is this going to take long? I should get back to Thomas. He didn't want me to leave.'

'He's safe, he's still with the pol—'

'It's not about him being safe! He should be with me. He was safe at home with his dad when I left him last!' Her face flushed. Her anger didn't last and she hung her head a little. 'Sorry, I don't mean to snap. I just want to get back to him.'

'Of course. This won't take long.'

Right on cue, Charley called them over. Alice edged forward towards where Charley was gesturing at a table.

'From the description, we worked out this was where he was sitting. Am I right?'

'Yes.'

'Do you remember which chair?'

Alice pointed. 'This one. He always sat in this one. He looked around a lot. People do though, don't they? In cafés, I mean. I think it's a big reason some people come to them. They watch people.'

'And he watched people, did he?' Maddie said.

'Constantly. It was more noticeable with him. I would see him staring over at couples in the middle of some deep conversation. I would catch him staring at me, too, when I was talking with customers. I didn't think much of it. He was just some man sat on his own in a café. Why wouldn't he look at what was going on?'

'And what did he have yesterday?' Charley said.

'Have?'

'Food, drink?'

'Oh! Sorry . . . He had a coffee. He always had coffee. But then he asked for a breakfast, too. I never gave it to him. There wasn't the chance.'

'The table was empty when we got here. Did he get his coffee?'

'He was here a while. He had a couple.'

'Same cup every time?'

'No. I always do the drinks in a new cup.'

'What do you do with the dirty cups, Alice?' Charley smiled, as if she was trying to play down the urgency in her voice. Alice might have picked up on it anyway. She moved quickly across the floor to stand on the threshold of the kitchen. She waited for Charley to stand next to her then she pointed.

'The table in the middle. I'm always on my own on a Tuesday, so I normally stack the dirty crockery on this table. I'll wash them when I have a lull. I've got a dishwasher, but I only use that at really busy times. Most of the small stuff gets washed up in the sink.'

71

Maddie moved to be able to see into the kitchen, too. Alice had gestured at a sink on the right side. There was still water in it from yesterday and a white mug was submerged and lying on its side. They had shut the café and put officers on the door to guard it overnight, preserving it as a scene while the CSI processed the main scene at Alice's home. Nothing had been touched or moved. There were dirty cups, plates and cutlery on the table and foodstuffs on other surfaces and discarded on the hob.

'Do you remember what you did with his cup?' Charley said.

'I . . . I'm sorry . . . I don't know . . .' She lifted her hands to her head.

'Take your time.'

'I gave him a new one. We talked about it being his birthday, so I gave him a coffee on the house. I didn't get to start his breakfast, but he had a coffee.'

'His birthday?' Maddie butted in.

'Yeah, I don't think it actually was. It was part of the ruse, an excuse to get the ID out.'

'So when you left, he still had his drink?' Charley said.

'Yes!'

Maddie's eyes dropped back to the mug submerged in water. Fingerprints are basically formed out of grease and residue. There wasn't going to be any of that left. The mug stood out to her. It could well be his.

'Did he go to the toilet at any time? Or move anywhere else in the café?'

'Not that I saw. He doesn't really move. He'd come in here and sometimes he'd stay for a couple of hours. He'd just sit with a coffee and watch people.'

'Okay, then.' Charley seemed to have come to the end of her questions. Maddie took over.

'Every day? Did he come here every day, Alice?'

'Pretty much. But only for the last few weeks. Maybe a month.'

'And you hadn't seen him before that?'

'No. That's not unusual, either. I've got a few older customers who are regulars. Somewhere to go, I suppose . . . I never thought . . .'

'Of course you didn't. Why would you? So he might have just moved to the area?'

'He might.'

'And how did he pay for what he had?'

'Cash. Always.'

'And did he ever tell you anything about himself?'

'No . . . Look, I've done all this! Someone asked me all this last night. Until late. I answered everything.'

'Sorry, Alice, I haven't had chance to review that yet. Sometimes it's good for different people to ask questions, you never know what might get missed.'

'I don't think I can help you anymore. He was here, every day. He sat at that table and he had a coffee. Then he stood up and showed me an ID with the details of my son on it. He stared right at me and he told me he was dead, that he had killed him . . .' She paused to inhale. She looked like she was fighting to keep herself together. Maddie waited her out. 'Who does that? Why would someone do that? And what he did to Justin!' Maddie gave her another few moments.

'Did you ever talk about Justin? Here, I mean, where this man could have got to know about him?'

'Sometimes I moan, I suppose. Nothing too bad. Justin causes me nothing but trouble. He lets me down, he lets his son down . . . But he didn't deserve that. I've given my story — all of it. Every little sordid detail about what Justin did to me, about how he walked away from us both. I've done this with the police. I suggest you go and have a look at that first and if they *have* missed anything, then you can come back and talk to me. I'm not going through it again.'

Maddie held her hands up. 'You're right. I'm impatient is all. With something like this, I just want to know everything straight away so I can start to make it all better. I want to find this man.'

'Good.'

73

Maddie met Harry's gaze. It seemed to be a warning glance. She pushed her lips together to show that she was done. Harry spoke.

'Thank you, Alice, you've been a great help. CSI are going to finish up. I am hoping to be able to hand the café back to you later today. I appreciate that you've lost a couple of days' trading now. You'll be able to open back up tomorrow morning.'

'Take as long as you want. I'm not opening — not tomorrow. Not for the rest of the week. Who knows after that.'

'I'm sorry to hear that.' Harry's tone seemed genuine. He strode to the door and gestured for Alice to lead the way out. Charley pushed the door shut behind them.

'Do you need a lift anywhere?'

'No, thank you. We're staying at my mum's with a constant police guard. Any chance your lot can leave us alone now? I think we could all do with room to breathe. The police sitting outside might be doing more harm than good for Thomas. It makes him think that someone's still out to get us.'

'I'll have to make a call up the command line,' Harry said.

'He isn't,' Alice said.

'Isn't?'

'Out to get us. He got what he wanted.'

'What was that?' Maddie spoke.

Alice turned her pretty eyes to her. 'He wanted to scare me. It was like he was drinking it in. He was loving every minute. He caught me off guard, when he said it was Thomas . . . He's not coming back for us, because he knows I'm not scared of him anymore. I *want* to see him again. I'd tear his scrawny head off.'

Maddie smiled. She didn't doubt her for a moment. 'That's the spirit that will get this place back open. I know it will. I'll pop in for a coffee when it is. I look forward to it.'

Alice didn't reply. She turned sharply and walked away.

Maddie watched her for a few paces. She could feel Harry staring at her. 'What?'

'I upset her yesterday by throwing too many questions at her. You were supposed to be the one she could talk to. That's why I brought you here.'

'She's okay. Like I said to her, I'm impatient to get up to speed so we can start tracking this man down.'

'I didn't need impatient. That is something I am quite capable of doing on my own. She wasn't exactly open when we spoke to her. I need her to feel like she can talk to someone.' Harry was using his unimpressed growl.

'She will. This is a bad time. I'll go and see her again in a couple of days.' Maddie turned to a movement — to where Alice reappeared. She looked a little unsure of herself.

'Maddie, right? Have you got a card or something? Just in case I think of something . . . You know, everything seems foggy at the moment. I know you're the good guys. I do want to help.'

Maddie beamed. 'Of course. You can call me any time, even if you just want a chat. Sometimes it can help to make sense of it all.' She held out her card.

'Thank you.' Maddie watched her cross the road and disappear between two buildings. She turned to Harry.

'What?' he said.

'What did you need from me, again?' She was smiling.

'You got lucky this time, Maddie.'

'No such thing! Let's get back to the office, shall we? I'm impatient, see?'

CHAPTER 10

'Mummy!'

'I know, Fern, I know,' Michelle Rice stammered. How could she not? Her eyes flicked to the clock on the kitchen wall as she strode out — 7:20 p.m. She had just put the kid to bed. This was now happening almost nightly. She walked down the hall to the bottom of the stairs. Her five-year-old daughter was back out of bed and blinking at the top of the stairs, the light bright above her, a dog-eared rabbit hanging limp from her grip.

'Hey honey, pop back to bed. I'll go see if I can get them to turn it down, okay?'

'Okay, Mummy.'

The music from next door was so loud, it might as well have been emanating from her own living room. A picture vibrated against the wall with each beat as she stepped to the front door. She pulled it open and cast a last look up the stairs to where Fern hadn't moved.

'Bed, I said!' Fern slunk towards her bedroom and out of sight.

The Rice family lived in a semi-detached house. The front doors for each of the joined houses were close together and in the middle, separated only by the length of two bricks. Similarly, the red-tiled paths up to them were split by a low wall with a black metal handrail running along its top. Michelle could lean over to knock the door. The music was even louder here. It was some sort of guitar music with a clattering drumbeat, the lyrics shouted rather than sung. There was movement a couple of houses down. Someone stepped out: an older man. He was wrapped in a dressing gown and his grey hair looked like it was stuck down with moisture. He made eye contact and threw his hands up in frustration. Michelle gave a reaction to convey her agreement. She knocked again. The old man crossed his arms to watch.

She got no response. She hadn't been expecting one. There was no way anyone would be able to hear her in there. She checked her pockets for her keys just in case her own door fell shut, then stepped over the low wall onto her neighbour's path. With a slight change in her position came a sudden sense of déjà vu. She had been here a couple of nights before and twice in the week before that. She had barely ever spoken to her neighbour and didn't know much about him. She knew he was a drunk, though. The music had started out as an occasional accompaniment to his drinking at first, but it was getting more common. And louder. Neighbours had told her that his mother had died, leaving him the house and making it far less likely he would ever leave.

She thumped the door again — still nothing but the roar of a heavy metal rock band.

'Mummy!' Fern appeared at the door, her bare feet on the cold tiles of the porch.

'Go back inside, honey. Go back to bed, like I told you. I'm just going to ask them to turn it down.'

'Why do they play it so loud, Mummy?'

'I don't know!' She smiled. 'Now get back up to bed. It's cold out here.' Fern pushed her rabbit's ear back into her mouth and turned away. Michelle could feel her anger rising, she took it out on the door as she knocked again. Then she rattled the handle. The door pushed in.

77

Instantly, the music was louder. The drumbeat from this close felt like it was pulsing outwards, keeping her back. She leaned in to where a second door also hung open. She couldn't get a clear view down the lit hallway. Countless jackets and shirts covered pegs on the right, more were on the floor underneath where they part-covered numerous pairs of shoes. There were boxes, too, that were marked up as coming from a storage company and overflowed with various trinkets and belongings. On the left side was a stack of old novels. She stepped into the porch. The size and shape mirrored hers, but this one was made to feel smaller by an out of control rubber plant with browned edges and a clear layer of dust.

'Hello?' she called out, taking advantage of a moment of quiet as a track finished. There was no answer. A second later and an earnest drumbeat announced the start of another song. She stepped back out to look at the front window, covered untidily by curtains. The man in the dressing gown was gesturing again. This time, Michelle ignored him.

'Hello?' She was back in the porch, shouting into the cluttered hall. Only the rock music shouted back. She tutted again, her anger propelled her forwards. She pushed the second door open wider and moved into the hall. A thick, musty smell greeted her. She lifted her hand to cover her nose.

'*Hello!*' The music seemed to be coming from the first door she came to on the left. The door was half open to reveal the living room. A bulb hung from the middle of the yellowed ceiling and burned a bright white. She could see a figure sprawled out on the sofa. Another was on his side on a filthy rug, his back turned to her. The stereo was against the back wall and close to the door, its digital display rising and falling with the beat. The volume this close was like a physical assault. She traced the wire from the stereo to a plug down by her feet. She pulled it from the wall. The silence was instant and gratifying. Neither of the figures moved. She recognised the man on the sofa as the regular neighbour. His breathing was now audible, more a hiss than a snore, and possibly the source of the sickly alcohol smell that hung heavy in the room. She held the plug in her hand and in a moment of clarity, tugged it hard enough for the other end to come away from the back of the stereo. She kept hold of the plug with the wire trailing from her fist, emitting a little mutter of triumph as she made her way out of the door, a mutter that turned quickly to a yelp of surprise.

The door pushed open. A man was stepping in through the open door as she was about to move out. He reacted with surprise, too.

'Oh!' he said.

'Sorry . . . I, er . . . I just popped round about the music!'

'The music?' The man scowled. He looked a little dishevelled himself, certainly not out of place with the part of the house she had seen. He had an untidy looking pony-tail made up of hair pulled tight from the back and sides, while the top looked a little thin. He wore glasses that were smeared.

'That's not why you're here?'

He smiled. He seemed to linger on her, his eyes chasing over her from top to bottom. He even leaned back a little to take her all in.

'Oh, I see. No! I'm staying here for a little while. Jeremy has been kind enough to put a roof over my head in my hour of need. I'm a little embarrassed about it, really. Only temporary. There's a problem with the music?'

'There was. It was loud, ridiculous really. These houses, the walls are pretty thin . . .'

'I can see you've sorted it!' He nodded at the power cable that trailed from her hand.

'Oh . . . I'll give it back. It was an excuse to talk to him about it. I was hoping to ask him to be a bit more considerate, you know . . .'

'I do, and I wouldn't bother if I were you. I don't seem to be able to talk to him about much. In fact, I would keep hold of that for now.' He grinned. 'And you are?'

'Next door!' she snapped. She felt uncomfortable, even though he was smiling. She was aware that he was between her and the door. His eyes still seemed to be chasing all over her.

'I assumed that. Well, I can't say I'm sorry if we have found a way to stop the music. Believe it or not, he says it helps him sleep!' The man wasn't moving.

'Well, it seems to have done the trick. Do you mind . . .' She edged forward.

'Sorry!' He stepped out of the way and she moved through to the path. She cast her eyes right, her neighbour must have been waiting for her to appear. He was still standing out in the cold, his arms crossed tightly over his dressing gown. He lifted his arm to give her a thumbs up signal, then disappeared back into his house.

'I'll make sure they keep it down. Jeremy has all sorts of people coming and going, it can get a bit rowdy. I think some of that might be my fault. He's letting me stay here and in exchange, I'm keeping him in booze!' he lifted a carrier bag that clinked like it contained glass bottles.

'I wish you wouldn't,' Michelle said.

The man shrugged. 'He'll get it from somewhere. And actually, it might not be a bad thing. He tends to drink until he's comatose. I reckon I can get him there by six at the latest every night, and then he'll sleep silently right through 'til morning. How does that sound?'

Michelle relaxed a little. At last someone in that house she could actually talk to. 'That sounds amazing, thank you.'

'My pleasure. I don't touch the stuff personally, and I appreciate a bit of peace and quiet of an evening.'

'Mummy?' Michelle snatched to her daughter's voice. She sounded unsure, scared even.

'I told you to go back to bed!' Michelle snapped.

'Are you coming back in? I'm scared and the wind is cold.'

'I'm just coming back in. The music has stopped now, you can go to sleep.'

'You have children?' the man said. He was leaning forward like he was trying to get a look.

'I have a child, yes.'

'How old?'

'Oh . . .' She hesitated. 'Five. Nearly six.'

'All the more reason to keep the noise down. Accept my apologies, I'll keep this lot on track.'

'My husband . . . He works late sometimes, too,' she said, cutting in too quickly. The man grinned.

'Well, he has a lovely family to support.'

She flashed a smile and mumbled a 'Thank you.' She concentrated on stepping back over the wall and ushered Fern back into the house.

'You're very brave.' The man's voice followed her into her porch. His voice had a higher pitch to it than most men. It was even more noticeable with more volume. 'Coming in here on your own, the smell alone would be enough to put most people off!' She detected laughter in his voice but there was something about him — an edge to his words.

Michelle looked behind her, expecting him to be leaning over. He wasn't. She couldn't see him. 'I don't scare easy!' she said, projecting her voice out of her own front door. She waited for a moment . . . There was no answer. She assumed he had gone into his house already.

The silence when she pulled her door closed was utter bliss.

* * *

Lance waited for the door to pull shut, but he didn't let his breath out. He waited for his heart to stop racing, for the excitement that was running through his veins and flushing his skin hot to dissipate. He had to lean forward onto the railing. Her image ran back through his mind. Her pale skin like fine china, her bright blue eyes, her plump lips, her long, straight hair . . . He'd struggled to speak at first. It was hardest when she had stepped past him, dragging her scent with her: floral but light and classy. It had lined his throat. He didn't want to breathe it out.

'You alright, mate?' A male voice, now, deep and verging on aggressive. Lance straightened to where a man was standing on the garden path that led to the same house she had just stepped into. *My husband, he works late.* This had to be him. He had a rucksack slung over his shoulder, his suit jacket hung open over a T shirt that looked like it was used in sports. It was a mish-mash of an outfit. Like an office worker who had gone to the gym straight from work and then slung his jacket back on to get it home.

'Old age. Catches up with us all!' He still felt flushed — he was burning up. He kept his face down to get his focus back. He could see the man was wearing shoes with the thin laces undone to show white sports socks underneath. 'Long day?' Lance concentrated on keeping his tone level. He was able to stand straighter now, getting himself back under control.

'A full day, sure.' The man's tone was guarded.

'Your wife . . . She said you worked late sometimes. She had some trouble with noise from in there but she dealt with it. I'm staying here for a little while. I told her I'd make sure there were no more problems while I was here.'

'I haven't seen you before.' The man looked to be eyeing him closely.

'I haven't been here for a while. I can barely remember the last time I saw Jeremy.'

'Jeremy. That's his name, is it?' the man snarled. 'He's a pain in my arse. You tell him from me that my wife is the only thing stopping me coming round and bouncing that stereo off his head. I've got a young family in there, we all deserve to sleep peacefully at night.'

'I agree. I agreed with your wife and I agree with you. She made it clear, too. She has spirit!' He could feel himself flushing again, he looked away lest his eyes might give away his desire to watch that spirit crushed.

'She does. Tell me about it. She won't be holding me back anymore, though. Like I said, I hear it again, and I'll be round for a little chat. With *whoever* is in there.'

'Understood.'

The extended hand caught Lance out a little, so far it had only been posturing and aggression. He took it up. The grip was firm, verging on painful.

'Nice to be able to talk to someone in there finally.' He said and he moved to his door. Lance gritted his teeth, his attention on his own hand. The handshake wasn't an offer of friendship or a sign of mutual respect between two men. It had been a demonstration of his strength, of his superiority.

When the door was pulled shut, Lance took back to leaning on the handrail. He needed another moment to pause as the adrenaline surged through him again. It was almost too perfect. And right next door! Normally he liked to work with distance, observing closer only when he chose to, when he knew enough to be able to. Maybe this was possible here? He shook his head, the spots that had gathered in front of his eyes dissipating. His mind flickered with visions of her again — how her eyes had filled with panic when her daughter had spoken from the doorstep and how he longed to see that again.

'I don't scare easy,' he mumbled through lips parted in a wide grin. Then he shook his head. It was a bad idea — right next to where he was staying. No separation. He would have to look elsewhere.

But when he stepped back into his own house, he turned and fixed on the thin wall separating him from the family on the other side. He reached out to lay his hand flat against it. He could feel the heat between his palm and the paper where he still burned with excitement.

The strong-willed woman, the whining young child, the posturing husband with all his superiority . . . It could all come away in an instant. And he could watch it happen.

CHAPTER 11

Thursday

Maddie was early enough to be able to pull up a seat for the daily 9 o'clock briefing. They were commonplace when a major investigation was underway and essential in its early stages. The first few days of this sort of job were always chaos, with detectives sent out with numerous tasks and the results all dumped back into a central computer system rather than being run through an actual person. The system was called *HOLMES*. It probably stood for something, but Maddie had never bothered to learn what. She hated it. If you would allow yourself to be governed by it, you would be forever doing singular tasks then returning to the police station to type your update. It took a lot of the 'following your nose' elements out, you had to justify every action before you took it, and sometimes, the last thing she wanted to do was to justify, or even put into words, why she was knocking on a particular door or shaking a particular tree. For good detectives, following your nose was how you made progress in a case. But it was also what made regular meetings necessary.

Detectives were streaming in steadily. All were clutching their daybooks. Harry stood at the front, his daybook laid out open in front of him.

'It's nine a.m. so I'll make a start!' Harry called out over the din of officers shuffling paper and talking among themselves. The large meeting room just off Major Crime was standing room only around the table that covered the middle. Harry was standing up one end in front of the large TV screen where he had shown Maddie the pictures of their first victim. Today it was switched off. The spindly looking flipchart was propped up to his left and was turned to a fresh page. The room fell silent.

'A lot has been going on . . . so this is an opportunity for us all to talk about what we know to this point. I know you've all been updating on the system — thank you for that — so I'll just run through a quick review. A quick summary first, as we have more resources joining us all the time.' He took in a lungful of air.

'Tuesday morning at 10:07 a.m., we received an email to the Crimestoppers account that stated we'd find two bodies at 19 Princes Way, Canterbury. We were told to expect an adult male and his young son. Patrols arrive to find an adult male suspended over the stairs by his neck. The method of killing is believed to be a combination of numerous stab wounds from a sharp implement, mainly in his abdomen, and asphyxiation. He was able to support his weight on the steps, albeit on tiptoe, until his injuries got the better of him. We now have confirmation of this male as Justin Wright. At 11:22 a.m., the patrol officer on scene was approached by a woman we now know to be Alice Oxley. She was very panicked and reported that she had been approached by a male where she works at the Westgate Café, St Dunstans Street, Canterbury, who had told her that her ex-partner and her son were both dead. He said that he had killed them and she would find them at her home address. Her home address is walking distance from her place of work — or, in this case, running. Her son, Thomas

Wright, was at the scene. He was found barricaded in his bedroom, however, and was not physically harmed. The attack itself had happened much earlier. From the boy's account, we think it was shortly after his mother left for work — she gets to the café around six thirty a.m. most days but is believed to have been a little later on this day, as she had to wait for Justin to arrive as her babysitter.'

Harry took a moment. He seemed to be checking he still had the attention of the room.

'The boy also reports the sounds of his father crying out in pain and begging for his life.' If there had been anyone not paying attention, Maddie was sure they would be now. Harry continued.

'CSI have almost finished at the home address and the café. Our killer appears to be diligent and knowledgeable of police processes and also forensically aware. He is also likely to be aware of CCTV locations as it appears he has managed to leave the area without being picked up on one. Where is Jen Russell? I understand you were doing a run to see if that's possible?'

'Yes, guv.' A woman piped up from the back. She had been one of the last to enter.

'The outcome?'

'It's possible to stay off camera in that area. Easy, even. You definitely won't get found on the council CCTV — most of their cameras are down the other end of the high street where you've got the shops. There are some private cameras around there — a newsagent, a hotel, a couple of entrances to first floor flats and a few terraced houses with them camera doorbells — but these are much further up. It all depends which way he went when he left, and how long he stayed on St Dunstans Street. If he walked up and down there, he would have been caught on a fair few, if he dipped straight down one of the alleyways, he would have been lost straight away. They were obvious, too — most of the cameras at least. If he did any sort of recce, he would have been straight down an alley. I know I would.'

'If he has been doing a recce, then that in itself might give us an opportunity. Alice Oxley says the offender was at the café just about every day for the last three weeks, so we will need to be reviewing all of the CCTV we can. I will be putting out for more resources to go through it, but everyone can expect to have a turn.'

Maddie heard some sighs and moans. Most didn't even try to stifle them. And why would they? Harry would already know that no one was going to be putting their hand up for that job. CCTV reviews were something everyone hated. It was boring, massively time consuming, and very often totally pointless.

'Barry, you were tasked with our victim. What do you know?'

'Justin Wright was born in 1981. He's thirty-eight years old. He has a record from his early twenties — some minor ASB-type offences out on the town on a Saturday night. Open source information from the web has been far more useful than police records in piecing together a more recent picture of who he is. He owns a company that supplies skips. Wright Skips, as it's known, was once part of Wright Demolition that Justin ran with his brother, Richard. The two brothers went their separate ways around six years ago with Richard continuing the demolition and Justin focusing on skip hire. Their split appears to be have been without any issues and there's evidence they still work together on jobs. Of more interest, it would seem that Justin is unpopular for two reasons . . . Skip hire appears to be quite the territorial market and he's been in dispute with other companies right from the get-go. This rivalry, if we should call it that, has continued and there's criticism online regarding his bully-boy tactics. This goes so far as a Facebook page requesting persons boycott his firm with examples of stories where he has personally been less than pleasant.'

'Anyone specific mentioned? Person or company?'

'Yourbuild Skip Hire seem to be the most overt critics of Justin and his company, but they are not the only ones. He may have been moving into house clearance and other similar types of work, too. It would seem that everything he does is met with some degree of upset. This includes his private life — which is not so private. And this is the other reason for his unpopularity . . . his activities with the opposite sex. A bit of a womaniser, it would seem. I found any number of dating site profiles. And there are defunct profiles that he appears to have ditched or disabled when they were the target of either jilted or disappointed lovers — or partners of disappointed or jilted lovers. Overall, the picture I am building is of somebody who seems to have a talent for upsetting people. If that can be a talent!' Barry chuckled and most people had joined in with him. Barry was nervous overall — he didn't enjoy speaking in front of his peers. His face was flushed with some mottled white in the centre of his cheeks. His hair was long enough on top to be pushed over into a parting through which he ran his fingers continually.

'It might be somewhere,' Harry said. 'Anything else of relevance?'

'That's what I have so far.'

'Okay, then, thank you for that. I'll be assigning a few of you to work with Barry on Justin Wright. A lot of people don't like him, as you have just heard, which makes our job more difficult. But someone strung him up and took their time with him. There might be some more specific candidates when we dig around him properly. I will want anyone linked to him spoken to, any known disputes thoroughly investigated. Maybe start with the intimate partners. And his brother. Knowing Justin Wright is just about the most important part of this investigation right now.' Harry looked round the room as if looking for someone specific. 'Andrew, do you have any more of an update from the child?'

Maddie looked over to DC Andrew McArthur. He twitched like he had been poked and had to scoop up the daybook that had slid from his lap before he could speak.

'Yes . . . I spoke to him again. We had to get him checked out at hospital and then his mother wanted him back with her, as you can understand. I didn't press him. He said what we already know, really. He was locked in his bedroom. He was awake in bed when his mum brought some warm milk in for him, as she always does. He heard his dad arrive and his mum leave. Then he described someone making a noise at his door. He heard his dad shout but he said he wasn't shouting at him and he was "far away." He couldn't remember any words and from what he described, it sounded like he was shouting out in pain. The loudest noise was the drilling sound. He said it seemed to go on for a while. The next thing was when the police opened the door.'

'Drilling sound?' Maddie said.

'Sorry, DS Ives.' Harry always used her title when there were other officers around. 'A point I may not have mentioned in our chat. Our victim was suspended on a wire that was through a loop on the ceiling. We think this loop was installed as part of the incident. There was a handheld winch left at the scene, too.'

'Understood, thank you.' Maddie said. She had follow-up questions but this didn't seem like the time.

'Anything else?' Harry spoke directly to Andrew McCarthur.

'No. The one thing the boy does give us is an idea of timescales. He said that he heard someone at his door straight after his mum left — he thought it might have been her coming back. His dad's shouting was shortly after that. Then came the drilling sound. He couldn't get out of his bedroom and he spent the rest of the time crying.'

'So, the offender was waiting for Alice Oxley to leave?'

Barry shrugged. 'He might have been. I got a good account, I thought, considering he's six. He's a smart kid and he said the offender arrived almost as Alice left. I guess he needed to . . . If we think about it, he put up the loop, then did what he did before making it to the café for nine. The kid didn't get a look at him. He didn't hear him speak. He didn't even make it out of his bedroom.'

'That's good, at least.' Harry said. There were nods around the room. A six-year-old was never going to make a good witness if he did get a glimpse of the offender and the fact he didn't meant that there wouldn't be a need to involve him in any court proceedings. It also meant that he didn't physically see the murder of his father. Already, his life was never going to be the same again, but the damage might have been limited by the thickness of his bedroom door. They should be thankful for that.

'Anything anyone else thinks they should add?'

'The talk about the timings and the circs, are we assuming it's just one offender?' A voice called out from Maddie's right.

'No. As with any investigation, we're not making any assumptions. We have one suspect as it stands but keep an open mind for more please. Anything else?'

Harry took a moment to look round the room. No one responded. 'Okay, then. I think we all know where we are. Most of you have tasks for today already. Those who don't will have shortly. Maddie and I are in Deal for midday today, so we will be out of the way for a few hours, but I'm on my phone for anything that can't wait. You know I like to be kept informed.'

Maddie glanced at Harry. They hadn't discussed a trip to Deal. He seemed to avoid her eye contact, still talking over the group, who were getting their gear together. She waited out the sound of scraping chairs and low mutterings until there was just her and Harry left.

'We have plans in Deal, then?'

'We do. I got hold of Vince. You said you wanted to come.'

'I did. I do. You did well to get hold of him. He's been ignoring my calls.'

'Mine, too. I sent a patrol round there to bang on his door. I don't care that he doesn't want to speak to anyone. I need to be making sure he's okay. You reminded me of that.'

'Ticking the box for welfare?' Maddie said.

'There is a requirement. But give me some credit, Maddie.' Harry stopped gathering up his things to shoot her a warning look.

'Sorry. That wasn't a dig at you, more at the organisation.'

'They do care. They just have a funny way of showing it sometimes.'

'You think?'

'I don't think it matters. *We* care. And we're the ones going to see him. I should have been already.'

'Do you think we should take him something? He's been off for three weeks now — he must be bored out of his mind.'

'Bored? He's got mirrors, hasn't he?'

Maddie snorted a laugh. She hadn't expected that. 'Fair point! I'll tell him you said that.'

CHAPTER 12

The shouting started almost as soon as she got back. She had gone out with their young daughter, carrying her school bag and stopping at the end of their front path to do her coat up. The child had dawdled behind her mother, dragging and scuffing her feet, her bottom lip sticking out like she might trip over it. She had done her best to hurry her up. She had been gone thirty-nine minutes, her coat damp enough to suggest that she had walked there and back in the steady rain. She had looked hassled on her way out, and she looked even more hassled when she returned, despite losing the sulking child. She slapped the gate open and it creaked as a spring pushed it slowly shut behind her. Lance watched until he couldn't see her anymore, then came the dull thud through the wall, confirmation that she had closed her front door.

Around him the house still slept. Jeremy always seemed to end up in the living room and, it would seem, never alone. Another hopeless drunk was always present and occupying the other sofa or an area of the floor. Lance had only been there a couple of nights now, but already he could see the pattern of Jeremy's life. The men who had stayed had been different both nights. By morning, a woman had appeared on the floor. No one took any notice of him. They were barely sober enough to be conscious.

He moved into the hall and listened for more raised voices from next door. It didn't take long. He heard the creaking of stairs, someone coming down them, then a deep voice. It was the man he had seen coming home. Lance couldn't make out his words. The voices moved towards the back of the house. The kitchens of the two properties were side by side so Lance moved to stay close, but it was harder to make out what was being said. Next door's kitchen had been extended so only some of it lined up with the thin dividing wall. Lance pushed himself up against it. He could hear the tap dripping over dirty cups and plates in the kitchen he was standing in. Nothing from next door. He lingered for a few more moments with his ear to the wall and his gaze outside, where a gathering breeze bothered the overgrown back garden. A fence panel hung loose on the right side. It had been patched up by a piece of wood that didn't match the rest.

He broke away to check the fridge. He was careful to hold his breath as he tugged the door open. He wasn't sure it was even working — the light came on but nothing seemed to be any more chilled than room temperature. He had put a crate of strong beer in there yesterday and a bottle of vodka on the table. It was all gone. He tutted. He would need to go out and get some more. That was the agreement: he kept Jeremy in booze in exchange for a place to stay. But that wasn't why he was being so diligent in keeping the alcohol well stocked. He wasn't about to be turfed out, but a drunken Jeremy asked no questions and retained no information. Just how Lance liked it.

He crossed the kitchen to head towards the front door and the shop that was a ten-minute walk. He froze. The male voice from next door was back but it was louder now, aggressive, despite being filtered through the brick. A female voice shouted back. It was shriller and it cut through clearly: *Just don't lie to me!'* Then a follow-up that was a little quieter. He thought it was maybe, *'That's all I ask.'* The male voice came

93

back, also quieter. He was back to not being able to pick out any of the conversation. He walked down the hall to where his coat hung near the door. Then came more shouting and the only voice he could hear was male. The shouting seemed to be coming closer. Lance was frozen, his jacket scrunched up in his hand. There was a final bellow of *'Have it your way!'* He heard the front door slam. Lance ducked into the living room. Jeremy and his companions still slept. Through the front window, he watched the man stomp down the path. Again the gate clanged open and squealed shut. The husband turned left and was quickly out of sight.

Lance waited, just a few seconds to see if the woman followed him out. She didn't. He heard a noise from within the house, it sounded like it was to the rear. He made it back to the kitchen, pulling his jacket over his shoulders as he went. The top of a UPVC door was now visible above the fence panel on the right side. He inhaled deeply, then cursed himself as the hand that reached for the back door handle shook a little. 'Calm yourself, Lance,' he muttered. 'You're getting worse.'

The air outside was tinged with cigarette smoke. The long grass and tall trees all shook and whispered to each other in the strong breeze that whipped through the rattling fence. He stepped over to it, aiming for the panel that had been badly replaced. He felt the tall, wet grass dampen his shins. The cigarette smell was stronger here — she was close. He waited for the breeze to die down.

'Everything okay?' He waited, his fingers running down the fence. The delay was long enough that he considered he was being ignored and he turned to go back inside the house.

'Oh, great, so now the neighbours can hear us!' The voice that came back was full of anger and hurt. Lance froze.

'I'm hardly one to make a noise complaint!' he said.

There was laughter from the other side that sounded like it was full of smoke. 'The irony, eh? Sorry we disturbed you. It won't happen again.'

'It will. It does, when you're living together. When you have a kid, bills . . . It happens.'

'Those are hard enough. But I was expecting them. It's keeping it in his pants that seems to be the challenge.'

'I see.'

'Sorry. I shouldn't have said that, either. We're fine, thanks for asking.'

'No problem. You want to talk about it?' There was another pause. Lance was back at the fence, his fingers again splayed against the coarse wood. He still had a shake. He could feel the excitement flushing through him. Maybe she would! Maybe he would be a shoulder to cry on! He could barely imagine where that might lead, how close she might let him get — and how *beautiful* that moment might be when he turned it round, when she saw what he really was.

'No. No disrespect, but we're strangers. It won't happen again.'

He heard footsteps, then a door pulled shut. The smell of cigarettes lingered, despite the breeze. He drew it in through his nose to savour it, the last remnants of her.

When he was calm enough, he moved away from the fence. His whole body tingled and the centre of his back flushed hot. He needed to go out and top up the alcohol supply. He couldn't have Jeremy sobering up and asking questions — or just getting in the way in general. Things were moving faster than he had hoped. *Strike and move* . . . A maxim that had always served him well. Jeremy might not be a concern for much longer. He could be moving much earlier than he had anticipated.

CHAPTER 13

Maddie stepped out of the car and stretched. Harry was already around to the pavement on her side of the car and making his way towards Vince Arnold's house, some way back up the road. Harry had grabbed the only space that seemed available within a square mile. She jogged to catch him up.

'Nice area,' she said. She meant it, too. It was a tight street and the houses either side formed two sturdy, unbreaking lines, but it had the feeling of a row of fishermen's cottages rather than a cramped terrace. She guessed that to have been their purpose, once. They had followed the main promenade to get here, the glittering sea close on their right side. The turn left was directly into Vince's road. It was a little way along, far enough for the sea view to be lost but the air was tinged with salt from a breeze that was straight at their faces.

'Shame about the parking,' Harry grumbled back.

'Could be worse!' Maddie pointed at an ugly, brightly coloured wheel clamp that was choking the driver's side of an old saloon car. It looked out of place in a row of neat little houses with gleaming doors and colourful hanging baskets.

Vince Arnold was breathing heavily when he answered his door. He wore a T shirt with the arms cut roughly shorter and shorts tighter than Maddie might have liked to see. He raised a towel to wipe the sweat from his face, turned away from his front door and moved into the house. Maddie took it as an invitation and followed him through. From the front door, it was two steps into a porch, then through another door straight into the living room. The house was small, as she had expected, but the space was used well enough for it to be cosy rather than cluttered.

The closeness to the sea provided the theme as she looked around. A modern-looking pair of oars crossed over as a display on one of the walls. As she got closer, she could see they were signed. Vince appeared in a few pictures, too, mostly in a long boat and seemingly as part of a rowing team. Overall, the room was welcoming: earthy colours, a comfortable sofa facing a log burner and a plush carpet. The stairs to the first floor came down the middle of the ground floor, dividing the room in two and turning away from the door at the bottom. Maddie had to duck under the stairs as she went through to the back of the house.

The seaside theme continued in the kitchen. It was modern but still in keeping with the cottagey feel overall. Through the window, Maddie could see a wood cabin in the garden that was side-on. The double doors at the front were spilling open and some loose weightlifting equipment was dotted around the grass area.

Vince was wiping himself with the towel. 'Kettle on then, yeah?' he said.

'We're not interrupting anything, are we?' Harry said.

'Just finished, boss. I put my own gym together out there about eighteen months ago. A bit of a godsend, really, I've been using it a lot.'

'Glad to see you're filling your time productively.'

Vince peered out towards his cabin. 'Not much else I can do.'

The kettle started its hiss. From the kitchen there was a door to the side. She followed Vince and Harry through it into a small conservatory. There were more sofas here, but they were made of a wicker material and the covers looked a little more beaten up than those in the lounge. The whole room in general had more of a feeling of being used, but that was no slight. It was pleasantly warm, the sofas were deceptively comfortable, and the views out into the neat garden were unobstructed. As Maddie sat, she was aware of a bundle of fur down to her right that moved as if it had been disturbed. A collie got to its feet and stretched, then moved to sit under Maddie's hand.

'That's Alfie. Ignore him and he'll go away. He belongs to the old boy next door — he's an old boy himself, mind!'

'Does the old boy next door know you've got him?' Maddie asked.

'He doesn't know much, to be honest. He's in hospital. Gets easily confused. I told his lad I'd look after Alfie for now, just until . . . well, just until they know what's going on.'

'You gonna get lumbered with him?' Maddie chuckled at the thought.

Vince didn't even break a smile. He simply shrugged, his gaze falling to where the dog still agitated for a stroke. 'Been nice having him around, to be honest. He's a good old boy — no trouble. Loves the beach. He can stay as long as he likes.' He stood as the kettle boiled. Maddie relented to the pressure and stroked Alfie's head.

'How have you been?' Harry shouted after Vince.

'Alright boss, thanks. Suppose you heard . . . the quack signed me off for a month?'

Harry hesitated a moment. 'I did, yeah. Probably a good thing, all in.'

'I thought so.' Vince appeared back at the door, holding a spoon that balanced a steaming tea bag. 'This visit off the record?'

'No. You have to have a visit. It has to be recorded that you did. The job has a responsibility to look after you. I'm sorry no one's been out yet.'

Vince waved Harry away. 'I ain't worried about that. I just hope they're working with the skipper's family. I meant you ain't writing down nothing I say, right?'

'No, Vince. I have to go back and say that I saw you and that you're okay. Ticks a few boxes. That's about it.'

'Well, I am. You can say that. I think the job were relieved when I said I was signed off, too. They suspended me to start with, then they were talking about having me back in the office, doing some case file stuff — whatever that means. They said I wouldn't be able to go out and about or even deal with prisoners. I've never wanted to be a detective. I *definitely* don't want to be a detective with one hand tied behind my back. No offence, of course!'

'None taken.' Harry said.

'I said I could do without it. I think the doc could tell I had the hump about the whole thing and he signed me off for a month — just like that: stress. He said someone like me should be taking the time off anyway, after what happened. I've never been one for all that, for being off work, but I was actually a bit relieved. I can't face being there at the moment.'

'We all understand, Vince. I don't think you should be back yet in any capacity. Take your time. This certainly isn't the time to be pushing you into a new role either, where you'll need to pick up new skills.'

'New skills?' Vince had moved back into the kitchen and was calling out now. Maddie could hear the humour in his voice. 'You mean like staying in when it gets cold and having a detailed map of the city's coffee shops to hand at all times?'

'Takes time to perfect!' Harry smiled. He finally sat down. His seat was opposite Maddie.

'You been okay, Mads?' Vince shouted from the kitchen.

'All good, thank you, Vince.'

'Not missing me too much?' She smiled. She had known something like that was coming.

'Not so much as I can't cope. Obviously it's getting harder the longer you're off. That's why I'm here, just to see if there's any light at the end of the tunnel.'

Vince re-emerged with two steaming cups. He smiled.

'You did that on purpose, Mads — setting me up with a comment like that when you know the boss is here. I ain't falling for it. I ain't taking the bait and this is my house now, Mads, you need to behave while you're here.'

Maddie laughed. 'I'll try. Just promise me you'll sit next to me and not opposite. I don't trust those shorts.'

Vince returned to the kitchen. He came back with his own cup and flopped next to her. 'These are my old rugby shorts. Sitting next to you won't make any difference either, I'm afraid. If this mouse is out the house, you'll all know about it.'

'Respectfully, Vince,' Harry said, 'I know I said everything was off record but, *for the record*, make sure the mouse is secured, please. We're only stopping for ten minutes.' Maddie struggled to control her laughter.

'Got a lot on?' Vince asked over the top of his mug.

'Yes, actually.'

'I saw the news about a body earlier in the week over in Canterbury. Kid was there, too, they said? Nasty business. What's that about?'

'We don't know much more. Our victim seems to have a talent for upsetting people, so we're not short on suspects.'

'I'm sure you'll get to the bottom of it. You always do.' Vince fell silent and looked a little pensive. Maddie knew what was coming next.

'Any news of the investigation on the skipper? Nearly a month down the line, I thought there would be something by now. No one's keeping me up to date. They said they would.'

Harry sucked in air through his nose. He took his time. 'I wish I had something to tell you. We're being kept right out of it, too. They figure we're too close to the investigation. They have a team they pulled together from all over. The SIO is from out of the county.'

'You mean me? Too close to me?'

'Not just you. Tim, too. We both knew him, we both worked with him and we can't help but have a personal attachment, a desire for a just outcome.'

'That's a good thing, surely?'

'It needs someone who follows their nose, not their heart. It's for the best.'

'And how are they doing? Following their noses I mean? They any good?'

'We don't even know who's working it. I've been told there's a lot of resour—'

'I was badgering them a lot, the first week after I came back from leave,' Maddie jumped in. 'I got told to wind my neck in, basically. They don't want us involved. I got the hump with it at first but there's nothing we can do.' She ignored the dirty look from Harry.

'They should be updating me,' Vince said. 'I'm a victim, too. They said they would.'

'They should. We all know that we're not very good at updating police victims. You might need to make that point.'

'I will be, don't you worry.'

'You're okay, though?' Maddie said. 'Really, I mean.'

'Yeah, I've got a few cans of man-up in the fridge. I've been supping on them of a night when I fancy.'

'Drinking on your own?'

'You asking me out, DS Ives?'

'Just checking you've got mates is all. I've never been confident.'

'Ha! Don't you worry about me.'

'Too late for that. You still seeing someone, Vince? Moved her in yet?'

'Nah. She's not on the scene for now.'

'So you are drinking alone?' Maddie pressed.

'Don't you worry about me. A cup of Darjeeling, occasionally a hot chocolate if there's a chill.'

'So I don't need to be worrying about you? There's someone out here you're talking to?'

'Nothing to worry about here. I can't say it again.' There was a change of tone, subtle but distinctive. Maddie was expecting a cheeky comment about how she could keep him company if she wanted or something similar. His sudden change in tone caught her out.

'You been asked that a lot?'

'Enough,' Vince conceded. 'I've got my sister. I see her most days for something or other. She's not shy in asking the same thing over and over either.'

'Okay, then, we won't be asking again. I can see for myself anyway. You keep a nice place here.'

'Never been tidier. Me and Alfie, there, have got quite the routine. Eat, walk, shit and then a bit of a tidy-up.'

'Too much information, Vince.' Harry said.

Vince chuckled. 'You know I meant the dog, right?'

Maddie's phone was a sudden interruption. She blushed and fumbled to switch it off, mumbling her apologies. She had a chance to read the screen — it was her mother calling. When she looked up, she caught Vince looking at her.

'You okay?' he said, 'seeing as how it seems to be the thing to ask these days!'

'Oh, yeah,' she said. 'I thought it was switched off. Sorry.'

'You really are rattled, Mads. This extended period without me . . . maybe I should have thought it through more. I could have set up a helpline, some counselling maybe!'

'Maybe you should.' She drained the last of her tea and reached to put it down on a coaster. Vince watched her, seeming to take it as a hint.

'Well, I guess you two have some police work to get back to, then. Can't be wasting too much time with the sick and wounded. Thanks, though — I *mean* it — for popping in an' all that. There's always a cup of tea here.'

Maddie stood up immediately. 'No probs. You've got my number if you need anything. Even just a drink away from here or something.' Maddie moved towards the door. Harry was following. 'I mean what I say.'

'And I meant what I said,' Vince said. 'If I had realised this was all it was going to take to get you out for a drink, I would have pushed the skipper in front of a gun a long time ago!' Vince's laughter seemed genuine. Maddie's certainly was. It felt like a good way to leave.

'In a rush all of a sudden?' Harry said, the moment the door was pushed shut behind them. Maddie had her head bent, studying the phone in her hand.

'Sorry. The phone call . . . It was my mum.'

'Something wrong?'

'I just know it's about going to see my dad. I said I would and now I wish I hadn't.'

'I see.' Harry paused like he might be considering his next words. 'We all have to do these sorts of things sometimes.'

'Do we?'

'Well, no. You have a choice. But sometimes a little bit of pain makes life easier in the long run.'

'If I just ignored her calls for long enough, she would stop. Then I wouldn't hear from either of them again. What could be easier than that?'

'We both know the impact that would have on you. You wouldn't be easy on yourself, not in the long run. Would you?'

Maddie sighed. 'No . . . I wouldn't. I'm going to have to do this, aren't I?'

Harry stepped out into the road for the driver's side as they made it back to the car and peered back over the roof at her. 'Call her now. Tell her you can make it whenever. I'll be waiting in the car.' He tugged open the door to get in. Maddie was still staring at her blank phone when she heard the car's central locking system clunk where Harry must have locked it again.

'So much for having a choice!' she said.

CHAPTER 14

5:33 p.m and she was already away from the house. He watched her down the path. Tonight she wore a scarf that looked expensive and a long sandy-coloured jacket that tailed off into a pointed shape at the back over tight, black jeans. There was a fashionable rip on both knees. The jeans tapered down to grip her ankles above a pair of low, black heels. She looked good, like someone out to make an impression.

It had only been seven minutes since the husband had come home. He wore the same suit jacket as the evening before. It was a straight swap, a tag team perhaps, one in to look after the young child so the other could go out. But this felt like something different. This felt like a woman who didn't want to be in that house. A marriage in trouble. He could imagine the conversation. He wondered if her husband even knew what she was intending. He might have been expecting to pick up where they had left off earlier that day. Maybe he had been hoping it would all be calmer. And here she was, straight out and looking her best.

The breeze was strong. Lance pulled the door to Jeremy's house and closed it gently behind him. It didn't matter. She had set off at quite a pace and no way would have been near enough to hear a door closing. He made it to the end of the path, to where she had turned left. He could see her in the distance. The breeze carried a hint of rain and she had pulled her hood up. She was having to hold it up, her head ducked down and tucked in. She wasn't taking much notice of anything going on around her. Perfect.

She was heading towards Canterbury's centre. This road led all the way to the high street. He was able to hold back far enough to see her with ease. He crossed to the other pavement for a better view. She wasn't looking back — she was barely looking out. Her movement off the street was sudden. Her pace barely changed as she veered a sharp right into a hair salon. Lance crossed back over to pass it on the same side. It was getting dark, enough for the inside of the shop to have a vibrant white glow. His neighbour had dropped her hood and now embraced a woman who had scissors hanging from her knuckles as she stood behind a seated client. The hug was lingering. His neighbour had her back to him but he imagined her to be upset. The woman holding the scissors was saying something, but he couldn't wait around to guess what that might be. He had a snapshot, a moment frozen in time, and that was all he needed to build his picture. She was upset, upset at the way she was being treated at home, upset that he was out cheating while she was left to look after their child, and now she was with someone who could make her feel better.

Lance continued until he came to a newsagent's. His pace was quicker, as fast as he could manage without attracting attention. He bought a pack of strong beer. He would add them to the alcohol he had gone out for earlier. He was just a guy out buying beer.

He saw her immediately as he walked back past the salon. This time, she was sitting over to the right, the seat reclined so her hair fell into a shaped sink. A different girl was running over it with a handheld showerhead. She looked quite a bit younger — the apprentice, perhaps. His neighbour had her eyes closed. The hairdresser who had hugged her looked like she was still talking to her, despite having a customer in front of her. The seated woman had a frown, irritated maybe that she wasn't getting all the attention anymore. Lance knew that women went to get their hair cut for the attention, for someone to take an interest in them and their lives. That was just as important as the result. His neighbour was being prepped for her own haircut and she would need a lot of attention. He had plenty of time.

He carried on, the beers swinging from his grip. The rain and the wind both seemed a little stronger and the layers of grey cloud above suggested it might get worse. His pace quickened again. It was nothing to do with the threat of the weather. It was excitement and it was knowing that he was now on the clock. He had never been spontaneous in his line of work — it was not to be advised — but recently, he was seeing the benefits. The highs were so much higher. He shook his head, his cautious self telling him that he should forget about the family next door, that it was too risky, that he still had the opportunity to move on, to find something more suitable.

But his pace didn't slow and his excitement didn't wane.

* * *

'Would you believe it?' Michelle Rice pushed the heavy, glass door of her best mate's salon open but made no movement to step out into the sodden world. The sound of the heavy rain was instant. She could feel droplets splashing back up onto her feet and lower leg. 'Maybe heels wasn't the best idea! My day's getting better and better.' She turned back to look into the bright shop. Angela Bennet glared back over at her, trying to look stern but the glint in her eye letting her down.

'Don't you dare take that work of art out into that deluge!' she said.

'You mean my hair?' Michelle ran her fingers through her new do. 'You like it, do you? I just had this done. Not bad, considering. I tell you what, though, I took one look at the girl who did this and I thought to myself, this isn't going to turn out well! Just shows, you can never judge a book by its cover.'

'Cheeky mare! You take that out into the rain and this will have been a waste of both our time. Give it a minute. It can't stay that heavy.'

Michelle rocked her head back to look up at the sky. She lifted her hand to run it over the back of her neck at the same time. She was so tired. She didn't know why she was in a hurry anyway, the only thing to rush back home for was another argument and more lies.

'I'm not so bothered about getting home, I just wanted a fag.'

'You smoking again?' Angela stopped what she was doing. She could be quite infuriating. She loved to talk, she was so well suited to the job from that point of view, and she was one of the best hairdressers around of course, but whenever she talked, she had to stop what she was doing. Angela had cut Michelle's hair for ten years or more now and she often had to make a decision as to whether she wanted good conversation or to get out of there in a reasonable time. Tonight had taken a couple of hours. They had talked about going out for a beer. Angela had said that she just needed to finish up with another client and she would be done for the day. But Michelle didn't like to miss bedtime. She knew Fern didn't settle all the time she was out. And she knew Scott would be getting angrier and angrier while he sat there on his own. She had deliberately timed the appointment for around the time he got in from work. He would have known that. He was meant to.

'I only smoke when I'm stressed, you know that.'

'I don't know why you let him stress you out. He's the one that should be at home bricking it, wondering what the hell he's going to do when you tell him to sling his hook.' Angela stopped her snipping to make her point again. Michelle was fidgeting with her packet of cigarettes. She was holding the door with her shoulder, her feet now visibly wet. 'You are leaving him, right?'

'What?'

'Scott. You're leaving him?'

'I don't know, Ange . . . Jesus . . .' She struggled to light her cigarette while the door threatened to push her back into the salon. It seemed the wind was stronger, too.

'You don't know?'

'I don't know!' Michelle snapped. 'I can't ditch five years of marriage, not just like that. There's Fern, too . . . and the house and everything.'

'He made a choice, though, surely, when he went off and slept with someone else.'

Michelle sucked far too much of the cigarette as part of her reaction. She had to close her eyes as her head rushed with the chemicals. She worked her mouth to try and help it clear. 'You wanna shout that louder? I think there's someone on the other side of the street who didn't quite catch what you said.'

Angela had stopped to the point where she had stepped away from her customer. 'It don't matter who hears me, they would all agree — they would all say the same. Look at you! You're gorgeous and it ain't just because of the genius who had a go at your hair. The man's a fool. And we don't think this is the first time, do we? He ain't about to change, not for no one.'

Michelle found a smile from somewhere. 'I never called you a genius.'

'You don't need to. You see enough of your own work and you start to realise. You're drop dead, 'Chelle. You could walk out of here into the nearest pub and you'd have them all over you! In fact . . .'

'No! I said *no*. The last thing I want right now is anyone all over me.' She turned back to where the noise of the rain seemed to be less powerful. It was slowing down.

'I'm gonna head home for another argument. See what he's got to say, at least.'

'And then kick him out?'

Michelle shrugged. 'I don't want him there tonight. He said he would go to his mum's for a few days, I think he wants to.'

'Of course he does! That's giving him the freedom he wants to go out and fu—'

'Ange! I get it, okay? I can't be thinking about what he's doing. That's down to him. I just need to worry about me and Fern. It's better if he isn't there for now — it's not a nice atmosphere. He can go to his mum's.'

'And not come back!'

'We'll see. I'm gonna head home. You sure you're okay for me to owe this one?'

'Don't matter if I'm not, does it? You said you were skint! I'm teasing you, babes. That one's on me, yeah.'

'It isn't. I'm good for it. I'm not quite at the stage where I'm the sad act spinster who needs a freebie!' Michelle was careful about putting up her hood so as not to ruin her new style.

'Are you not?' Angela called after her. 'You should have said that before I did your hair! I thought that was the look you were going for!'

Michelle lifted her hand away from the hood momentarily to show her middle finger. She heard laughter and something called out in response, but the door fell shut half way through.

The rain was harder than she had thought. She flicked her cigarette into the gutter where the running water swept it up instantly to tumble end over end. The whole scene seemed a lot more vivid now, with the artificial lights of the shops and passing traffic reflected off every sodden surface. Her feet couldn't get any wetter and her shoes were starting to rub as a result. She considered taking them off but would wait until they became unbearable. It was only a ten-minute walk.

When she got to her own street, she realised how dark it had become. It was just as wet here, but there was no light leaking from shopfronts and fewer car headlights to remove the blocks of shadows. Her own house looked to be in darkness from the front. Fern's bedroom was on the first floor at the back. Scott would probably be up there listening to her read. She was too late to be able to take over. She would leave him to it, wait for him to come down and then they would talk. She stopped to lean on her gate, partly from hesitation and partly due to the pain in her heel where her shoe was rubbing. Next door was in darkness, too, aside from a white light clinging to the underside of the porch that was so covered in grime and dusty webs that the light was largely ineffective. There was no noise, at least. The man had been true to his word at keeping them quiet. She should be glad of that. She couldn't be sure how she would react if they upset her now.

She pushed the gate open and it gave off its usual squeal.

* * *

The sound of the gate took his breath away so hard he almost choked. He knew what it meant. She was back. She was *here!* The excitement had started to wear off. Getting into the house has been so easy, too easy almost, and he had taken it as another sign that this was fate. That this was meant to be.

He heard the key in the lock. He had pushed himself as far back into the cupboard as he could and something was digging into his back. He couldn't quite see the front door, but he could tell it had been pushed open from the way the light had changed. He held his breath. He leaned forward a little. He wanted to hear every single sound. She stepped in. *He could see her!* His view out into the hall was restricted through the slats in the cupboard door, but it was enough for him to see her as an outline. The light was weak, just what was leaking in from the street through a heavily frosted glass panel above the front door. She hung her coat on a peg and sighed as if she was tired. He saw the dark outline of her arm as she reached for a switch. Suddenly the hall was flooded with light. She squinted and put her keys down in a pot on a side unit almost directly opposite him. There was a full-length mirror on the wall, right where she had hung her coat. She checked herself in it, pushing her hair up, scrunching bits in her hand. She sighed again, her mouth falling into a sort of pout. He could see her whole reflection at a slight angle. He had to bite his lip to stop a gasp of utter ecstasy. It was perfect. She pushed her top so it fell off her shoulders, her new hair trailed down her soft skin, her full lips curling into a smile that also seemed to light a sparkle in her eyes. He could see the confidence flowing back into her, the life with it.

Then!

Just like that, she must have caught something in the corner of her eye. Lance knew what it was. Her husband's form was right where he had left him: suspended from their banister above, his toes brushing the bottom step, his head rolled forward on a tight ligature, his tongue hanging out, his skin drained of colour, washed out of the blood that pooled around him.

'Scott?' Her voice shook. At first glance, he might have looked to her as if he was standing on the step, waiting for her to come home. Lance had even tried to fashion him so he had his hands on his hips, as if ready to continue their argument. He had envisaged her coming in and having a go at him, maybe even walking right past him and through to the kitchen. But he had dismissed that. People knew the dead. It was the stillness.

He had run through her coming home in great detail — over and over. He knew she would turn the light on first and then he had been certain she would see Scott right off. He was straight ahead of her with a slight lean forward, his skin so white, in stark contrast to the angry red around his neck where the ligature had tightened. And then there were the wounds in his chest. The blood that had flowed from them saturated his white shirt. He hadn't even considered that she might turn to the mirror first, that she might check her own beauty, that he would be able to watch the confidence flow back into her before he got to see it snatched away again. It had been incredible. More signs that fate was working with him to ensure perfection.

The early discovery of the slatted cupboard had made him so excited, he had let out a little whimper at the possibilities. When he had stepped in and first seen that view out, his legs had nearly given out, his back had flashed so hot he had needed to get back out again and pull the front door open to cool himself off. He had listened to the rain, counted backwards from twenty to get his breathing back under control. Then he had got back in the cupboard to wait. It had been nearly an hour. It had been worth it.

She had frozen still, just a few feet away from him — *touching distance!* She could see her husband now. And Lance could see her.

He must have moved forward slightly. He jerked back as his nose bumped the wood of the door.

'Scott?' She said again, her voice a little louder.

'*Mummy! I can't get out!*' A terrified voice came from upstairs. The child had stayed quiet so far. Her dad had been stern when he told her to, enough that she would have felt that she was being scolded. The sound of her voice now was like a prod to her mother's side. She sprung forward, her scent disturbed as she did, pushing through the wooden slats. He inhaled, long and deep. The delicious woody scent of the door mingled with hair products, perfume, rain and the essence of fear. It was unbelievable. As good as anything he had ever inhaled. He wanted to preserve that moment — that smell — for the rest of his life. His eyes fell shut.

'*Scott!*' She was out of sight now, her voice a shriek. There was a moment's pause then another shout. '*Fern!*' The wooden stairs thumped and scraped as heels sprinted up them. '*Fern!*'

He pushed the cupboard door open. He inhaled deeply through his nose as he stepped out. There were more sounds from above. He moved to the bottom of the stairs. He lifted his hands to his wig. His head was itchy, the ponytail trailed down to where his back ran with sweat under the layers. He stopped to stare into Scott's dead eyes.

'She won't be coming back down for you,' he muttered. His voice shook from the adrenaline.

'*Stay here, baby, stay here with Mummy!*' There was a pause, then she spoke again. '*Yes! The police! You need to come right now. I just came home . . . My husband . . . I think he hung himself!*'

Lance's gaze flicked up the stairs. He stepped away from Scott. He felt a pang of disappointment — *hung himself?* She must have missed the blood, the gaping wounds that leaked into his clothing. He licked his lips, his mind racing with an idea, about how he could prolong this moment, about how he could tell her what he had done. *Show* her, even!

He lifted his foot to rest on the bottom step. She was talking on the phone — to the police. He shook his head. This was too much. He needed some control. He counted back from five. Then he took his foot off the step and turned away. He moved slowly back to the hall mirror, to where she had stopped on her way in. He wanted to see if her scent lingered. There was nothing of her left. He lifted a gloved hand to disturb her jacket, inhaling as he did. Better.

It was time to go.

He pulled the door open roughly, then stood still. The sound of the beating rain rushed in.

'*Hello! Is someone there?*' The fear in her voice! The terror! *He had done that!* His desire to stay, to tell her, to show her who was in her house and tell her *exactly* what he had done returned in a rush. But he couldn't. There hadn't been the time to plan, not like he normally did. This had been better than ever. And it wasn't over yet.

He stepped out into the rain. The wind took hold of the door behind him and bounced it off the wall. There was a sound on the stairs, heels coming back down the first few but slower, tentative. Then her voice again.

'*I think there's someone here! Oh, God! The door's open — there's someone here!*'

He had already stepped over into the shadow of next door's porch. It was just a hop over the wall. His hands were shaking so much, he couldn't get the key in the lock for

Jeremy's house. It didn't matter. There was no way she was going to come out of that house, not with her child in there. He counted backwards from twenty. It worked to calm him enough and he opened Jeremy's front door. He paced past the living room, where Jeremy and a male friend were already comatose on the sofa.

'Strike and move!' he muttered.

He needed to get his stuff together. This wasn't finished yet.

It was going to be incredible.

* * *

The police seemed to arrive all at once and Michelle felt like she was swept to one side. They filled her house, moving from room to room, turning on her lights, pointing their tasers, shouting '*Police!*' Fern was terrified, her grip so tight on her mother's leg that she wanted to cry out in pain. But Michelle didn't want to push her off, she didn't want to send that message and besides, it was the only thing she could feel through the fog. They were at the top of the stairs and Michelle was looking down with Fern tucked in tight behind her legs. Michelle had meant to walk her away so she couldn't see her dad, but Fern had crumpled like a dead weight when she had tried to move her. She hadn't had the energy to force her and now she was transfixed herself.

Scott looked different from behind, more natural even, as if he was leaning forward to see the front door under the bit where the ceiling dipped in the way, like she had seen him do before. His arms gave him away, though. They hung off shoulders that slung forward and his legs were slightly bent. The ligature was thin, a cable of some sort, barely visible. She could almost pretend that he was stooping, that she had imagined what she had seen when she had come home. That it wasn't his blood that dripped onto the sodden carpet of the bottom step. That he wasn't dead.

But he was.

The police, who had entered as a frenzied mass through the door and split in every direction off the hall, were back as a mass again at the place where they had begun. They all approached Scott. One broke off to step around him and come up the stairs — a woman. She held her hands out, trying to block the view. She had a high-visibility jacket on. The landing light was so bright, it flared her edges, making her look bigger. At least, that was how it looked to Michelle through her tears. They came now. Shock, realisation, desperation. It all started to leak out from her.

* * *

The sirens had drifted in like distant thunder on the edge of an approaching storm. The top bedroom of Jeremy's house was nothing more than a storage room. The bed was so cluttered with junk that the only part of it that was visible to Lance was one of the legs of the bed frame. Even that stuck out at an angle where the whole thing had collapsed under the weight of old bike parts, tube televisions and more alcohol bottles than he could care to count. All of them were empty and discarded, a reflection of the room in general.

But Lance stood in it now. He had stripped down to the waist. He had needed to — his body had felt like it was almost reaching boiling point. He always felt like this when he was high. This was the rush. Normally it was starting to diminish by now, but tonight had just been so . . . *perfect*. And it wasn't over yet. The window was a deep bay, made up of two windows pushed out at an angle and the third in the middle facing him square on. All three were sash windows made of old wood that had swollen over time to make their mechanisms choppy, but he had been able to force them open. Each one was lifted as far as it would go. The wind pushed in the rain and the sensation across his bare torso took his breath away. He inhaled long and deeply. The smell of stale air and discarded liquor had been sucked out the window instantly and now all he could smell was the freshness of the rain. The drops were so big, he could see them individually. Suddenly they pulsed blue. The first of the strobe lights were arriving. The sirens stayed distant. The police cars were killing their noise some way out as if they didn't want the bad man inside the house next door to know they were getting close. They had no idea he had an elevated view from a neighbour's darkened window.

A couple of cars arrived together, a third just behind. They parked untidily, the occupants pushing doors open before the wheels had even stopped turning. Heavy boots sploshed into puddles, then pounded up the path. When they got to the door they bellowed, power in their voices. '*Police!*'

More cars arrived and braked hard, stopping short to block the street behind them. More heavy boots stepped out, more shouts: '*Police! Police! Police!*'

Lance inhaled. There was no mistaking fear. You could hide it in your voice by shouting louder. You could hide it in your body language by puffing out your chest and moving forwards. But you couldn't hide the scent. The air was thick with it. The droplets flashed with it. The drains gurgled and filled with it.

He had done that.

He turned away from the pulsing streets and driving rain and found a T shirt. He slipped it over his head then wrenched his wig off in a sudden movement. It picked and pulled at his hair and skin as it came away, but the feeling of relief was instant. He had a bag readied at the door. He shoved his wig into the main compartment, having to focus to work the zip shut. His body still surged with the adrenaline that was burning him up. He couldn't bear to wear anything more than his T shirt and trousers.

Stepping out onto the garden path, he was saturated instantly. He lifted his head to the rain, half expecting every drop to steam as it struck him. He walked to the pavement. Some of the police cars were ticking over as they littered the road. He turned right and walked past them, glancing back to where the door to the neighbour's house hung open, to where every window was lit with shadows moving behind them, to where fear leaked out like the light from the bulbs.

He made it to the end of the road. A distant siren approached at speed, then a high revving police car gave two honks on the horn as it came into view. The siren stopped and the car flashed past him. He stepped out behind it, turning in the middle of the road to watch as the brake lights, sudden and powerful, gave the standing water a deep red glow. The rain seemed stronger still, the drops hitting him so hard it was starting to sting. He liked the sensation. He lifted his arms out, increasing the surface area, increasing the sensation, turning his palms up. He felt every strike, not just those on his body but all around him — he felt *everything*. It was all here for him . . . *because* of him. For a moment, he was convinced that if he dropped his arms, the rain would stop with it. He was a god. He had life and death in his hands.

He turned away from a whole street that glowed blood red, every inch soaked in fear.

He had done that.

CHAPTER 15

Maddie stripped off her coat and dropped it in a heap. She moved to stand by the radiator. It was fiery hot, too hot for her bare hands but pleasant enough to lean against, for a few moments at least. Soon, the searing heat was through the seat of her trousers and she had to fidget.

'You should hang that up,' Harry growled. He was still in his waxed coat and it dripped from the cuffs onto the floor.

'You should take yours off. Are you not staying?'

'I figure we'll be sticking around for ten minutes or so,' he grumbled. He pulled his jacket off. 'Time to put a pot on at least.'

Maddie smiled at his sarcasm, but it was strained. This had the makings of a long night that hadn't started yet. She watched him cross the floor to the kitchenette. Major Crime was quiet. It ran with an eighty-twenty split, meaning that the vast majority of their available resource worked a day shift, leaving a handful of DCs working lates. There was also one DC assigned to work the night — and he was already showing as sick from the night before. Maddie looked to the blackened window running with constant raindrops and considered that it was highly unlikely their night duty resource would find any motivation to cut his sickness short. She wasn't expecting him in later.

'Coffee?' Harry's growl cut across the empty space to snap her from her thoughts.

'Strong,' Maddie said.

Right on cue, the door was pushed open and two DCs appeared to shake the water from their jackets. Their hassled faces showed surprise as their inspector leaned out of the kitchenette to offer them hot drinks.

'Yes please, boss,' Helen Smithers answered. She was in front of Barry Carter. Both were experienced detectives. Maddie had been relieved when they had turned up as reinforcements. They had both been on the day shift as well and had seen their enquiries run over to the point where they had been available to ask. Both had agreed to stay on — she'd expected nothing less. This was what Major Crime was all about. There were a couple more still at the Rice family home but they shouldn't be long. The scene belonged to CSI for now. Major Crime had pulled back to regroup. They would need to have a plan for first thing in the morning. Maddie rubbed her eyes. Even the semblance of a plan seemed a long way off.

They took their drinks into the briefing room. No one spoke. Harry was last in, having doubled back for his daybook. He rubbed his hand over his head as he walked back in, his closely cropped hair making a noise that could only be heard in a room silenced by tension.

'Right then, people . . . I know we were all due off a couple of hours ago. I don't intend on keeping you too much longer, but be warned . . . the boss may have different ideas. I think the most important thing is to be fully prepped for the morning so we're ready to go with a full house of detectives. CSI have the scene tonight. We have initial accounts from those who matter and we can revisit the key witnesses in the morning.'

Harry fiddled with the laptop that was left in the room to power the screen. Or at least, it would have done if the

operator had known what he was doing. 'Talk among your-
selves a minute.' He tutted.

Maddie's attention was drawn to movement out on the
floor. DCI Julian Lowe had walked in. Major Crime for the
area was his responsibility and he had been one of the first
calls Harry had made. He was tugging at a scarf, his movements hurried and clumsy, and it looked like it was strangling
him as it came away. Helen Smithers was closest to the door.
She tipped out to make the chief inspector a hot drink. When
he bundled through the door, he still seemed to be fighting
with his clothing — now a damp jacket that was refusing to
unzip. He ditched an umbrella in the corner.

'Evening all,' DCI Lowe said. Helen wasn't far behind
him. She put a cup down on the long table where he was
spreading out his damp outer layers. 'Awful night — in more
ways than one.'

'It is at that, boss,' Harry said. 'Sorry to drag you in.'

DCI Lowe waved him away. 'You didn't. I couldn't take
it all in over the phone and when you said those words, I was
pretty much putting my shoes on to come in.'

'Those words?'

'"*Serial killer*," Harry. If that's where we are . . .'

Harry grimaced. 'It's very early. I said "*might*" and I mean
that. We're running two murders after today. I'll show you
what we have and we can talk about similarities. That's all.'

'Okay, then. Show me what you have!' Lowe slumped
into a seat and crossed his legs, sitting at an angle to Maddie.
He wore jeans, a jumper and trainers. It seemed wrong.
Maddie had never considered a man like DCI Lowe had
anything to wear that wasn't a suit.

Harry turned on the large screen at the front. It came
on as a bright white. Then it was a far darker image: Justin
Wright suspended by the neck, his bare torso an ugly mess
of white puncture marks and dark red staining. This was the
image Maddie had also been shown. Their first murder victim. Harry introduced Justin, talking directly to DCI Lowe.
He used words like *frenzied* and *helpless*, all the words they had

used before. The picture changed. Lowe uncrossed his legs to plant both his feet and sit straighter. He looked more and more like a man braced.

The picture changed. Tonight's victim was presented. Scott Rice took up the centre of the screen and the similarities were stark. It was like an audition for the part of *suspended man stabbed to death in the hallway* and these were the last two candidates. Choosing between them was going to be very difficult. The stripped torso was the same. Even the pattern to the numerous puncture wounds was similar, as was the red staining down the front. This time, the man's tongue protruded from the side of his mouth. His eyes were bulging a little, too. He had a large tattoo on the right side of his chest, a woman on horseback that reared up. The rider had one arm up with a defiance that contrasted with the words '*RIP MUM*.' There was a date written underneath it. The image told of a woman who went down fighting. Maybe it was a family trait.

'Okay, then.' Lowe cleared his throat with his first word. 'So I can see we have similarities.'

'The key part to determine for us is any sign of motive that links the two,' Harry said. 'It might just be that the victims have both upset the same offender and the debt is now repaid, as it were.'

'Or it might be that we've some psycho out there hanging men up and stabbing them to death? I assume the cause of death is the stabbing?'

'Predominantly. The first victim, for certain. Charley Mace was the CSI officer on duty. She suggested that Scott, here, looked more like he had survived the stabbing long enough to asphyxiate.'

'CSI still there?'

'Yes. They were still working on the Justin Wright job when they were called out to this one. I think they were only there to draw up some sort of plan for the morning.'

'What about resources?'

'I've already put a call in to the central resource unit. They know what we have — and what we might have. They'll start channelling everything they can to us tomorrow. It won't be enough. They warned me there's a lot going on. We'll get more officers for sure but no guarantee of their area of expertise or experience. These jobs are always the same . . . You get sent a load of resources that take more effort to manage than they add to the investigation. CSI are also massively stretched, as you can imagine. They're going to appeal to Essex for resources to cross the border and assist.'

'Okay. I'll put a call in myself to see if I can have an impact on what we get sent. The Area Commander will want uniform patrols for visibility, too. The moment this hits the press, we're going to need to be out in force. Any update on the media?'

'The first was reported locally but barely made a ripple in the nationals. We didn't release too many details and we weren't really asked to. The media are aware of a lot of police activity at the second address today and we're getting questions from bigger outlets. I think the answer to those questions will determine how big this goes and how quickly.'

'We won't be able to keep a lid on this.'

'I agree. One of our tasks tomorrow morning will be to revisit the informant from tonight's job. She's given an account, but we couldn't push her for detail — she was falling apart. She wasn't keen to speak to us again but if we were to tell her that we have had another death in similar circumstances, she might be more encouraged. The issue with that is it means our secret is out.'

'It is.'

'I don't think we have a choice. She may not have seen anyone, but we need so much more from her.'

'Of course we do. And a little leak to the press might not be such a terrible thing. We can use the press to put out public appeals, et cetera.'

'We can and should. We will need to try and control *when*, however. The problem is the amount of work it always generates. We'll be looking to send good detectives after bad leads, something we can ill afford.'

'We shouldn't wait too long for that though, Harry. We open ourselves up for criticism if we leave it too long. You'll just have to try and triage the response as best you can.'

'A few more days though, boss. I think we need to know a little bit more about this latest job before we put out requests for information.'

'We'll keep that under constant review.' Lowe was clearly not making any promises. 'So what else do we know at this stage? I mean from the point of view of suggesting this is one offender carrying out a series?' He shifted forward. The strain on his face seemed to be increasing.

Harry cleared his throat. 'What we know? Okay, well I know that you are aware of the first job already, but it's worth repeating. We were first alerted to Justin Wright at 10:07 hours, when we received an anonymous email to our Crimestoppers account sending us to the victim's address. Alice Oxley owns and runs a café a few streets over. The victim is her ex-partner, who was there looking after their son on his last day off before going back to school after the half-term. We understand the offender gained entry to the property shortly after Oxley left to go to work. This could suggest the home was under surveillance and that our offender waited for her to leave. Method of entry is unknown — no signs of forced entry. The child at the address was aware of a noise and then was unable to get out of his room. The door was tied shut from the outside and there is no evidence that the offender entered the child's room. We believe the victim may even have been responsible for the barricade. The method of killing is described as a frenzied attack with a short, stubby blade of some sort, combined with asphyxiation by hanging. Charley Mace was on scene as our CSI officer, and it was her that used the word "*frenzied*." Her early thoughts were that the bruising and marks were consistent with a very sharp blade, stabbed with as much force as one could muster. She thought that could become quite significant.'

'Significant?' DCI Lowe said.

'Overkill. I'll use her pun. A knife stabbed into the chest and abdomen up to its hilt with far more force than was required. Repeatedly. And from behind.'

'So someone very angry?'

'Or excited.' Maddie broke the tension that seemed to be building between the two men. DCI Lowe snapped his attention away from Harry as if he had forgotten there was anyone else in the room.

'Excited?'

'If we're talking about a serial killer, then we will need to consider that this is someone who gets off on what they do.'

'We will.' Lowe shook his head. The load on his shoulders seemed to increase in front of her eyes. It seemed that the last thing he wanted right now was a serial killer on his patch. 'You said ex-partner?' he said. 'Are there any new partners on the scene for this Miss Oxley?'

'Like I said,' said Harry, 'she hasn't helped us massively to this point. There was clearly some animosity there. She's upset by his demise, but I got the impression it was more the nature of the killing and the fact that her son was in the home at the time. Maddie?'

'Yeah, I didn't get any love lost there. No suggestion of anyone else, either.'

DCI Lowe sighed. 'And today's incident?'

'This evening at 6:20 p.m., we received a call from Michelle Rice,' said Harry. 'She reported how she had come to find her husband hanging. She initially seemed to think that he had done it himself. Again, they have a young child, a daughter this time, who was in the house and had been barricaded in the bedroom using a very similar method. She then reported that the offender was still in the house. Patrols were quickly on the scene and there was no sign of anyone by that time. Unfortunately, she didn't get a look at anyone. She just reports hearing the front door open. When Maddie was speaking to her earlier, however, she conceded that she might not have closed it properly and the wind could have got hold of it.'

'Sir, if I may?'

Harry gestured for Maddie to continue.

'Michelle Rice was very much in shock. Her first account was a mess. I'm back with her first thing in the morning to make a bit more sense of it. I'm sure there's information from her that will be key. I'll need to take my time with her, but I will bottom that out.'

'It doesn't change too much at this time, anyway,' said Harry. My two officers here have been conducting house-to-house. Helen, Barry, anything to add at this time?'

Barry gestured at Helen to speak. 'There is, sir,' she said. 'We conducted house-to-house in both directions away from the house. We have two separate reports of a male seen in the vicinity of the house at the material time. He stood out as his behaviour seemed "*odd*."'

'Odd?'

Helen flicked through pages of her notebook to read from it. 'One witness sees a man walking down the road carrying a bag, wearing a T shirt. It was freezing cold and raining hard. He was in no hurry, according to her. Then I spoke to a male who was standing at his top floor window on a junction, looking directly down the road towards the address. He describes seeing an old man stop in the middle of the road, facing him directly, with his arms out.'

'Arms out?' It was Harry's growl that was first to cut in, but DCI Lowe had also spun around as if he wanted to question her.

'"Like *Christ the Redeemer*."' Helen looked up from her notes, then closed her book with a thump. 'His description, not mine.'

'Excitement,' Maddie repeated. 'Feeds into the idea of someone doing this because they like to.'

'It might.' Harry said.

'Old man? That was the description, right?' Maddie said.

Helen opened her book back up. 'Old, yeah. White-skinned. That's it.'

'Any mention of the hair? Glasses?'

'No,' said Helen. 'They didn't get a great look, I don't think. There were parked cars and it was dark and raining. Visibility wouldn't have been great. I can go back and ask again?'

'It's fine,' said Harry. 'I think we are at risk of leading our witnesses. At the moment, we have obvious similarities between the jobs, but we also have some differences.'

'Go on?' DCI Lowe prompted.

'From what we know of the first job, the man in the café had taken a lot of time and effort to get to know Alice Oxley. He must have been stalking her for a reasonable amount of time to get the information he had. There's no suggestion of that with today's incident.'

'So far, you mean?'

'That is true. DS Ives may get something more tomorrow, but with Oxley it was obvious immediately. The offender made sure Oxley knew who he was and told her what he had done. We think he then calmly left the café when she ran home. There's no suggestion that Michelle Rice knew the offender, not from what we've been told. How we were informed was different, too. After the first job, we received a timed email from an anonymous account. After the second, we were called by the victim's wife on her return home.'

'He might have been there, though!' All eyes suddenly turned to Maddie. 'Sorry, I'm just thinking out loud. At the home, I mean. She said that someone was there while she was on the phone. That means the offender might have been at the house when she got back.'

'He might. And that's relevant?'

'It might be. That would mean he was there when they both found out their partners were dead — or exes, or whatever — you get the point. Helen, this witness who saw Christ the Redeemer out in the street, when was this?'

'He didn't know an exact time, he did say—'

'I mean, when was it in relation to the police arrival?'

'Oh, yeah. I was just gonna say, the police were already there. That was why he was standing in his top window in the first place. He said there was a lot of flashing lights and he was trying to see what was going on.'

'So he *was* there. The slamming door was him leaving.'

'Assuming that was our offender,' Harry warned.

'I think we suspect it was, don't we? When I spoke to the informant, she was really muddled — all over the place, as you can imagine. I'll go back through it with her tomorrow.'

'Yes please, Maddie. We need to have a good understanding of a timeline here.' DCI Lowe rubbed at his face. Maddie noted his empty cup.

'Can I get you another coffee, boss? Maybe a strong one!'

'No thank you, Maddie. I have some writing to do. The SMT will want an update ready for them in the morning. I think I know enough to get me going. Harry, can you stick around while I put this all into some sort of order?'

'Of course.'

'And I assume the scene is resourced for the night?'

'We have two scenes. The house and an alleyway where we think our offender might have gone. That will be searched at first light, but anything out in the open will have been washed clean immediately.'

'You never know your luck. I assume that means there is little more your investigators here can do for now. I suggest we get them home for some sleep. You'll need a fresh team tomorrow, that's for sure.'

'You heard the boss.' Harry stood up, his voice projecting over the scrabbling movements of Maddie and her two colleagues. 'Maddie, 8am start tomorrow, please.'

'You don't want me in earlier?'

'No. I'll need to see what resource we have and then get them all briefed. It might be a slow start, but be ready for a later finish.'

'Maddie smiled. She knew what that meant. Certainly she shouldn't be making any plans for her evening.

'Anything I can do to help tonight?'

Harry snapped his fingers. 'Yes, one action for tonight . . . Can you send a brief summary of the MO to the national crime analysts? Just to see if this method's been used somewhere else. Never know your luck.'

'Will do. I'll follow that up with a call tomorrow, too — make sure they understand the urgency. They can be a little blasé.'

'Thanks. And Barry, you were looking at the victim for the first job? I think it makes sense to task you with the victim here, too. Let's see what we can find out. It'll be interesting to see if he has any involvement with skip hire for a start.'

'Yes, sir.' Barry replied from the door.

'Okay, then. Get some sleep tonight. We need to be on it tomorrow. Best case, we have two victims who managed to upset the same man and he's now in hiding. Worst case? Well, the worst case really is something much worse.'

CHAPTER 16

Friday

Gavin Walker woke to the familiar sound of pebbles rolling and bumping onto other pebbles, pushed around by a heaving sea. The sound merged with a distant call of a gull. He often ended up here. It was a changeable environment, like nowhere else, and he wasn't always guaranteed a good sleep, but this morning the ocean was breathing calmly in and out as if it was sleeping, too. Gavin loved the sea, whatever its mood. It was always there when he woke, ever reliable, the only constant in his life.

It was cold. After the sound of the seaside, that was the next sensation he was aware of. He was laid out on his side on a solid bench. The sun was well-hidden behind thick rolls of cloud that covered the vast expanse of sky stretching out before him until it met the horizon. The sea always seemed to colour itself to reflect the weather. Today, it was a washed-out grey that smudged into brown where it met the beach. Further out to sea, Gavin could see dirty streaks hanging from the clouds like strings bending in the prevailing winds: it was raining in France. No doubt it would be coming this way, too. The night rain had been torrential. It had driven

129

him home to start with, but not for long. He had still preferred to step out into the torrent than stay at home with his demons. He had walked to a late-night alcohol supplier then onward to find somewhere out of the worst where he could consume it. He couldn't go home — he could never cope there for long. It was the silence, the loneliness. It followed him around the house, was waiting in every room, stalking him, pushing him out, then ready to shut the front door after him. He wasn't welcome there.

When he sat up, the freezing wind struck him in the back of the neck. He lifted his collar to pull it tight. The shelter was barely befitting of the word. It was a semicircular structure with the open side to the sea. The back had slits shaped like windows but with no glass installed, there was nothing to stop the cold winds whipping through. They were designed as a place to rest for the casual Sunday walkers along the promenade in the summer months, not for a hopeless drunk trying to pluck up the courage to survive another day of winter.

Gavin had some carrier bags on the bench next to him. He checked the contents. All the cans had been opened and were empty. He would normally try and leave at least one can of lager for when he woke up, as there was rarely a time when he needed one more. More cans had spilled out of the bag and were on the floor. He reached down to gather them up, checking each one in turn before putting it in the bag. They were all empty. He tied up the bag for the litter bin.

His head hurt as he sat up and he needed to be still for a minute to clear his vision and wait for his breath to come back from the exertion of leaning forwards. He held his head in his hands.

'You out?' Gavin looked up to see a blue beer can a few inches from his face. It was held out for him to take. He did. He looked up at the man who had given it to him. He was smiling. He gestured at the tied-up carrier bag. 'Looks like it's your brand, too!'

Gavin hadn't seen him before. He thought he knew all the drinkers. A lot of them tended to hang out together, moving or sitting as a group. They only split up to sit in the precinct where the foot traffic was highest so they could beg for spare change. He tended to avoid them now. When he had spent time with them, he would find himself pitying them, judging them even for the life choices that had got them to this point. And then he would realise that he was no different. He could kid himself that by not sitting on a street begging for his next drink he was better, but he was no less desperate. He had been avoiding facing up to the truth his whole life. That was how he had started on the alcohol in the first place.

'Can't say I have a brand.'

'I understand. Whatever you can get, right? Mind if I sit?'

'Sure.' Gavin moved the bag of empty cans from the bench to hold it between his feet. The man peered out to sea. He had long hair that ran down his back in a ponytail. It was untidy, the hair scraped together from where it circled a thinning patch and it caught in the wind to flick towards him. He was older than Gavin, probably older than sixty, even, and with the classic drinker's pot belly. He opened his can and took a swig, pulling his lips back as he swallowed.

'Quite a view,' he said.

'Keeps me coming back.'

'You from here? Deal, I mean?'

'Man and boy.' Gavin looked out to where the deeper waters of the horizon had turned a dark green. 'I just never left . . .'

'And why would you?'

'I've not seen you before.'

'Funny you should say that . . . This is my first day in Deal! It's a long story. I'm trying to work the place out. I just need to survive for the next few days and then I intend to move on again. I figured I would find someone who might know the tricks and learn what I could. In exchange for a drink or two, of course!'

'Tricks?'

'Food, shelter, medication.' He lifted his beer can to shake it gently. 'Just the stuff you need to know!'

'Not much to tell you. The Salvation Army does a bit round here. They have a kitchen once a week — twice sometimes, in the year. The church opens when it goes below freezing. They were giving out blankets, too. I've got a place so I don't . . . I've got a place to live but can't stay there much.'

'Oh?'

'It's my place . . . I mean, it's just not good for me. My head. It's all messed up. I need the space. I don't do walls. People think I'm crazy . . .'

The man tapped his can against Gavin's. 'Say no more, my friend! No one gets to sit on this bench, drinking this *utter shit* at this time in the day unless their heads are messed up. We all have our story, my friend, and we're all as crazy as each other!'

'I guess you're right.'

'The forecast for tonight . . . it's getting colder. I need to have a plan in place. I like Deal. It seems nice. I wouldn't mind making it through 'til the morning. Did you ever consider renting out one of your rooms? A doorway even, just something that keeps me out of the worst?'

Gavin didn't like being put on the spot. He took a swig from his can. He barely noticed the strong taste by now. He would flick it to the back of his throat so most of the liquid never went anywhere near his taste buds. But now he held it in his mouth, playing for time, considering his answer. He grimaced when he finally did swallow. 'This *is* shit,' he said. 'Look, I don't live with people. It doesn't go well. I know I said I wasn't there much, but it's still a place I can be . . . alone. I need that.'

'Of course. I'm sorry, I didn't mean to be so direct. I'll find a place. I don't suppose you know someone else who might take someone in for the night? Someone who could do with a paying guest? I'd chuck in a hot takeaway and a bottle of good wine, too. Nothing like this shit!'

Gavin hesitated. The thought of hot food with red wine accompaniment lingered, as did conversation with another human being. Like normal people did. 'One night?' he said.

'That would be a start. I'm only here for a few days. I'm just looking for somewhere where I won't freeze to death when the sun goes down. I don't live with people well, either. I could do with someone who takes no offence from me leaving a crate of beers on the kitchen table before I shut myself away all night. I'm no burden.'

'A few days, then?'

'That's all. I pay my way, too. Do you think you might know someone?'

Gavin hesitated again. He could always leave the house and come back here. He did it most nights, anyway. He could still be alone.

'Maybe we could try it, but you should know that my place . . . I don't do much with it. It's no hotel. It's a bit of a mess.'

The man chuckled. 'Don't you worry about that. Drier and warmer than this bench is all I am after. And you don't realise who you're talking to, seems I make a mess wherever I go!'

'I'll have to make some room somewhere.'

'And you'll get nothing but appreciation from me, no matter where it is.' The man slapped Gavin's knee. 'In fact, how about I start showing my appreciation? A seaside town like this has to have a good café, right? You fancy a slap-up breakfast? Least I can do.'

'A café?' Gavin wasn't sure. He didn't do people.

'Sure! I always look out for a café whenever I go to a new place. Sitting in one of those places and watching the sort of people who go there tells you all you need to know. That's how I get a feel for a town. I like to people-watch. Is there one?'

'A café? Yeah, there's a few.'

'Breakfast, then?'

Gavin looked down over his front. He was wearing a battered and stained light blue jacket over torn jeans. He couldn't exactly remember what he was wearing under his jacket. His hair was unkempt, most of it flattened under an old grey deerstalker. He looked like shit. His new friend did, too. They would stand out. People would stare. The people working there would rush them out or he might even see someone he used to know. That wasn't something he dealt with well.

'I . . . Those sorts of places . . . I don't like all the . . . It's not for me.'

'Yes, it is. That's exactly who it's for. I'll do the talking, the paying and the waving if anyone wants to take a look at us. I do it all the time and you know what? The more you do it, the less you care! Trust me on that one, friend. Let's go and have a look. If the place isn't right to stick around or you don't like the look of it, I'll get us something to go. Either way, let's go get something hot to eat.'

Gavin found it difficult to argue. It was a freezing morning. A hot meal and ten minutes sitting out of it could set him up for the rest of the day. He took one last look at the sea as he stood up. It would still be there when he got back — his one constant.

'Okay, then,' he said. 'Let's go and have a look.'

CHAPTER 17

'I take this for granted, you know. I forget it's here, even.' Rebecca Arnold looked like she was lost in the view. She was staring out to sea, her legs swinging against the thick wall that ran along the edge of Deal's promenade. Her heels made a knocking sound. When Vince didn't reply, she turned to his wide smile.

'What?' she breathed.

'You look like a little kid sitting like that!'

'I wish! Forty-one next week.'

'I know. I've got you nothing.'

'Just as I expected.' His sister was smiling as well. She turned back towards the view, to where the sea heaved in and out, slapping lightly against the pebble beach.

'I know what you mean, though.' Vince said. 'You get so busy you don't see what's right on your doorstep. Alfie and I must have been down here every day since.'

Alife was a few metres in front of them on the beach and he seemed to be chasing a scent downwards, using his nose to dig through the pebbles. He jerked his head up to peer over at the use of his name. His nose was twitching and his tongue appeared. He was soon back to his digging.

'What's the plan with him?'

'I think he'll be staying put, to be honest, Becks. Can't see any other way. Just waiting for the news.'

'That's good. For you, I mean. And him.'

Alfie's head suddenly twitched backwards. He changed his stance to increase his grip. A tattered piece of carrier bag appeared in his mouth, though most of it was still under the pebbles. It was a tug of war — him versus the beach. He emitted a little growl and his tail wagged.

'A couple of idiots together, you mean!'

'What's the plan with you?' Rebecca said.

Vince left the question hanging in the air. He had known it was coming. It had been pretty regular from his sister and every time he'd met it with a joke or throwaway comment. Today, he didn't feel like joking.

'I don't know. I've gotta get myself back to work, I suppose. Can't be having too much time on the ol' Tom Dick. They'll think I've gone soft!'

'We can't have that, can we! Do you want to go back?'

'I don't know. They might not even have me.' This sentence was uttered more softly and he regretted saying it the moment it fell from his lips.

Rebecca seized on it. 'What do you mean?'

Vince chuckled. 'I don't know . . . Not sure the job's for me anymore. I've got another week and then I'll go have a chat. See how the land lies.'

'I've never known a man more suited to a job. Never!'

'Ah, but you only know the stories I tell you! It's all made up, Becks. I watch a lot of action stuff on Netflix! I just adapt the stories so you'll be impressed. I don't really have lasers behind my eyes!'

Vince felt a bump against his arm. 'Be serious for a moment, would ya?' Rebecca pushed off to drop to the stones. 'Come on . . . This was supposed to be a walk! And you still need to buy me breakfast!'

Vince dropped down, too. Alfie detected their movement, gave the shredded bag one last tug before conceding defeat and trotting after him.

Vince patted his stomach. 'You mean at your place? They only do them filthy breakfasts. I've got a stature to present.'

'You still on porridge and egg whites for breakfast?'

'Yup. You tried it, yet?'

'God, no. A coffee, then? You can watch me eat!'

'Hang on, how come I'm *buying* breakfast in there? Surely there's some staff concession?'

'Because I'm the one who works there, not you.'

'But it's your breakfast.'

'And you're paying!'

* * *

The eyes that met Maddie's were wide and frightened as they peered around the side of a solid-looking front door. Maddie smiled as warmly as she could muster. She had only left Michelle Rice the previous evening. She'd told Michelle that she'd be back in the morning when she had dropped her back at her mother's house. It had been the easy thing for Michelle to do: it had meant the police would leave and all the questions with it. But sometimes, letting a tired and traumatised witness sleep was the worst thing you could do. Maddie wasn't sure what sort of reaction she might get this morning.

'Hey!' Maddie said.

'It's early.' Maddie could see some of her hair, crumpled and slept-on. The pristine new haircut had already dropped out overnight. Her eyes looked heavy, her skin washed-out and pale. She looked tired, like she had barely slept a wink.

'I thought I would get this done. I figured you wouldn't want to be sitting waiting for me to come round. Once I'm gone, you can get on with your day.'

It was just past nine a.m. Maddie had been in for six thirty despite the boss telling her to take a lie-in. Of course, she had found Harry already at his desk. They had both had the same idea — the key to this was getting to know their

137

victims. A good detective knows that a victim is always chosen. Find out the reason why, and you're a big step closer to finding out by whom. Harry had agreed to her request to miss his briefing so she could get out to talk with Michelle Rice. They both knew she was the person who would know Scott Rice best.

'I don't know . . . I don't know if there's much more I can tell you . . . I didn't see anything. It was all just . . . It was just Scott.'

The mask of shock from yesterday, the one that had stopped her being able to string sentences together, that had blunted her recall, was still very much present.

'Have you had breakfast?'

'Breakfast? No, I just . . .'

'Is Fern being looked after?'

'Fern? She's here with me and her nan.'

'How about I take you out for breakfast? We don't have to talk about anything from yesterday. We can just talk — about *Love Island*, if you want to! Have you been watching that?'

The question didn't seem to register. Michelle checked over her shoulder though, like she was considering it. Maddie couldn't imagine the pressures inside that house. Fern was at the age where she would be constantly asking questions but when answers would be impossible to word.

'I need to . . . I'm not ready.'

The door hadn't opened any further. Maddie felt like it was the right time to back away.

'Take your time. I'll be in the car. I've got a couple of calls to make, anyway.'

Michelle hesitated. She looked beyond Maddie, out into the country road that led past her mother's house. Then she nodded. Maddie smiled and turned away instantly — before she could change her mind.

* * *

Gavin Walker sat back from a plate wiped clean with thick, crusty bread and exhaled his satisfaction. He eyed his coffee. It had come as part of the breakfast. He used to like coffee. He couldn't remember the last time he had drunk one. He was considering it, now. Maybe it would be nice, like when he used to take the time to hunt out a place that sold good coffee, not that machine crap, like normal people did.

The man opposite must have seen him staring at his cup. He reached out with a silver hip flask. A clear liquid poured from it to fall into his coffee — a good measure. The man winked.

'It looked like it could do with livening up is all.'

Gavin smiled. Who was he kidding? He didn't want to drink a coffee, not a *normal* one at least. This was what he wanted. Oblivion. Another day avoiding normal people and what they did, what they thought. People were looking over now. The hip flask had attracted some attention, some shakes of the head, even some tutting. He made a point of savouring his coffee for anyone watching. He exhaled and licked his lips. His new friend seemed to approve.

'How's that? Better?'

'Better.' But Gavin wanted to leave now that he could sense that people were looking over. He wanted to go back to being the blur of homelessness on a bench that people walked past while avoiding eye contact at all cost. 'I should get off. Can't be too long in the warm and comfortable, don't want to soften up!' Gavin snorted laughter. It ran out quickly.

'Of course. I'll go and square this up.'

'Thanks. For the breakfast, I mean. It's been a while. My place isn't far from here. I'll show you. Just remember what I said — it's no palace.'

'If it's dry and warm . . . I'm not looking to be choosey, here.'

'How long do you think you'll be in Deal?'

The man leaned back, picked up his own coffee and took his time with it. Gavin didn't recall seeing him pour from the hip flask into it. He certainly scowled at it like it had an aftertaste. He seemed to be contemplating his answer.

'I shouldn't be long. A few days, maybe. But breakfast every day is a given — on me! Is that okay?'

Gavin shrugged. He had been good company, nice enough at least. Not much chat but someone to talk to if he wanted — just about right.

'Sure. I mean, we'll play it by ear.'

The man waved his hand. 'Oh, absolutely. I used to live on my own, too. I had my own place. It was no palace — a bit like yours, I bet — but it was my space. I was okay with guests for a while, but they can outstay their welcome. I have no intention of doing that.'

'Okay, then. What brings you to Deal, anyway? You never said.'

'Didn't I? And you mean aside from the beautiful sea-front and the greasy cafés? I came here to meet someone.'

'Meet someone? An old friend? Your kid? I've seen that before.'

'Nothing like that. A friend of a friend is all.'

'Okay, then. I know a few people round here. Maybe I can help?'

'I'll bear that in mind, thanks.'

Gavin didn't persist. It was obvious the man didn't want to talk about it anymore. He respected that.

'I reckon I should be able to sort it out on my own. I wouldn't want to involve anyone else — not a friend, at least. You never know how these things are gonna go!'

Gavin shrugged. He watched as the man walked to the counter. He paid with a twenty and waited for the change, dropping some in the service pot. Gavin was normally good at working people out, at putting them to a back story — a life on the street gives you that ability. But he wasn't sure about this one. He looked the part: ragged clothes, unshaven and with an understanding of the street, but there was something different about him. And it wasn't just the twenty. It didn't matter. Gavin had nothing to lose, nothing of value to be stolen or defrauded.

Whatever this man wanted, there was no way it would be from him.

*　*　*

Michelle had put on a layer of makeup, enough to disguise the worst of her exhaustion, and the mask of shock looked to have slipped a little. Maddie had hoped that getting her away from Fern would be enough to do that. She had seemed reluctant at first, as if she didn't want to leave her daughter, but she'd caved in quickly. Quickly enough for Maddie to understand that it might be a relief to get away from her for half an hour. Not that she would ever admit it.

They were in a place called Quex Barn on the outskirts of Margate. It was a short drive from Michelle's mother's place in the village of Minster. Quex Barn was a mash-up of a farm shop and a café. The prices were at the higher end of the spectrum for a hearty breakfast, so Maddie had high expectations. She had left her statement forms, daybook and even her pen back in the car to set the scene for an informal chat. She wanted Michelle to relax enough to talk about what she knew.

'So what do we do now? I know you want a statement from me, you told me that last night.' Michelle dipped her head and sipped from a wide teacup that she held in both hands, her eyes flicking round the room. They were upstairs, a mezzanine level that had been fitted in around the eaves. There were a couple of other tables occupied, but they were some distance away. That was the reason Maddie had led them up here. She wanted to be able to talk freely — more importantly, she wanted Michelle to be able to talk freely.

'I do. I want as much detail as I can get, even the stuff you don't think is important.'

'I can't tell you much. I said that last night. I didn't see anything.'

'You saw *something*, Michelle. We know that. What we don't know is just how relevant it is. I do this all the time, talking with witnesses and sometimes it all seems totally irrelevant. But further down the line, when other pieces of the puzzle come in from other places, you can start to see which bits fit where. You're important to me. No one's more important. You were there.'

'I saw Scott.' Michelle said. Her voice was distorted where she was trying to hide behind her teacup. Maddie struggled to hear her.

'So tell me about that,' Maddie said.

'Tell you? I don't want to ever talk about it again!' She dropped her cup back to the saucer. It clunked so hard, the liquid slopped over the sides. Her hand was shaking when she lifted it to push her hair out of her face.

'Okay, then. Let's not talk about that. Let's start *before* that. Let's talk about what you were doing before you came home.'

'I'm s-sorry,' Michelle stammered. 'It's just . . . the last thing I told him, the last thing I said . . . I would never have said those things if . . .'

'You argued?'

Michelle lifted her eyes to fix on Maddie. They were heavy. The red around them was back. 'He was cheating on me. I mean, he denied it, but I know he was lying. I've had my suspicions for a while but last night was the first time I actually . . . I'm sorry, this isn't important, is it? You want to know who was in my house, not in my husband's bed.'

'Actually, it might be,' Maddie said.

'You think it could have something to do with all this?'

'I think he might have upset someone. Maybe this is how.'

Michelle seemed to take a moment to consider. 'I suppose he could be messing around with someone's wife. That's what you mean, right? I never found out who she actually is — I just have a name . . . *Jenny*. Do you think that's what happened? That he brought this to my house?' She was getting more animated and Maddie held up her hands in surrender.

'Let's not jump ahead. It's my job to consider everything, to question everything and to find the answers. I can't be sure that's what happened, Michelle, but I need to consider everything. I want to catch the person who did this and I want to stop them.'

'Stop them? You think they will do it again?'

Maddie checked around her again. She exhaled as she leaned forward. 'The person who did this is clearly a very violent and dangerous individual. I'm a police officer. We're here to keep the public safe. It might be that there's another family out there on course to go through the same thing you are. I want to stop that happening. So let's go through what happened in detail. We'll do it here and now over an expensive breakfast, then I'll charge Lennockshire Police for it and go back and write up what you've said. We'll meet again and you can check what is written to make sure it's right. We can take as long as we need. Will you help me?'

Michelle sat straighter and rolled her hair between her fingers. 'I went out to get my hair cut. I found out what was going on a few days ago. I have a friend who runs a salon. I talked to her about it and she told me to challenge him. It took a few days for me to pluck up the courage. Yesterday morning, she got in touch to egg me on. She told me she would fit me in for a free cut if I spoke to him that day. That was the plan. Challenge him and then have somewhere to go to be out of the house. I know Scott . . . I know me. I knew exactly what it was going to be like in that house after I told him.'

'Okay. So you found out about this Jenny. How did that happen?'

'I saw something on his phone. A week ago. It was a thank you for a gift, like it was for something thoughtful. There was no more detail, but it just stood out as different . . . romantic, you know? I got into his phone and it was the only message — so any previous conversation had been deleted. That looked odd in itself. I did some hunting round on his Twitter and Instagram and there was nothing. Then I found something on a picture-sharing app I didn't even know he had. I've never heard of it. Anyway, you can direct message people. And there was a much longer conversation on there with this *Jenny*. It was all very obvious.'

'Obvious?'

'Nothing explicit, but it didn't need to be. Mostly it was plans on where to meet but the more telling stuff was the conversation about *how* to meet. There was some talk about what he would tell me so he wasn't questioned. The piece of shit did it, too . . . One of the excuses she had suggested for being late, he had used. I remember him telling me, the lying bastard.' She turned away and flopped back into the seat rest. 'Sorry. I don't know if I can be angry — if I'm even allowed to be after what's happened. I don't know how to feel.'

'You should feel angry. Betrayal is betrayal. What happened since has robbed you of the chance to get past that. I can't imagine how difficult this is for you, all of it.'

'It's Fern. The fact that she was mixed up in all this, the fact that she saw what she saw. I should have left her in that room. I wasn't thinking straight.'

'Of course you weren't. You can't blame yourself for that, either. So you challenged him?'

'We argued in the morning. I wasn't going to mention it until later but it was on my mind and he came right out and told me he was going to be late home from work. There was hardly even an excuse. It was like he was getting bored of lying and wasn't even trying anymore. Maybe he thought he didn't have to as I'd been so gullible.'

'Did you tell him what you knew?'

'I asked him for more detail. I said that was a reasonable thing to do. He got really defensive really quickly. I knew then. I knew what he was planning on doing after work. I called him a liar and told him to make sure he was home on time. He stomped out like he always does when we argue.'

'So he didn't know what you knew about this Jenny when he left for work?'

'I never said it. Not her name, or even that I knew he was being unfaithful, but he might have had his suspicions. I said I thought he was lying about why he was going to be late. He said he was playing squash. I put him on the spot and he couldn't remember who with.'

'So what happened then?'

'He was home on time, just after five p.m. I was ready to challenge him the moment he came in, but he didn't even take his coat off. I'd been building myself up to it all day. Fern was already in her pyjamas and playing a game on her iPad. I don't let her play it at night normally, but she shuts out the world when she's got her head in that thing! I was going to sit down and talk to him about what was going on. Then the cheeky bastard swanned straight in and told me he was heading back out to watch a football match at the pub. He said he thought it was best to give me "space" so I could calm down. Like it was all *my* fault and I was just being silly. He was better prepared than in the morning — he had all the details, the pub, the game he was seeing . . . I was so furious, I couldn't even speak at first. The football thing was one of the excuses this Jenny had suggested previously and here he was, coming home after getting angry about being called a liar and using it. Right to my face!'

'What did you say?'

'I said I had spoken to Angela and I had an appointment.'

'Angela?'

'Angela Bennett. She's my mate who runs the salon. She gave me a hair appointment that was half an hour after he came home. It was deliberate.'

'Did anyone else know?'

'About this Jenny?'

'That you were upset with Scott, that you were going to challenge him about it all?'

'No. I'm not one of those who plasters their issues all over the place. This is my business. I felt a bit humiliated, to be honest. Angela's my best mate, I can tell her anything.'

'So you never talked about it with anyone else? Even that you're having problems?'

'No! I told you already.'

'Okay. So you were ready to challenge him?'

'I was. I told him I had to ask him a question and then I was going out so he would have to stay home for Fern. I told him I could still get the "space" he thought I needed. His reaction caught me out. He was gutted! I was expecting him to back down, to accept that sometimes you can sneak out, sometimes you can't. But he practically begged me, telling me this was the most important match of the season. The bastard! I told him that I had something important to talk about and he replied with that! And I knew that he wasn't begging me to go see some football match . . . He was desperate to meet his tart. He must have been on a promise, eh?' She paused, her face suddenly contorted in horror. 'Or maybe he really loved her.'

'And did you tell him?' Maddie was desperate to get her answers, she tried to keep her on track. There would be time for Michelle to reflect on the rest later.

'I asked him why he was so desperate. That was when I asked for the details . . . who was playing, where and why it was so important. Then I asked him who he was watching it with. He was right in the middle of his lie when I just said it straight out . . . I asked if Jenny was watching it with him. He shut up. It was instant. His lies had been so fluent, so off the cuff, but that name closed him up completely. A part of me still wanted to believe that he was going out to watch the football with his mates but in that moment, I knew for certain. It was all over his face.'

'How did he react?'

'He got angry. I think he was angry at being caught out. He accused me of spying on him, going through his phone blah, blah, blah — all the usual stuff. He denied it, too, said it was just a friendship. I told him that I was going out and that he should start making plans to move out of the house.'

'How did he take that?'

'He was getting angrier and angrier right up to the point where I told him I wanted him out. He's moved out before. Our relationship hasn't been a simple one, as you can tell!'

'Is there such a thing?'

'I guess not.'

'So he wasn't angry when you told him to move out?'

'It all faded away. I think the penny dropped for him. He started talking about Fern, about breaking up our family unit, but it was like he was telling himself — almost telling himself off. He got upset. That was when I left. I could feel myself feeling for him and I didn't want to do that. I didn't want to show a single bit of weakness. I know I can be weak. That's how he got back last time. I wanted to stay angry. Angela knows what I'm like . . . She was the one who said about the appointment. She has a way of keeping me angry! So I left . . .' She leaned forward to rest her head in her hands, her elbows on the table. 'I told him to leave me and Fern alone. I told him to go. I told him that if he couldn't see how special our family was, then he wasn't the man I fell in love with. I told him he had let Fern down.' Her head stayed in her hands, she had uttered her words downwards. She lifted her eyes. 'Then I called him a bastard, and that was the last thing I said to him.'

'You were angry.'

'I was. Now I don't know what I am.'

'What happened then?'

'I left. I went to the salon. It's a ten-minute walk from my house. Angela looked after me. She kept me angry, like she does, but she also made me feel better — more positive about myself. When I got back, I looked great. My confidence was back, I was stronger . . . I was ready to tell him to leave that night, to tell him that someone else was going to be lucky to have me. I had it all practised in my head. But then I opened that door and there he was . . .' She sat back, her eyes glazed. She lifted one hand to rub at her mouth and face.

'Then what happened?' Maddie's tone was soft and encouraging.

'I think about it now and it doesn't seem possible, but there was a lot that seemed to happen in, like, a second. I saw him. I can't have been looking right at him. I thought he was on the stairs waiting for me. I caught him out the corner of my eye at first. I still had time to be angry — angry at myself. I thought he was waiting for me to say sorry, to plead with me to forgive him. I could already feel myself weakening and he hadn't even said a word and that made me angry at myself. How can that all happen in a second?'

Maddie smiled gently. 'Because they're feelings. It's not an internal dialogue. We can experience a lot of feelings almost instantaneously, it's how we're built. It's what keeps us safe.'

'He didn't speak. I was waiting for him to start. The first thing I noticed was his nipples. That sounds odd, doesn't it? I thought he was wearing a red top but it was . . . His white shirt was hanging open. Then his head . . . it was at a funny angle. His eyes were open, they were staring towards me but not at me — and I knew. I just knew all at once. And then I thought of Fern. I thought he'd taken it out on her then done himself in — because of me! You hear of it, don't you?'

'You do.'

'But she was okay. Oh, God, she was okay . . .' Michelle started to break. Maddie was desperate for her to continue with the recollection and kept the pressure on.

'That's good. She was safe and well. What happened then?'

'The door banged and I thought someone was still in the house and I called you. That's it, like I told you last night.'

'Tell me about when you got home again. Really try and think of that bit in detail.'

'When I got home?'

'From the salon.'

'Detail? I don't know what else to tell you?'

'Okay, let's start with the basics. Was it dark?'

'Dark? Yeah of course, it was night time. Darker than normal, too — it was raining hard.'

'Okay, so it was raining hard. The rain recently has been very heavy, very loud. Do you remember closing the front door?'

'I don't know. You do these things on autopilot, don't you?'

'The sound . . . Do you remember hearing the rain?'

'Yeah, I do. You're right. I closed the door. It was loud — I would have known if I hadn't. I shook some of the rain off my hood.'

'So your hood was up?'

'Yeah. I was holding it off my hair. I looked in the mirror! I remember now. There's a mirror in the hall. I checked my hair, that it wasn't ruined. That was when I saw Scott, you know like when you can sense someone is there? I must have seen him out the corner of my eye.'

'You said you turned the light on?'

'Yeah.'

'Before you looked in the mirror?'

'Yeah, of course. The switch is right by it.'

'So you turned the light on and then you saw Scott?'

'I did. I think I spoke to him. Then I saw he was . . . His face was weird . . . Fern was shouting! I remember that. I ran up the stairs to her voice. She was in her room. There was a bit of rope tied to it from the banister. I opened the door and then I called the police.'

'Was it easy?'

'Easy?'

'The rope. Was it a big knot?'

'No. I just pulled on it and it came away, I don't really remember what I did, I was so desperate to get in there!'

'Her bedroom . . . It's at the top of the stairs, is that right?'

'Just off to the right. The bathroom's right in front of the stairs, hers is next to it.'

'Did you go into her room?'

'No. She sort of threw herself out at me. I remember she nearly had me over and I was near the top of the stairs. I had to reach for the banister to steady us both. I remember looking back down at Scott. I thought he might start talking to me, telling me it was all a wind-up. Then I called the police.'

'You were on the phone to us when you said someone was still in the house.'

'I heard the front door bang.'

'Just a bang?'

'What do you mean?'

'No other noises?'

'It banged open . . . Then I heard a car go past and the rain. I hadn't heard that before. Oh, God! He *was* in my house, wasn't he! He was still there! He opened the door!'

Her hands fell to the table, her head hung between them. Maddie reached out to put her hands on top of them.

'If he was, he soon ran! You must have terrified him. Nothing like a mother clinging on to her daughter. You did amazingly.'

'He was right there!'

Maddie squeezed her hand. 'Let's think about where. The layout of your house . . . I had a quick look. The living room is the first door on the right. The kitchen is at the back of the house at the end of the hall. All the internal doors were wide open when I was there — it was busy with people. Police people — our CSI and a load of other colleagues. Tell me about it when you got home.'

'Tell you about it? Tell you what?'

'The living room door . . . Can you remember if it was open?'

Michelle's eyes seemed to scan the tabletop. 'No! There was no light. The street lights come in through that window. We don't ever close the blinds at the front. That door is always open. You can walk all the way through the house using the light from the street. I do it all the time. So both the doors must have been shut.'

'Okay. When you heard the door bang, that was the front door. Was there anything else? Any other noises?'

'Like what?'

'Do the other doors make a noise when they open?'

'The kitchen door, it sticks! We never close it. You have to kick the damned thing open! I would have heard that.'

Maddie sat back. 'The living room door?'

'That one's fine, it doesn't make any noise. I didn't hear anything else. He must have been in the living room! What if I had gone in there? What if Fern had run downstairs to her dad? He wouldn't have been able to get out without coming right past us. What if he had hurt Fern!' She was starting to dissolve again and Maddie gripped her hands firmly, massaging her at the wrist.

'He wasn't there to hurt Fern. Or you, Michelle. He was there for Scott. He got Scott. Then he left.'

'You seem sure. How can you be so sure he isn't coming back? He ran out when I was on the phone to the police. Maybe that's why he ran? What if Scott was mixed up in something — something they need to come back for?'

'There's nothing to suggest he was mixed up in anything.'

Michelle suddenly fixed on her. 'You seem awfully certain. You talked about him doing this again to another family, too. You said that! He's done this before, hasn't he? Something just like it?'

Maddie hesitated. Michelle's body slumped, her eyes rolled and she exhaled a long breath. 'We weren't his first.'

'You weren't.' Maddie conceded.

'So why haven't you *stopped him*!' Michelle's anger was sudden and unabated. She sat up and pulled her hands back.

'We are doing everything we can, I promise you that. That's why you are so—'

'Scott would still be alive! Fern would still have her daddy! If you'd stopped him, if you'd caught him earlier! How many others?'

Maddie held her hands out. 'This is early Michelle, we need your help and then—'

'*How many?*' She stood up. Her teacup rattled. She was suddenly making a scene. The people at the other occupied table were looking over. A waitress appeared at the top of the stairs with two steaming plates of food. She stopped dead, waited to see what Michelle did next. She was leaning as far forward as the table would allow, looming over Maddie.

'We have one other case. It's similar enough for me to think they might be linked — but we don't know that, Michelle.'

Michelle's head shook, her lips pulled back in a scowl. 'You do. You know that for damned certain. I can read you like a book. That's how you know he's done with us. But now he's off after someone else, some other family. And he'll get them, too, won't he? Because you lot haven't got a *fucking* clue where to start!'

She pushed off the table. It rocked and thumped as she did. She swept past the waitress to make her way down the stairs. The waitress stared over to where Maddie slumped back in her chair.

'It's okay. Put them down. I'll give her a minute!' Maddie smiled. She was sure it didn't look genuine. The waitress dropped the plates untidily on the table as she was asked, then scurried away.

Maddie stared out of the nearest window. She had an elevated view of a rolling green field. She felt anxious as she ran back over Michelle's words in her mind. Their investigation was all about what *had* happened and they were still piecing that together. And what did they have? Two victims in two days, and everything to suggest that he was going to strike again. Michelle was right: they really didn't have a clue. Somewhere, he may already be lining up another victim. He could have started already. He could be watching them right now, plotting his next move. And when it came to stopping him, Maddie really didn't know where to start.

* * *

Vince swilled his coffee. He could feel Alfie lying across his feet. They seemed to have developed a set routine for their coffee stop. Alfie would sit patiently next to him and watch him stir his drink. When Vince was done, he would carefully unwrap the small biscuit that always came out with it. He would be painfully slow and Alfie's only reaction would be to suck in his tongue, lick his lips and twitch his ears. Vince would then exchange the biscuit for a shake of his paw. Only then would Alfie lie across his feet to silently watch the rest of the punters for any other spilt titbits.

Rebecca's presence had done nothing to change the order of things. She had looked on indulgently throughout the whole transaction.

'Done?' she said, when Vince brought the coffee up to his mouth for the first swig.

'Yeah, you?'

'Me? What do you mean?'

'Are you done questioning me? I'm fine, okay? Just like I said.'

Rebecca lingered on him, waiting for his eye contact. 'I can't help it. I can see you're hurting. Under all your macho posturing, I mean!'

'That's all I got, sis! I'm nothing more than a macho posture. You should know that better than most!'

'You know what I mean.'

'I do and you're right. I lost someone and it should never have happened. That's gonna hurt for a bit.'

'But it wasn't your fault.'

Vince smiled. He patted Alfie as a way of avoiding having to give an answer straight away. Rebecca saw right through it.

'It wasn't your fault,' she persisted.

Vince straightened back up. 'When you do that job, you sort of get hardened to all the crap — all the bollocks. It happens quickly. You join up thinking you're gonna save the world one emergency call at a time, but it's so rarely like that. We're not always there for the victims and most of the time, the last thing they want is saving. But we are there for each other — all the time. It's us against them. Nothing else comes close. I should have stood next to the skipper, because that's what you do. You stand together and you fall together.'

'That's ridiculous. To me, I mean. I know I'm an outsider — just someone who works in a café or a doctor's surgery, but "fall together?" What would that achieve? And you told me you split up to look for someone, to have a better chance of finding them? That makes sense to me. It wasn't like you got scared and ran! You didn't let anyone down.'

'But that's exactly what it feels like to me. I can't shake it. I've had three weeks to think about all this. About me. I have a role in that team, in the force — I'm the one who looks out for everyone else. They always put newbies with me or the petite girls on the weekend late shifts who are gonna get stick because they're turning up to drunks in a copper uniform. It's always *"Good ol' Vince"* that will look after them. I know that. I like that. I live for that, even. Then I let the skipper down. I wasn't there to protect him when he needed me and that's all I have. That's what I do. I'm not the brightest. I don't have a detective head. I'm just a lump who's got everyone else's back. Except I haven't. I didn't this time. I don't know how I walk back into that team, that force — I'm terrified of it, Becks.'

Vince could feel the emotion welling in him. He knew there would be tells on his face. He turned away to pat Alfie again. Then the waitress appeared holding a plate of breakfast for his sister and he was glad of the interruption.

The waitress grinned. 'You coulda gone and got this yourself, Becks!'

'Cheeky! I'll be in later. Plenty of time to make up for it then!'

'I heard you been picking up a few extra shifts. You planning a holiday or summin'?'

Vince looked on as her sister continued to humour the girl. He could tell she didn't want to talk to her, but he was glad of the change in subject. It took another couple of follow-up questions before she finally left.

'Looks good, sis!' Rebecca didn't make a start on her meal. Her attention was back on him. He had seen that look on her face a lot recently, but prior to that he hadn't seen it since growing up together in the same house when she'd had the role of big sister. He had thought that role was long gone.

'Look, I'm fine, honest! It's good to take some time out to think stuff through sometimes. I'll be back stronger. I'm not sure what happens at work, but that stuff will sort itself out.'

'I'm just glad you're okay,' she said, but Vince could tell from her expression that she was some way from satisfied.

'You know me, I'm always okay.'

'You are. And I won't be sad if you leave that job. I could put up with you sitting behind some desk in a safe office, working nine-to-five!'

'Ha!' Vince huffed. 'I'm too good at upsetting people to be wasted behind a desk. Like I said, it'll sort itself out.'

Rebecca chewed a mouthful of food. Vince could tell she had a question. He waited for it.

'These people . . . They're done with you, right?'

'People?' Vince played dumb, but he knew what she meant.

'The people who shot your mate, who shot that other man.'

'They had their chance, sis. They weren't there for me. There's no reason they'd come back for me, either. Not worth the risk. The job are looking into it, to be sure — that was another reason they were happy to see me signed off for a while. I got told to stay at home and keep my head down. That's why it's just me and Alfie against the world for now!'

Rebecca sat back and smiled. It looked genuine now, like she was satisfied. 'And anyway, even if they weren't done with you, no way anyone's finding you in Deal! Nothing ever happens in this town.'

Vince grinned back. 'That's why I like it so much!'

155

CHAPTER 18

'DS Ives, you summoned me here?' Everyone looked ridiculous in the standard issue, bright blue and oversized shoe covers that were part of the kit required to enter a crime scene such as the Rice family home. Somehow, Harry Blaker managed to look more ridiculous than most. Maddie smiled, not just at his look but also at the use of her rank. He only ever used it when they were in a formal meeting or when he needed to remind her of it. She was guessing today was an example of the latter.

'I'm not sure I *summoned* you anywhere, *boss*. It was a friendly request.'

'With good reason, I hope.'

'I wanted to run something past you.'

'Okay, then. And how did it go with our informant? Was there more cohesion in her account today?'

'There was. She's still very much in shock and very emotional — all to be expected, of course. But some of her information might be very significant — hence my *summons*.'

'Go on?'

They were in the hallway. Maddie had been greeted by two CSI officers. Charley Mace was the most senior and had given a quick summary of their work so far. All of their initial focus had been on the body of Scott Rice. They had completed a full body map, swabs and photos in situ. Then a fingertip search of the area with Scott still suspended above them in case they found something of significance that they might need to match up with his final position. They had taken photos of all the bloodstains and marked out the smaller stains or spots of blood with tape for the same reason. The next area of focus was on the ligature. This included the metal loop that had been freshly bolted to the ceiling specifically as part of the method of killing Scott. They hadn't checked it for prints yet, but Maddie was once again expecting to hear that the victim had held it in his hands at some point. Again, there was a hand winch on scene as part of the setup. When she arrived, it was being photographed.

Charley had made it clear that there was still a lot of work to do and had moved away to get on with it. Maddie had come in firing questions and it was obvious that this message was for her, to manage her expectations. Processing a scene took time and they were going to need to be patient. Maddie held back on sharing her thoughts — that the quicker they got answers from this scene, the more chance they could have of stopping another. It probably wouldn't help the situation.

Scott still hung over the scene as a whole, his presence dominating the atmosphere. Charley was waiting for a few more colleagues to assist her with lowering him down. Mercifully, he was wrapped in a body bag as part of Charley's obsession with losing nothing that he might shed, but it was made of a white, reflective material that gave it the look of a giant, hanging chrysalis.

Prior to moving away, Charley had explained how she had made a start on the kitchen and that the entry points at the front and rear were the next priorities. The front door had been processed already to ensure the numerous comings and goings did nothing to destroy evidence.

The final focus would be all the areas their offender was known to have been, then a generic search and assessment on any areas left. But Maddie was here to interrupt those plans and to give Charley a new focus.

'Charley!' Maddie called out towards the kitchen, now that Harry had arrived. 'Could you come down here a moment?' Charley appeared rolling gloves carefully from her fingers. She pulled another pair from her pocket to replace them.

'Jesus, Harry, somehow you manage to make that forensic get-up look good!' Charley wore a beaming smile, as ever. Maddie had never met someone so keen to get in among the most filthy or violent of crime scenes. Maddie had also been at the Rice home when Charley had first arrived to survey the scene the previous evening. She had positively clapped her hands at the sight of the suspended figure of Scott Rice, quickly counting out his numerous stab wounds and then making a noise where she sucked through her teeth, like a mechanic kicking a car tyre before telling you an extortionate price to fix it. 'He really upset someone!' she had said, all the while beaming. Maddie could hardly disagree.

'Thank you, Charley. I tried not wearing it at all once and got firmly told off.'

Charley held the twinkle in her eye. 'Don't you ever forget that, either, sir. The crime scenes belong to me until I tell you otherwise. Now then, how can I help?'

Harry gestured at Maddie. 'Nothing to do with me. Chief Superintendent Ives here would like to discuss matters with you, I believe.'

'One day I will be SMT. Then you'll all be sorry!' Maddie grinned. 'I spoke to Michelle Rice again this morning. I just want to run something past you both.'

'Go on.'

'Michelle went out to a hairdresser last night. She came back in through this door.' Maddie turned to point at the front door. It hung open and the light leaking in was strong, despite the day's cloud cover. 'Last night it was dark and it was raining hard. She can now be sure she closed it after her, the rain was so noisy there was no way she could have left it open without knowing.'

Maddie moved to stand at the door. She turned and stepped in like Michelle must have. 'She'd just had a new haircut and she had her hood up. The first thing she did was take a step in and check her hair in this mirror.' Maddie did as she described. 'Over there, her husband was already dead and suspended on his tiptoes on the stairs. But she didn't see him straight away, she was too busy taking in her own reflection.'

'Okay?' Harry's growl was an impatient one. Maddie had come to know it well.

'Then she saw him.' Maddie gestured towards Scott's chrysalis. 'So now, all her attention is forwards. First towards her husband, then her daughter, who is shouting from an upstairs bedroom directly behind him. She runs past the living room door. Now, these internal doors are always open, Michelle is sure of that.' Maddie pointed out the door to the living room and the kitchen that was visible at the end of the hall. They were both open now, assisting with the natural light. 'Last night, they were both shut. She knows that for certain because it was as good as pitch black in the hallway when she came in. Normally, there's enough light coming in from the street lights through the living room window and the kitchen window for her to move through to another room without turning on a light. Last night, there wasn't.'

'So?' Harry said, his impatience growing.

'When she was on the phone to us, she said the offender was still here. I think we can say that for sure, now. He left when she went upstairs. She said the kitchen door sticks — she would have heard that being opened. The living room doesn't and is silent—'

'So he was in the living room?' Harry shrugged. He plainly couldn't see the relevance.

'We haven't been in there yet, but we'll make sure we do it properly.' Charley said, her tone carrying a warning for anyone who might be trying to suggest otherwise.

'I spoke to an officer who was first on scene,' Maddie continued. 'He and his crewmate did a full sweep of the house. He remembered it well. He said his mate pushed the internal doors open, then he rushed in with a torch and his taser drawn. The one who pushed the door followed him in and worked the light switch.'

'Maddie, I don't see the—'

'The living room door was shut. He's certain of it.'

'So he closed it behind him? You said it was silent?' Harry moved over to it. He reached in with his gloved hand and pulled it shut. It barely made a noise.

'Maybe. But what do we know? The one thing that has been bugging me about linking the two jobs together the whole time was just how the informant discovered what had gone on. Alice Oxley was told her family were dead. From nowhere, out of the blue, and by a man who was standing right in her face. Her account said he was so close it was uncomfortable, that she was *"freaked out"* and that she thought he enjoyed telling her — that's what she said, right?'

'That's right.'

'So think about why he might have stayed here, at this house. She was out for two hours. He should have had enough time to put some distance between him and this house before she got home. But he wanted to see her, when she saw what he had done. And if he had shut himself in the living room, he would have been here in the house but he wouldn't have *seen* her.'

'Okay,' Harry said.

Maddie pointed at the mirror. Then she moved to stand directly in front of it, taking in her reflection. She spun 180 degrees. Charley caught on first.

'The cupboard,' she breathed. 'We haven't processed this yet. It was going to be a wipe over the handle and a visual search. That's it!' Charley pulled open the door. It was floor to ceiling and slatted. The wood was painted a bright white. Maddie moved so she was on the outside of the door.

'Can you see me? Through the door I mean?'

Charley took a step closer behind the door. She moved back away from it to speak. 'Most of you!' The excitement was clear in her voice.

'If he stood in there, he could have been just a few feet away from her when she came in, when she realised what he'd done — like he was with Alice Oxley. That's what this man wants. He wants to see the reaction.'

'Well . . .' Harry ran a hand over his close-cropped hair. 'That would be a new one on me.'

Maddie was on a roll. 'The witness down the road who saw Christ the Redeemer . . . At that time, he said there were already three or four police cars here, at least. I checked the CAD for when the patrols TA'd. There was seven minutes between the first car and the *third*. If there were four cars here, it was nine minutes. The first car took four minutes to arrive from the time the call was made.'

'So he stayed in the area.'

'He did. He stayed and he waited for the police. He could have been well clear in four minutes. He must have stayed close, too. The witness is a few doors down and he was walking past, his direction away from here. Maybe it wasn't just Michelle Rice or Alice Oxley . . . Maybe he wanted to see our reaction, too.'

'Okay, then.' Even Harry's tone had a little excitement in it. 'This gives us a better understanding of who we're looking for.'

'It's just a theory.' Maddie suddenly felt the need to back down. She didn't want the whole investigation to tilt on its axis based on what she thought.

'We don't have a better one.' Harry produced a ringing phone from his pocket. He scowled at it. 'No caller ID. I need to get this.' He gestured at Charley. 'All your attention on that cupboard. If he dropped a fleck of skin, we need it found!'

'Yes, boss.'

'And Maddie, call the office. Have the CCTV from the first job reviewed again, but with particular attention to after

— including when the police turn up. I want someone looking specifically to see if anyone was hanging about in the area. Do it now!' He turned, his phone now silenced and thrust to his ear. Maddie was left staring at Charley, whose smile had returned.

'I think he means "*Good work, detective!*"'

Maddie laughed. Both women fell silent. Both stared at the cupboard door. Harry's reappearance came a few seconds later and was clumsy, the front door bouncing off the wall in his haste.

'Maddie! We need to go.'

'Go?' Maddie said.

'That was the Central Analyst Unit. They might have something similar. They're sending the details through. Sounds like our man could have been busy elsewhere.'

He was gone again. Charley sniffed. Maddie turned to it.

'Go on, then!' Charley said. 'He who must be obeyed! You go do the exciting bit and I'll just pop in that cupboard on my hands and knees to look for flakes of skin!'

* * *

'DI Kimberly Hart.' The answer to the phone was abrupt, as if the answerer had already been talking to someone else. It was projected into the interior of the car on the hands-free. Harry and Maddie both sat still. Harry had the car ticking over for the heater.

'Good morning. This is DI Harry Blaker from Lennockshire Police. I'm here with DS Maddie Ives . . .' He paused, waiting for an acknowledgement.

'Lennockshire?' She sounded hassled.

'That's right. Down on the coast. I'm sorry to call you out of the blue, I was hoping you might have a few minutes to talk about a case you're working?'

'Sure. I tell you what, could you give me a second? Or maybe I could call you back? I'm just getting to a scene — you know how it is.'

Harry made eye contact again. Maddie certainly knew *how it is* with senior officers arriving at a scene for the first time. They would have a million questions, both fired out and received in. There was no way she would be getting back to them any time soon. Harry must have had the exact same idea.

'Actually, this is important. Maybe for both of us. It shouldn't take a minute.' Harry stopped. He had been effective at putting her on the spot. There was only one answer.

'Okay, what have you got?'

'I've been made aware of a brief summary of a murder scene you attended and subsequently became the SIO for. Janet Foreland. A white female, forty-five years old, found with a wire ligature round her neck and stabbed in the neck in an apartment overlooking Bristol canal.'

'Janet . . . Yeah, okay. A couple of months back.'

'So I see.'

'Did you have some information for me?' The woman's voice was more levelled now, as if they had a little more of her attention.

'We might have. We have two sus deaths in a couple of days. Both victims were found by their partners with frenzied stab wounds in their torsos. They were trussed up by the neck by a wire over a loop and lifted up onto their tiptoes.'

'Okay. And you think that's relevant to my job? Janet received a clinical cut to her neck She was also seated on the floor when we found her. Probably moved after she died and positioned against the wall.'

'Positioned?' Maddie cut in.

The DI took a moment to react to the new voice. 'That's what I said. What makes you think it has anything to do with your job? I mean Lennockshire, that's three hours from here — four, maybe.'

'How was she positioned?' Maddie persisted.

'Sitting. One leg pulled up. Her head was held by a wire that was tied off on the ceiling. She was against a wall but the offender used her blood to . . . well . . . to make a statement, for want of a better word.'

'A statement?'

'It was a white wall. But there wasn't much white left. It was covered in her blood. A random pattern, to me, at least — swirls. The offender used a decorating sponge. It was left at the scene.'

'Your victim, Janet . . . Was she found by a loved one? A partner, or member of her family?' Maddie said.

'Was that not included in what you have already?' DI Kimberly Hart tutted. Her tone had been getting more and more curt. It was clear this was a call she could do without.

'We took a quick call from the Central Analyst Unit. It was just a brief MO and victim details. We're heading back in to see if there's any more detail on our email but we thought the best way was to call you direct. We might be able to help each other out, here.'

'I see. Well I think an email request might be the way to go if you need anything more from me. With all due respect, you could be the press, for all I know.'

'I appreciate that.' Harry's growl cut back in. 'I've already sent you an email from my phone. It's from my police account and might be with you already. It has contact details in there, so you know we are who we say we are. We don't have time to be wasting. We have two victims that were strung up and left facing the front door of their own homes for their loved ones to find. Is it possible the killer was still on scene when your victim was found? Looking at the worst-case scenario here, we have a serial killer whose thing is watching the reaction to what he has done.'

There was silence on the other end of the phone. Maddie wasn't surprised. She wasn't sure what you could say to that.

'It's just a theory,' Harry continued. 'The link with you is just a theory, too, but us detectives . . . we all like to make sure we explore every one, no matter how unlikely.'

'That might not sound so unlikely . . . It wasn't something we . . . I hadn't considered that.'

'We have a set of circumstances here that makes that scenario possible. You didn't. Until now, perhaps.'

'No. We didn't, not in isolation. Hold on.'

Harry again made eye contact with Maddie. There was a brief pause. The speaker made a sound, like Kimberly Hart was dragging her phone against a rain jacket. Then came a *clunk* that might have been a car door closing. When she spoke next, there was wind noise.

'I'm at a scene. It's probably an OD. The patrol here called it sus based on the back door being insecure. I don't think there's anything more to it. I should be away from here very quickly. Maybe it would be better to call you back from my desk when I have everything to hand?'

'I'm sure you're right. We're right in the middle of it here, though. Is there anything that springs to mind, anything we can take away and use now?'

'Well, no. I mean, yeah, some things certainly would make sense if your theory was correct. Janet was found sitting up against a wall in the living area of her flat. It's the penthouse apartment with a view over the canal. She was worth a lot of money — a bit of a local celeb. On the day she died, her sister received a message from the victim's phone asking her to come over straight away. It suggested there was something wrong with her marriage and insisted she tell no one of her visit. We now believe this message was sent by the killer, around the time of her death. The sister has her own key to the place. When she went in, she found her sister sitting up against the white wall of her living room — but, as I said, there wasn't much white left. Forensics have found very little to assist . . . No sign of forced entry, no clear motive or disputes, no sexual assault . . . The only thing of any interest was traces of bleach on the victim's cheek.'

'Bleach?'

'That's right. It matches the type found in the victim's kitchen.'

'Did anyone else have a key?' Maddie jumped in and couldn't hide the urgency in her voice.

'Her husband, naturally. But that was all.'

'And where was he? When she was found, I mean?'

'Away on business. He travels a lot. He works as a diplomat for a tech company. Very senior. His alibi was solid. Their relationship was less solid, it would seem. There's some evidence from the victim's phone that she was a little closer to her sister's husband than she should have been. This led me to speak with him under caution as a potential suspect. He didn't match with the description we got, but—'

'Description?'

The DI did nothing to disguise a huff. 'A neighbour saw a man walking away from the building. She said he walked with purpose and looked "crazed," like he was on something. There's nothing else to link him. He just didn't look like he belonged in the area. She hadn't seen him in the building before and we've established he didn't live there.'

'This description . . . Was it of a white male, around sixty years old with a ponytail and glasses?' Maddie could barely breathe.

'Was that in the summary you have?' The DI asked. Her voice was distorted by the wind.

'No. We have a description from one of our scenes.'

'Well, no. That isn't right. The age could be right, but his hair was short. "Closely cropped," it said. No glasses either. He was a white male, slim build, aged around sixty. He was described as "like a tramp" by our witness. He was in the area at the material time and we wanted to speak with him, but no one can put him in the room — or even the vicinity of the top floor at the time of the offence. It's quite possible it was just a homeless man passing through the area.'

'Slim build?'

'That's what I remember.'

'Did he have a bag?' Maddie kept the questions coming quick while she was getting answers.

'Yes, from memory. A small bag.'

'Our man might have a bit of a belly. Can you double-check his build with your informant?' Maddie said.

'Not right now, DS Ives. Like I said, I don't have everything to hand and I've just arrived at a scene. It's a very busy time. I'll call you later. It does sound like this might just be a similar MO but with a very different offender. Happens all the time.'

'What about the sister? And her husband?' Maddie said, ignoring the tone that had turned patronising.

'I think I covered them already. Look, I'm not sure we have a link after all. We must be two hundred miles from Lennockshire and I don't see anything more than coincidence as a link. This love triangle is slowly revealing itself. There'll be a strong motive in there. No one was being completely open with us to start with. The sister's husband remains the focus for me. The suggestion of an unrelated serial killer is not something I can support, from what I know. Maybe keep in touch if you learn anything you think I need to know. I'll send over what I have later. I have your details.'

'I tell you what . . .' Maddie rushed her words before the DI could hang up the phone. 'How about I send a detective down? She can review your material. I'll make sure she's well briefed on what we have here so she can make any comparisons. That way, you don't really have to get involved at all. I can tell you're busy.'

For a moment, the only answer was wind noise. 'Look, fine. Send someone down. She can poke around the case file, by all means, but I don't have time to be briefing her on the ins and outs of everything we know. This is very much a live investigation — I can't have anyone in the way.'

'I'm sending my best. You won't even know she's there!'

There was another sigh. 'When?'

'Tomorrow morning. She'll leave first thing.'

'You should have just said from the very start if this was your plan.'

'It wasn't!' Maddie laughed. She ignored the constant attempt from Harry to make eye contact.

'It's Saturday tomorrow. I'm not in. I'll make sure someone knows she's coming. That's probably not going to be enough time for me to arrange anything and we run light at the weekends. She'll be put in a room with the file at best.'

'That's all we need.'

'Fine. I'll need her details.'

'It will be DC Rhiannon Davies. She'll—'

'Send me her name. On email. I need to get this scene processed. Send her details and I'll try and find time to reply with where she needs to go.'

'Thank you, Ma'am. I really appreciate it. We'll make sure we write up anything you might need for your case file, too.'

'I would expect nothing less.'

The call ended. Finally, Maddie relented. Harry's glare was expectant. She knew why.

'Rhiannon will go. I know she will.'

'DC Davies of CID will go as part of a Major Crime investigation?' Harry replied.

'Hardly the first time we've asked for CID support.'

'We haven't asked, have we?'

'No. But she'll go!'

'It might be the first time we've sent them without a consideration for our own. She was your first thought?'

'She's always my first thought! All our DCs are tucked up anyway, Harry. I know that. We're already asking for overtime to work the weekend to try and cope. This might be a complete waste of time. Surely we're better off wasting CID time?'

'Can CID even release her?'

'She's on rest day. I know she is. It won't be an issue.'

Harry shook his head.

'She doesn't need a weekend off, not at her age! She'll be fine. I'll talk to her.'

'You don't think this is a waste of time, do you? There's another reason you're not sending one of our own.' Harry said.

'Rhiannon's thorough is all. I'm a lot more likely to believe her if she comes back and says it was a waste of time.'

Harry huffed but was clearly done arguing. 'When you talk to her, are you going to tell her that you've already upset the SIO?' He spoke over his shoulder as he drove out of the space and away from the Rice family home.

'She's been working a case for a month or so and then two detectives from a county two hundred miles away call her out of the blue to suggest she might be barking up the wrong tree entirely. She was always going to get the hump. And she won't be there tomorrow, anyway.'

'I get that. But you know she'll be briefing someone to meet our Rhiannon and she might not be too positive about it.'

'You're right. I just won't tell Rhiannon that!'

Harry shook his head.

* * *

'Rhiannon! I made you a coffee. White, weak, one sugar!' Maddie sung her words the moment Rhiannon entered the Major Crime floor.

'You wanted to see me. Now I'm worried.'

'Worried?'

'You want something.'

'Ah, you see, this is *why* I wanted to speak to you. Because you're sharp, Rhiannon. You might just be the sharpest detective I know.'

'Okay. So you want something and now I know it's something shitty! That's how compliments work with you.'

'That is very unfair.'

'Tell me I'm wrong.'

'About what?'

'About wanting something.'

'Okay, you're not wrong about that.'

'And it's shitty.'

'It . . . It's a Saturday.'

'Tomorrow?'

Maddie grinned. She pushed the mug towards her colleague. It caught and scraped on the table. 'Delicious coffee.'

'I have plans tomorrow.'

'No, you don't.'

'How do you know?'

'Because this is juicy. Trust me, you're going to want to be involved. What cases have you got on the go down in CID at the moment? A few burglaries, right?'

'I'm leading on the burglary series. Asian Gold. It's a big op. I've been presenting direct to the chief on community tensions. But thanks for belittling it.' Rhiannon tried to look hurt but it only took a grin from Maddie to break it down. 'What do you want, Maddie Ives?'

'There was a murder, you know, a proper crime. Not some crack addict crawling through a window for trinkets . . .' Maddie paused for Rhiannon to laugh, she was relieved when she did. 'A woman positioned against a white wall, her blood smeared all over the place with a decorating sponge. Proper stuff.'

'When?' Rhiannon's eyes widened a little.

'A few months ago. In Bristol.'

'Oh.' Rhiannon visibly deflated. 'Months ago and in a different force? What do you want me to do about that?'

'I think it might be linked to what we have here. You know about the murders?'

'Of course. I've heard bits about it. We're all braced to be stitched up with shitty enquiries Major Crime can't be arsed with. If this is CCTV reviews, then—'

'It's not! I wouldn't waste you on CCTV reviews and that's not me kissing your arse anymore. I need someone thorough, someone whose judgement I can trust. You were the first person I thought of.'

'Judgement? About what?'

'The woman was cut, her blood smeared all over a white wall and then she was sat up to face the door that her sister then came through. Her sister got a text message from the victim's phone asking her to come round. She was *supposed* to find her. The two victims we have here, they were both hung up to face the front door. Both were found by family members and it was fashioned so they were *supposed* to.'

'So that's why you think they're linked?'

'We have an offender description from one of the scenes. Bristol have a description, too — they don't match, but they're close enough that I don't want to discount it. Not until I've had someone look over it who I trust. I spoke to a DI over the phone. She's the SIO. I think I gave her the hump and she got a little defensive. She probably won't want me to be right — I don't blame her . . . Roles reversed, I wouldn't want me to be right, either. She's granted you full access to the case file. You'll see everything they have. I'll get you a summary together of what we have. I'm not expecting a clear link, maybe just what your gut tells you.'

'My gut?'

'You have good instincts. This DI Kimberly Hart might have, too, but I don't know that. She's nothing more than a voice on the phone to me.'

'And you want me to go tomorrow?'

'I said you would go first thing.'

'Of course you did!'

'I can send someone from here. I know a couple who would jump at the chance. We've already got a load in for overtime, but they are doing the shitty jobs — those CCTV reviews you mentioned.'

Rhiannon sighed. 'It's fine. I'll go.'

'It'll be a long day. I can't really justify a hotel on expenses, not at this point, not when she could just send it all on email.'

'Why don't you do that, then?'

'Because you never get it all. There's nothing like being in the actual office where a live investigation is going on. Digging around in daybooks and post-it notes, maybe calling a number or two to clarify something with a witness . . . You know what I mean.'

'I think I do. You want me to go and upset a whole force by snooping around?'

'That's not what I said!'

'So you don't want me snooping around?'

'Snooping — definitely. I just want someone who can get what I need without upsetting anyone.'

Rhiannon hid her laughter behind her coffee mug. It was enough for Maddie. She could see she was enthused and that was all she needed. An enthused Rhiannon Davies was quite something.

CHAPTER 19

'Like I said, it's no palace.'

Gavin pushed open the door and the familiar, stale smell of his home swept outwards. Normally, he would step into the dimly lit interior beyond without even noticing, dragging his feet through the layers of unopened post to move into the living room. But today someone was with him and he suddenly felt self-conscious. Embarrassed, even.

'What a curious building!' His guest had stopped a few paces back outside the front door and was looking up. If he was disgusted, he was hiding it well. He seemed to be taking in the building as a whole. Gavin could understand why — it was always a talking point when someone saw it for the first time. It was highly unusual: a long slim design, punctured by front doors along its side. Each dwelling was marked out by high walls, which wrapped around a small, stone yard. The interiors were cramped. You could easily see right through to the identical-looking back yard with the same high walls. Anyone who came up here for deliveries, to read meters or more often, just lost, would comment on it.

'Chicken shed,' Gavin said.

'Sorry?'

'This whole building was a chicken shed. My post even has it on it. This is Number 5, *The Chicken Shed*. Redwall Farm is further down the lane. This used to be part of it. It isn't right for housing, that's for sure, but that didn't seem to stop the council buying it up. I hate it.' He did, too. It was nothing more than a slim barn separated into cramped dwellings by poorly insulated walls. He didn't reckon there had been a big change to the building from when the animals lived in it.

'It's certainly unique. It's dry, though. Warm, too, I bet. No complaints from me.'

Gavin shrugged. 'With the heating on. I can't afford the bills, so it isn't on much. The bench is colder, though, that's for sure.'

'Thank you for this. And here, like I promised!' He placed a bag on top of a pile of clothes that covered a sofa. They'd stopped at a nearby off-licence to purchase a crate of strong lager and a couple of bottles of red wine. It should be enough to see them through the day, at least. 'And I assume there's a takeaway that delivers for later.'

'Okay, well there's a bedroom at the back. The kitchen's there, too. You can find the shitter just through there. It should all work. The bedroom's yours to use, but you might have to clear a space. You can't hurt anything in there — just push it out of the way.'

'I am very much obliged.' His new housemate moved to the window and seemed to take in the view. His place was on the outskirts of Deal, a good twenty-minute walk back to his bench on the seafront. The first row of terraced houses where the town started was visible through the bedroom window, but all you could see from the front were rutted fields that ran into a golf course.

'You're a bit isolated up here, aren't you, my friend?'

'Isolated?'

'People. Community. We seem to have left it all behind.'

'I got what I was given. I waited long enough for this place. I couldn't say no. It does feel like nowhere up here.

That's why I head back into the town, I suppose, and the area where I grew up. Odd, really. I don't really like people no more, but I can't bear to be away from them.'

'I don't think that's odd. That makes sense. A lot of people have the need to feel a part of *something* at least. This pastime that we have chosen for ourselves can be a solitary one. Do you have any friends who come up here? Any reason I should be aware of my state of undress?'

Gavin forced a smile. 'No, there's no one who comes up here to see me. It's peaceful. Not all these places have got people in them, either. There was some junkie a few doors along. He used to get the police up here a lot — he was stealing from the shops and not very good at it, by all accounts. He might still be there, but I heard he was in prison. They used to put people up here that they didn't want in the town — at least, that's what I reckon. A lot of the places have problems and they can't be used for housing at the moment. Apparently I'm one of the lucky ones.'

'And you are.'

'Well, whatever. I don't have people up here.'

'So I should feel honoured?'

Gavin took a moment to consider. 'You might be the first person who's been in here since I moved in. I used to have people — friends. When I lived down in the town, they would come round. Some of them had a go at getting me off the booze. They thought they were helping. I was younger then. I think when you get older, people seem less bothered. I suppose they think you're old enough to make your own decisions. No one wants anything to do with you anymore.'

Gavin was suddenly self-conscious again. He glanced up to where the man moved back to the sofa and took two beers out of the crate. He opened them both, then knocked them together like he was toasting. He handed one to Gavin. Gavin took a long, deep swig.

The man did the same, then doffed his tin. 'To staying committed to the only true friend that matters . . . alcohol!' They knocked tins again. 'And to not being disturbed.'

CHAPTER 20

She was confident, verging on brash. The doctors' surgery was busy with a regular stream of people coming in. Most of them seemed to be displaying attitude of some sort and Rebecca Arnold met each one with an expectant stare and a slight lean forward that was designed perhaps to disarm them, to let them know that she was not about to fold to their will. Her name was displayed on a name tag that hung a little lopsidedly on her top. Her latest customer was a fat mother. Her excess flab pushed out against her tracksuit and she was towing a plump little boy along, his face so swollen from his diet that it looked like it was starting to close up. Soon he would hardly be able to push whatever it was he was holding in his hand through the layers to get to his mouth. The woman was loud, too. The room was busy, the seats all taken, but it was hushed, as if everyone understood the need to be quiet — but not the woman. She seemed oblivious to the impact she was having on the room, her business shouted for anyone to hear. Lance watched her, careful not to show his disgust. She had come in to get an appointment for her son, but it very quickly became about her, about how she could never get an appointment and how the system was letting her down.

Rebecca was calm, quiet and stern. She directed the woman to a touchscreen appointment system, then ignored the tuts and huffs.

Lance wouldn't have been able to. He had to hold himself down as it was. He wasn't there to make a scene — he was there to blend in. He had stood outside for a while and counted ten people in with no one coming out. That was when he had decided to go inside and just sit, that he might be able to blend in and no one take any notice of him.

He had been right. When he'd pushed through the door, no one had even looked up. Most were on their phones, some flicking through magazines. He had walked right past a clump of people gathered around the desk. Rebecca's colleague had been in front of the reception when he had walked in and she didn't even look up. He had taken one of the last seats, right beside a low table that held a brightly coloured wire fashioned into a spiral. There were small, wooden beads in differing colours along its length. Other children's toys were stacked in boxes on the other side of the table. The few children present were taking no interest in them. They probably hadn't even noticed. They were all in the same state of distraction as their parents, peering down at a handheld device of some sort. Oblivious. It was the way of the world, now.

The two reception staff swapped out seamlessly. Rebecca gave her replacement a brief smile and pushed through a door at the back and out of sight. Lance checked his watch. It was three p.m. The local schools were preparing to kick out their masses of squawking, squabbling children with the colours of their day dripped down their shirt fronts and plaid dresses. Rebecca would need to be there to meet her son. Her day ran like clockwork: an early morning shift in the café, then lunch cover at the doctor's surgery three days a week. Today being a Friday meant it was her last. She sometimes did a split shift, going back to cover the evening at the café when she could get her kid looked after.

PC Vince Arnold had become quite the reliable babysitter for her. She had seized on the opportunity presented by his leave of absence.

It had been easy to find him. Mason had provided an address that he had said was 'a place to start.' It had turned out to be Vince's home address. Then he'd needed to find his weakness, the person who would allow him to get close. That had been just as easy. Rebecca Arnold was it. Her regular schedule made it easier still, and she would emerge from the side door to the surgery at any moment to continue with her day.

Lance was as ready as he needed to be.

He stood up and made for the door. No one looked up. No one noticed — he was just another frustrated punter who was tired of waiting. Except he wasn't. The fact that everyone was so oblivious to him, to what he was, to what he could do, should he choose, made him flush a little with excitement. His exit through the door was hurried and clumsy. He needed to slow down — to calm down. The air outside was much cooler but did little to put out the fire that seemed to be growing under his skin. He tried to focus, but his thoughts moved to where this could all end, and how. He told himself again that he needed to be calm. There was plenty still to do. His groundwork to this point had been ideal. Fate really had been on his side. The police should have applied their label by now — they were always so quick to do that. '*Serial killer*' they would say, albeit under their breaths and far away from the media. He reminded himself that there was time to relax, that he was way ahead of schedule.

He moved to where he had a distant view of the side door. Rebecca was always in a hurry. She never seemed to have the time to stop and take in her surroundings. Next, she would pick up her son, then take him round to her brother's house. They would stay in and play X-Box, while she did an extra shift to cover the teatime rush at the café. She would be back at her brother's house just after seven p.m. She and her brother would have a glass of wine, then Vince Arnold would carry his sleeping nephew out to her car so she could run him the short distance home. Saturday was a similar pattern. Sunday was her only day off.

Suddenly, he considered that Saturday could be his opportunity. That was tomorrow. He felt his skin bristle with heat again at the thought of it.

'Why not?' he murmured to himself. Just then, he heard the scrape of a door pushed open. Rebecca Arnold appeared. Her head was bent over a phone. She turned away and moved quickly over the road to pull open the door of a car. The engine fired and the car pulled away.

Lance stood next to a battered old Vauxhall saloon. It was black — for blending into the shadows when he needed it. Today he was hiding it in plain sight. He had a bright yellow metal clamp marked *DVLA* chained to his front wheel that perversely served to make it all the more invisible. He unlocked it, the heavy chain scraping as it came free. He slung it in the boot. It lay flat next to two brand new hand winches. His back flashed hot again at the sight of them.

Lance's walk to the driver's seat was casual. There was no rush, not anymore. Today he would let her go, he didn't need to follow her any longer. He knew enough. He would pick her up again tomorrow morning in the café. Her son usually had a play date on a Saturday morning. This week, it was her friend's turn to host. She would be meeting her brother.

He wound the driver's side window down so the air could move around him when he got moving.

'Oh, yes,' he said. 'I think we're ready!'

CHAPTER 21

The house looked shut-up and vacant. The sound of Maddie's knock reinforced the impression of an empty space behind. She was back knocking for Michelle Rice at her mother's house. The silence was long enough for her to turn away and start towards where she had parked her car in Minster's tight roads. Then there was a sign of life that came all at once. The front door scraped and Michelle herself leaned around it to call out with anger in her voice.

'There's nothing more to say. I've done it twice. I won't do it again!' She pushed the door back shut. Maddie let it happen. She gave it a second, then stepped closer, so close her mouth was almost against it. She spoke in a raised voice.

'I'm sorry, Michelle. I only came here to say that. I want to be able to pick up the phone and talk to you about how we're doing with all this, about how we're getting closer to finding him . . .' She let her words make their way through the door and sink in. She was certain Michelle was still there. She would surely be interested as to why Maddie had returned. The door moved again. It made Maddie jump and she jerked backwards, stumbling off the step.

'And are you?' Michelle leaned around the door. 'Closer, I mean?'

'It feels like it, but I've got nothing tangible. Nothing I can show you or tell you.'

Michelle held her stare. 'And you drove out here from Canterbury to tell me that?'

'No. I drove out to apologise and to talk to you about safeguarding. About Fern. There are some things I have to do, some forms I have to fill out. It's a referral. But if I come out and talk to you, then I might be able to avoid all that.'

'What forms? What referral? This has got nothing to do with Fern.'

'I get that. That's why I wanted to come out and explain. In any incident like this, we have to make a referral to child services. It's force policy. Fern was present when her dad was murdered . . . We need to make sure she's getting what she needs—'

Michelle lunged forward. She was too quick and Maddie didn't see it coming. The slap jerked her face to one side. Her cheek stung and her vision blurred temporarily. The door slammed. That part, Maddie had been expecting — the slap had caught her out. She could have sent a form to Social Services who would then have had this experience, but she had seen this as an opportunity to come back out, to try again with Michelle. She had expected that their relationship might get worse before it got better.

Maddie raised her hand to her stinging cheek. She left it a full minute, then raised her voice for another go.

'I know why you're angry. I would be, too. I know Fern has you — she doesn't need anyone else. She doesn't need Social Services at the door, and nor do you. But if I send this referral in, they will . . .' She paused. There was no more movement at the door. 'I could have done that already. But if you speak to me for just a few minutes, I can cover off a few points and then they don't need to come out. That's why I'm here. To try and make this easier.' There was no reaction. 'And I still want to apologise.'

Maddie stepped away from the door. The house was large and detached, with neighbours' houses distant and hidden behind thick hedges. She checked all the windows in turn. Still there was no movement. She considered her options. There was only one she hadn't tried yet. She moved back to the door and hammered on it with the bottom of her fist. She kept hammering until the door flew open. Maddie was quick to step back out of range and to speak first.

'After today, you can ignore me all you want. But talk to me now for a few minutes, or you'll have plenty of other people to ignore. And if you do, they'll go to Fern's school, to her GP — anywhere they can, to get what they need. Your business will become everyone else's.' Maddie ran out of air. She stopped her rant for a breath. The door closed again. Maddie swore. She started her walk down the drive. She was making mental plans to refer this family to every Social Services project and agency available when she heard the door again.

Maddie turned but stayed where she was. Michelle stepped out. She was pulling a coat over her shoulders as she did. She stopped to pull the door shut firmly behind her. Then she lifted her hands to her mouth. When she pulled them away there was a puff of smoke. She didn't look over at Maddie. She did turn a sharp right to make for a wooden bench that was a few paces into a neat lawn. She sat down, crossed her legs and stayed looking away. Her position on the bench was over to one side. It was about as close to an invitation as Maddie might have hoped for.

'I didn't know you smoked,' Maddie called out.

The woman gestured with the packet — that was more like an invitation. Maddie walked over and took one.

'Only when I'm stressed out. The last few weeks, I reckon it must have been twenty a day.' Smoke fell out of Michelle's mouth in a stuttered pattern as she spoke. She was looking away.

'I'm exactly the same.' Maddie pushed the cigarette into her mouth. It had been a few months since her last, and she desperately didn't want it but recognised it was something to bond over.

'Are you going to arrest me?'

'Arrest you?'

'I never hit a police officer before.'

'Oh, I see! Don't worry about this.' She gestured at her cheek that felt like it was burning up. She had been resisting the urge to touch it. 'That would kind of go against what I'm trying to achieve, here.' Maddie had certainly considered the option, though, when the door had been slammed shut. She only dismissed it when she realised that she would then have to break it to Harry that she had arrested their witness.

'Okay, then. I thought you would. That was why I came out here for a fag. I know you can't smoke at the police station.'

'Been arrested before, have we?' Maddie laughed.

'No. I went through a stage of watching a lot of the police programmes on TV. Every time someone got arrested, it seemed all they wanted was a cigarette. I couldn't do your job.'

Maddie felt the coldness of the bench as she leaned back. 'Most coppers I know aren't sure they can do it, either. Not all the time. Not when you turn up to some jobs. When you find out what one person is capable of doing to another.'

'You mean like us? Is that what's got you stressed?' Michelle's tone still carried an edge. She pulled her jacket tighter. The temperature seemed to be dropping fast as the evening approached.

'Yes. I can't imagine how you feel after what you've been through, but the possibility of a serial killer out there is definitely enough to get me sucking on one of these!'

'Serial killer?' Michelle faced her for the first time since stepping out of the house.

'Maybe. And don't tell my boss I said those words. Or the press. We're kind of hoping to avoid the circus that comes with it.'

'But that's what you think?'

'It seems to have some of the hallmarks. We have a few incidents that are similar enough to suggest it's the same person. And we think he's . . .' Maddie paused to search for words that might have less of an impact on Michelle. She couldn't find any. 'We think he's getting off on it. Like that's his motive. That's part of what makes a serial killer . . . someone who hurts people without the traditional gains.'

'Traditional gains?'

'Money, jealousy, love rival, pride . . . People hurt other people for all sorts of reasons. Most of them, you can understand on some level. You don't get that with serial killers. There's something they get out of it you could never hope to understand. It's what makes catching them so difficult.'

'Getting off on it? Like some sicko stealing underwear and playing with himself dressed in it?'

'Maybe!' Maddie laughed, she couldn't help it. 'Sorry, it's not funny, not at all. These people . . . It's not necessarily a sexual thing, although the excitement is the same and the compulsion certainly is. There's no suggestion of any masturbation here, though. Shame, really.'

'Shame?'

'It's excellent for DNA.' Maddie was wistful. It finally prompted a giggle from Michelle. It dropped away quickly.

'Why did he target us? That's what I don't understand . . .' Her voice seemed close to breaking. She took a moment. Maddie waited. 'That's the most important thing for me. Once I know that, once I know what we did — or what Scott did — for him to pick us out, I can make sure we never do that again . . .'

'We're building a picture. That's a question I might be able to answer in time, but I wouldn't let that consume you too much. It could just be wrong place, wrong time.'

'That's certainly been the wrong place.'

'Your home?'

'Yeah. It's never felt like that, though. Some places you just don't gel with. It gave us problems from the off. I remember the heating problem. When we moved in, it was the middle of a cold snap and the heating was dead. Took a few weeks to sort. We found a load of issues with old pipes.

Anyway, that was my first impression of that place — empty and cold. I guess I never got away from that.'

'That is a shame. It looks homely now, from what I saw.'

'Even if I had gelled, we can never go back there. Not now. Not after what I saw. The neighbours stress me out. The house still doesn't get massively warm on the coldest of nights and now I'll always have that image — whenever I step through that front door.'

'It'll fade, over time. I know it's a bit of a cliché, but it gets easier with time. All of this will.'

'Maybe you're right.' It was clear from Michelle's tone that she didn't believe that for a moment. There was a natural pause. Both women took another drag. 'What's all this about a form?' Michelle sounded tired now, resigned maybe.

'It's really nothing to worry about. Social Services get a referral in every instance where a child has suffered the loss of a parent or if there has been a violent incident in the home. This ticks both those boxes. I just need to be able to say that Fern's safeguarding is being managed by the police.'

'Managed by you?'

'Poor turn of phrase. I mean we're happy that it's being managed by you — that you don't need Social Services to step in. Some of the people we deal with . . . Well, let's just say they should never have become parents.'

'I can imagine.'

'I assume you're staying here for a while now? Is it okay with your mum? Living with her I mean?'

'Yes, of course!' The edge returned to her tone.

'That's good. I couldn't live with my mum is all. She's . . . Well, she's probably a very different person from yours.'

'My mum loves having us here. Well, she loves having Fern here — I think she could take it or leave it when it comes to me! She understands that we can't go back. We'd been staying here every now and then anyway, when next door was bad.'

'Next door?'

'Some drunk.' She waved her hand dismissively. 'It was an elderly couple when we moved in. They were lovely, actually. The old man died a few weeks after we moved in and then his wife gave up shortly after that. I guess they wanted to be together, eh? Anyway, the son inherited the place. He's a drunk. He gets obliterated and plays rock music — no matter the time. Scott was at the point of putting his head through his stereo, I think. When he was away with work, we used to come here. Assuming he was away with work, of course . . . I suppose I shouldn't really complain, somehow *we* became the noisy neighbours!'

'You did? How do you mean?'

'I told you we argued. Me and Scott. Our last day on this earth together, and we spent the morning arguing. It must have travelled through the walls. He'd stressed me out, so I went out in the garden for a smoke. I was sitting in the cold having one of those moments when you wonder where it all went wrong and someone called out from over the fence. Asked if I was okay! He even asked if I wanted to talk about it. That's how low I got, some old drunk offering me a shoulder to cry on.'

'He wasn't drunk then? Was it very early morning?'

'It wasn't him, actually — the son, I mean. I've never said two words to him. He's got some bloke staying with him. There's always loads of people stumbling in and out, but this one seemed okay. It was actually nice to have someone in the house I could talk to about the music. He caught me turning it off the night before. It seemed like he was on my side overall.'

'Did you talk to him? About Scott, I mean?'

'God, no! He caught me at a weak moment is all. I was upset, but I didn't tell him why. I saved it all up for Angela, poor cow. I wouldn't talk to some stranger about my personal life. He looked like a sex pest for a start!'

'Sex pest?' Maddie said.

'All drinkers look like sex pests to me. He must be a drinker, they all are in there.'

'What did he look like?'

Michelle shrugged. 'Old . . . long hair — like in a pony-tail. He should give it up, if you ask me. There wasn't much left on top!'

'Anything else you remember?' Maddie was half aware she was sitting straighter. She tried to hide her hunger.

'Why does he matter?' Michelle seemed to eye her with suspicion.

'I just want to be sure we've spoken to everyone. I know we knocked on that door, but I'm not sure we got someone with that description.'

'Well he had glasses, too. They looked cheap. Like the sort you get free on the NHS, you know what I mean?'

'Did he have a pot belly?' Maddie cursed her own haste and the leading question.

'He had a bit of a belly, yeah. Like I said, he looked like every other drinker.'

'And how long had he been there?'

'I'd seen him twice over a couple of days, I suppose. Although I didn't actually see him the second time. He was just a voice over the fence. No one ever stays there long.'

'And he was staying there?'

'Is there something about this bloke? You don't think he . . .' Her head started shaking. 'No way. Scott would have snapped him in half! He was nothing. Some old man with a scrawny neck.'

'I want to make sure we've spoken to him is all. He might know something. So, was he staying there?'

'He said he was. But people there come and go. Most just happen to collapse on the sofa, from what I've seen . . .'

Maddie felt light-headed, partly because her mind was running with thoughts and theories and partly because it was flooded with cigarette smoke. She was out of practice. She stood up, considering that it might clear her head. 'I should get back to it. I can tick off what I need to with Social Services. I'll make sure they stay away. I do need to make you aware that they are there. They can be useful, if Fern could do with speaking to someone . . .'

Michelle's head was shaking.

Maddie didn't want to press the point and undo the work she had done to rebuild their relationship. 'Michelle, you guys have been through quite a trauma. What I mean is, if you need us . . . if you need me . . . don't hesitate, okay?'

'I know what you mean. I think getting hold of the bastard that did this is the best way to make us all feel better. Me, Fern, the lot of us. She's old enough to know about good and evil. It's on every kids' programme she watches or story I read her, but good *always* wins. That's the bubble a child lives in. I can't have that burst, not yet.' Michelle finally made eye contact. Her breath was visible as the temperature dropped further. 'Please, detective . . . Bad things happen, but good has to win out in the end. You have to catch him. That's the only way I can think of her coming out of this without lasting damage.'

Maddie smiled. She dropped her cigarette among a smattering of others in a metal bucket resting against the leg of the bench.

'All the more reason to get back to it, then!'

CHAPTER 22

Lance was waiting. He leaned on the arm of the sofa in Gavin Walker's living room, the main seating area too filthy for him to consider sitting — even in these trousers. The smell of damp was a permanent fixture in his nostrils. Gavin had been asleep in the room until a few minutes before. Lance was still breathing heavily with the exertion of having dragged him out. He had woken enough to clumsily work his legs but not to complain, resist or even be truly aware he was moving. The red wine had been effective and Lance had made sure he had been topped up all day.

The door thumped.

He had seen them arrive. That had been some time ago. They had walked past a couple of times and knocked on doors leading up to this one. Lance knew the other houses were largely empty — and those occupied were not the sort of places where you would get an answer. Then they had walked right across his window and turned up the path.

He stayed still. Long enough for them to thump again. This time, it was louder, more intense. There was frustration behind that door. He understood why. They needed to speak to him and they had come a long way to do it. He stretched as he got to his feet. He was not a man who would be rushed by anyone.

* * *

Robbie Holt rubbed his hands together. It had already been a long day and he had spent most of it cold. Mikey was not a fan of the heater in the car and Robbie knew better than to make it an issue. They had met at nine a.m. after Robbie had worked late the night before covering the poker tables. Mikey had been extra grumpy, too, before his meeting with the boss, that was. When he and Mason had talked, Robbie had been forced to wait outside in the car like a little boy while his mother shopped. He had been dozing when Mikey returned. He seemed to be in a slightly better mood — though he didn't seem any keener on conversation. Instead, Mikey had told him of their task and made it clear that there were to be no follow-up questions. It all seemed pretty simple, anyway: drive down to Deal on the south coast, speak to Lance, find out what was going on, chivvy him up and take the update back to the boss. A simple day out — maybe two, as he'd been told to bring an overnight bag in case. Not quite a road trip, perhaps and not with Mikey in this mood, but a day or two away from the norm. He had managed to get Mikey to make a grudging stop at a McDonalds for a breakfast at least.

Now it was late afternoon and he was hungry again. Mikey had refused another food stop. Robbie stepped back as his colleague hammered on the door, already hoping that this wasn't going to take long. The environment didn't help — this place was a shithole. They had driven past a couple of times and Robbie had been unsure if it was even a place you might find a person living rather than an animal. They were out of the car and up close, he could see the filthy windows and smell the overflowing beer cans and general detritus from the bins that could only come from human habitation. When the door was tugged open, the smell that rushed out was even worse.

The Tax Man stood among it.

'Gentlemen! Anyone would think you were trying to wake the dead!' Robbie stepped to one side to get a better view of Lance. He looked dishevelled. He wore faded jeans and a jumper with a round collar that gripped tightly around his scrawny neck. He stood in battered boots. He'd shaved his hair shorter since he'd last seen him. It only served to make his face look even more sucked-in and pale.

'Jesus, Lance, you're a wealthy man! What's going on?' Mikey leaned around Lance to glance at his living conditions then looked him up and down.

'I'm working. You know that. I like to blend in. I'm good at it, too. The only way I tend to stand out is if I forget myself and have a little strip wash, or if two men in expensive leather jackets start hammering on my door.'

'The boss wants an update.'

'I suggest you come in, then.' Lance stepped back. The smell seemed to intensify. Robbie hesitated, but Mikey didn't. The door led straight into what might constitute a living area. It was dark. A pair of roughly pulled curtains blocked most of the natural light. Bundled up clothes and random boxes blocked the rest.

'If I'd known you were coming, I'd have had a little tidy-up!' Lance grinned. His eyes flitted to Robbie. They were just as Robbie remembered: small and dark, like a rodent scanning a room for morsels of food. His smile did nothing to warm his expression.

Mikey got straight to the point. 'You're taking too long. The boss wants this over.'

'Well, of course he does! It would seem he is determined to go to prison. I know you agree with me, Mikey. You're clever. You know this needs to be done right and that's what I'm doing. We need to be sure that when this officer falls and people start pointing, no one points at Mr Mason. That's not easy. Not with the history.'

'I get that. I watch the news, though, Lance. I know you've made your mess. The media are already talking about two murders with links. You've made your point, now finish this.'

'Finish this?' Lance smiled. His tongue appeared to wet his lips. 'You found me okay, then?'

'We did.'

'How could you possibly know where to come for me?'

'We have our ways.'

'Of course you do. It was the first thing I found.' Lance plunged a hand into his pocket. Mikey flinched. Lance pulled out a small, square piece of plastic. 'You need to relax, Mikey! What did you think I've got in my pocket, a snake perhaps?'

'I'm relaxed.'

'Speaking of snakes, this is a tracking device right? Accurate to within . . . what, ten metres? That would be about right, judging by the way you've been trudging up and down the road out there. I found it a few minutes after our meeting was concluded. Who stitched it into the money bag you left me? Your work, Mikey? 'Cause it's kind of sloppy, to be honest!'

Lance turned his beady little eyes to Robbie. 'I don't reckon it was your boy over there, judging by his face. Am I right, boy? Did you know about this?'

Robbie shrugged. He didn't. He was still trying to process the information. He wasn't surprised to see the tracker, but he was a little miffed that no one had told him. He'd asked Mikey that morning how they were going to find Lance and he'd got nothing back, just a grunt like it was none of his business. He'd assumed that Mikey had been going to call Lance or that he already had.

'I got sent down here to chivvy you up,' Mikey said. 'The tracker was my idea. I said we might need a way of finding you if you were taking your time, if you were enjoying yourself too much. So here we are.'

'Enjoying myself?'

'That's what this is to you, isn't it? You get off on all this mess.' Mikey swept his arm at the room. 'What *is* this? You living with some tramp, here? Someone else you're playing with.'

'You think this is a game?' Lance's tone was suddenly deeper, darker. 'You think I like living here like this? This is a job and I do it right. Four weeks ago, I took your job. First thing I did then was find your target. That wasn't difficult. But then I have to find his weakness, a way in. That's a little bit more tricky. A few days' work and I find out he has a sister that he visits where she works in a café. A few more days and I find she's got a young child and they live on their own. Your PC Arnold babysits. So I figure that's my way in. Then I went back to the city to find someone with a similar setup. This is a shitty little seaside town. Make a mess here and it would be the biggest thing to ever happen. It would change the town. Best is a city, where people keep their heads down a bit more, where everyone isn't something to everyone else. You keeping up?'

'Do I need to be?'

'You came down here to ask me a question and with doubt in your mind. I'm answering it. In the city, I go to a few cafés until I find a girl of a similar age. She's moaning about her man. She tells everyone who'll listen that she's got a young kid, too. So she's the first. I strung up the feckless partner for the girl to find. The kid gets me in the door. Then I move. Always strike and move — remember that, kid!' He flicked to Robbie. It caught him out and he flinched a little, Lance seemed to smile and Robbie felt his cheeks flush.

'I use places like this. Drinkers, see? Most of them don't give a shit. They'll take anyone in, as long as they get a few beers out of it. And lady luck really does seem to smile on the bold. The next place I go to, just like this it was, but . . . *right next door*, Mikey! A young woman, a young kid and some marital issues screaming right through the walls! Some things are just meant to be. That was beautiful. So there we have two and the setup close enough even for the local plod to start making links. And now here I am, Mikey. Ahead of schedule. And what do you think I do next?'

'When, Lance?'

Lance had been getting more and more animated, to the point where he was fidgeting on the spot, his hands gesturing in time with his words that had sped up as he talked. Some spittle had gathered between his lips to stretch as he spoke. Robbie watched it now as it stretched between a big grin. The eyes above were small and black.

'I did a little research.' He brought his speech back level. He lifted his hand to where he had the tracking device between his thumb and finger. 'The battery life on this particular model is what . . . five weeks, tops? Four is the recommended max. And here we are. Almost four weeks to the day after we last met and you're knocking at my door.'

'Okay. So I wanted to talk to you while I could still find you. So what?'

'Talk?'

'When is this being done, Lance? You've had your money. The boss paid for a service. You've been clever and I get that that takes time. But you're there now. String him up for his sister to find — that's your end game, right? So it looks like the others? Whatever it is, just get it done.'

'You make it sound so trivial. This will be beautiful, Mikey. I don't think you appreciate that. I don't think you respect me for what I am, for what I am capable of. I don't like that about you.'

'I use clinical. That's what I prefer. This is just messing about.'

'And then what?'

'Then what?'

'When I've completed your task? That's why you're here, is it? For the *then what?* You find me, chivvy me up as you call it, get me to commit to a timescale and then wait until PC Vince Arnold is a dead man.' Lance took another step back. 'Ready to take your boss's money back the moment it is done?'

'Don't be ridiculous!' Mikey scoffed. 'We've done this before, me and you. Don't forget that. I've hired you, paid you, then hired you again.'

'Not recently, though, Mikey. I'm not your go-to guy anymore, am I? You only came back to me because of Mason.

That's right, isn't it? You've made no bones of talking down my methods.'

'So what? Get this done right and you put yourself right back in the running.'

Lance chuckled. It was carefree, like something silly had been said between two friends out for lunch, belying the tension that now hung thick in the room. 'Well okay, then! Seems like I'm getting paranoid in my old age. Your message has been delivered. You can head back to Mason and tell him that. I need a few more days, I reckon. Like I said, this is all set up for the big finish.'

'A few more days,' Mikey repeated.

'That's it.'

Mikey lingered for a few more moments. Robbie thought he was going to say something more but he turned back towards the door. Robbie was by it. He reached for the handle.

The noise of the gunshot was so loud and so sudden, it almost took Robbie off his feet. He spun back. His ears were nothing but a ringing noise. The air suddenly had an acrid smell, like burned earth and Mikey was laid out on the floor, floundering on his side, bumping against Robbie's shins. Robbie's hearing came back in a rush, like someone sighing in his ear, instantly followed by Mikey bellowing in pain.

'*What the fuck?*' Mikey reached down his leg. Robbie looked up to where the gun was pointed directly at him.

'Are you carrying?' Lance's voice carried no emotion at all. He was looking straight at Robbie, those dark, rodent eyes suddenly boring a big hole through his skull.

Robbie shook his head and pushed his hands out instinctively to show he had nothing in them. Lance had him lift his top and spin slowly then step away from where Mikey was writhing on the floor. He was a little quieter but cussing and murmuring threats of revenge.

Lance shifted his attention back to Mikey. He dropped onto him, putting all his weight through Mikey's injured thigh — Robbie could see that he was bleeding from it freely.

Mikey bellowed in pain. He stopped when Lance pushed the barrel of the pistol he was holding into his cheek.

'I really don't like these things. Guns are so impersonal. Anyone can shoot a gun. But I know that you like them, Mikey, because you're a filthy coward who has only come down here to shoot me in the back when I've done your bidding. So . . . Where is it?'

Lance didn't wait for an answer. His free hand moved quickly over Mikey to search him. He pulled a pistol from an inside pocket of his jacket. It was similar in style to the one Lance had pushed against Mikey's cheek: black metal, a squared barrel, modern-looking. Lance threw it on the sofa behind him. He continued with his search and the next item he pulled was Mikey's mobile phone. He grabbed Mikey's hand and pushed his thumb against the fingerprint-reader to unlock it. Mikey looked like he was resisting to start with, but there was no struggling once Lance pushed the pistol harder into his cheek.

The phone unlocked. Lance stood up, the underside of his chin lit by its screen in the poor light. Mikey was back to moaning on the floor. Lance's thumb moved over the screen with his left hand, his right still by his side with control of the weapon. It was pointed at the floor. In a split-second, it could be lifted to point at either one of them. Robbie stayed still. Even if he had been considering a rushed assault, he didn't know if he would be able to move. His feet felt planted. If they weren't, he didn't think he could be quick enough, anyway. His eyes flicked from the silent Lance to his mate on the floor. Lance seemed to take an age. Then he threw the phone to rest beside Mikey's gun. He sighed. It was long and dramatic. He gave Robbie a lingering stare.

'Your phone,' he said.

Robbie took a moment to process the words, then jerked his hands to slap his pockets.

'Slowly!' Lance actually laughed. 'And unlocked.' Robbie slowed himself down. His phone was in his right pocket. He took it out with his fingertips, unlocked it and held it out. The gun pointing at him felt like a heat source. Lance lowered it when he took his phone. Again, he took his time inspecting the device. Robbie stared on. Lance twitched, then sniffed and his head made a barely detectable shake. One eyebrow lifted in apparent surprise — but just for a second. Finally, he looked up. Robbie had been holding his breath. The gun jerked back up to be level with his head. Robbie threw his hands up, pushing out with his eyes tightly shut, waiting for the inevitable.

'Nothing on your phone says you knew.' Lance's monotone voice cut through his panic. Robbie waited another second, his thighs burning where he had leaned back in a sort of squat. He dropped to his knees.

'Knew?'

'Mikey, here . . . His phone says different. He and Mr Mason were in agreement. It was like I said . . . You're here to get your money back once I've done the job. I've been betrayed, it would seem. Did you know?'

'No!' The magnitude sank in for Robbie. The gun was pointing straight at him. 'We were told to come down, to find you! I asked how and I wasn't told nothing. I got told we were coming down here to chase you up for the boss! They made me sit in the car. I swear!'

'Mikey? Your boy, here . . . Is he part of this?' The gun still pointed at Robbie. Mikey stared right at him, too. He was clutching his leg.

'No.'

'I believe you. Which is a minor miracle, really, in the circumstances.' He dropped the gun back to his side then he gazed up at the ceiling. Robbie did the same. He was drawn to a polished metal square that stood out from the yellowed ceiling as looking brand new. There were four oversized bolts on each corner and a metal loop in its centre. Lance dragged a low table from the shadows to position it underneath. He moved to the window, bending to pick up a length of grey wire that was anchored in the floor. It ran through his hands as he stepped up onto the table. He wasn't holding the gun anymore. Robbie had no idea where it was.

The end of the wire was a fixed loop. Lance pushed it through the loop on the ceiling and brought it back down with him as he stepped off the table. He kicked it out of the way. Robbie watched as he moved out of the room and out of sight for a few seconds. When he came back, he dropped something solid on the floor and out of sight. Robbie's attention remained on Lance's hands, where he now grabbed the looped wire to hold it tightly in his fist. He looked down at Mikey.

'I think I might need your help here, Mikey!' Lance said.

Mikey had been watching him, too. His moaning had become quieter but his breathing louder where he was forcing it through his nose. He was still pushing down hard on the wound in his thigh. He was on his side, his head lifted.

'Put this over your head.' There was plenty of slack on the wire. Lance held it out for Mikey, who dropped his head to look away. He didn't lift his hands. Lance's face twisted into a grin. 'You playing hard to get, Mikey? After all we've been through!' The grin was gone in an instant. He snatched to Robbie. He held the loop out towards him. He knew what it meant, what he wanted. He didn't move.

'Normally, this is the easy bit. You'd be surprised what people will do when you have their kids shut in a room and a gun in your hand. The problem here is that our Mikey doesn't have any real motivation, does he?' He took a step closer so Robbie couldn't ignore him anymore. He reached out. The wire was cold and smooth to the touch. Now it was in his hand, he could see it was actually coiled steel. It felt strong and unforgiving, strong enough for the job, no doubt about that.

'Over his head,' Lance said. He stepped back so he was in the internal doorway that led to the back of the house. Robbie was close to the front door, close enough to consider making a run for it. But he still didn't know where the weapon was. There would be no outrunning a bullet, and he couldn't leave Mikey. Not like this.

'Mikey here is on thin ice, no doubt about that, but I may have a use for you. If you won't do as I ask, then you're no good at all.' Lance cut through his hesitation.

'Do it, lad,' Mikey growled through gritted teeth from the floor.

Robbie bent towards him. Mikey kept eye contact the whole way, not even breaking away when he ducked a little to make it easier for the loop to find its place. Lance stepped right past him to squat back under the window. A moment later, Robbie heard a ratcheting sound. The coiled steel started to gather itself up. It became shorter with every ratchet. Soon the slack from the floor was all gone and it was pulling under Mikey's chin. He had to sit up, his face contorted in anguish, his gaze upwards as the wire seated him straight.

'Help your mate up, then!' Lance sung. His voice was gleeful and it cut through the fog that was consuming Robbie. He stumbled forward, his hands reaching out to support Mikey under his shoulders as the sound of the ratchet kept coming. Mikey clambered to his feet. The wire moved with him, any slack taken up instantly. He kept his injured leg bent, his weight shifting to his good leg and steadied himself by reaching up to grip the steel wire. The noise stopped. The cable was tight around his neck and pushed his ears flat. He was flat-footed, his breathing unrestricted but still loud through his nose, his face a grimace of pain. He moved one of his hands down to scrabble at the wire round his neck but it was hopeless.

Lance moved behind Mikey to stare right at him, his teeth trapped his bottom lip, his head slightly tilted — as if he was studying him. Robbie took the chance to talk to him, to try and reason with him.

'This ain't necessary. Look, Lance. Me and Mikey . . . We can go back to the boss, tell him you're doing the job like we talked about and nothing's changed. Please! You still have the money, right?' Robbie petered out. There was no strength in his voice, no confidence. He couldn't think of a single reason why Lance might agree. It was desperate.

'The Tax Man, right? That's what they call me. Did you hear that?'

'What? I mean, yeah, I heard that.'

'One of life's certainties. That's where that name comes from. Not from me but I really rather like it! I'm reliable, boy. Consistent. If you're going to be one thing in your life, be reliable.'

'But you're not here for Mikey! Listen—'

'Take off his shoes and socks!' Lance snapped.

'What? Lance, I—'

'*Now!*'

Robbie flinched. He made brief eye contact with Mikey. His shoes came off easily, his socks, too.

Lance squatted back to the floor. Mikey's wide eyes strained to see, but he couldn't move his head enough. Robbie could see, however. He could see that Lance had picked up two solid blocks of worn wood, shaped like two triangles. One side looked smoother and more polished than the others. He bumped one against the back of Mikey's foot, polished side up. Mikey winced, then lifted his foot enough for Lance to push the block all the way under. It changed Mikey's stance, pushing his right foot up onto tiptoes. His left foot was a little more difficult. Lance bumped the wood as before, but Mikey struggled. The thigh on his left side was still bleeding freely. Mikey slammed his eyes shut, his whole face a grimace and his breathing loud through his nose as he wriggled his weight up onto his toes. The soles of his feet squeaked on the polished wood as he swung by his neck. He reached up to steady himself on the wire above. Robbie could see he was struggling to get his weight onto his right side. Lance moved back under the window. There was another ratchet sound and any slack was gone.

'My old man was a cobbler,' Lance said. 'Do you even know what one of them is, boy?' Lance got back to his feet to stand next to Robbie. 'Of course you don't. A cobbler was someone who would mend your shoes. But people don't fix things anymore. Your shoe breaks and you just buy another pair, right? There was no future in it, even when I was a lad, it was going that way. So, what was it that my father handed me? *Nothing*. No future, no hope. It wasn't his fault and he was very sorry, I could see that. He wanted me to have the life he did . . . a trade, a career that could last me my whole life if I worked hard.' Lance turned a beaming smile towards Robbie. 'I've made more money out of his old tools than he would ever dream of!'

Robbie didn't reply. There was nothing he could say. Lance was becoming more erratic. He was staring at him closer, too, leaning in inches from his face, like he was studying him for the slightest movement. Robbie was scared — terrified. He knew he was showing it and it felt like Lance was enjoying every moment.

'Mikey here was right about me,' Lance said. He took a step away to put a hand on Mikey's shoulder like he was embracing an old friend. Mikey reacted with a grunt. Lance leaned on him. 'You were right about me. I *am* escalating! The simple, *clinical* jobs just don't do it for me anymore. I *do* like to make a mess! But better than that, I like to watch the rest of the world clean up after me. The power, Mikey . . . Choosing who lives and who dies, watching them, deciding how . . . That's not just my *job*, that's my *purpose!* I don't think you respect that. I think you underestimate that.'

He moved past Mikey, bumping his shoulder as he did. The steel wire swung and creaked where it was tight against the loop. Mikey groaned again and was back to clawing at his neck with Lance now out of his sight. Then Mikey fixed on Robbie, his eyes wide with fear. Robbie broke to look beyond him, to a scraping sound where Lance had picked up a crowbar from the floor. He pointed the hooked end at Robbie and winked. When he moved around in front of Mikey, his eyes burst wider still.

'So then, Mikey . . . I've seen your phone and your conversations on there. So I know what's been going on. It was your idea, too. Seems like your boss was rather impressed with your thinking! Maybe he wouldn't be so impressed if he knew that it was you who messed this up. I had my suspicions from the moment you called me back, when you accepted my ridiculous fee without blinking and then your boss agreed to travel all the way down to a Canterbury multi-storey car park to meet me! Of all my demands, that one was a joke. I just threw it in when you were agreeing to everything. We're all from the Bristol area, Mikey. You know that and I know that. Something just wasn't right, not right at all.' Lance licked his lips and his head jerked to one side as he studied Mikey closer.

'I wasn't going to take the job. I smelt the rat and I didn't fancy it. But I went along . . . I was interested in where it was going to go. I turned up expecting a negotiation, to be told I was asking for far too much, to be told how he wanted it done and for Mr Mason to use the fact that he had come out of his way as a sort of bargaining tool. But what did I get, Mikey? You and your boy here throwing money at my feet — and all of it upfront . . . no question. And Mr Mason? Barely a flicker when I pointed out his son's brains. I mean, granted, they probably weren't his brains — I don't even know if that was the right car park — but no matter what I did, no matter what buttons I pushed, I got nothing. I'm good at people, Mikey. Reading them, I mean. But you lot gave me nothing.' Lance moved in even closer, their noses almost touching.

'When you get no reaction, it's because there's something already decided, something that renders the whole conversation pointless. Mason knew that. You knew that. And by the end, I knew it, too. So now we all know! But I want to hear it from you — that would mean a lot, you see. It's the least you can do. So, what is this all about?' Lance gestured at the room with the bar in his hand. 'This visit?'

'Fuck you!' Mikey spat. He had moved his hands back above his head to grip the coiled steel. They were so high, his fingers looked to be butting up against the loop. Lance shifted the crowbar to lean on it like a crutch. He only settled for a moment, then he pushed off to walk back around behind him. He kicked out with his foot, swiping the wooden blocks out from under Mikey's feet. They clattered into an untidy pile. Mikey made a noise like a cough as he suddenly had to scrabble with his toes to take his weight. His face changed colour to a deepening red, his hands moved to clutch at his neck. Lance moved back to the window. This time, the noise was a half-ratchet, lifting Mikey further so when he settled, he was on his toes to keep his airways open.

'The idea of you coming here today . . . That's all I'm asking. What was the plan, Stan?' Lance chuckled, again as though he was chatting with an old friend. Mikey looked like he was fighting to breathe.

'How about we keep the questions easy?' Lance said. 'Yes-no answers only? I'll start with an easy one . . . Did you come to kill me once this job was done then return with the money?'

Mikey was wobbling from side to side, battling to stay on the ends of his toes, trying to take the weight on the leg that wasn't bleeding from a gunshot wound. His mouth was flared open, the skin on his neck white where it was pinched by the wire and flushed everywhere else. His eyes were wide and bloodshot. He stared at the man in front of him.

'I'm not . . . playing . . . your games.' Mikey's voice came out a strained gurgle.

Lance tutted. He stepped back. He was back to leaning on the crowbar. He flicked it round in one movement and brought it down hard and fast towards the floor. The bar smashed into Mikey's left foot and he screamed. When his breathing came back, it was harder and faster. The jeans on his left leg were already a soaked patch of red. The bleeding from the gunshot wound wasn't so obvious. It had either stopped or was just soaking straight into the material. Robbie looked down to where two of Mikey's toes were now a waxy white and sticking out at obtuse angles. His breathing worsened. He pushed out with his right leg — the good one, trying to take all the weight through the tiptoes on his right foot. He was fighting for balance. The loop creaked as he swung around.

'Let me break it down a little . . . Did you come here to kill me?'

'Yes,' Mike gurgled. White froth leaked from his lips.

'After I had completed our agreement?' Lance said.

'Yes.'

'Your idea?'

'Yes.' Mikey said. He had managed to lock his right leg out in front of him. It pushed him backwards and gave him some sort of control, enough to keep the pressure off the front of his throat, just enough to keep him breathing.

'Did the kid know anything about it?'

'No.'

Lance shook his head. 'After all we've been through.'

* * *

Gavin Walker woke with a start and with some confusion. He had no idea where he was, nor why he had snapped awake so suddenly. He thought he'd heard a loud noise, a bang of some sort, like someone had kicked the door he could see, from where he was laid out on the floor. He struggled to sit up. He was in his bedroom. His head had lifted from a pillow. He never came in here at all, certainly not to sleep. He didn't recall having any pillows, either. The area around the door had been tidied, or at least the old clothes and random belongings had been pushed out of the way to allow the door to shut. No way he would have done that.

He lifted his hand to his head. It thumped with a pulse. He had started drinking early. His housemate had started him on a bottle of red wine. That wasn't his normal choice, not during the day That would explain the headache and dizziness.

He got to his knees. He had a sudden urge to urinate. His head beat harder with the movement. He heard something — he strained to listen. There were voices in the next room. Nobody else should be here. His guest was out most of the time during the day and he knew that he couldn't have anyone back here. Gavin flashed with anger. He used the energy to get to his feet. He made for the door.

* * *

Robbie snatched to the sound as the internal door pushed in. Lance reacted to it, too — he leapt across the room. There was just time for a dishevelled face to appear, a thick beard and an expression that contorted in shock and surprise as Lance was on him. He led with the crowbar. The first blow struck the dishevelled man on the top of the head and forced him back out of the door and out of Robbie's sight. He heard a crash like the blow had taken him off his feet. Lance threw the crowbar down, then walked through the door. When he reappeared, he was shuffling backwards with the man's boots under his arms, dragging him back into the room. It looked to be a struggle but he got him far enough across the carpet for one of his feet to rest against the front door.

Robbie could see all of him now. He was filthy. His hair was like his beard, long and untidy. He had a thick flash of red down his forehead where he looked to be bleeding heavily. His head rolled from side to side where he was lying on his back. He was barely conscious. Lance stood over him. He put one foot either side of the man, peered down and squatted to retrieve the crowbar.

The man's eyelids flickered. His eyes had been rolling in his head, but they seemed to focus now. He narrowed them and his hand lifted to rest on his head as he mumbled nonsense. This seemed to be what Lance had been waiting for. He raised the crowbar in both hands high above his head. The man on the floor raised his hand, his mumble louder, protesting or begging, maybe. It made no difference.

Lance brought the crowbar down as hard as he could. Robbie slammed his eyes shut. The noise was bad enough. After the sound of the third strike, Robbie turned away to drop to his knees and vomit. The noise had stopped. All Robbie could hear was the heavy breathing of someone trying

205

to catch their breath and the squeaking of a tight wire against a metal loop. Then came footsteps.

'You need your eyes open from now on, boy. You understand me?' Lance wasn't smiling anymore and his face was splattered with blood. His tongue shot out to wet his lips and those black eyes ran all over Robbie. Robbie couldn't answer — it didn't seem to matter.

Lance turned back to Mikey and swung the crowbar towards the floor again. This time, the impact was through Mikey's right foot. Mikey gurgled in agony again. The loop squeaked where he bucked and swung as much as the wire would allow.

Lance moved quickly back to where Robbie was still on the floor. He was so close, he filled his vision. Mikey's breathing sounded different, now — a permanent gurgle.

'Mikey there's not going to make it. He's trying to hold up his own weight on broken feet. He's a fighter, though, I'll give him that.' Lance moved from a squat to a kneel and planted the crowbar to lean on it. He pushed the thick end into the floor a few inches from Robbie's face. It ran with clumps of blood that slithered down the smooth metal.

'Watch it,' Lance snarled. 'You need to understand.' Lance inspected him. Still facing away, Mikey was fighting for his life. It was a battle he was losing fast. Lance stared directly at Robbie as he watched. He was so close, he could feel his breath on his cheek. Mikey's fight was done. The wire rubbed on the loop for a final twitch. Robbie wanted to look away, to slam his eyes shut, to block out the horror in front of him, but Lance still stared. The room was silent. Lance waited another minute or more. It seemed like an age.

'Now, then . . . What to do with you?' He stood up. His stare fixed on Robbie. His chest was heaving from his exertions, the crowbar hanging from his right hand. 'I'm really not sure. Maybe I should take my time? Sleep on it, even. Where's your wallet?'

It took Robbie a few seconds to make sense of the question. He dug his hand into his back pocket and took out his wallet. Lance grabbed it, took out his driver's licence and dropped the wallet to the floor.

'So that's what I'm going to do. I'm going to sleep on it. That gives me the time to consider this betrayal and how I react from here. You have three options, the way I see it. You can stay here tonight and wait for the morning when I might have a use for you. You can make a run for it when I'm asleep and take your chances that I don't turn up at the address on here to find you and anyone else linked to you . . .' He leaned back lower, his right knee taking his weight. 'Or you can kill me in my sleep. Search hard enough and quietly enough and you'll find Mikey's gun. But I will say this to you, boy . . . If you kill me, you'd better kill me properly. Do you understand? Have you ever killed anyone before?' He held Robbie with those beady black eyes for a few more moments. Robbie wanted to break away, but he couldn't. He wanted to speak, but he couldn't. Lance finally stood back up.

'I didn't think so. You can sleep in here for the night. I'll have the bedroom.' Lance discarded the crowbar. It struck the floor and bounced into Robbie's leg. He flicked out to push it away. Lance was already at the front door. Robbie heard him lock it. He came away, rattling the keys at Robbie. 'They'll be in my pocket. Should you need them.'

Robbie looked across to the body of the dishevelled man laid out on his back. His head was turned away. It looked to be an unnatural shape. He snatched from him to Mikey. He looked so different now. His legs had been stretched out. Now they both had a bend, and the ends of his toes brushed the floor lightly with the slightest swing. His morose eyes peered down, his tongue lolled out and his head was a changing colour of purple. The coiled steel that had claimed his life was so tight, it was almost completely hidden under a fold of skin on his neck.

Robbie looked away and peered across to the front door. The dishevelled man's feet were resting against it. Mikey was also in the way and Robbie knew it was locked. He could have got out easily enough in normal circumstances, but this

207

was far from normal and right now, he was too terrified to even consider it. He turned to lie on his side, his back to the worst images of that room. The air was heavy with a metallic odour and there was an irregular dripping sound. He knew it was blood. The room was running with it. But he knew he was going to lie there all night until morning. He didn't have options at all, not where the Tax Man was involved. If he tried to run, there could only be one certainty.

CHAPTER 23

It struck Maddie how different an impression you could get of a home just by studying the frontages side by side. Michelle Rice's house was attached to Jeremy Wilson's and ought to have been a simple mirror image. The two front doors were close together in the centre and both had large bay windows that completed the rest of the downstairs. There was another bay directly above that looked identical in style and size. The first floors were completed by smaller windows above the front doors that provided light to a box room. She also knew from her time in Michelle's house that there was another large bedroom and a bathroom at the back.

Michelle's frontage was neat and welcoming. Jeremy Wilson's home looked shut-up and foreboding, with aggressive weeds that mingled with the grass then broke out on their own to wrap tightly round a cast iron boot scraper next to the front door. Curtains were pulled roughly closed at every window. Maddie had got the name *Jeremy Wilson* from the voter's roll and had it confirmed by the agency that paid him his income support there. But a name was all she had. There was no police record. A colleague had spoken to him as part of the initial house-to-house but he had been intoxicated and quickly dismissed. Maddie now knew that he could be the most significant investigative lead they had.

Uniform officers now had a view of the back, confirmed by their monotone radio transmission. It was what Maddie and Harry had been waiting for. They moved forward together. They were losing daylight fast. It was dark enough to see white, artificial light leaking through a small gap in the curtain at the ground floor bay window. Maddie hoped that it was a sign of life. She stood among the weeds at the front window.

'There's no way to see in,' she said.

Harry stood out on the path, arching his back to take in the top floor. 'Suggest you knock, then.' He slapped his hands together. The collar of his waxed jacket was lifted to cover his neck. He wasn't normally a man to feel the cold but the sudden drop in temperature as night had swept in seemed to have caught him out.

Maddie thumped on the door. It was made of a solid wood and made a loud sound. The only response was a noise from a few doors down. An elderly man stepped out of his house.

'Can I help you?' he said.

'I don't think so, sir, thank you,' Maddie said. 'I was really hoping to speak to the occupants of this address. Do you know them?'

'I used to. I was friends with Bill and Lizzie. Their son lives there now. I don't have much to do with him — no one around here does.'

'Do you see him? Do you think he'll be in?'

'Oh, he'll be in alright. The door's never locked, either. Give it a twist. Normally we hear him. You're not from the council, are you? We've all complained around here about the noises and comings and goings. I'm too old to be knocking on a neighbour's door in the small hours.'

'We're not from the council, no. We're police officers. We'd like to speak to the occupant. It's Jeremy, right?'

'Jeremy, yes. The police, eh? Is it about the noise?'

'Not today, sir. But I'll be sure to mention it.' She hit the door again.

'Is it about that horrible business the other night? We've already spoken to your lot. They were here knocking everyone's door. They said they talked to Jeremy. I told them about the noise and they made a note.'

'Okay. I was hoping to speak to him again. Does anyone else live here?'

'People come and go, and at all hours. They're all the same. All drinkers. I never have anything to do with any of them.'

'Thank you.' Maddie thumped the door again. Harry stepped up beside her and twisted the handle. The door pushed in.

'Suggest we check and make sure there hasn't been a burglary, then.' Maddie said. Harry didn't argue and followed her in.

The hallway was dark. Maddie noted that the large cupboard under the stairs was the same as next door — albeit on the other side. It looked a lot more dilapidated, too. The internal door to the living room was shut. She noted how dark it was. Somebody could easily be standing just a few feet away from her and she might not see them. She certainly wouldn't if they were in the cupboard. She tried a light switch. Nothing happened. The living room door was on her left. She paused by it. The same white light she had seen from outside was pushing out from under it. Harry stepped past her to move through to the back of the house. She waited for him. His torchlight cut through the atmosphere like a laser. It fidgeted and flickered as he searched. His final act with it was to flash it twice out of the rear window. A torch flash in reply told them their colleagues were at the back door. They had been briefed to stay there. For now.

Harry was back at her side and Maddie pushed the living room door open. The room revealed itself, but Maddie had to take it on board in stages, there was so much of it. It seemed to consist of bundles of mess. As she stepped in, her foot crunching on the carpet, she was able to start picking out people: someone asleep on the floor, a woman with long hair falling over her face, another figure, obviously male, stretched out on the sofa. Both were asleep. The man on the sofa was snoring gently. Maddie stepped closer for a visual check for any weapons. She gripped her PAVA spray in her pocket and stood over him.

'Police!' she shouted. There was no response. *'Jeremy! It's the police! Wakey-wakey!'* she shouted louder, chancing this to be her homeowner. Nothing. Harry moved in beside her. He reached out and grabbed the sleeping man's eyebrow in a tight pinch and twisted. The reaction was instant.

'What the hell? Who are you! I ain't got nothing here, okay?'

'It's the police.' Harry growled. 'Seems you don't hear your door when it knocks.'

The man sat up. His face creased into a million wrinkles. He rubbed at the stubble on his face and head. His eyes seemed to be searching for something to focus on. He stank — the sickly-sweet smell of alcohol. He belched and instantly smelt worse. Maddie had to take a step back.

'We didn't mean to wake you,' she said. 'We were knocking and not getting any answer. 'We were getting worried about you.'

'Don't need to be worrying about me. I'm always alright. Sorry about the door. I mean, I sleep heavy.'

Maddie had kicked two empty wine bottles together when she had stepped back. 'I'm not surprised. Were they both today?'

'This afternoon. I have a problem you see. I drink.'

'So I see.'

'Can I help you? Is that all you needed? To be sure I was okay? I appreciate that . . . You people are nice people.' His words were a little slurred. He seemed to be searching the room. Then he patted his pockets and pulled out a tobacco pouch that was folded up tightly enough to suggest it was as good as empty. He managed to get a miniscule amount in a pinch and had to close one eye to get it on a waiting Rizla paper.

'Who's here with you at the moment?'

'Molly over there. She's worse than me for sleeping — look at her!' He giggled.

'No one else?'

'Not that I know of. It can be a bit of a surprise house sometimes, though! You know, you wake up, go for a tinkle and . . . *Surprise!* There's people here you don't even know. Some people come here to crash, especially this time of the year. I don't mind so much. As long as they go again. Most people know the deal . . . if you come here you need to be bringing a little drinky-poos with you. They look after me and I look after them, you know how it works.'

'You had someone here recently . . . A man . . . Glasses, ponytail. Do you remember him?'

'I do. He was good to me. Stayed for a few days, a week maybe. Never let me go short. Kept me in my drink — pouches, too. I think this is the last of it.' He gestured with the tobacco. 'All good things have to come to an end, I suppose.'

'He's gone, then?'

'Seems to have.'

'What do you know about him?'

'Know?'

'His name — What was his name?'

Jeremy scowled. 'Do you know, I don't think he ever told me his name. And I didn't ask. The people that come here don't come here as a *name* . . . They just come here as a person, as a drinker. For shelter, to get out of the cold.'

'Did he tell you where he was from?'

'From? We're all from the same place, right? Our mother's womb an' all that! I know nothing more than that. Where you're from doesn't matter to me.'

'Did he sound local? When he talked, was there any accent?'

'Maybe. I don't really remember. We didn't really talk. It wasn't that sort of agreement, see. He stayed here. I think he was here most nights at least, not sure about the daytime. All I really knew is that when I went to the kitchen, there was always a little present waiting for me. He was a good man. I don't reckon he's the sort of bloke the police want to bother themselves with.'

'When did he leave?' Maddie persisted. She was trying to hide her frustration.

'Leave?'

'He's gone. When was that?'

'I don't know. Just one day there was no presents and there was no *him*. Couple of days ago, maybe?'

'Where did he sleep? In here?'

'No. There's a room upstairs. I think he was in there? I don't know. I didn't really see him that much. People go about their business, not for me to ask what that is.'

'What did he look like?'

'Look like? You tell me. You said about the ponytail, the glasses. That's right, that's what he looked like.'

'Anything else you remember about him? Anything distinctive?'

'Distinctive? He knew his red wine! That was a real treat. He got the good stuff. I don't know what else to say, really. He was a good guy, a bit older. If you're looking for him, that's all you really need to know. Now then, I think those two bottles were the last ones, so I'll need to be popping out. Is there anything more you might need from me?'

'Your DNA.' Harry's tone was even gruffer than usual. Maddie was surprised his patience had lasted as long as it had. 'We'll be getting that. It's what we call an elimination sample. You need to stay with us for now.'

'Limination?' he slurred back, seeming to find the word funny. 'Why do you need that from me?'

'You were spoken to about what happened next door, am I right?'

'Spoken to? Oh, yeah. I heard something bad happened. I don't really know them, to be honest. I keep myself to myself.'

'It happened Wednesday — early evening. Have you seen him since then?'

'Who?'

Harry's jaw rippled where he looked to be swallowing his first response. 'Ponytail, glasses . . . Has he been here since?'

'No.'

'Was he here on that day? On Wednesday?'

Jeremey seemed to give the question genuine thought. 'You know, I think he was. Had some good wine that day, so he must have been.'

'But you haven't seen him since?'

'Nope. Not a dicky. Maybe he doesn't like all the noise. I hear your lot banging around in there, slamming the front door at all hours. It's been like a circus! People are trying to live next door. This is a quiet neighbourhood round here, maybe you could pass that on to your mates!' His words were still a slur.

'I'll go get the kit!' Maddie cut in before Harry could respond. 'You okay in here for a sec?'

'I reckon I can cope. I'll get the patrol in here to do a quick walk around upstairs, see if this really is a surprise house. I may need to leave them here, too. Personally, I think any chance to preserve this as a scene might be long gone, but I'll let CSI make that decision. We'll need to get someone here tonight.'

'I'll give Charley a call.'

When Maddie stepped out, the chilly temperature was suddenly a lot more welcome than on the way in. It had a freshness to it. Charley picked up the call before Maddie had even made it to the end of the path.

'Hey.'

'Charley, sorry to bother you. Are you still on shift?'

'No. But I'm still at work.'

'More overtime! You must be able to retire and live on your savings by now!' Maddie laughed.

'You didn't call me at this time of the day for small talk. What do you want from me, Maddie Ives?'

'Fine. But one of these days I am going to call you when I don't just need your help. I revisited a witness earlier. Long story short, we think Scott Rice's killer spent some time next door. He might have been living there while he was making his plans.'

'Okay.'

'We're here now. Our offender's not, but this must be where he popped out from when our lot arrived on Wednesday. I wanted to speak to you about what we can do in here.'

'You mean what *I* can do?'

'Yes. That's exactly what I mean!'

'Is the occupant on board?'

'The occupant is drunk. Permanently. And we have people coming and going at all times to join him, people that are unknown to the occupant, so we've got even less chance of working out who they are. Does that answer your question?' Maddie was aware of a groan from the other end.

'Is it the house that's attached? With the noise complaints and the front window with a layer of fuck-knows-what?'

'I can always tell when you're upset. You get all sweary.'

'I assume it's a shit tip inside, too?'

'There you go again! And yes. Think of a shit tip and double it.'

'And how many occupants have you got there now?'

'Two or three. And some bundles we still haven't disturbed . . . so maybe more.'

'Jesus . . . And do you have a specific area he stayed in? A bed or sofa?'

'Not sure yet.'

Charley sighed. 'I'll need to come take a look. I'm not sure how much we can help, though, to be honest. It might be very little.'

'Okay. We need to get elimination DNA from the occupants here anyway. We can do it, but it's better for CSI to do it properly, you know — if you're coming out anyway . . .' Maddie grimaced as she waited for more swear words.

'My days of scraping the cheeks of some old drunk are long gone. I'm far too important for all that. I've got a junior working with me for a bit of experience. This sounds like it could tick that particular box very nicely.'

'Oh! So there was me worrying about putting you out and you can just palm any *actual* work off to someone else!'

'Don't push your luck, Ives. I'll need to be asking questions to see if any property can be attributed to the suspect and then it's a needle search in your filthy hay stack from there. God knows what we'll find if we start swabbing that place. I can't have a junior doing it all.'

'Okay. It could be worse . . . I could be pointing you into some dark cupboard to look for flakes of skin or something!' Maddie laughed.

'I needed to talk to you about that, actually. You were on my list to call before I finished today.'

'About the cupboard . . . Tell me your news. Tell me you've cracked it wide open!'

'I'm not sure about wide open. But there is something that might be interesting.'

'Go on?'

'That cupboard you had me looking in. I found some hair. Just a few bits.'

'Hair . . .' Maddie repeated before biting down on her lip to stop her blurting out a million questions. She knew Charley would have more to say.

'Yes. Hair's no good on its own, as you know. You need the root ball for DNA. Even then, it can be a little hit and miss. The first few I checked brought no luck. Then I got one with a clump at the end. It didn't look quite right, but I took it anyway.'

Maddie was fit to burst. 'Okay . . .' She hoped that would prompt Charley enough so that she wouldn't have to shout *spit it out!*

'Then another one . . . The same thing . . . A clump at the bottom. I've seen enough roots and it wasn't looking right. I took them back to the lab and I still wasn't sure — the colour was off. Anyway, that doesn't really matter. I sent them off priority, just in case.'

'And you have some results for me?'

'They weren't roots. So no DNA. Hence the result being so quick. I rushed it over and I think they took one look and picked up the phone.'

'I see.' Maddie had been holding her breath. She let it out in a sigh that Charley would have picked up.

'It was glue.'

'Glue?'

'The hair was from a wig. It must have been. The lab thought that was likely, too. They are going to run some tests to get more of a breakdown so we should be able to confirm it. That won't be so quick.'

Maddie was interested again. 'A wig?'

'To look like greying hair. I can't tell you much more than that.'

'What if we had a wig? Would you be able to match the hair to it?'

'Do you?'

'Well . . . No. I'm thinking ahead.'

'I love your positivity! I don't know, is the honest answer. Go find me an offender and give me his wig and I'll accept the challenge of linking the three beyond reasonable doubt. Until then, I'm not sure it helps, really.'

'No, it does. It helps massively. Shit . . .'

'You okay?'

'Yeah. It's just what it might mean is all. Doesn't matter. That's for us to figure out.' Maddie turned away from the house to pace a little. It helped her think.

'Okay, then. I need to get some stuff together here then head over.'

Maddie was lost in her thoughts. She snapped out of it to reply. 'Anything I can do until you get here? Maybe I can soften the blow? Get something unpleasant ticked off, at least?'

'Just try and ask some basics — common sense stuff, the sort of stuff that other detectives can struggle with. If there are shoes in the hall, try and ascertain that they belong to whoever you have there . . . Check the bathroom for a toothbrush, the kitchen for a special set of cutlery that the suspect was very specific about using and left unwashed. Oh, and check the bins for anything bloody or soiled.'

'Soiled? Really?'

'You're right. I'll save that for the junior. Oh, and don't touch *anything* that you might want us to look at. Just leave it in situ.'

'Don't worry. I've seen it in there . . . The less I touch, the better!'

'Can't wait,' Charley huffed.

'From what we know, our offender is forensically aware. He's brazen, but he's clever. I don't think we're going to find anything left of him.'

'Oh, I agree. None of the items I just said will be there, but it'll give you something to do. But if he was in that house there will *definitely* be something left of him — forensic science tells me that. Experience however, tells me that identifying him among what everyone else might have left is the difficult bit. Probably impossible.'

'Okay.'

'I'll be half an hour. You don't have to stay.'

'I do. I feel bad enough as it is calling you late on a Friday. I'll try and send the grumpy old bastard home, though. There's a uniform patrol here, too. Should I keep hold of them?'

'Yes, for now. Just in case I do find something groundbreaking and we need to keep it as a scene overnight. If they leave, it'll take hours to get anyone back.'

'Fine. See you shortly. And thanks, Charley.'

'No need for thanks. It's my job, after all. I'm only two hours late off already.'

Maddie's phone was bright enough to make her squint in the darkness, where she stayed a moment as her mind raced.

'Everything okay?' Harry's question made her jump. She hadn't seen him step out of the house.

'As okay as it can be.'

'Did you get hold of CSI?'

'Charley. She'll be half an hour. She doesn't have too much hope, either. They'll take the elimination samples. Charley has some junior with her. So we don't have to.'

'Good news. That's an unpleasant job avoided. So how come you look so unhappy?'

'Something Charley said. She did what she could in that cupboard next door and found hair. She thinks it's from a wig.'

'A wig? Any links to any person?'

'No. Just hair with some glue. That's why they think wig.'

'I see.'

'He's changing his appearance, isn't he? The description of the Bristol job, the sixty-year-old male seen walking away — slim build. In the café we have a sixty-year-old white male, long hair, glasses, larger build. Here we have the same description from Michelle Rice, but a neighbour sees an old man walking away with a slight build and short hair. It's all the same man, isn't it?'

'If we assume the wig is his, then yes.'

'If it isn't, where is it? Charley would have found it in the cupboard.'

'I'm sure you're right. We'll need to ask Michelle Rice to be sure.'

'I can do that. I think I already know the answer. I want to head back in and check the CCTV again. The review was for a very distinctive look. He could have been missed.'

'What are we reviewing for? A white male aged around sixty years old?'

Maddie sighed. She ran her hand over her mouth. 'The St Dunstans CCTV alone . . . Think how many matches we will get for that. We've got nothing that covers the entrance to the café, anyway. All we can show is who was in the area at the material time. We're a week in or so. Bristol are a few months down the line for their job, we have three dead between us and that's the sum total of what we have — a white male, aged around sixty, slim build. It's not a lot, is it?'

'It's more than we had,' Harry said. 'That's progress.'

'It just doesn't feel like it. Michelle Rice saw right through me earlier. She knows we're a long way off. It doesn't matter to her — her life is already changed forever. But there are other people, other families out there, Harry . . . This is a long way from over.'

'I agree. We need to be on top of our game to get closer still. That means getting some rest. There are officers coming in first thing in the morning to start back on the CCTV. We're back in first thing, too. I can brief them with the new information. There's nothing you can achieve tonight other than ensuring you're exhausted for tomorrow. Head home, Maddie. You'll come back fresher and maybe even a little more positive.'

'Was that a dig? I'm not being negative for the sake of it.'

'No, you're being negative because you're tired and you're in the middle of a complex investigation. You can't see what we have done, what we have achieved. We're a lot further along.'

'What if this happens again? Another murder? Another kid trapped in a room while his dad screws his own noose to the ceiling? Jesus, Harry, we're supposed to stop people like this!'

'And we will. Get some rest.'

'I said I'd wait for Charley. She's not far out now.'

'And you'll go home after that?'

'Yes.'

'Straight home? Without reviewing any CCTV?'

Maddie hesitated. 'Yes.'

'I'm only thinking of you. It's been a long day, I know I'm feeling it.'

'I did say to Charlie that I'd send _you_ home, actually. There's no need for you to be here too.'

'Ah yes, I remember . . . You're in charge these days.'

Maddie thought she detected humour in Harry's voice. It was too dark to read his facial expressions. 'Don't you forget it!' She chanced.

Harry's reaction was to turn back to the light from the front door. She could see he was smiling.

* * *

When Harry pushed open the front door to his own house, he immediately dropped his hands to cover his groin. He had a dog. A recent addition to the household and one who was the perfect height and bounce to really catch him in the most sensitive of areas. He was now well aware of that from experience.

Jock was as reliable and consistent as ever. He sprinted the length of the hall, a dark shadow that jumped the moment he was close enough, his nose and paws aimed for the midriff. Harry turned away and ignored him like he had read on dog owners' forums. He waited for as long as he could resist before turning back to Jock and bending over him to make a fuss. Jock rolled onto his back, legs splayed, his bulging eyes fixed on Harry with the expectation of a belly rub.

'Not now, boy.' Harry stepped over Jock, gratified that his eyes were the only part of him that followed. Harry was tired. His chair was calling him. His hand reached out to feel the radiator as he went. He quickly moved it off to prevent it blistering from the heat.

'Christ alive! _Melissa!_' He bellowed for his daughter. She had only been back home for three weeks and he was certain his utilities bills were already double what they had been for the rest of the year. He took a right off the hallway and into the dining room. The living room was to the right of this, the kitchen straight on. The lights were on in every room and there were smells from the kitchen accompanying the sound of music. He switched the light off in the dining room and reached around to do the same in the lounge as he passed. Jock was back under his feet.

'You're home!' Melissa beamed. She was stirring something on the hob. The oven glowed. The doors out to the conservatory were wide open and the light was on out there, too.

'I am. The national grid called me. They said something about needing the energy for the rest of the village?' He paced through to turn the lights off in the conservatory. He pulled the doors shut as he stepped back into the kitchen.

'I got hot. That's why they were open.'

'Did you consider turning the heating down? Or off, even? It's not even cold yet.'

'Not in here it isn't, because I've got the heating on. It's like I have said to you before, Dad . . . You don't live in a cave, so you should make the most of a few creature comforts!'

'I don't want to live in a cave, just a house where *you* can't reach the thermostat.'

'Are you going to be grumpy all weekend? And after I made you dinner!'

'No. But I might be working all weekend. We've got a job on. There's a lot to do.'

Melissa sighed. 'Isn't there always. So our dog walk and dinner is off the cards, then?'

'I'll still try,' he said. It was planned for Sunday. They were going to take Jock out for a decent walk and stop a couple of villages over at a pub that did a nice Sunday lunch. It had been Harry's idea and he wanted it to happen. Since she had come home, they hadn't really talked about how she was doing. She had been living with a boyfriend, but that had broken down recently and rather suddenly. Melissa didn't always cope well with changes in her circumstances. She had a history of mental health episodes. She had hurt herself and battled depression. Her boyfriend had been an important part of keeping her level. When they lost her mother, they had very nearly lost her, too. He was worried that the breakup of her relationship would knock her again. She seemed okay — she seemed strong, but he hadn't really asked. Sunday was going to be the day when he talked to her properly. He wanted to know if she was still taking medication, if she was still managing her own health. He would need to be sensitive about it. He was dreading it.

'I've heard that before! What's going on? I assume someone had to die for you to be working a weekend?'

'Two, actually.'

'I see. There's no chance of Sunday going ahead, is there?'

'I really don't know. I've got to go in first thing tomorrow — just a meeting. There's nothing else planned at the moment, so we might be okay.'

'What are the chances of you not getting tucked up for Sunday between then and now! What about if we do it tomorrow? I'll book you in for straight after your meeting. Tomorrow looks to be the better day of the two, anyway. Then if anyone calls, you have a whole day free on Sunday.'

Harry looked down to where Jock was now sitting on his feet where he had been still too long. The dog gazed upwards and as he looked into those big, brown eyes, he was in no doubt that he was in cahoots with his daughter.

'Okay, yeah — tomorrow. It's a breakfast meeting, so we'll head out straight after. I'll need to be checking in with work fairly regularly, but I want the walk to happen. I've been looking forward to spending some time with you both. It'll be nice.'

'It will! And in the meantime, I've made you a curry!' She stirred a spoon through the saucepan that was bubbling on the hob. She lifted some out to slop it back in the pan. 'Which might not be . . .'

'Great,' Harry mumbled. 'I'll be in the living room in shorts and T shirt.' He flapped his shirt away from his chest to emphasise his discomfort.

'It's not even warm in here!' Melissa called after him and, not for the first time in the last three weeks, Harry felt he missed living alone.

CHAPTER 24

Saturday

Robbie snatched his head away. He had finally managed to fall asleep, but it hadn't been settled. The floor was hard and uncomfortable, the air thick and stale and the silence of being on the outskirts of the town seemed, rather bizarrely, to have made his sleep more disturbed. He was used to the dull roar of a nearby high street that somehow lulled him to sleep. Out here, he had been woken by the scrabbling noise of a single rodent that stood out from the silence.

Something touched his face. It must have been what he had jerked away from when he had first woken. His eyes took a moment to adjust. When they did, they settled on a shiny, black cable.

'You're still here!' said Lance. 'I think you made the right choice.' Robbie was still facing the wall, his back to the scene that he could remember as vivid as a photograph. The voice was behind him, too. For a moment, he allowed hope to creep in, hope that the monster who had made the mess had also spent the morning silently clearing it up and that when he turned around, there would be nothing but a couple of sofas and the smell of disinfectant.

He was disappointed. Mikey was swinging from the ceiling like a redundant puppet. His colour had changed enough overnight for him to look unreal in the early morning light, like a wax model had been strung up in his place. His face and hands were the only exposed part of his body. Robbie could see the tips of his fingers were a reddish-purple. Beyond him, the dishevelled man who had crashed the party was still lying on his back. Mercifully, his face was turned away. He had one leg raised so that a foot rested against the front door.

'What's this?' Robbie asked. He was looking back down at the strip of plastic that had stroked his face. He recognised it now as a cable tie.

'Insurance. For me. I'm going to have to ask you to move over to the radiator over there. I need to be out this morning. There's something I cannot miss, but I'd prefer it if you were here when I got back.'

'Okay. I'll stay here, I swear.'

The man's face hardened. He shook his head violently and tutted. He looked like he had to gather himself before he spoke. 'Don't be *swearing* anything — not to me, not to anyone. You go giving your word to people like me and it ends badly when you have to break it.' Lance leaned in so close, Robbie could smell minty toothpaste. 'And when you break your word to me, I tend to string you up and take your breath away. Do you understand?'

Robbie managed a jerky nod. Lance walked over to the radiator, still with the cable tie in his hand and gestured for Robbie to follow. 'This way you don't have to promise me anything that you'll be tempted to break the moment I leave the house. You see, if you're gone when I get back, then you got out fair and square and it's my fault for not fixing it right. I can't blame you for that and maybe I don't have to hunt you down and kill you. Maybe. But if I leave you to your own free will and you let me down . . . I take betrayal very personally. Get over here.'

Robbie did as he was told. He knelt in front of the same solid metal pipe that he could see was acting as a ground

226

pin for the steel wire that rose up from the other end. Lance secured the plastic tie so tightly that Robbie had to suck in a breath to stop from crying out. He still had full movement with his left hand, however — until Lance produced another zip-tie and trussed it to the pipe also. This one was pulled even tighter.

It left Robbie on his knees with his head bent forward, his elbows digging into the thin carpet to take some of his weight. He wasn't sure where Lance was. There were noises behind him, then a plate slid under his face and his nostrils filled with the scent of buttery toast.

'What is this?'

'Breakfast!' Lance said. 'Don't ever let it be said that I am a poor host. You must be hungry. I need to go to work.'

'Work?'

'Work. Your boss Mr Mason has paid me to do a job.'

'But . . . I thought—'

'What? That I would just take the money and run? I'm not like your friend Mikey. I'm a very simple man with simple rules. I get a job and I finish it. Everything is in place and the Tax Man always collects — that's what they say, right? I'm still considering what happens after, with you, with Mr Mason. I still need to consider the depth of this betrayal.'

Robbie kept his eyes down, fixed on his breakfast, not wanting to look into those dark eyes again — or what was on display in the rest of the room. He was aware that Lance had moved in closer to him. He could feel the heat on his face. He spoke directly into his ear.

'Right now, you're a loose end, boy. I will need to be sure that is not the case. You remember what I said about being reliable? You show me that you are reliable and maybe you're not a loose end anymore. At least, not one that I need to worry about. Clear?'

'I w-will!' Robbie stuttered. 'This is j-just a job. I was told to come down here with Mikey to speak to you, to find out when you were g-going to do the job. That was it!'

Lance moved away. Robbie dared to look to his left. His eye dragged to movement: the dishevelled man, he twitched his foot! Robbie flinched. Then he heard a grunt and strained to see the source. The grunt was from Lance, the twitching foot was the result of him yanking the body away from the door.

'I didn't think this through, did I? You could have helped me out here.' Lance's laughter fell away as quickly as it had started. He moved the man from the door in a series of shuffles. Then he fixed on Robbie, those rodent eyes looking right at him, but overall he looked distant, as if his thoughts were already elsewhere. 'I have work to do. I'll be back later.'

Robbie relented to the pain in his neck from craning over his shoulder, turning back to face the wall as Lance left out of the front door. He was aware of the sound of it being locked after him.

Robbie focused on the wall. The sweet smell of the toast mingled with the stale room and made him feel sick. He looked at his wrists, at the cable ties that held them. Even the slightest movement was painful. He gritted his teeth and tried to pull his arms back together. Instantly, his skin was pinched white and both wrists flared in pain. The ties scuffed along the metal slightly and the pipe rocked from the right side. His eyes followed the pipe along. At the far end, it seemed to dip into the carpet. He now saw he had been wrong. The wire holding up Mikey was tied off against a *different* pipe. He had assumed it to be the same one.

He pulled back against his ties again, this time watching the pipe. *It lifted!* He was sure of it. He turned back into the room, starting at the front door then straining his neck as far as he could. He had got the impression that Lance was going to be out for a while and anyway, he had pretty much said that if he could get free then it was on him, it was Lance's fault. Like he might not even be too bothered.

The strain in his neck was too painful. He had to turn back to the wall. He rested it for a few seconds, then tried again. Directly behind him on the sofa, he could see something that might have been the handle of Mikey's gun sticking out from a bundle of clothes. He must have left it where he had thrown it. He couldn't quite focus. The pain in his neck was too bad. But Robbie dared to consider that there might be possibilities. He edged right, using his knees to propel him. The pull on his wrists was instant. He dragged them along the metal — just an inch — and it was agony. The plastic dug in, pinching the skin like a Chinese burn, only far worse than he had experienced from any playground bully. He looked along the pipe. It was quite a distance and he would have to cover it inch by inch. But he had time.

His gaze shifted back to the door. His breathing was heavier from the exertion and from managing the pain. His mind ran with doubt, suddenly concerned that this was a test . . . Lance didn't seem the sort to make mistakes, to truss him up to something he might be able to escape from. *And to leave a weapon in the room?* He thought of what he had said, about proving he could be reliable. And Mikey, too, and how he had toyed with him until he died, like he was having the time of his life. Maybe this was another game to him, a bit of sport?

Robbie didn't know. He considered it didn't matter. He couldn't just stay there and wait for him to come back. If there was the chance of an escape, he had to try.

CHAPTER 25

Rebecca Arnold was obvious to Maddie. She looked awkward half sitting, half leaning on a pillar painted black with Deal's town crest in gold. It was one of many dotted along the promenade. She was facing away from the view out to sea and was looking directly at the alleyway from which Maddie had emerged, having parked her car. Harry had been waiting by his car for her when she arrived. He was instantly a step behind her and sullen.

'Saturday morning, Harry. So much for a weekend off.'

Harry grunted. Maddie knew better than to try again. She made straight for the seated woman, who stood up to greet them.

'You must be Harry and Mads?' the woman said.

'Maddie Ives,' Maddie said, accepting the hand she was offered to shake.

'Sorry! My brother . . . He always calls you Mads!'

'Not always.' Maddie laughed.

'I can imagine. He can be a cheeky one, but he's a good guy. He talks highly of you, too. He's not just about pet names and sexual innuendo.'

'Really? That's kind of all it is to my face! Until I tell him off. Then he's very quick to back away. I guess that means he likes me.'

'Thanks for coming over,' Rebecca said to Harry. He was the one who had taken the call and set the meeting up over the phone. The call had been out of the blue and when Harry had told her about the arrangements, he only gave the time and place. Maddie had asked follow-up questions, but either Harry hadn't asked for any detail himself or he simply didn't want to share what had been discussed. Maddie wished she had been the one to take the call.

'I know what we talked about . . . I couldn't. I didn't tell him. I was going to, like we said, but when I spoke to him last . . . I dunno, he was more guarded, if anything,' Rebecca said and immediately Maddie got the confirmation that there was more to Harry's call than he had revealed.

'Okay, don't worry,' Harry said. 'At least this way, we can be sure he'll turn up.'

'He should. It's become a regular thing. I work here a few days a week and we've done Saturday mornings since I started. I've seen more of him since he stopped working. Sometimes he doesn't talk much.'

'That's okay. I've a feeling he'll have something to say today.' Harry's standard growl had deepened.

Rebecca led the way. When they entered the café, she smiled over at a man on the other side of the counter. He gestured at a table that had a *reserved* notice across its middle. It was just gone eight on a Saturday morning and the café was busy. Maddie wasn't surprised, not with this location. When she sat down, her right shoulder brushed up against the window that dominated the frontage. It was on a corner. Two sides were glass and the counter was down the opposite end to their table, near to the door where they had come in. Her view was over a road with only an occasional car to obstruct the glittering sea beyond. It was a crisp, bright morning — for now, at least. More rain was forecast for later and it looked like grey clouds were already starting to gang up out to sea. They would need to increase significantly in number if they were planning an assault on the land. The low sun gave the sea a twinkle in its eye.

A man appeared at their table and Rebecca ordered drinks. Both officers declined food, despite Rebecca's insistence and promises to pay. There was a brief argument where Harry gruffly insisted there was no need. He seemed to pick up on Rebecca's facial expressions at the same time as Maddie and softened his tone to offer some explanation.

'It's fine. You don't need to buy us a coffee. We're happy to be here. And I have lunch planned with my daughter later. She'll be upset if I turn up full. She's always upset at me, it seems.'

Some of the warmth returned to Rebecca's expression. 'A daughter? How old?'

'All grown up. Early twenties now.'

'Ah, okay. I have a little boy. He's seven. They're a pain in the ass at that age, but lovely. I wouldn't change him for the world.'

'They never stop being a pain, I'm afraid. They just find a different angle.'

The drinks arrived. Maddie's attention was still out of the window but no longer towards the sea. She wanted to see Vince approach. She didn't think there would be a big reaction but he would know instantly why they were there. Beyond that, she wasn't sure how he would be.

'This is him,' Maddie said. He was a distant figure, but his build and his walk were distinctive enough for her to be sure. He was walking on the pavement parallel to the promenade. Despite the chilly morning, he was in a grey hoodie, board shorts and a beanie hat. His hands were pushed into the front of his top as he crossed the road to walk directly over the roundabout, seemingly oblivious to the two cars that had to be quick on their brakes as he stepped off the pavement. He pushed through the door and instantly made eye contact with Maddie across the café. She waited for his reaction. It was a fleeting smile that he broke to give a thumbs up to the man behind the counter.

'Ollie!' he bellowed, with his usual lack of volume control. When he got closer, Maddie could see that the hairs on his legs were standing up as if he was cold. His hat had a weathered look with frayed edges.

'So, what have you come as, Vince?' She chanced a light-hearted introduction.

'Fancy the chances,' he replied. 'So this is why you wanted to pin me to a time today, sis? You two not working today? I heard the shit was hitting the fan at our place.' He stood behind the free chair, his hands still pushed into his top.

'I reckon I might have to check in later,' Maddie said.

'You've got a meeting first, I see.'

'It's my fault, Vince,' Rebecca said. 'I asked them to come along. I wanted to talk. I'm worried. I know I've told you that, but I don't know what more to say. I don't understand it all, this world you lot inhabit. When you talk about it, it's . . . well, just like . . . a different world! I thought it might help me if I had some people here who know what it's all about.' Rebecca's reply sounded like a well-practised script, as if she had thought hard about the first thing she was going to say and that was it. Maddie watched Vince closely. He was looking around the interior of the café as if assessing his options. He still stood behind the chair.

'Me and the boss here are supposed to be seeing you again, anyway,' said Maddie. 'Welfare . . . You know how it is. Made sense for us all to get together.'

'My sister, too?' Vince's tone carried an edge for the first time 'I wasn't aware you were friends?'

'We're not. First time we've met. But it turns out we've got a few things in common.'

'Oh, yeah, what's that?'

'We're all worried about you for a start.'

'You don't need to be worried about me.'

'We both said you would say that. Like I said . . . A lot in common!'

'How did you find her?' This question was directed to his sister.

'I didn't. Not Maddie. I got Harry's details from your phone. When you were making the tea.'

Maddie smiled up at him. 'Another thing we've got in common!'

'Yeah, she's a devious cow, too. So what is this? Some sort of intervention? Let's get it over with, then!' He dragged the chair out. He was rough and it clanged off the table. The noise was loud enough for the occupants closest to turn towards it. Vince took his seat. Everything he did was heavy. Maddie couldn't tell if it was heavier today. He wore a grin, but she was finding him hard to read. He leaned forward on his elbows to show fingerless gloves.

'I just want to make sure you're okay,' said Rebecca. 'That's all. That's why we're all here. You talk about your friends like you respect them and they're worried, too.'

Vince didn't reply immediately. His gaze moved to the view out of the window. 'I know where you all are. I saw these two just the other day and we talked. It's a shit thing, but shit happens.'

'Did you tell them about your sleep?' Rebecca said. Vince snapped back to her.

'There's nothing to tell.'

'You're not sleeping. You told me that. I know what you're like . . . You keep it all bottled up, but that just means it doesn't get dealt with.'

'Dealt with? What do you want from me, sis? A scented candle and crossed legs while I talk about my feelings? That's not how I work things out. I'm okay, I know it.'

'I know you, Vince. Better than you like to admit. You're not okay.'

'I'm alright to be babysitting for you, though, ain't I? You still dropping Sammy off later so you can pick up an extra shift in here?' There was anger in his tone now. 'Oh, yeah, I'm okay to help there, that suits you, doesn't it?' Vince sat back, his arms crossed. The table fell silent.

'I knew it, too.' Harry's growl cut through the low din of the chatting diners to snatch Vince's attention. 'When my wife died . . . When I was pulled away from her so the paramedics could take over, when her head rolled to the side so she was facing me but looking right past, when I knew that she would never look at me again, not with those eyes.' Harry paused. The whole world seemed to pause with him. Maddie was caught out. She could tell Vince was, too. He stuttered the beginning of a reply.

'Boss, I—'

'I knew I was okay, too,' Harry cut back in. 'And the more people told me I shouldn't be alright, the more determined I was to ignore them. I don't know why we do that to ourselves. I didn't sleep. Not for months. A few snatched hours but never at night. I could only sleep during the day. The nightmare came at night. Always the same ending. The last moment of our life together in a flash of white.'

'What do I say to that?' Vince chanced a nervous smile.

'It hit me hard, I nearly didn't make it, Vince, and I'm smart. You're not. You're like some big, dumb Labrador with sloppy chops, bumbling through your life bugging the rest of us for treats. And you've got this massive heart — Lord knows, it's the only feature that redeems you. And we all love you for it, but listen to me, Vince . . . It can bring you down. You can't do this alone.'

'I . . .' Vince stammered. 'Was that a compliment?'

Harry huffed, but his tone suddenly seemed a touch warmer. 'Only you, Vince . . . Only you could listen to all that and pick out a compliment.'

Vince beamed back at him. 'And you just said you love me. You know that, right? You all heard that?' Vince leaned back to take in Maddie and his sister. The tension was gone, replaced by laughter around the table. The drinks arrived. The timing was perfect. It gave a purpose to the silence as everyone fidgeted with sugars and stirrers. Vince spoke next. Maddie stayed silent to allow him to talk. She reckoned Harry was doing the same.

'So . . . What did you do?' Vince peered over the top of his mug towards Harry.

'Nothing. For a long time. It was only recently that I started talking to someone about it. I was suffering, of course I was. You expect to suffer after something like that. But what you can't know is what is normal, not when you're in it. You need someone to tell you what is normal and what's unhealthy. Maddie pointed it out. She made me see sense. But, like I said, I'm smart . . .'

'Okay, then,' Vince said.

'Okay?'

'I'll call your boyfriend. Maybe take him out for a steak dinner — who knows where it will end up!'

'Of course you will. Just take it seriously, Vince, if you're capable.' Harry stood up. His tone was agitated. He plucked his wallet from his back pocket and dropped two items onto the table in a pile.

'The card gives the details of the fella you're taking out. The tenner is for the drinks.' Harry held up his hands to meet Rebecca's protestations. 'Please, I insist. You were right to call, no matter what the slobbery Labrador here says the minute we're gone.'

Vince shook his head. It looked like his face flashed with anger, like he might bite back, but he settled to leaning back, his arms crossed. A lopsided grin appeared to point up at the inspector. 'So that's it? You've been here like five minutes! You came all the way out here to call me a slobbery dog and now you're done?'

'I called you stupid, too, Vince.'

'Was it even worth the drive out?' The edge was back in both men.

'Call that number and it will be. We do have somewhere else to be, like you said, but we still came all the way out here for five minutes with you. Think about that.' Harry made for the door.

'Yes, *boss*!' Vince called after him. His voice had a natural boom and it attracted looks from most of the other occupants of the café.

236

Maddie jerked to her feet, suddenly feeling like she might be the spare part. She mumbled her goodbyes, made a promise to keep in touch with both of them and stepped out onto the pavement. Harry was waiting. He had moved to one side so he couldn't be seen from inside the café.

'You think he'll call?' Maddie said.

'Yes. He's a lumbering idiot who doesn't like to take instruction, but he will. He'll just leave it long enough so he thinks it was his idea.'

Maddie considered pointing out that maybe Harry could have presented it differently, seeing as how he seemed to know Vince so well. It was only a fleeting consideration. That could only lead one way. 'Is there another coffee shop around here somewhere?' she said. 'Only I had one, but there wasn't the time to finish it!'

'It was time to go. Like I said, Vince needs to be told something then left alone for it to sink in.'

'Well you certainly told him.'

'You would have done it differently?'

'Maybe it's the telling part that gets his back up.'

'You need to be direct and simple. Just like he is.'

'Good copper, though.' Maddie left a gap for Harry to agree. He didn't take it. 'He's talking about not coming back. I can't imagine him doing anything else.'

'He *is* a good copper. He'll be back at it, too. It's more than just a job for him. Although it sounds like he's been filling his time with babysitting duties. Maybe there's a new career there somewhere.'

'He might not be the sharpest,' Maddie said, 'but I can't think of anyone better to protect someone you love.'

Harry held her in a stare for a few moments. 'You're probably right. I need to be getting back to my daughter. I have a dog walk planned.' He set off towards his car.

'How is Jock, talking of loved ones?' Maddie called after him.

'The perfect height.' Harry called back.

'Perfect height?'

'He gets me every time I walk through my own damned door.'

Maddie grinned. If she hadn't been sure what he meant initially, Harry assisted with a slight adjustment of his walk. She smiled at the back of his head. He might be a grumpy old bastard, but he cared about Vince just as much as she did. This was his day off, too.

CHAPTER 26

Adam Yarwood seemed smaller. His outline as a whole was a little less imposing, his clothes hung looser, the impression overall was of a forgotten balloon that had been left to deflate. His shoulders were less wide, the arms that hung off them less thick and the chest less defined. He seemed to carry himself differently, too. His head was slightly crooked, his stance not as straight. Even his smile was lopsided. But those eyes . . . There was nothing different about them. They still smouldered their mischief.

'You sizing me up or letting me in?' His voice was exactly as she remembered. Maddie was frozen in her own doorway. She stayed that way until he moved forward, breaking the spell, forcing her to step backwards. He hesitated, his lips pursed and his eyes narrowed. 'Second thoughts?' he said.

'No.' Maddie said, without a moment's hesitation.

'Okay, then.'

'I guess I didn't realise . . . I didn't know it was *this* weekend?' They had talked on the phone a handful of times over the last few months. Adam had seemed keen to keep her up to date on his recovery from a head injury that had nearly taken his life. Maddie hadn't seen him since. He'd said that he was getting closer to being strong enough to come down. She'd told him that she didn't work weekends anymore, that they should sort something out for him to come down on a Saturday. And now he was here. Eighteen months before, she had sneaked into a busy London hospital to stare down at his lifeless body, talking nonsense while a machine supported his breathing. Then she had sneaked out again. She'd had no choice. At that time, he'd still had links to an organised criminal gang, one of the most dangerous in the country, and in a previous life she'd had been tasked with getting close to him in her capacity as an undercover police officer. This was something she had taken too far. It had been against everything she knew and believed in, but she couldn't resist him. She still couldn't. This was just like him, too . . . turning up from nowhere.

'It wasn't. I mean, we didn't set a weekend.'

'I might have been away! I could have been anywhere — this would have been wasted.'

'I didn't know I was going to make it.' The mischief in his eyes seemed to fade for a moment. Maddie didn't want to talk anymore. She stepped into him, reaching out to push the door shut behind them, then moved her hands to rest on his shoulders, her eyes falling shut as her lips found his. She took air in through her nose, inhaling his scent, feeling his warmth. She felt the embrace in every part of her body. It might have been eighteen months, but it was instantly familiar, as if he had just left a moment ago. And now he was back.

Finally, their lips parted. She stayed close, enough to only see those eyes.

'I can't touch your face. I used to like that. I'm working on it!' Adam's words were a little slower — more deliberate. She only noticed it now. She licked her lips. She didn't know what to say, didn't really understand. 'My arms . . . I can't lift them above my shoulder. I could barely move them at all. I can't tell you how much progress I've made. My physio, she said I needed to have targets. You're it now. I want to be able to touch that beautiful face of yours. To rest my thumb on your lips.' He paused and seemed to swell with emotion.

'I took stuff like that for granted once . . . I won't do that again.'

She kissed him again. She felt his hands slide into the small of her back. They lifted slowly then fell back.

'Maybe I just need to move my face.' She grinned against his lips, the movement of her hands more urgent as they moved down his body. She moved her kisses to his neck, then his chest. She felt him take hold of her wrist to stop her moving down any further.

'We need to talk before . . . before anything.'

Maddie stopped. She wasn't sure if it was irritation or frustration in his voice. She did as he asked and stood back to meet those eyes. They were tinged with sadness.

'There are limitations,' he said. 'For me. It's all temporary, but some things have been slower than others . . .' His face flushed. Maddie didn't think she had ever seen him embarrassed.

'You're right . . . Shit! I'm sorry. I got carried away! I want to know everything. We have plenty of time.' Maddie's words stumbled to a stop.

'We do. I can still drink coffee . . .' He lingered on her. She took a moment then snapped away.

'Coffee! Where are my manners! All this time and all you've been through, you make the effort to come all the way down here and the first thing I do is try and sexually assault you in the hallway! Coffee . . .' Maddie felt her own cheeks burn. She cursed herself as she turned for the kitchen. When she looked back, Adam was following with strides that were slightly elongated, as if he was walking with stiff legs. It was slow and deliberate. They made eye contact. She snatched away and flushed hotter still.

'It's okay. I want you to see. I can walk. I had to learn again, which means I'm getting better all the time.'

'How did you get down here? I could have come and picked you up. It would have been no—'

'Train. All by myself. No mother, no nurse, no one. It was utter bliss. It took me all day, but I did it.'

'All day?'

'I came down yesterday. I'm in a hotel.'

'A hotel? Why would—'

'On my own.' He cut in. 'I came down to see you, Maddie, no other reason. I want to spend every minute I can with you, but those limitations I mentioned, they make some things difficult. And you don't need to see those things because they won't be difficult forever.'

'I don't care what—'

'I do. And anyway, it's been a while. It wouldn't be right for me to just turn up and assume . . .' He seemed to run out of words. She'd never known him do that before, either. Her mind flicked back to where she had got caught up and carried away at the front door just a few moments before. Her cheeks burned again. 'It's the same reason I didn't tell you I was coming this weekend. I might not have made it. No shame in turning back if you didn't even know I'd started out. But I made it. I'm still recovering from the journey, but I did it.'

She moved to the coffee pot, desperate for the right words to say.

'Coffee, then. Seems there's a lot to catch up on!' She tried to giggle. It was forced and fake and she knew it would sound like it. She busied herself. This wasn't how this was supposed to go, the first meeting after all this time. She spilt some of the coffee on the counter and tutted at her own haste. Suddenly she felt hands on her hips. Adam pushed himself into her back. He kissed her head, inhaling the scent of her hair. She leaned back into him. All of her movements stopped.

'This is as hard as I can grip you, right now. You have no idea how much I want to just wrap you up, carry you through to the bedroom. But I can't. And that's okay. Just being here . . . I never thought I would be here again.'

Maddie turned on the spot. Again, their lips were close. 'I'm sorry. I thought the same. It's overwhelming. I mean it was, opening the door to you.'

'Maybe we should go out for a walk? I'm supposed to do it as much as I can.'

'And I can't sexually assault you in a public place, can I?'

Adam laughed and his eyes sparkled. 'It's not that you don't have my permission. I just don't like being sexually assaulted when I can't sexually assault you back!'

Maddie kissed him hard. She felt his hands move back around her and lift a little. Again they fell. He pulled away and his eyes dropped.

'It's so frustrating! I can't hold you.'

'You've had a hold on me from the day we met, Adam Yarwood. Let's go for a walk.'

CHAPTER 27

Vince swore when the doorbell rang for the third time. It was a double press, too. Whoever it was, they weren't giving up. He dropped the dumbbell he was holding onto the grass. A towel was on the wall by his back door. He swept it up and dabbed his face as he walked through the house. It was over his heaving shoulders by the time he answered the front door.

His sister stared intently at him. There was clear anger in her expression. 'You forgot, didn't you?'

'Shit!' Vince flicked to where his watch had been. He had ripped it off at the start of his workout. It was arm exercises today, which could make his wrists swell. He could remember exactly where he had placed it on the wall. That didn't help him now, with his sister glowering at him and his nephew Sammy standing at her hip. Even he was looking up from the electronic game in his hand to stare at him expectantly.

'Sammy! Good to see you lad! You remember you said you wanted to play on Uncle Vince's gym? Well, I made a start without you!'

'Bullshit, Vince!' Rebecca hissed. 'You forgot. And there's no way you'd let anyone near that gym of yours.'

'I just lost track of time is all. It's no biggie, okay. I'm here, aren't I? Quick shower and I'll be good to go.'

'I have to be at work, Vince. I don't have time to wait around while you sing in the shower.'

'You don't need to stick around, Becks. I'll sit Sammy down for a minute, stick the kids' channel on and I'll be back down in five. There's some new movies on Netflix for us to watch. I was looking earlier. See, I ain't forgotten about nothing!'

Rebecca glanced at her watch again and sighed. She gestured at a brightly coloured satchel on her son's back. 'In there is all you should need.'

'Bet I don't even need that. We're gonna have fun, trust me on that! And you're sure you don't wanna stick around? Only when I get to singing in that shower . . . Honestly, I've had questions from the neighbours asking me if that Adele bird pops in for a rinse.'

Rebecca found a smile. 'I have to get going. Maybe some other time, yeah?'

'Suit yourself.'

Sammy stumbled over the doorstep where his mother had shoved him in the back. His attention moved back to the device in his hand. Vince gave a reassuring wave, then closed the door as his sister hurried away. Sammy moved into the living room but remained standing, his head buried in the flashing screen, the repetitive noises of his game blinking.

'Hey Sammy, you wanna take a seat, mate? I just need to get a shower quick.' Sammy didn't look away. He backed into the sofa to perch on the edge. He was still wearing his bag. He had a long coat that hung open and shoes that trailed laces. Vince shrugged. He reckoned he might be able to get a shower and change before the lad even noticed he was gone. He made for the stairs.

* * *

Maddie often found herself here. She was in Enbrook Park in Sandgate, just a short walk from her apartment but with enough trees surrounding her that she could forget there was anyone or anything around at all. Running down the west side of the park was a small stream with a miniature waterfall that was perfectly positioned to take advantage of a small clearing. On a summer's day, it had everything: natural surroundings, strong sunlight and plenty of shade. Today she was having to make do with the pleasant splashes and gurgles — and the company of Adam Yarwood.

The stream was more swollen than normal due to recent heavy rain, but it was a tiny force of nature going about its business no matter what. Maybe that was what Maddie liked about it. She found the process reassuring — calming, even. The water ran from the top of the park, obeying the rules of gravity, falling where it was pushed. Sometimes her work could have her convinced that the whole world was intent on pushing back against the flow. This was the spot where she would bring a coffee and find some perspective. From here, she would often walk further up into the park, but already Adam was looking tired. They had come far enough.

She smiled reassurance and he smiled back. She sat on the same flattened rock she always did, ignoring the names of young lovers etched into its surface. It was angled towards the murmuring stream, enough that she needed to lock her legs out to stay seated. Adam seemed to have problems doing the same.

'Are you okay here?' she said.

'It's nice . . . but don't you have miles of seafront here? I thought you were going to take me for a stroll along the promenade!'

'I thought about that, but the coffee shop is over this way!' She lifted the two cups to highlight her point. Adam took one. She wasn't quite telling the truth about the promenade, about her reasons for staying away. It was long and flat and very beautiful, but it was tainted for her. The great expanse of flat sea had been her previous source of calm, but in one violent incident it had come to signify the opposite. Now she made do with the most miniature of waterfalls surrounded on all sides by mature oak trees. She felt safe here, as if nature was on her side, flexing and straining to keep her hidden from anything that might pose a threat.

And now Adam was here. She moved her hand to fall onto his. She felt a squeeze back. The interruption of her phone made her jump.

'Shit!' She had meant to turn it off — to silent, at least. She broke off from Adam's hand to scrabble for it. The screen glared with a name: *Rhiannon*. She cut her off, then sent a hurried reply: *Call you later.*

'Sorry!' she said. Adam didn't reply. She flicked her phone to silent. It vibrated in her hand almost immediately. She read Rhiannon's short reply: *Ok, it's important.*

'Dammit. I need to call her back. Just a minute.' She stood up and managed to take two paces.

'Who?'

'A colleague at work. She says it's important.'

'I thought you had weekends off.' Now Maddie was a little further away she could see how awkward he looked, how uncomfortable. He looked like he was pushing against the rock rather than resting on it.

'No such thing with this job!' she chuckled. Adam's expression didn't change. He looked stern — pissed off, maybe. She felt like she needed to offer more. 'I sent someone to another county at the last minute to do me a favour — she's supposed to be off, too. The least I can do is answer her call. It should only be a minute.' Adam turned back towards the sound of the falling water. Maddie moved further out into the clearing.

'Rhiannon, sorry about that. What have you got?'

'Can you speak? If you're busy—'

'It's fine.' Maddie cut in and instantly felt sorry. 'I've got a minute, what do you need?'

'It's not so much what I need, it's what I have. I just wanted to give you an update. I think they're linked.'

'Linked?'

'The scenes, the murders.'

'Okay.'

'I looked through the case file for the jobs. One of the last updates was from one of your team about the pull winch that was seized from both your crime scenes.'

'Pull winch?'

'A handheld winch that your offender used to lift that sort of weight from the floor and keep it there.'

'Okay, yeah. Sorry. I didn't know that was what it was called, but I know what you mean. The orange-handled thing.'

'That's it. Maybe they should just call it that, sounds so much better!' Rhiannon chuckled. Maddie could hear the excitement in her voice. She was starting to feel it herself. Adam was still facing away.

'What about it, anyway?'

'Yes. So you found this pull winch at your two crime scenes, they're likely to be from the same supplier . . . Toolstation. They're not the only stockists in the UK, but they are the only one where you can walk in and get one from one of their outlets. Otherwise you're online. I figure that if you go online, you're putting in credit cards, giving addresses — you're traceable, so you wouldn't do that, you'd—'

'Rhiannon! The short version?'

'Sorry! I'm babbling. I don't mean to babble. So down here, they have a crime scene where a woman was left sitting up against a white wall. Her blood was then smeared all around her. I've seen the crime scene photos, someone was definitely trying to make a statement—'

'And the same winch was found?' Maddie cut in again. Adam shuffled on the rock. His new position looked even less comfortable.

'No. I figure he didn't need a winch this time. He still used wire around her throat but only to hold her head up.'

'Okay . . . You've lost me, here. You seemed sure of a link?'

'I haven't finished! So first, the wire was tied off on a steel loop that they think was drilled into the ceiling specifically for that purpose — just like you have. But the wider MO is the same, too — at least, I think it is. She was positioned to face the door and her top was changed after she was killed. The one he put on her had no blood on it. One of the pictures in the CSI pack is from right back at the front door. She looks like she's just sitting up, Maddie! I read the statement that covers when she was found. The witness said she got right up close to the victim before she knew there was anything wrong at all. Even with the blood, she didn't put two and two together straight away, didn't know what was going on. The witness only went there after she got a text message asking her to come round. The layout of her home too . . . He could easily have been there when the victim arrived, hidden somewhere he could have witnessed the discovery from and then stayed hidden until he could walk away. Another witness reports someone moving away like he was on a high *after* the call was made to the police. The description isn't quite of the same person, but the behaviour . . . The witness said he was stripping off.'

'Stripping off?'

'I mean, not completely. He took two layers off his top half, just down to a vest apparently, and it was like he was desperate, like he was burning up.'

'Burning up?'

'Yeah. I guess smearing walls and lifting heads is hard work. It wasn't a warm day apparently, but our man didn't seem to notice. Sound familiar?'

'It does. Our man walked away in freezing rain wearing just a T shirt.'

'I know that!'

'Of course you do. Well, that's good work. There's still a lot of conjecture in there, Rhiannon. Circumstantial bits. But I think it will help us with building a picture.'

'There's more. These pull winches . . . I made some calls to Toolstation's head office. I had to be persistent, but they finally agreed to help. They're not a massive seller, but Toolstation have an outlet in an industrial unit just outside of Bristol. Five weeks ago, they sold four pull winches as part of the same transaction. The customer paid cash.'

'Four?'

'Four. And that's unusual in one go. I got them to look back through — I was pushing my luck. They're going to send it all through, but I managed to get them to check there and then. The only time they've sold more than one of these winches in one transaction has been to commercial customers — that is, traders that have accounts with them. Builders and the like. Even then, the most sold was three.'

'You think it's our offender?'

'That wasn't all he bought. He got a length of coiled steel wire rope at the same time. And four square ceiling mounts — heavy duty. I have an image. They're the same as what you have.'

'Okay. So that sounds a bit more positive!'

'I think it's a lead that needs bottoming out.'

Maddie beamed into the phone. 'I totally agree with that. That really is good work. Five weeks ago, you said?'

'Yes. The head office are pretty sure that the CCTV deletes itself after twenty-eight days so we might not get anything, but I'm on my way there now. Even if it's gone, it's an unusual order, so someone might remember something about the bloke who made it.'

'They might.' Maddie was beaming. 'I don't remember the details of the winch being in the summary I gave you?'

'It wasn't. I'm never too keen on a summary. I don't like feeling I'm missing something. I pretty much copied the whole file.'

'I know what you mean.' She would have done exactly the same thing. Why trust a summary of what someone else thinks is important when you can see everything and decide for yourself? 'This was the reason I sent you down there, Rhiannon. You know that, right? Excellent work. Keep me updated.'

'Will do. I'm a few minutes away from the store. I'll see what I can get.'

'Couldn't you have just called them?'

'I could. I prefer to speak to people face to face. Also the person who sold those winches might not be there, so I might need to do some door-knocking. It's the other side of the city from the police station. They're bound to live near to the store. I don't reckon a shop assistant at Toolstation commits to a long commute. Oh, and I sent the SIO a request for the source unit to be tasked down here. I noticed no one's done that. You never know, someone out here might have an idea of what's going on. Do you think she'll mind? I don't want to overstep my mark.'

'Having spoken to her on the phone, I'm pretty certain she'll mind immensely. But I bet she'll put your request through.'

'Well, that's all I need. I was always going to upset someone, somehow, by coming here.'

'Yes, you were! Keep me up to date.' Maddie was smiling as she moved the phone around to end the call. Rhiannon's tinny voice had her moving it back to her ear.

'Oh, Maddie!'

'Go on?'

'I know you probably worked this out already, but . . . *Four*. If this is our offender, he has four winches.'

Maddie's smile dropped away. She had already started walking back towards her seat on the flattened rock, her mind moving away from the double-murder case she was running at work and back to Adam. She had missed the significance of the number completely.

'And we have two victims.'

'One winch per victim,' Rhiannon said.

'So he has another two planned. At least.' Maddie was thinking out loud. 'Two more families about to have their lives turned upside down. Jesus, Rhiannon, he could be watching them right now!'

'Or stringing them up.' Rhiannon's tone was different, too. It had been a jovial call, Rhiannon excited with her update, Maddie delighted with her young colleague's demonstration of her ability. Both women were now seeing the bigger picture.

'I need to get back to work,' Maddie said. 'Like I said, keep me up to date. Speak soon!' Maddie ended the call.

'That girl has some talent,' she murmured. She rubbed her face, contemplating their next move. She considered that she should call Harry. Going back into the station was a move that would do nothing more than make her feel better. There wasn't really much else she could do at the moment that the team of detectives on duty and the Major Crime team were not doing. And Adam was here. She looked over to where he seemed fixed on the bubbling water. He didn't look away, even when she sat back next to him.

'A stroll, then? I know you said it was good for you,' Maddie said.

'Are you going to turn your phone off?' Adam's mood seemed to have darkened. Maddie's mind was still on developments from Bristol. She snapped back to Adam.

'I can't turn my phone off, Adam. That's not how this works.'

'How does this work, then?' He scrabbled to stand. Maddie watched, resisting the urge to help. She stayed seated.

'Are you angry with me?'

'Have you any idea the effort it took for me to come down here? To come and see you?'

'I think I'm starting to understand, yes.'

'It's not much to ask, then, is it? For your attention I mean. Just for one day.'

'I don't do that sort of job. Sometimes life gets interrupted. Most of the time, it doesn't. But there's a big job that—'

'Of course there is!'

'I don't understand why you're angry at me.'

He started to walk away. 'I'm not, okay. Just forget it. This was a mistake. It's too early.'

'Adam?' Maddie called after him. She pushed off the seat to walk after him.

'Don't . . .'

'Come on. We can talk about this! Sometimes I have to take calls. I remember when you used to do the same and—'

'*Used to!*' All of that power, that dominance Adam had once worn effortlessly on his sleeve, came surging back. He stood straighter as he faced her. For a moment, even his shoulders seemed broader, his chest pushed out. It lasted a moment, then his body slumped to hang on his frame. 'And now I'm useless . . . Redundant.'

'I don't think you're useless.'

'I think I'm useless. You just remind me how useless.'

'That's not my fault, Adam.'

'Well, shit, I'm sorry. I can't imagine how awful this is for you.'

'You don't need to be sarcastic. Or an arsehole. It's not my fault. I can see you're struggling, I can help if you—'

'I don't want your help!' Adam continued his walk back towards the path. 'This was a mistake.'

Maddie watched him go. She recognised someone who was angry at her mere presence. She knew there was nothing she could say that would make it any better, not while his biggest fight was with himself. She found the flat of the rock to sit on and focused on the burbling water, her one constant, her one place of calm. Suddenly it seemed like anything but.

* * *

'That damned doorbell!' Vince spat shower water as he leaned out. He tried to listen for anything other than the sound of the water. For a moment, he considered that he hadn't heard it all, that he was being oversensitive listening out for his nephew. Then the bell chimed again.

'She knew I was getting in the shower,' he mumbled. His sister must have forgotten something. She could have just texted him. No doubt this was her way of making sure his shower was cut short.

The water sound changed from a blur of noise to a fast drip as he spun the tap to turn it off. He reached for a towel and wrapped it around his waist. The heavy mist in the room was sucked out the door as he leaned out of it.

'Sammy!' he yelled. 'Sammy?'

There was no reply. Vince cussed again. Then he heard the distinctive scrape of the internal porch door. From there, it was two paces to the front door.

'Sammy! *Don't open the door, Sammy!*' Too late. Vince was on the top of the stairs when he heard the sound of the street leaking in from outside. The front door was open.

'*Sammy?*' he yelled. There was no reply. He bundled down the stairs, his left hand gripping the towel. His wet feet reached the turn in the stairs from where there was an elevated view down to the front door — to where he could see Sammy.

He was facing out towards the street, towards where Vince could just see that the light was brighter. Vince couldn't see the front door from his angle, but he could see his nephew's stance. Even from behind, he looked frozen to the spot. He managed a step backwards but it was a part stumble. Vince was stuck. Moving would mean taking his eye off Sammy for a moment. Staying put kept him out of reach. The breeze that was rushing in from the street turned the water on his back cold. He shivered. There was movement from Sammy. Not his feet — they looked to be stuck in the carpet — but from his arms.

He put his hands up.

CHAPTER 28

He was a boy. Nothing more. Vince moved his own arms but out, not up, as he edged along the carpet. He had made up his mind to throw himself down the last few steps and sprint round to the front door. The sight of the youth at his front door had stopped him dead. He stepped forward to reach for his nephew. He wrapped his arm round Sammy's chest to pull him backwards. He was rough and Sammy stumbled over Vince's bare foot, his shoe scraping over his toes. Vince barely felt it. He pulled Sammy behind him, then pushed his hands out towards the boy at the door, towards the black pistol that was clasped firmly in both his hands, pointing directly at him.

'Be calm,' Vince said. 'I've got a kid here. What's this all about?' Vince stared at the youth. He felt Sammy move. He moved his right arm back to keep him still. He could feel his hair against his forearm and kept enough pressure to hold him against his back. A trickle of water ran from his hair into his eyes. His movement to wipe it away with his free hand was smooth and deliberate. He didn't want to spook the youth on his doorstep. But he did want him to talk. The longer he didn't, the worse it looked for him.

'Y-you're PC Arnold,' the boy said. His voice matched his build: meek and slight, and he had a stutter. He was still holding the weapon, but it looked like it had a slight shake now. Vince had handled firearms and knew they were heavy to hold up for long. The gun looked real to Vince, real enough that he didn't want to assume anything else. He tried not to focus on it. Instead he locked on to the frightened eyes that were looking down its barrel. Vince didn't like frightened. He had dealt with people at the extreme of every human emotion and frightened was always the least predictable.

'Right now, I'm a bloke in a towel. That's all. I'm no threat to you, lad. Don't do something you'll regret for the rest of your life. Talk to me.'

'You handcuffed a man to a railing. He couldn't get away and he was shot dead. His dad is Alexander Mason. He sent someone to kill you. For what you did.'

Vince took a moment, trying to make sense of what he had said. 'There's more to it than that. There's more to understand. And the boy behind me . . . He's seven. He had nothing to do with it.'

'The men who pulled the trigger, who killed Mason's boy . . . They're all dead. Mason did it himself. I know he did. You're the only one left.'

'Okay, then. Well I'm happy they got 'em. They shot my mate, too. He didn't make it. I got no allegiance. I was just a copper doing my job, okay? I didn't know what was going on. I'll tell you about it, I'll tell you all about it if you just stop pointing that thing at me. Put it down, okay? You've got my attention.'

'The man who was sent to kill you . . . He was supposed to have done it by now. Me and Mikey were sent to hurry him up. Mikey's dead.' The boy's voice started to break. His fear was increasing if anything, his unpredictability with it. 'If I go back to Mason, he'll kill me too. Unless . . .'

'I can help. You know what I do. Talk to me about what's happened. Tell me what you know and I can keep you safe. You have my word on that.'

The gun lowered. The boy had been staring straight at him, but he broke away. His eyes seemed to glaze and drift towards the floor. Then all at once he snapped back, the gun back to head height, his chest tensed to take the weight, his finger back on the trigger, his focus back on Vince.

'I can't. The Chicken Sheds, out at Redwall Farm — you know it?'

'What? I, err . . . I mean, yeah, I know it, but—'

'He's been staying there. The Tax Man . . .'

'Tax Man?'

'You won't be able to stop him. He's killed two people already — before Mikey. Strung them up, he said. Stabbed them, too. He wanted the coppers to think they had a serial killer, that it was all random. But it was all about you. You were next. They wouldn't look at Mason if they thought they had a serial killer. The things they say about him . . . Once he has you as a target, he gets you. That's why they call him the Tax Man. A killer for hire and he loves it. It's not you anymore.'

'What's not me?' The boy wasn't making much sense to Vince. He seemed to be getting more animated with every word.

'His target. He talked about a Plan B. He was proper excited! I don't know what he means. I don't want to know! But now he knows me, he knows my *address!* You're the cops — you have to stop him. He killed Mikey . . .'

The lad took a step back, his eyes wide with fear, his finger covering the trigger. Vince took a step closer while he pushed Sammy further back behind him.

'*Stop!* I have to hide! You can't help me. If you come after me, I'll have to shoot you . . . And then the kid'll be a witness. Don't make me do it!' His voice was pleading, enough for Vince to believe he might. The boy was edging backwards. Vince was almost close enough to slam the front door. He watched as the boy edged away. The gun was firm in his grasp. The boy seemed to hesitate. He had more to say.

'Whatever this Plan B is, it's soon. You have to get to him!'

'Who is he?' Vince demanded.

The only response from the boy was to raise the gun higher as a warning. He continued backing away.

'Sammy — run to the back of the house,' Vince hissed. 'Do it now! Go!' There was a delay, then he heard the footsteps that told him his instructions were being followed. He didn't take his eyes off the boy in front of him, who got to the end of the path and broke into a sprint. Vince leapt out of his front door and up his garden path. The running lad swerved into the middle of the road as he made for the general direction of the town, away from the sea. Vince flicked to his open door, then back to the figure getting more distant with every passing moment. He could see the outline of the weapon still in his hand. He wanted to follow. He could hang back, see where he went, maybe get a linked vehicle or sight of him entering an address. But Sammy was his priority now. Maybe this was just a ruse to get him out of the house? He looked down at his bare torso and beyond to his feet. He certainly wouldn't be chasing anyone down wrapped in a towel.

He jogged back into the house and snatched up his phone. The first call was 999. The second was to DS Maddie Ives.

CHAPTER 29

Maddie leaned forward, her back tense, her grip firm on the grab handle above the passenger door. She suddenly realised her back was stiff where she hadn't changed position the whole journey.

Firearms would be leading the assault on the Chicken Sheds. She had researched the full address to be on Redwall Lane, Deal. The moment Vince had reported a handgun, there had been no other choice. It had worked out for her. A spontaneous firearms operation took time to get together. The delay had meant she could get into work and then out to Deal. Adam had removed the necessity to make up any excuses for her sudden dash back into work when he walked away from her. He had kept walking, too. She had seen him from a distance when she had broken into a jog towards her home while still on the phone to Vince. She considered going after Adam, taking a minute out of her day to catch him up. Maybe she could have made an arrangement to see him again, to try this all again now that she could understand his situation and it could go better. But it had been a fleeting idea, which she had dismissed before it had even properly formed. She needed to get to work. She didn't want to waste a minute.

She had met up with Harry in a small police station that was still in use in the centre of Deal. Firearms had convened there, too. The investigators had needed to take a back seat as the talk had switched to tactics. Maddie hid her frustration badly at the amount of time this part took. If their man was up there — if he was at the address — he might not be for long. Harry needed to remind her twice of what was at stake, of how they needed to prepare for the worst. He was right, of course. A couple of local officers were also present at the briefing and they knew the address. There was general incredulity that they were now in use as dwellings but nothing of any use. Their input only added to Maddie's frustration.

She had done her own background checks on the address. There were six dwellings that came under the banner of the Chicken Sheds and any number of people associated with them. Most had records for petty crime. The Chicken Sheds seemed to be a place where the council housed their problem individuals from the town, but none of them seemed to stay there for long. Most of the associated people had new home addresses. There was one exception: Gavin Walker. The police system held a record of a spot check by a PCSO checking on his welfare after a concerned local called to report someone laid out on a bench on the promenade on a particularly frozen morning. He had given the Chicken Sheds as his home address. The report didn't cover why he wasn't at his home at six a.m. in minus three degrees. The spot check was dated the previous winter. They had no idea if this address was current.

At last, they had streamed out of the speed gates at Deal police station in a convoy of marked cars. Maddie and Harry were in a police van with the tactical team. The atmosphere was tense. Initially, there had been excited chatter as the six officers in the back discussed their roles between them, but that had quickly run out. Now they were just a minute away and the only sound from the rear was the last-minute tightening of Velcro pads and the click of helmet straps. The scenery on the right opened up as fields. This was their final approach.

When the sergeant's voice broke the silence, there was clear tension in it. 'Target is that building on the left. Firearms go first. We de-bus but we stay with the van until we're called forward. Everyone understand?'

Confirmations bounced around the interior. Maddie stared ahead. The road had a gentle gradient down to the Chicken Sheds from here. They were just as she had seen on Google Earth. The steep banks dropped away to be flat to the road by the time they were opposite. The target was a long, slim building with high walls jutting out to meet with the road. With no idea which of the properties they needed to focus on, firearms planned to go door-to-door. As with any firearms deployment, a silver commander had been assigned. Today being a Saturday, this was a chief inspector plucked from doing something else who was suddenly asked to remotely manage the risk of an armed team and an unknown number of civilians. Overkill was always likely and, sure enough, he had insisted that every dwelling was to be entered and every person turfed out. Doors that were not answered were to be put in by the team sitting behind Maddie. The approach was to be with weapons drawn and ballistic shields. The firearms sergeant was assigned bronze commander, and he would take the lead on the ground. His vehicle sped past them now to signal the start.

Three firearms vehicles passed in total. The front one sprinted to the far end of the row, the next positioned itself in the middle and the last pulled up just in front of the van. Maddie was aware that a pair of riflemen had been sent to cover the back. In the van, someone pulled the handle on the side door so the team could spill out. Maddie stayed in her seat. Her view from the front was good.

The doors to the cars ahead swung open the moment they stopped. Two officers spilled out of each car, the doors staying open. They emerged with weapons part-raised, a ballistic shield plucked from the rear seat by one of each of the pairs. Six men to approach a multi-occupancy building of this size didn't feel like enough, but firearms were stretched. Most of their resources were out conducting an area search for the armed teenager in the area of Vince's home address.

Maddie had voiced a different tactic for the assault — a quiet approach. She had proposed that she and Harry, as plain-clothed detectives, knocked the doors and peered in through the windows with the armed team sitting up around the corner. She had been ignored — of course she had. It would be a brave commander sending unarmed detectives to what was technically a firearms incident. Now they were here, she was back to thinking that her idea might have been a better one if they wanted to avoid an escalation. If there was an armed offender in any of those dwellings, he would now be in no doubt that they were here for him and he might see only one way out.

The officers moved quickly. Six dwellings, two for each pair, the knocks staggered so a second pair could provide cover from the road. They saw something of interest early. The break to their pattern was obvious. Maddie reckoned their focus was on the third property — in the address linked to Gavin Walker.

Two members of the tactical team sprinted forward in response to a raised arm signal. The lead officer was carrying a red steel battering ram for the door. It went in almost instantly. The two officers who had forced entry leapt back as four of the six firearms officers filed in.

Maddie got out of the vehicle. Considering the major police operation that was unfolding in front of her, she was caught out by the tranquillity of the country lane in the hour leading to dusk. The tranquillity was not to last. The birdsong was interrupted by urgent yells.

'*Contact! Contact!*' She felt herself moving forward. The rest of the tactical team moved with her. They had found someone. The two officers who had forced entry got sucked into the building and went out of sight. The officer in front raised his arm to stop their advance until there was an update.

Maddie twisted the bezel on her radio to turn it up. A beep told her it was on maximum volume already. She exchanged a glance with Harry, fighting with herself not to move forward, her back aching with the tension, waiting for the gunshot that now felt inevitable.

It seemed like an age. Then an officer reappeared. He had a ballistic helmet under his arm and sergeant stripes on his shoulders — the bronze commander. He was pulling at his balaclava. The tension lifted in an instant. They all walked towards him.

'You'd better come take a look, boss.' The sergeant spoke directly to Harry as soon as he was close enough. Harry set off at a pace, Maddie right beside him.

The Chicken Sheds seemed to get smaller as they got closer — slimmer, certainly. The front door to number three was wide open. The first thing to hit Maddie was the smell. The light was poor and it took a moment for her eyes to adjust and work out what was going on. Then the scene started to look familiar.

A male was suspended from the living room ceiling. He was side-on, the leg closest to her a dark shade of crimson, his face lifted upwards slightly by a slim wire caught round his neck. Further into the room and crumpled in a doorway was another body, another adult male. He lay on his side, his eyes peering back at her from under wisps of hair that had fallen over his face. He had an unkempt beard and his clothing looked to be in keeping with his surroundings. He matched the description she had read of Gavin Walker. There was an overwhelming smell of damp mingling with the oppressive stillness that always seemed to accompany the early stages of death. Maddie didn't think they had been here long.

'There's no sign of life. I've called an ambulance to confirm life extinct.'

'Okay.' Harry's reply was calm, any sign of surprise at finding two dead bodies well-hidden. His hands remained pushed into the pockets of his waxed jacket, suggesting he was in no doubt that any life in these two men was long extinct. 'We need to get everyone out,' he said.

'Yeah, I get that. My lads have conducted a prelim search but only for persons. These two are it for this dwelling.'

'Did you finish the others?'

'Three out of the six. You could see through the window what we had here. We'll finish the other three, but I think we've found what we were going to. I suggest you free up a couple of my patrols to do an area search, see if we've got anyone in the area who might stand out as having moved away from it quickly. We should cover the area between here and PC Arnold's place. Did you see this?' The sergeant stepped towards the body that was suspended upright. He pointed with his little finger at the left thigh. 'Gunshot wound.'

Harry leaned in. Maddie was just behind him. 'Okay,' Harry said again.

'Looks like small arms. The sort of thing PC Arnold described as being pointed at him. I'll update the silver.'

'Good. Then send two of your cars out for the manhunt. Just leave us one out front and the rifles at the back for another half an hour or so, just in case someone returns or is flushed out from another property. I'll keep the tactical team for the door knocks — no need to keep you all here.'

'Okay, thanks,' the sergeant replied.

'You okay down there?'

Maddie had been half-listening. Harry's question was directed towards her and she focused on him. She was squatting down under the front window, her head against a long radiator. When she looked up, the firearms sergeant was shuffling out of the room.

'The winch.' She pointed to a silver metal handle tipped with orange plastic. The wire ran through it, then rose up to a steel loop drilled into the ceiling. The tension in the wire suspended the winch a few inches from the floor.

Harry moved so he could see it. 'This is all looking very familiar, isn't it?' His voice came over the sound of a number of heavy boots leaving the room as they followed their skipper.

'The third winch, Harry.' Maddie got back to her feet. 'One more to go.'

* * *

Robbie was beginning to think he had been duped, lied to, despite doing exactly what had been asked of him.

Mikey's phone had been left where Lance had said it would be, the security removed so he could access it — specifically the GPS tracking app that Mikey must have been using all along. It was a simple mapping app with a pulsing blue circle that he was now right on top of. He lifted his head to look around again. He was on a road packed with cars in central Deal. They stretched out in front of him on both sides of the road, bumper to bumper, packed as tightly as the houses that overlooked them. Lance had told him the GPS would get him close enough for the car to be obvious. He had walked one side on the pavement. Now he was walking back down the other. Something caught his eye. One of the cars on his right side, maybe twenty vehicles up, had a bright yellow blur on its front wheel with a black smudge in its centre. When he got closer he could see the smudge spelt out four letters: *DVLA*.

He reached in his pocket for the key he had been given. He moved to the back. The key caught on his pocket and clanged onto the ground. He took a deep breath to compose himself then bent to pick it up. He made himself pause again, using the time to take in his environment. Dusk was not far away and was being hurried along by the thickening cloud cover. He had ducked away from at least three marked police cars that had flooded the area since he had left PC Arnold's house. It was to be expected — Lance had told him as much — but then, Lance had told him a lot. He had come back from his morning outing talking fast and excited. He had said that there was an opportunity, something had come up and that Robbie could choose to help him or not. In reality, he'd had no choice at all. Robbie's spirit was sapped. His wrists burned with the pain of edging along the pipe, only to find that it dipped into the floorboards and continued out of sight. There had been no end. He had been trapped. He had edged all the way back, shooed a brazen mouse who had taken nibbles out of the discarded toast and wept. Then he had waited. His weight had been pushing through his knees and elbows to add to his discomfort.

Lance had set him free. Then he had told him he could go back to Mr Mason and explain that they had failed, that Mikey had got himself killed and that Vince Arnold was still breathing and see what sort of response he got. He didn't fancy that. He already knew how that would end. The other option had caught him out. Lance had told him to go to Arnold's house, watch for a girl to drop off a kid and then count to one hundred. Then he was to knock on the door, point the gun at the big lad inside and tell him what he knew. And when he was done, Mason's money — the money Lance had been paid for completing the job — it would be his, to just drive away with.

Despite the incredible offer, Robbie had never doubted that he was serious. Lance was excited, talking so fast that Robbie had struggled to keep up. He'd seemed to be delighted with himself, telling Robbie everything. It all came out as a rant, about how he dotted battered old cars around to use as storage when he was working a new area. He would buy a few old cars with cash — cars no one wanted anymore. He said no one looked twice at the old, beaten-up things in life.

Then he had talked about the money. Lance said that he had returned the tracker, that he would find the car with the money in it by following the GPS to the right street. The car would stand out due to the DVLA clamp attached to the wheel. He said it served a purpose, making it even less likely that anyone would take any notice. But it was clear that he liked the irony, too, that it was all part of his game.

Robbie had been excited himself at first, swept up by Lance, by the thought of a sudden fortune. But now he was wary. Now he was at the point where he would be driving the money away — assuming it was even here. It seemed to go against everything Robbie understood about the world. He half-expected Lance to emerge from the shadows to claim his bounty and to tie up his loose end.

Robbie recognised the Volkswagen badge on the back, despite the fact that most of the W was missing to reveal the black rubber behind. It also had the word *Bora*, which he assumed to be the model of the car. It wasn't one he had heard of. It was a saloon car with rust around the wheel trims. The seals along the doors carried a good layer of moss and the windows looked to be as damp on the inside as they were on the outside. The paintwork was faded, scarred and scratched all at the same time — just as Lance had described.

He slid the key into the boot lock. It didn't move. There was no button for central locking and the lock was difficult to find. He bent to an awkward position to try again. Still it wouldn't move. There was a silver button next to the lock. He pushed it in. The boot clicked.

'Wasn't even locked!' Robbie shook his head. He straightened up and cast another look over the roof of the car and then behind him to be sure no one was close. The road was steady with traffic. A few people had passed on foot, too, but no one was taking any notice of him. After the night he had experienced, he was just a beaten-up bloke standing next to his beaten-up car. Satisfied, he lifted the boot door. The bags he recognised as the ones he had dropped on the floor of the car park in Canterbury were both there. Lance said he had dipped into the money a couple of times for a few expenses, but most of it was left. Robbie held his breath as he tugged at the zip of the first bag. The air came rushing back out in a long sigh that ended with an excited whimper when the bag fell open. He plunged his hand in, dragging his fingers over the neatly stacked wads, pushing them around to see how deep they went, to check it really was all piles of banknotes, right to the bottom. He did the same with the second bag. It didn't look like anything was missing at all.

'Holy shit! I'm rich!' He spoke quietly, resisting the urge to bellow the words at the top of his voice. He had never been told the fee, he'd had no idea what someone like the Tax Man might command for taking out a copper, but he had assumed it to be a lot. He still didn't know how much was in there — it had to be hundreds of thousands! He slammed the boot shut and rested his fingers on the top. Suddenly his confidence about how he was blending in evaporated and he felt like he was standing out like a sore thumb for everyone he could see, all ready to wrestle the contents of the boot from him. He couldn't let that happen. After what he had been through, he deserved it. Every penny.

He made sure the boot was locked. There was a smaller key on the same loop as the car key. Lance had told him it would fit the clamp on the wheel. It did. It was fiddly, but it came away. He threw it on the back seat. The engine fired first time. His eye was drawn to the rearview mirror, where white smoke rose up from the exhaust. It was gone after a few seconds.

'Just had to clear your throat, old girl!' He was cheery as he patted the top of the steering wheel, then rolled out of the space to accelerate away. When he got to the next junction, he angled the car to take a left. A car passed across the front of him — it was a marked police car. The two coppers inside looked to be in deep conversation, their focus on each other and not out the windows. They were moving right to left. Robbie tugged at the wheel to turn the car right. The saloon gave another puff of white smoke as he changed gear and picked up speed. When it cleared, he could see the rear of the police car in his mirror. It was moving away with no signs of brake lights, deviation or spinning round.

He would need to take the long way now, but that wasn't a problem. Lance had asked him for one final task before he was done. Then he was free to take his money anywhere he wanted.

He patted the steering wheel again. The excited giggle that fell from his mouth was totally involuntary. Now he was starting to believe.

CHAPTER 30

Harry pushed his phone roughly into his pocket, then rubbed at his chin. His eyes lost focus as if his mind was elsewhere.

'Bad news?' Maddie asked.

'No good news. Area search can find no trace of Vince's gunman. He was it. The last link to anything.'

'We've got other lines of enquiry.'

'You know what I mean.'

She did. Finding that boy and getting him in custody had been their best chance of making major advances quickly. Otherwise, they were falling back to the same slow enquiries: CSI swabs, fingertip searches, CCTV reviews and hoping someone saw something relevant. Judging by the remote location of Redwall Farm and its surroundings, Maddie didn't think that was likely.

'Are we still monitoring the main roads in and out? He might turn up.'

Harry shook his head. 'They were never set up. Silver command figured he was seen on foot and road checks would be a waste of resource. He wanted mobile patrols instead. It could be the right call. That's the thing . . . We know nothing about this kid.'

'Or the bloke he was referring to.'

'Assuming there is one.'

'You don't think there is? Vince was pretty convinced. He didn't think he was lying. He said he was terrified, too. Doesn't sound like he could be capable of the things we've seen. It just feels like we know nothing about this, full stop. If he had gone after Vince . . . We were a long way from stopping him, Harry. I keep thinking that.'

'It's crossed my mind. We're a few steps behind, but Vince is okay. He's safe now. There'll be time for reflection on what could have been when this threat is behind bars.'

'Whether that's before or after he does what he has planned with that last winch.'

'There are answers here. It's a crime scene. There always are. We process it like any other. We're closer than we were.'

Maddie didn't feel it. They were standing out the front of the Chicken Sheds. She had her back against the wall. Harry leaned on the doorframe. He kept glancing back in as if he was checking the two bodies hadn't stood up and made off out the back. They had made a cursory search, despite Charley being on her way and calling ahead to make it clear that no one should do anything with the room until CSI had done initial photos and swabs. Nothing obvious was standing out. The place was a hovel, typical of the sort occupied by a drinker who didn't have the will or the ability to look after it anymore. Maddie intended on going back in there for another poke around, but the smell and feel of the place was so oppressive that she had needed a break for a gulp of fresh air. They were losing the daylight fast. The cloud cover was enough to block the sun, but not completely — it was still able to outline the clouds in blood red above the fields in front.

'He could have stood out there in the distance and watched the whole thing. Us, I mean.' Maddie said, voicing a thought that had suddenly come to her mind.

'Who could?'

'Our offender. We know he likes to be involved. He could have been out at that treeline. Laughing at us again.'

'If he has any sense, he will be long gone.'

'What about the other scenes? He waited for us there.'

'This seems different. Those were staged, carefully planned. This feels more reactive — rushed even — Walker could have disturbed him. And I don't get the impression that anyone would have been coming up here to find what he's done for some time, if at all. It's that sort of place.'

'We did, though,' Maddie said. She felt her phone vibrate in her pocket. The screen showed a stream of numbers with no name attached.

'Hello?'

'Maddie.' The voice made her push off the wall to stand straight. She walked out into the road, carrying on away from the building until she was sure she was out of earshot.

'Adam,' she breathed back.

'Hey, this a good time?'

'Always a good time!' she lied.

'About that . . . I just wanted to call and say sorry. I was a shit earlier. I can't just turn up out of nowhere and demand you all to myself. I should know better. I did once.'

'It's fine. It's not a problem. You got angry. It didn't seem to make sense to me.'

'I did. I get angry easily. The doc said it can happen with knocks to the head, but I got a lot of frustration, too. I know what I am now. I'm getting there. Don't get me wrong, but I miss the simple things and it makes me angry.'

'Simple things?'

'Just buttoning up my own shirt would be a start! I wasn't entirely honest with you. I brought someone down with me, one of the medical team. One of the physios. I've been working with her a long time, someone I trust. Otherwise it wouldn't even have been possible. Maybe it was too early.'

'Someone you . . . Did you tell her about me?' Maddie's question was rushed, her tone suddenly serious.

'I told her why I was coming down. She had questions.'

'What did you tell her?'

'Nothing. Nothing for you to worry about. I'm not stupid — I still remember all that you told me! I gave her some flannel about being an old flame I knew from school. I said you had moved down here and we were sort of seeing each other before the accident.'

'Did she ask why I hadn't come up to see you all the time you were recovering? What if she asks your mum about me? Your sister, or worse, Adam, what if she asks your *brother*?'

'What would she ask? Calm down, Maddie. Worst case, she asks my ma what she knows about a girlfriend down on the coast. My mum knows nothing and I fob her off. Job done. And my brother's out in Spain — I told you that. I don't speak to him anymore.'

'It doesn't sound ideal, Adam . . .'

'Ideal? What do you mean *ideal*? It was the only way I could possibly do a couple of days away. I don't think you understand what this is to me. You're only upset because you can't control this and I've had enough of people controlling me.'

'Control? You think this is about controlling you? If that bothered me in the slightest, I'd have been gone a long time ago. I never knew your movements from one day to the next — never have done. And I never complained. I never felt like I could.'

'Look, I didn't call to argue with you, I called to say sorry for arguing with you before! For getting angry like that. That isn't me.'

'I've never known you to apologise either — there's something really fishy going on here!' Maddie's laughter was strained. This was out of character. All of it. He was different. She preferred the aloof version of Adam. The one she knew nothing about, who didn't ask anything about her but who gave her absolute confidence that he wasn't breathing a word to anyone about their relationship. If any associates of Adam were to find out that all the time she spent among them, she had been working undercover for the police, they would think nothing of extreme violence. And they wouldn't care that it was in the past, that she had changed roles and moved some distance away. Organised crime gangs survived on reputation, on keeping face. They kept that at all costs. Her concern far outweighed the pang of guilt she felt about caring more about that than Adam's welfare. Of course he was different. After what happened to him, it wasn't fair that she should expect him to be the same person, to just pick back up where they had finished.

'Maybe the bang on the head brought with it some improvements.' Adam's laughter was just as strained. It was all strained.

'Maybe.'

'You don't sound so sure. I tell you what . . . Let me make it up to you. Can you do dinner tonight?'

Maddie turned back to face the Chicken Sheds, her attention lifting from the phone to where she had left Harry. He was now out of sight and, somehow, someone had managed to sneak a small van right outside while she'd been engrossed in her conversation. CSI had arrived. She cussed under her breath. She knew Harry would already be briefing Charley — she should be in there.

'I'm not sure I'm going to be around this evening. I had to go into work in the end . . .' Maddie left that sentence hanging. She had been going to explain, then she had been going to apologise. In the end, she did neither.

'Oh . . . You actually went into work? I thought it was just a phone call?' Maddie didn't have a reply. She was walking quicker now, her mind back on the job in front of her. 'I was planning on staying one more night anyway. How about you let me take you to breakfast in the morning? That place just down from you?'

Maddie knew she was going to be back to work in the morning, maybe even still there from the night before. There was no way she could commit to a social breakfast. And even if she could, she didn't want to.

'I'm . . . I'll be working in the morning. We've had some major developments. This was a shitty weekend to come down! I guess it works like that sometimes. I'm really sorry. How about we sort another one and I'll put in for leave either side. That way, we'll get a long weekend and I can't be pulled back into all this!' She forced a chuckle again but she was gritting her teeth for the reply. It was instant and it was angry.

'You'll always be pulled into that.'

Maddie reeled. 'Some of what I do is important.' It was all she could manage.

'You mean unlike me?'

'No. That isn't what I meant.'

'Would you come back with me? Would you ever consider that we could be together? Where is this going, Maddie?'

'Going?' Maddie was struggling for what to say. Adam had never been a man who was concerned about where anything was *going*, let alone a relationship. It had frustrated her at first, the never knowing where she stood, when she might see him again, even. But she had come to like it, to rely on it almost. It fitted in with her life. When the stars aligned, they would spend some time together and it would be amazing. For the rest of the time, she was free to do what she wanted.

'You don't even want me talking about you. You don't want to spend time with me when I come down, your work rules your life . . .'

'What would you have me do?'

'Would you come with me? I have a place. We can have a life.'

'No.' Maddie's reply was instant. Had she taken a moment, she might have softened it but she would not have changed it. Her mind ran with different reasons, different explanations, but she couldn't get any of them in order. Instead, Adam spoke.

'The truth. At least I can say that the trip down here wasn't wasted.'

'You can't just turn up and ask me that, to choose to up and leave everything to be with you. It isn't fair.'

'You mean I can't just turn up like this? Weak, hardly able to lift my arms. We talked about it before. I thought it was what you wanted. But I guess that was when I was stronger, when I was worthy of you.'

'That isn't what I meant at all, and you know it. I've built a life down here, a job I love.'

'Love!' Adam spat the word back at her. 'That's your reason for staying? Because you have found something you love?'

Maddie could feel herself getting angry. Everything she was saying was being thrown back at her. She was done with being reasonable.

'Go home, Adam. Don't come back unannounced again. I can't promise I'll be happy to see you.' She ended the call. Instantly, she had a flash of regret, but that was all it was. She needed to focus. Nothing was more important than her work, not right now, and she couldn't focus with him around. If there was still anything left of the Adam she remembered, she knew he wouldn't stick around after that.

When she got back to the front door to number three, Harry was coming out of it.

'Sorry about that,' she said. 'Phone call.' If Harry picked up that she was rattled from the call, he didn't mention it.

'Charley's making a start. She's going to do what she can tonight, but it won't be much. She's talking about just doing an assessment for the morning when she might have some help. We're not getting any answers anytime soon. We might as well head back.'

'To the nick?'

'Yes. I want to see what we've got overall. We'll need priorities for the morning. Is Rhiannon still in Bristol?'

'I haven't heard back from her, actually. She should be heading back soon.'

'Ask her to stay there. I want to go through everything we know tonight before we go off duty. Some enquiries might come out of it where she is.'

'Okay. I told her we couldn't put her up. I didn't think there would be budget.'

'Four murders, Maddie. I don't think we need to worry about budget anymore.'

He moved towards two marked cars. Maddie could see two officers in the first one. They looked bored. Harry waved and the officer in the passenger seat gestured with the scene log. Harry tugged open the driver's door to the marked car behind. A patrol that had assisted with door-to-door enquiries had left it for them to use after the tactical team had left in their van. It jogged Maddie's memory.

'Did you get an update from the house-to-house?'

'Yes. Nothing. There's some druggie a few doors up and the rest are empty. He was out of it. The patrol reckons he spends his whole life in that state. He's not going to be any use.'

'Still feels like we're at square one, Harry.' Maddie slid into the passenger seat. She had to move a fleece top and a ticket folder onto the back seat from the previous occupants.

'We go back and review what we have. We know a lot more than we did. We just need to put it together, work out what to focus on.' He pushed his phone into a cradle on the dash. It beeped to confirm it had paired with the car. Maddie peered out of the window. Darkness was setting in.

'What do we have?' Maddie sighed. Her reflection peered back from the glass. 'We have a man who we can be sure is an experienced killer, who is changing his appearance, staying at places where we may never detect a trace, leaves nothing obvious behind and is clearly enjoying his work. White male, around sixty, may have been in the Bristol area in the last few months, hired by a gangland boss who's, shall we say, averse to assisting police with their enquiries, seeing as he blames us for the recent death of his son. That's if we could even find him. That's my summary. Feel free to add anything in.' Harry didn't reply. She hadn't expected him to. She was thinking out loud, to herself almost. She continued even quieter. 'Among all of that, Harry, which bit needs to be our *focus*? Which bit stops him carrying out whatever the hell he meant by—'

The sound of a ringing tone erupted through the speakers. Maddie turned to it momentarily, to where *MELISSA*

MOB appeared on the screen. Harry seemed to hesitate. Maddie looked across at him until he pressed to answer the call. She turned back to look out of the window. Her reflection appeared and faded as they passed street lights.

'You're on speaker, Melissa. I'm just driving.'

'Okay, thanks for telling me, otherwise I might have got all sweary!' The voice was chirpy. Maddie couldn't help but smile. It was such a contrast to her father.

'Everything okay? I'm going to be late home.'

'Of course you are! You weren't even supposed to be working today. I told you, didn't I?'

'You did.'

'At least we got our walk in. I'm still full, but I will do something in a bit. Did you want me to leave you some dinner in the oven?'

'Oh . . . No, don't worry. I'll get something here.'

'It'll be better than last night. I know what I did wrong.'

'No, its fine. Last night was fine. I might be very late here so I'll have to get something. What did you call for?'

Maddie looked over at him, she was humoured and trying to catch his eye. He kept looking forward.

'What do you mean? I got your message! You're going to be late off and to give you a call. Then I thought I would ask about dinner.'

'Message?'

'Yeah. Someone came round to tell me you were held up and to call you.'

'Who?'

'No one I know. A copper, I suppose.'

'Did he say he was a copper?'

'He didn't say much! You okay, Dad? Why so serious? Some bloke knocked on the door and said you would be late off. Then he just left. I assumed you'd sent him.'

'What did he look like?' Harry snapped.

'Look like? Jeez . . . It was just some old bloke. Ponytail. Bit messy. I thought he was going to ask me for money to start with!'

Harry stiffened in his seat. Maddie did, too.

'And he left?' Harry said.

'Yeah . . . Hang on, he's coming back up the drive now. I can ask him who he—'

'*Don't answer it!*' Harry's voice was raised and strong. He came back quieter, his tone reassuring. 'Honey, don't answer the door. Stay at the back of the house. I'm sending a patrol round and I'll be just behind them. Is the door locked?'

'Locked? What's the matter?' There was fear in her voice.

'Nothing. It's probably nothing. Where is he now?'

'He was walking towards the front door. I've lost him. I'm at the front window, I can't see the door from here.'

'Did he see you?'

'I'm standing at the window! It's the only place I can get reception — you know that!'

Harry cussed again. The car slowed while he was thinking.

'Go to the back of the house. Someone will be with you in a few minutes. Stay on the phone with me. I'll have Maddie here call it in.' Maddie was already scrabbling with her radio. It was in her bag, the aerial caught as she lifted it out and it fell into the footwell. She scooped it back up.

'Okay, but I don't get reception anywhere else. It's your fault for living in the arse end of nowhere!'

'The landline. Get the home phone and take that with you. Call me straight back on it.'

'I don't even know where it is!'

'On top of the speaker. Right behind you. Do it now, Melissa!' Harry had cut over her. Maddie heard her huff, then start to speak. The call cut. She must have lost reception. The silence was instant.

Maddie stared over at Harry. The car was rolling slowly forward, veering to the left. Someone overtook and gave a toot of their horn. Harry didn't seem to notice. He was gripping the steering wheel tightly with both hands, his eyes looked glazed as they stared forward. Ten seconds passed, then ten more. Melissa should have called back by now.

Harry must have thought the same. He jabbed at his phone again. The speakers filled with a dialling tone this time. The number selected was labelled *HOME*. It rang until an automated voice cut in. Harry was back on his phone. Maddie watched as he tried Melissa's mobile again. The car swerved untidily into a raised kerb and came to a stop in the silence between dialling and connecting. The speakers announced: '*The number you are dialling is not available.*' It cut out.

Harry sat back as if he was frozen in time. Maddie was in the same state, her police radio in one hand, her mobile in the other. Harry's phone beeped. His whole body twitched like he had been jabbed in the side. He had a text message. It was labelled as coming from *MELISSA MOB*. He opened it. Maddie could see it as clear as he did . . .

PLAN B.

Harry wrapped his hands back around the steering wheel. He pressed a panel and the blackness of the evening was fragmented with a frigid blue. The siren wailed.

* * *

Robbie couldn't wait any longer. He wanted to be a long way from here. He had parked as per Lance's instructions in a farmer's yard with an elevated view across a muddy field to the front door of the house he had left a few hours before. It was the focus of a lot of police activity. There had been police cars and even a police van outside when he had arrived, but their attention had been all on that house and he'd had no concerns about bumping up on an area of flattened mud in his battered old saloon. He had fitted in among the broken-down farm machinery behind an abandoned horsebox that had an even thicker layer of moss on it than his car had.

The police activity was constant. He had watched as cars had arrived, their occupants alighting to knock on surrounding doors or walk out into the field opposite. A couple in plain clothes had walked right past him to the farmhouse that was further down the track. He had ducked down in his seat but even that had probably been unnecessary. They had passed at a distance. They seemed to be chatting — laughing even — with no concern of what might be near them.

Then dusk came. His confidence had increased as the light had slipped away. He'd been sitting up straight, gazing across the field, watching the whole time as the police activity dwindled. A CSI van had been the last to arrive and looked to be parked up for the night. From his reckoning, there were four officers left. Two were in uniform, sitting in a car out the front. They stepped out of their car and wrote something down whenever someone arrived or left. The other two were the plain clothes officers he had seen earlier in the bright daylight. They seemed to move together: if one went in the house, both did. The same when they reappeared back out the front. The only exception was when the woman had walked away with a phone to her ear. Robbie had known straight away that they were the reason he was here. They were just as Lance had described: the woman with long, dark hair, the older man with a dark, waxed jacket that hung open over broad shoulders.

Robbie did as he was told. He'd watched until the man and woman got into a police car and pulled away. Then he'd made the call. He had said three words: *'They just left.'* That was it. The phone had gone dead instantly and Robbie was left to assume that he was finished.

He was supposed to wait fifteen minutes. It had been almost five and he couldn't see the point of waiting any longer. He could see the house but not much around it. Light from the inside leaked out of the front window. He couldn't shift the image of Mikey. He had been left under the main ceiling light and he hadn't seen anyone remove him. He could still be there. Robbie didn't want to think about that anymore. He didn't want to think about anything. He considered that he might go and find a nice hotel — somewhere distant. Then he would have a long bath and a longer drink.

Lance had given him some tips on how to disappear. And he intended on doing just that.

CHAPTER 31

Harry killed the lights and they slowed, despite being some way out. The A256 ahead of them was a black strip washed in artificial white with darkness either side, but the tall lights now drifted past them rather blurring as they had a few moments earlier. Maddie had driven this way to Harry's home before. She remembered the large, white house that was lit up across a small field on her left. A roundabout came into view in the distance. From there, it was a right turn and then a twisty road through fields and past an industrial estate until the houses started. Harry's was the third or fourth on the left after entering the village of Eythorne. It was probably two miles further in total, far too early to be slowing down.

'Are we easing off?' Maddie said.

The journey had been in complete silence, Maddie letting Harry concentrate on his driving. It had been every bit as frenetic as she would have expected to start with — verging on scary. She hadn't said a word, of course, just clung onto the handle on her door with a silent wince when they had come close to other traffic while pushing their way out of Deal.

There were other response cars making their way there. Maddie had put out the call over the radio and the silver commander had been quick to call up and divert just about everything he had. He was insistent that firearms be the first patrol to approach the house. Harry had made no reply. Maddie had acknowledged the instruction but said nothing more. The A256 was the most direct route from Deal to Eythorne. The firearms cars that had been in the town had popped out at various points on the same stretch of road. She could see blue lights ahead and behind. They had been keeping pace with them, but now the lights pulled away, their brake lights mingling with the rear reds on the roof as they slowed for the roundabout. A blue and red blur passed them. She got a glimpse of a questioning look from the passenger. Why was the boss slowing down to let them get ahead on the welfare check on his own daughter?

'Yes.' Harry's growl seemed to fall from his mouth without it moving. His jaw looked clenched, his attention fixed forward. Another car flashed up the outside lane. They were slow enough now to hear the whine of the siren as it approached. The flashing blur then passed them to merge quickly with the horizon. It was as if they were standing still. They made the roundabout and Harry's pace around it was steady. The change of direction pointed them directly at a full moon that had broken from the cover of the clouds. It hung low over flat fields that lay out in front of them and sloped away. From the higher ground, Maddie could see the powerful lights of an industrial estate angled down on a yard full of sleeping lorries. More lights marked the perimeter of a food packing factory. They approached slowly. The roads got narrower and Maddie knew this was where they would enter the village. Suddenly, she was pushed forward in her seat as Harry brought the car to a squealing stop.

'What's going on, Harry?' Maddie snapped.

'When he sends the message . . .' Harry hesitated, his cheek rippled where he was biting down. 'From what we know about him . . . When he sends a message, he's already . . . He knows he has time. We know he plans it like that . . . and he spends time getting to know an area.'

Harry checked over his shoulder and shifted into reverse. The car whined, the urgency back in his driving. He reversed ten metres or so before braking just as roughly. He spun the car to the right. Maddie looked across to a turning that led into woodland. It seemed to have emerged from the shadows now that they were stationary. No way would she have seen it at any speed. Harry gunned the engine and they lurched into it. The headlights ran over thick foliage in the tight turning that almost sent them back on themselves. Down the track were a couple of street lights, but the trees had them wrapped up with leaves and branches, suppressing their reach. From the poor lighting emerged a row of terraced houses on the left and a smattering of cars parked opposite. The closest car on the right was an old black saloon that looked abandoned, rather than parked. Harry pulled in front of it.

'They're calling you on the radio, Harry. They're in position. They're struggling to get to the back, but they have it covered as best they can. They want some direction.'

'There's a silver commander?'

'There is. Seems they're waiting for you to give the word.'

'Full entry. Through the front door. Take it off its hinges.'

'Without you?' Maddie said.

'Tell them to do it *now*.' Harry snapped. He killed the engine and pushed his door open. It shut firmly behind him, leaving Maddie holding her radio in the dark. She spoke into it.

'This is Alpha One, One. From Inspector Blaker . . . Full entry. All officers through the front door. No delay.'

Maddie waited for the silver commander to jump in, to insist that he was running this show, that he gave the orders. Maybe everyone else was waiting for the same. There was a collective silence, then a male voice confirmed the order and barked his own at individual units. The assault had started.

Maddie pushed her door open. Harry was standing out in the middle of the darkened road. The rough tarmac had cut up and become loose.

'What the hell is going on, Harry? Your daughter might be in there—'

'She *is in there!*' Harry's shout caught her out. The anger and emotion behind it was entirely to be expected. Their position, standing out on a darkened track, wasn't. 'You can't get to the back of my house — you can't cover it. It backs onto a wood. There's an old rail line that used to run to the pit — it goes along the back of all the houses. Take a right and there are gardens and fences to get past to go into the village. He won't do that. He'll come out the back and he'll take a left. It's a short path to come out the other side of the road here. The woods run right up to the road. He'll cross over. This is where you would park. He has to have a car. This is right.'

'His car is here?' Maddie ran her eyes over the neat line of maybe ten parked vehicles.

'It is.'

'You know this, do you?'

'*We* know this! We've been following him around, a step behind all the time. He's waiting for *me*, to see what he's done . . . And it *is* done, Maddie. I can't see that. Not again. We both know my Mel . . . It's already too late.' His voice shook with emotion. Maddie had never heard him tremble before. She didn't have a response. Harry was right. She'd known it the whole way but had suppressed it, telling herself instead that there was still hope. Maybe he hadn't got in. Maybe he'd been spooked and had run if he had seen her on the phone . . . *They just needed to get there.*

But she hadn't called back. Why would she not have called back?

Everything they knew about this man told them that Harry's daughter was dead already. And he was right — her killer's getaway would have been meticulously planned. So far, he had demonstrated an incredible ability to be part of the aftermath just long enough to be able to slip away in the confusion he created.

'So what, then? We just stand here and wait? We hope you're right and that—' Maddie stopped dead. The radio interrupted with an anxious voice and the sound of rhythmic thumps in the background.

'*Contact, contact! Female in the living room area. Visible through the front window. She appears . . . She's not moving. A ligature is visible. Medics to stand by please, for when the house is clear.*' The voice was heavy with shock. The sound of smashing glass marked the end of the transmission. It sounded like the door was giving them trouble. The man with the key was unmoving a few paces away from her. The silence that followed seemed more silent than before, the darkness darker — as if someone had thrown a blanket over the pair of them. Harry's head was bent. Maddie stared at him. She had never felt more helpless.

'*Entry gained! Stand by!*' Another update . . . It sounded breathless. Maddie had turned her radio up as far as she could — it came through like a shout.

'Turn that down,' Harry growled. 'We need silence.'

'So we're just standing here waiting?'

'I am. It's a short jog to my house. You know where it is. You should go, you need to manage that scene.'

'Manage the scene? It's your house, Harry . . . It's your . . . I'm not leaving you on your own, Harry. Of course I'm not!'

Harry's head lifted, he stepped towards her, almost into her. '*Fuck off, Maddie!*' he hissed. 'Fuck off, *now*. You go and you don't come back here. Not until I call you, *understand?*' Maddie recoiled. She felt the globules of spit on her cheek. Her eyes were as accustomed to the dark as they were going to get and Harry was little more than an outline. His eyes reflected the lights behind her with two small, silver glints. She had never seen him like this. Every word was like venom. She didn't argue. She stepped round him to make for the road.

* * *

Lance had heard the distant sirens and had almost instantly had to stand up to help with his breathing. He had been crouched behind a bush in the front garden of a neighbouring house that was all in darkness. There had been some lights on at the back when he had checked earlier, but the front of the house was dark and silent with blinds pulled across for the night. They might start twitching soon, with what was coming. He would be long gone by then.

He was burning up already, his excitement peaking. He could see across to the living room window. He just about had the angle for him to see his display. The daughter was in the very centre of the window for anyone approaching straight on. The blinds were pulled right back, the powerful spot lights in the ceiling giving the whole display a backdrop of vivid white. And the police were on their way. More importantly, the boss was on his way! The man they called Harry. It was a work of art. Perfection.

He felt a run of sweat down his forehead. His navy baseball cap suddenly felt heavy. It gripped his head too tightly at the sides to be comfortable and he'd zipped his dark fleece right up to cover his chin so that only a few inches of his face were visible. His 'uniform' would never stand up to inspection, but he wasn't about to be inspected. He was about to mingle with the darkness and confusion, where all eyes would be forward, wide and fixed on what he had done. The sirens were closer. The black of the night suddenly had a blue tint. It got stronger. They were here.

The first car arrived. The drive burst with white light from the headlights but they stopped short. Nothing came onto the drive. He heard doors pushed open and slammed shut. Engines were left ticking over. Another car arrived, and another — maybe even three in convoy. The peaceful village, its occupants having closed their curtains to the world for the night, was suddenly a cacophony of whining sirens and pulsing blue. He backed himself further into the hedge. The white headlights flickered where officers ran across the front of the cars and the first black outlines appeared on the drive. They stopped dead, frozen by what he had done! It took his breath away.

He had to get closer!

He stood up straight and jogged through the darkened garden, stopping just short of the fence line. He could hear excited chatter from where they had moved to the front door: '*Contact, contact!*' someone shrieked. He heard more boots. They passed by him — they were the other side of the hedge. The officer in the lead carried a long, heavy bar. He wore a helmet. They attacked the front door. The sound of smashing glass added to the mayhem that peaked with shouts of '*Police! Police!*'

A number of black figures suddenly funnelled into the house. He moved along the hedge to the end of the drive, to where the lead police car was pulled roughly across the pavement. The front door of the car hung open and a flat police hat was squashed against the dash and the windscreen.

This was where he should walk away. The police were all occupied, their tunnel vision focused on that house. Frantic hands would be trying to cut her down. The brightly lit room would be their whole world for now, as if there was nothing outside in the darkness. Her dad would be in there, his face a shocked mask, locked in a silent scream, begging his daughter to speak to him . . . to be okay . . . anything. He could slip away. Now was the time. But the pull to see that, to watch it through the lit window like a movie theatre, was too strong.

He reached into the car and grabbed the police cap. It was better than the one he had. A better fit, too.

Another car arrived behind him. Two doors popped open, then came the sound of more running boots. They ran past the other side of the car. The officer at the back slowed to stare over at him.

'Medics kit!' he blurted. They kept running, both of them, towards the bright lights of the living room. Lance burned so hot he felt like he might combust there and then. He watched them, waiting for them to go in. The officer who had slowed now stopped. He was still outside. He took a single step towards the window, his hands lifted to his head, then he spun away as if he couldn't look anymore. He seemed to be looking over, back towards Lance.

It was time to go. He was struggling to breathe, close to not being able to function at all.

He turned away to walk among the scattered police cars, keeping his head down, the rim of the police hat protecting him from the bright headlights. He lifted the boot of a patrol car that had been untidily abandoned half on the kerb. It gave him another moment where he could glance back towards the house. He drank in one final look at the chaos. It was his finest moment, no doubt about that. He flushed hotter still. Sweat ran into his eye and made him flinch and the boot door squeaked in his clammy hands as he slammed it shut. Exhaust fumes were warm against his legs. The car was ticking over where it had been abandoned.

He slid into the driver's seat. The sound of the engine revving and his front wheels scrabbling for grip only added to the confusion. He glanced over for one last time. He had wanted to see this Harry. He had wanted to be there for that, but it didn't matter . . . He didn't think the night could have been any more perfect.

* * *

Maddie hung by the edge of the junction where they had turned off the main road into the village. She faced in the general direction of Harry's house and could see the wood-land on the opposite side that he had talked about. It ran along a field in which she could make out three horses in the silver light of the moon. They all had their heads bent to the damp grass. They were part of the team, now, an early warn-ing system: they would surely lift their heads to the sound of someone crashing through the woods to make their escape.

She peered back over to where Harry was a distant sil-houette, still standing in the middle of the road. He had done nothing to move out of the light. He was facing her, his outline broad, his hands hanging by his side and, even at this distance, she could tell they were balled into fists. Despite what Harry had told her, this was as far away as she was going to go. She had her radio down so low she had to hold it to her ear for updates.

'*Control, the house is clear. We have one female, not conscious, not breathing. Medics have cut her down and are working on her now. Visible stab wounds to her chest and neck. Confirm SEKAS are en route?*' The man sounded exasperated and exhausted at the same time. Beaten, maybe. It sounded like chasing up the ambulance was more an act of desperation than any real belief that it was going to make any difference. The confirmation was monotone. The operator sounded flat. There was a general feeling of acceptance. They had all been here before.

The Tax Man. The phrase ran through Maddie's mind. She had picked it out of Vince's hurried phone call. It had lingered with her ever since.

Maddie took in Harry's outline. Nothing had changed. She had no idea if he had heard the update. She moved away from the junction, staying in the shadows of the woodland as she watched for anyone approaching.

She looked back over to the field. She could see two of the horses — and they had their heads up! She held her breath. All her attention focused on the wooden sty on the other side of the road. The footpath that led away from it became invisible under the cover of the tall trees. The next sound wasn't of someone sprinting down a woodland trail, however. It was a diesel engine being revved hard.

As the car burst past her, its brake lights were already illuminated. The tyres sounded like they were struggling for grip and it suddenly lurched left and into the junction she was covering. The POLICE livery was bright and unmissable as it flashed past. Maddie was confused. Were they in pursuit? Could she have missed him?

She ran after the car. It pushed into the road, then braked hard enough for the wheels to lock and skid on the loose surface. It ground to a halt just a few metres into the muddy verge. She made it to the passenger window and slapped on the glass. There was no one in the passenger seat but the driver looked over. His eyes burst wide for a moment like she had given him a start. Maddie locked eyes with a sixty-year-old man with a slim build and short hair wearing a plain, black fleece. He had a police hat on his lap. His face suddenly contorted into a big smile. She had seen him before. She knew where.

The car moved forward. She went for the handle and missed. The car picked up pace. She broke into a run. She looked up to where Harry was standing out in the road, the headlights from the patrol car lighting him up.

'*Harry! It's him!*' Maddie shrieked. The car revved harder, surging forward. She had caught up enough to grab the handle on the passenger side. It dragged her forward and she stumbled on the loose stones and crashed to the ground. Pain jolted in her knee.

She lifted her head. The car surged on, the passenger door still hanging open. There were no signs of any braking and then it hit something solid — hard. The whole clearing seemed to resonate with the sound. She could feel the ground shake under her palms. The rear of the car rocked up in front of her and the orange street light above it twitched backwards, flickered, then spluttered out.

Maddie scrambled to her feet to sprint forward, stumbling on the surface. She heard a door open. The car had bucked left from the impact. The passenger door had fallen back shut. She tore it open.

'*Harry?*' She could see right through the empty car. '*Harry!*' she screamed again. She heard what seemed like grunts from the other side. She sprinted around the front of the car to be blinded momentarily by the one working headlight.

She could see a bundle of something dark. There was movement. She could make out Harry. He was kneeling, his right arm pumping up and down. She moved closer. She heard a series of rhythmical thuds. Now she was closer, she could see a man lying under the open door as if he had been dragged out, one leg still up and bent into the footwell. The car's weak interior light was enough to light up his face. Blood was gushing from his head. The man's arms lay limp by his side offering no resistance. Harry's huge fists were still coming down on what was left.

'*Harry!*' Maddie screamed again. She threw herself forward onto Harry. His arm came up to throw another punch. She grabbed it and tried to wrap herself round it. The sharp point of his elbow caught her hard in the face.

'Harry! *Stop!*' His fist dropped for another blow, she tried to catch it on the way back up. She got a hold of it. It was solid like steel. He shrugged her off — it seemed effortless. He threw another blow downwards.

'Harry! He's dead!' she screamed, trying to break through his fog. He seemed to hesitate. When he raised his fist again, he didn't shrug off her attempts to hold him.

'Please, Harry! That's enough. We got him!'

Harry's arm stayed tense, his focus still downwards. Maddie chanced a look, too. The man's cheek looked crushed on one side, his jaw protruding at an obtuse angle, his lower teeth permanently on show. His hair and chest were slick with blood.

Maddie planted her feet. She still had her arms around Harry's. She moved so she was in a position where she could hook him under the shoulder. She pulled him up. He came with her, his feet stumbling to hold his own weight, his head hanging forward. She stepped backwards, away from the man on the floor. Harry stepped with her. She pressed the red emergency button on top of her radio and it vibrated in her hand.

She shouted into it. 'This is Alpha One! We are in a road off Wigmore Lane. Approximately two hundred metres from the target address. Patrols can find us if they take the turning opposite the railway bridge. We have one in custody. . . We will need a medic!'

CHAPTER 32

Five days later

Lance Askew leaned back, crossed his arms across his bony chest and held his bottom lip between his teeth. His eyes were half closed. He looked every bit like an elderly gentlemen in contemplation, as if he had just been asked a question on the political state of the nation by a friend over a pint. He let go of his lip as a smile broke free. The only clue to what Lance Askew was, to what he was capable of, came from the empty black eyes that shifted to the camera in the corner of interview room three, Canterbury Police Station.

Maddie wanted to look away. He had walked into the room already looking up, seeking out the cameras so he knew to where he should play. Maddie couldn't say she hadn't been warned. The officer who had led in both interviews had told her it would not make pleasant viewing, that it probably wouldn't be what she was expecting. It wasn't, either.

'I knew I was going to get caught,' Askew said. 'I think I even wanted to be — I just didn't know how. I could never quite work that out, I never really knew what might be the best way.' He took his time to contemplate. 'As it turned out, it all came together naturally! I couldn't believe it, the way it happened. In a stolen police car. And when I pulled around to where I had my own car parked up, he was right there! He's an inspector, right? Someone told me. I thought I'd missed him, but there he was! *The boss.* Your boss, is he? Anyway, he knew what I'd done. The moment I saw him, I could see that. It was beautiful.'

'Beautiful?' The screen was split. The voice came from one of the two detectives who leaned back in their own seats. Her voice had been maddening throughout, monotone to the point of sounding disinterested. Maddie knew that wasn't the case, she knew it was the style of a lot of good detectives. If your voice was the same pitch throughout, it was more difficult for your prisoner to detect when they might have said something you were interested in or to pick out which questions were more important among many.

Maddie had expected to hear disgust in their voices. They had to be utterly appalled — the whole force was. But even after watching a few minutes of footage, it was clear to her that disgust would have delighted their prisoner. He was all about the impact he was making on others.

Askew was badly bruised, enough for it to be clearly visible on both camera angles. Harry's beating had dislocated his jaw, cracked a rib and knocked out a number of his teeth. His nose had been broken so badly that they couldn't set it straight and it was going to have a permanent kink once the swelling went down. Askew had been asked three times at the beginning of the interview if he was fit to answer the questions and twice if he wanted a solicitor present. It had been he who had prompted the interview and had also requested his early transfer from a hospital bed to the custody cell, having waived his rights to legal advice. He couldn't wait to tell his story.

'Beautiful!' he said. His eyes flickered back to the elevated camera. 'His reaction! The way he looked at me! He knew what I was capable of! He knew what I had done. I let him grab me. I aimed for him with the car first, though — that was a natural reaction. If I'd thought it through, I think

I'd have stopped and walked towards him. But, like I said, it just worked out so perfectly. He had all this adrenaline mixing up with the anger. I was looking right into his eyes all the while he was hitting me, and all I could think about was how perfect this all was. How this was the way I wanted it to end.'

'Why his house? His daughter?'

'Ah! A pertinent question. Just recently, I've learned to let fate hold my hand. It seems to be so much more satisfying. I was in a café. It was to be my final observation of your PC Arnold. I was angry about my betrayal, still undecided on how I was going to play it, but all the arrangements were already in place. Then PC Arnold got put down by a bigger man, a more powerful man. I saw PC Arnold, how he reacted — a man of that build and apparent arrogance — and yet he responded like a scolded child. Your inspector Harry controlled the people around that table — every one of them. I knew straight away that he was the one I wanted to see broken. I was so excited, I could barely stand. I followed him. I knew I'd be starting again, but I had time. I wasn't dancing to Mason's tune anymore . . . His betrayal had seen to that. Harry went to his home. He was going to be my target at first. I was going to string him up, to lift him onto his tiptoes. The moment you do that, you take away their strength. They know it, too. You can see it! But then . . .' Askew's eyes clamped shut and his head tilted back.

'Then?' The officer shouldn't have prompted. She should have let Askew speak in his own time, but Maddie would have done the same. He was enjoying himself, savouring the moment, knowing that they were hanging on his every word. She would have wanted to get it all over with, too.

'Then . . . there was a daughter! A dog walk. Picture perfect. No wife, otherwise she'd have been there. Just the two of them. Harry and all he cared about in the world, out for a stroll and with fate leading the way! I knew instantly . . .'

'So that's why you killed Melissa? Because you wanted a reaction from her dad?'

Askew stiffened to sit straight, his smile dropping away. He looked rattled for the first time. '*Reaction?* It's so much more than that. A reaction is a moment in time — an instant. What I do resonates with people for the rest of their lives. Him, his colleagues, you two in here, anyone watching this tape. I have the power and the ability to take lives, to change them forever, or to walk on by. I am fate.'

'Fate?'

'Fate. I select their course. I choose who lives and who dies.'

'Who lives?' the detective prompted.

'Take the kids. I told the mother in the café that her child was dead, but I chose that he lived. There wasn't the need. I knew she would believe me. The second time, I didn't have the time. But I planned it with the third, with PC Arnold, his little nephew — if fate had allowed! Can you imagine? Coming home to that? To your brother and your child? Askew sucked in a lungful of air and it pulled his shoulders straight. His face twisted into a smile. 'Do you have children, detective?' He leaned in again, desperate to see the reaction. Maddie didn't know whether she believed him anymore. She didn't know what to believe. He would say anything to get a reaction. This was his last chance, perhaps.

'So you choose who you kill? How?' The lead detective was still monotone. Maddie knew her. She was a mother of two, one still in nappies. She was doing an incredible job of avoiding his traps.

'You play it down,' Askew said. 'You don't do it justice with your words. Don't underestimate what I do. Alexander Mason underestimated me. Mikey underestimated me.'

'And you killed Mikey.'

'I did. I was his fate. Betrayal must be met. But not his boy.'

'His boy?'

'Sidekick, then — apprentice. Some boy terrified of his own shadow. I allowed him to live.'

'And this was the same *apprentice* who conveyed a message to PC Arnold?'

'The same.'

'What happened to him?'

'This is about me.' Askew gestured with his hand towards the camera. 'All of this is for me . . . I'll only talk about me. All you need to know about *him* is that he was nothing until he met me. Now he's something.'

'And Mason? He was a big part of that.'

Lance snarled this time. 'I told you, I knew I was going to get caught — or killed. I couldn't help myself. I stayed longer after . . . Stealing police hats, cars! My preparation, too . . . I was leaving more things to chance — rushing. I haven't done that in the twenty years since I started. I was going to square up with Mason. That was where I was going. I made sure you knew about him in case I didn't make it. I actually envisaged it would be your firearms team who would be the ones to find me. I saw the way they stormed the Chicken Sheds . . . They were desperate to shoot someone! That could have been fitting.'

'What do you mean by *since you got started?*' The monotone voice cut back in. Maddie watched the two detectives as the question was asked. The lead detective had been sitting back with her legs crossed. She shuffled now to plant both her feet. This was a key question. It was a key answer.

'I am fate.'

'Which means?'

'Killing people, detective. Since I started *killing people*. I know how you like to have things right, how you need me to say it!' He lifted his grin to the camera again. 'You would never have caught me. Not if I had continued like I was. Like I told you . . . I wanted to get caught.'

'And why is that?'

'Why? What do you mean, "Why?"'

'Why would you want to be caught? I've been a police officer a long time. It's not often you find someone who wants to get caught.'

'I'm sixty-four years old. My health is not what it once was. My weight loss has been sudden. Sometimes I struggle with my breathing, like I can't catch my breath, and I'll have chest pains with it, too. I used to cut a far more impressive figure than this, let me tell you that. My life is about blending in, being invisible. I can hardly just pop along to a GP, and even if I could, what then? Hospitalisation? Treatment? It's coming for me. I can feel it. You can't retire from hiding. Now the state will provide three square meals a day, Sky TV and all the hospital treatment I could ever need. That's right, isn't it? And all I had to do was kill your boss's daughter!' Askew leaned forward onto his bony elbows to study the two officers seated in front of him. He was still trying for a reaction. Even now. Maddie couldn't see one, not from the angles the camera allowed, but she didn't have to be so restrained. She snatched the headphones out of the socket and clicked to close it down. She had seen enough.

She swigged at her full cup of tea and balked that it was cold. She checked her watch and sighed. She couldn't put it off anymore. It was time to go.

* * *

It was always a strange feeling walking through a prison, but today was stranger still. All police officers will visit a prison at some point as part of their job. Maddie had been less often than most, perhaps because a large proportion of her career had been undercover. She remembered being caught out the first time she visited after changing to a detective role. She had expected segregation from the other prisoners, to be led in via the back, into a room with her prisoner already produced. It wasn't like that at all. Police were led through the front, often after waiting with family visiting one of their own and being made to hold up their police ID to the Perspex window that separated them from the bored looking guards.

Today she had only needed to show some civilian ID. She was the family waiting to visit her own.

The hospital wing was a long walk from the entrance. It felt like they had done enough distance to do two laps of the whole building when they emerged into an area that was obviously reserved for medical purposes. The polished brick walls were the same, as was the two-tone paint, the cast iron industrial radiators and black rubber flooring. But the rooms were different. Her dad was in one of his own, the door wide open. Another waiting room was near to it. Her mother must have seen her approach. Her face was stern and she sniffed before she spoke.

'Maddie . . .'

'Hey, Mum.'

'You made it.'

'I did!' She didn't tell her that she couldn't put it off any longer. Her mum had given her a reprieve. She had come down with a cold that had delayed them by a couple of weeks. She had made a lot of it: told Maddie that, following his cancer treatment, even a common cold could kill her dad. The word *dad* was still the one that made her most uncomfortable in that sentence.

The guard who had walked Maddie through pointed at the room. 'He's in there. You first!'

Maddie stepped in. The doors had been wide open and the only guard in the vicinity was the one who had walked through with her. Maddie's police instincts had her expecting security at a prison to be better.

It was very quickly apparent why it didn't need to be.

She had been desperate not to feel sorry for him, not to feel anything at all. But now she was here, looking down at him. His skin pulled so tightly against his cheeks that the white of the bone was pushing through. Dark circles ringed his eyes and his tongue darted out to try and wet his rasping, dry lips. He was pathetic — nothing like in the memories she was desperately trying to keep at the forefront of her mind. Her mum's heels clicked in behind her. She walked around to stand the other side of him. Maddie looked up to where she was staring over. Her expression had a hint of '*I told you so.*'

'Dad . . .' Maddie said.

A smile flickered across his lips. He wet them again.

'Hey, girl. Glad you could come. I didn't think you would.'

'I didn't know . . . Mum told me.'

'So what? You would have come earlier!' He grinned. It turned into a grimace and then a weak cough.

'Probably not.' Maddie said. 'She said you wanted to see me.'

'Of course I did! My only daughter . . . My firstborn.'

'And part of the reason you're here.' Maddie looked away from him, taking a moment to flash her eyes around the room. There were charts and containers for medication. It seemed far from modern. Overall, the feeling she got was of a field hospital.

'That may be so. I've spent a lot of time in here, always in and out. I reckon I've done my time, my Maddie, but you may not agree. That's okay. I didn't get you here to talk about that. Prison has been hard. It's no place for a man like me. I just wanted you to know that I don't blame you, that I love you as my daughter. I wanted you to know that before I went.' He coughed again. His words seemed to be more strained. Talking was clearly an effort. Maddie hated that he was so pathetic. He licked his lips again, then reached his hand towards hers, his bony fingers feeling for her grip. She took them. The other hand lifted towards her mother who stepped forward to take it, her face beaming down at him.

'Families should be together,' he said. He fixed his eyes on Maddie. Her mother did, too. She knew it was her time to speak, to make her peace, to make his transition easier, perhaps.

Her throat felt tight and she had to cough to start the words off. 'Recently, I feel like all I am doing is losing people from my life. Good people. I don't want to be losing people anymore.' She could feel her throat getting worse, the emotion of recent events leaking out. 'Maybe you caught me at a weak moment . . . but I am glad I came.'

His smile grew wider, her mother bit down on her lip and shook her head like she was going to cry, then she nodded at her husband. Maddie leaned in closer to hold her dad's attention. His grip tightened on her hand. It was cold.

'You're right about prison,' she said. 'It's no place for men like you. But don't worry, 'cause hell is waiting. Fuck you and your idea of family.' She straightened up and jerked her hand away in the same movement. Her mother's smile was dropping away, in slow motion it seemed, as if the words were still registering. 'And fuck you, too, *Mum*. You can't lose something you never had.'

The guard who had walked her through struggled to keep pace on the way out. Maddie left her mother holding her dad's hand and didn't look back. The guard fumbled over the first security door.

'These visits can be hard. They don't always go well, not in the sick bay.' He was trying to break the silence, like he felt awkward. Maddie wasn't feeling it.

'I thought that went very well.' The rest of the walk was completed in silence.

* * *

Maddie was back in the passenger seat, her belt secured and her hands on her lap. She expelled a deep breath before Vince spoke to her.

'All done?' He was gripping the steering wheel. The car had been started the moment he had seen her.

'All done.'

'It go okay?'

'I think so.'

'I take it you got your message across?'

'Oh, yes.'

Vince grinned. 'That's my girl!'

Maddie stared out of the window as they moved off. She watched the grey of Brixton's prison walls blur into the grey of the terraced houses that pushed right up against it. She sighed. Vince seized on it.

'No regrets, Mads. We said that on the way up.'

'I don't regret what I did. I don't regret anything about him. Maybe just that it came to that. A normal family isn't too much to ask for, is it?'

'No such thing, is there? Every family has its issues.'

Maddie didn't reply. She'd run out of energy.

'You still want to do this now?' Vince said.

'Yes.'

'Okay, then.'

Silence returned. They had a ninety-minute drive, maybe more if the traffic coming away from South London was snarled up. She glanced over at Vince. His focus was fixed ahead and his lips made a faint popping sound in time with the music that was low on the radio. She reflected that they had spent the whole of the journey on the way up talking about her.

'How have you been, Vince?' she said.

'I've been good!' He burst into a grin. His head dipped to the music, where a beat kicked in. His movements became more pronounced. The comparison with the slobbery Labrador flashed back through Maddie's mind. The boss had been spot on with that one.

'Did you get your update, yet? Mason and the rest?'

'Some.' The smile dropped away. 'I heard they nicked that Mason fella. A lot of people round him got hit, too. They all got the frighteners. A few have squealed him up for taking out the men who pulled the trigger on the skipper.'

'That's about what I heard, too. Seems they've been building intel around this group for a while and they just needed that spark to move from intel gathering to positive action.'

'I never got that. We're the police. We know someone's up to something and we just sit back and watch.'

'We do. I used to be part of the intel gathering, don't forget. I know that forces monitor these groups. Sometimes for years. They only act when they step out of line.'

'Criminality isn't out of line?'

'No. Not when you're an OCG, it seems. As long as your drug dealing, trafficking and violence is only towards each other, it's only affecting the underbelly and trading is only on the black market. We had a group in the North we were following. There was a vicious assault on a lorry driver — mistaken identity. He had nothing to do with the drugs that had gone missing — it wasn't even the right lorry. There was a big uproar about a family man beaten half to death while he slept in his cab and suddenly we were in the positive action phase. Twelve arrests overnight, nearly forty search warrants by the end of that month and all the undercover assets and sources were pulled in the shortest time.'

'All above me, Mads. Being a copper for me is simple. You find someone doing something wrong and you nick 'em for it.'

Maddie could hardly argue with that. This wasn't the time, anyway. 'How do you feel about it all? This Mason fella, the rival gang he shot up who were responsible for Tim?'

'Good. I mean I would have liked to have got hold of them myself, but we're all about handing them over to the courts, to the justice system. They'd have ended up in a hotel like the one you just left.'

'Three square meals a day, Sky TV and all the health treatment they could ever need.'

Vince glanced over. 'Sky TV?'

'Doesn't matter. Just something someone said. Maybe the Alexander Masons of this world have got it right.'

'Someone killed his son. If it were me, my first reaction would probably be the same.'

'My dad in there . . . The setup around him . . . His own room . . . People helping him die with dignity. He doesn't deserve any of it. Not for what he's done, for who he is. But I didn't see him. When I walked into that room and I saw his clean bed, the tray on the table next to him with a yoghurt sat on it and jug of water, I saw Lance Askew. The people he left for us to find — the boss's daughter — there was no dignity there, was there?'

'No.'

'Justice, the idea of it, what it is . . . it was all so simple before I actually took this job and became part of it!'

There was a period of silence, as if both were taking a moment to think. Vince spoke first. 'I hear he's been talkative — this Askew. How many murders has he committed?'

'He has been. He figures that prison is the best place for his retirement so he might as well make sure he stays there. And you know what? He's probably right. Imagine a world where that's the truth.'

'We can't think about that. We just have to think about the people we save by getting him off the street.'

'I suppose we do. I can't. Not right now.'

'So how many?'

'Oh, no idea. We've only interviewed him for our jobs. There are forces all around the country lining up to talk to him. Seems he's in the mood to make his admissions, though. A twenty-year career, he said.'

'Twenty and out. That can only be a good thing.'

'A *good* thing?'

'You don't think so?'

'I just wish he wasn't enjoying himself quite so much. I'm struggling to see any good. It's like he's showing off. He wants everyone to know he's been getting away with it all this time, that he still could be if he hadn't got sloppy on purpose.'

'He would say that!'

'He might be right, Vince. We were nowhere near him. If the boss had gone chasing him at his house, we still might not be. He was so brazen. He just used the chaos, took advantage of the fact that we're predictable, that we come running when we're called and we don't always take the time to look around on the way in.'

'We learn lessons, then. That's what matters.'

'It does make you think differently.' Maddie was back to staring out of the window. They were picking up speed on a slip road to join the motorway. 'I know the boss is.'

'You think he's serious? I heard he chucked his badge in.'

'He did. You can't blame him for struggling to see a way back to work after this. I don't know how he'd come back at all.'

Vince seemed to have an instant reply that he swallowed.

Maddie leaned back into the headrest. She let her eyes fall shut. She felt drained, physically and mentally.

'I've got no thoughts of going back. Life on the outside is just . . . easier.' Vince said.

The silence returned. Maddie lifted her head away from the headrest as Vince's words struck home. The exhaustion that had suddenly pushed her eyes closed was just as sudden to leave. She didn't know what to say. '*What about me?*' and '*What am I supposed to do now?*' came to mind, but she realised how selfish that would sound. This wasn't the time. 'I do get the easier bit,' she said.

'You thinking about it, too? Maybe we could start a vigilante group? You, me and the boss. Like the A Team — only less jewellery!'

'Maybe, Vince.' Maddie's mind was busy again. She had hardly been able to silence it since that night. 'That evil bastard was sitting right next to us in that café. He was close enough to know exactly what we were talking about. Then he followed Harry home, watched him pick up his daughter and decided she needed to die — and all for his pleasure. So he could prove his own worth to himself. People like that shouldn't even exist. The two murders were over in Canterbury, two families ripped apart. I never considered that he could move to another town. We weren't just blinkered when we were first called to those scenes . . . The whole investigation was blinkered. Maybe if we'd done something different, if *I'd* done something different . . .'

'What, though? Sometimes you've just got to accept that an arsehole is an arsehole. And he holds all the cards.

The plans are his. We're always gonna be a step behind. He ended up with Harry mashing him into some dirt track — he hardly got away with it. You will learn from it because you're smart. And next time, their face will be part of a dirt track even quicker.'

'Next time?' Maddie couldn't help but laugh — with incredulity rather than humour. 'I'm not sure I've got the energy for a next time, either. Most jobs when you come up short, you tell yourself to learn from it and move on. This one, you come up short and the boss's life gets turned upside down. His youngest daughter . . . Gone.'

'You can't be beating yourself up, Mads. This ain't on you. Wasn't so long ago, you were telling me the same thing when we lost the skipper. Took me a while, but you were right about that.'

'I'm always right. I thought you'd know that by now!'

Vince grinned. 'You were gonna doze. I think I might prefer you when you're asleep, Ives! Get some rest if you can. I'll wake you when we're there.'

Maddie was smiling. The voices in her mind seemed a little quieter. The sun that had done nothing to raise the temperature when she was outside was pleasant now as it came through the window to combine with the heaters. She felt sleepy again. She pushed back into the headrest and closed her eyes.

* * *

Vince ratcheted the handbrake firmly enough for Maddie to wake with a start, as if something terrible was happening in front of them. She sat up and stared forwards, then turned to a grinning Vince.

'You alright, Mads?'

She huffed, then stretched. When she looked out of her window, she could see the village of Coldred. The village green stood out from the grey drizzle. It looked colder out there than it had been in the built-up town and any trace of sunshine was gone. They were facing away from the pond that was its focal point, with the pub on her right side.

'Here already!' She grinned. Vince shook his head then pulled himself out of the car. Maddie hesitated, enough that she was still belted in when the driver's door was shut hard enough for her to feel the car rock. Vince never did anything lightly. She watched as he walked round the front of the car to appear beside her door. He was wearing the same battered hat that he had worn to the café and the same fingerless gloves, which he pushed into the pockets of his jacket. He stood by her window, leaning down to mouth something, his breath visible. A light breeze swept it away. Maddie couldn't delay any longer. This was a day for getting things done.

The door of the Carpenter's Arms in Coldred was solid and heavy. It was made of a dark wood that continued as a theme when they stepped in. It was typical of a traditional British countryside pub with the dark wood beams dissecting a low ceiling and white walls. It was dim overall, due to small windows, but was cheered by a fire in a large fireplace of exposed brick. It was early afternoon. A few punters were strewn around, a couple in the corner, a few older gentlemen at the bar on high stools, close enough to talk to each other but seemingly choosing not to, their pints of ale sitting under their chins. Everyone took a moment to look up or over. It felt like a local pub where everyone knew everyone else. There might have been some suspicion behind one or two of the glances directed at Maddie and her large-built companion. They weren't villagers. They certainly weren't locals.

The woman behind the bar looked over and gestured to a solitary figure, the only one who hadn't reacted to their entrance. He was sitting over by the fire, a long leather sofa pulled around to face right into it, his back to them. Maddie made eye contact with Vince and they both walked over together.

'I told you to stay away.' Harry's growl was low, barely audible over the gentle crackle and hiss of the bright flames.

Movement dragged Maddie's attention right where she watched a large tractor sweep past. The road was at its closest point to the pub here, enough for the tractor to rattle the panes and send vibrations through the floor. They would have passed the same window just a few moments earlier.

'So that's how you knew we were here!' she said.

'I told you to stay away.' Harry said again, his tone a little darker.

Vince moved round to sit on the closest chair on Harry's left. Maddie took his lead to sit to his right on the same leather sofa. It was firmer than it looked — uncomfortable almost, but this was likely because she was perched on the edge with her back tensed.

'I know you did,' she said. 'But we're family. The only one I've got left, anyway.' She was suddenly aware of what she had said. 'I mean . . . I didn't mean—'

'Forget it,' Harry said. He was still facing forward. His whole body looked stiff. His waxed jacket hung over the seat next to her, dripping steadily onto the carpet and his trousers were water-stained below the knees. His cheek glistened in the firelight, a single track where tears had been left to run. It looked every bit as permanent as his existing scars.

Maddie reached out, her left arm reaching around him as best she could. She had to shuffle to get closer. She met no resistance and felt encouraged to reach further. His head turned towards her, just slightly but enough. She held him tighter, noting how cold he felt.

'Just driving past, were you?' Harry said.

'Something like that.'

'How did you find me?'

'You come here everyday round the same time. You have since . . . your daughter. Faye . . . I spoke to her. She told me, so I called the pub. They said you were drying out by the fire. I reckoned it might take a while!'

'Faye?' Harry said.

'I got her number. Personnel have her listed as your next of kin . . . When we couldn't get hold of you, I mean . . .' Maddie stopped. This was the point where he might explode if he was going to. She had run this through in her mind, expecting him to be angry, telling her she had no right to go through his personnel file or to speak to his daughter. But Maddie was worried about him. They all were. She didn't know if that would be enough to placate him. She needn't have worried.

'This was the last place. Melissa and I . . . We went out for a walk. We ended up here. When they were kids, just little girls . . .' Harry took a moment. She felt his shoulders rise as he took in a deep breath. 'This was our bike ride. All of us. Here and back with a pub lunch. Saturday, we walked it. We talked here, Mel in front of the fire with the dog . . . They only lit it for her. I swear that girl was cold-blooded! She was doing better, so much better. And now . . .'

'Now?' Maddie prompted.

'It feels like there's nothing left. It's all gone.' He was back staring at the flames. The deep breath he took, his words, none of it seemed to be tinged with any emotion. He just seemed empty.

'Talking of the dog . . . Where is Jock? I was hoping to say hello.'

Harry's voice came back as a sigh. 'He's at home. He stinks when he's wet. I didn't want to push my luck with this lot in here. As it is I've been sitting here for an hour with just a pint of orange.'

'You still have Faye. You know that, right?'

'She blames me. For bringing this to our door.'

'That isn't fair.'

'I don't understand fair, not anymore.'

'I bet that isn't what she thinks, either.'

Harry shrugged as if dismissing it. 'She's devastated.'

'Of course she is. I just want you to be okay. Recently, I've been thinking that this isn't a world for good people. I think we're outnumbered. You have to look after the good ones, keep them close. What else is there?'

'Yeah, it's just us and them!' Vince's big, clumsy arm suddenly lunged across, grabbing Harry in his own version of a hug. Harry's expression darkened for a moment. Then there was the flicker of a grin.

'For God's sake, Maddie, did you have to bring the big, dumb Labrador with you?'

Maddie laughed. 'Yeah, I can't leave him at home. He isn't house-trained.' She giggled. So did Vince after initially trying to look hurt.

'Anyway,' said Vince, 'I'm gonna get a drink. This is a pub, after all. Boss, you wanna top up that orange juice and lemonade you're nursing, there? Or maybe I can get you something proper?'

'I'm okay, thank you, Vince.'

'Mads?'

'Do they do a coffee? Flat white, if they have it.'

Vince rolled his eyes, 'I doubt it, Mads. Bet they do pitchforks, though. Right up the arse for out-o'-towners who come in asking for *flat whites*.'

'Perfect. Give that a go. Then it's either a drink or some entertainment.'

'Fine. I might go feed the ducks first, though. I've got some biscuits in my pocket. Them ducks looked cold out there, all huddled together. I might be able to brighten their day at least.'

Maddie watched him leave. He veered away from the bar and disappeared through the door. He had said on the way up that he would find an excuse to leave her alone with the boss, said it wasn't his forte: 'All that soft-skill shit.' He'd warned that he was just going to hug the old man and then make his exit. He had been true to his word.

'He's more sensitive than he would have us believe, you know.' Maddie said.

'Sensitive? Maybe. Subtle? Definitely not. One of the good ones, though. You were right about him.' Harry still faced towards the fire. He had leaned back a little but seemed a long way from relaxed. 'What's this about you running out of family?'

'Oh, it hardly matters. Not here and now.'

'Your dad?' Harry said.

'My dad, yeah.'

'Has he passed?'

'No. I went to see him this morning. Shouldn't be long now. Not long enough, anyway. That's the last time I'll see him. I think I managed to lose my mum at the same time. She had this big idea that we should all get together at his end, to pretend he was anything other than a piece of shit so he could rest in peace. I couldn't give him that. He doesn't deserve it. She won't ever forgive me, though. Not now.'

'I see.'

'And Adam, too. He was back on the scene.' Maddie was thinking out loud more than anything. This was hardly the place to bring that up.

'Yarwood? The Manchester guy with the links to bad people?'

'Yeah. But it doesn't matter. It's sorted.'

'Sorted? You liked that one, right?'

'Not enough, it would appear. He was a different bloke. Needy . . . scared . . . I think he came down here for me to make everything alright. And I didn't.'

'You don't seem too upset about it. I guess that tells you what you need to know.'

'I'm not. The job got in the way, but I let it. I need to find something that I love more than this job. I guess I realised that he isn't it. I thought I would feel bad about that, but I don't.'

The silence returned. Harry finally huffed, 'You came here to discuss something. I assume it's something about where we go from here, is it?'

'Go?'

'This family, as you call it . . . Us two and the family dog out there. I might not have the answer you want, I'm afraid. Come on then, let's get this over.'

'Are you coming back?'

'I don't think I am, Maddie.'

'Okay, well I'm not going to say it again. The thing about giving it time.'

'I appreciate that. The chief inspector already has. Just after he told me that I've been referred to the Independent Police Complaints Commission.'

'He said that?'

'Excessive force. He doesn't think it'll go anywhere.'

'I see.'

'Your face . . . Was that me?' Harry looked at her with the first sign of any emotion. Maddie lifted her hand. The swelling on her cheek had gone down just about all the way, but the discolouration was still there. It was at the point where she had a green and black smudge around one eye but no pain, so she would forget why people were reacting to her.

'It was my fault, to be fair. I shouldn't have put my face in the way of your elbow.'

'I'm sorry. For hurting you. It could have been a lot worse for me. You stopped me. Thank you for that.'

'Thank you? Really?'

'He wanted death. At the end, I could see it. He was revelling in me. That makes sense with what we know about him now, doesn't it? With what he is? I think being beaten to death as a reaction to what he had done was just what he wanted. He was smiling, Maddie. I couldn't knock that off his face.'

'This isn't about him. He's off the street.'

'He is. He can rot in a cell. I have to believe that he's not smiling anymore.'

'He . . .' Maddie's mind flashed with his interview, with his reaction to the officers, his explanation of prison and his glee at the end. 'You're right . . . He can't hurt anyone. Not anymore. That's the main thing. We have no idea how many people he's killed in his lifetime. He does seem determined to tell us, though. I think it'll all come out.'

'Before this job, I wouldn't have believed that people like that existed,' Harry said.

'I know. Me neither. You know what this all means, right?'

Harry turned. The flames from the fire burned in his eyes. 'Means?'

'This family we got here . . . Us two and the Labrador — and all the others back at the nick . . . We can't stop. This man was all about the impact he can have. If his final act was enough to make us all walk away, well . . . he wins, Harry.'

Harry turned back to the fire. A log shifted in the moment of silence. 'Nice try, DS Ives. You got anything else?'

'Dammit!' Maddie clicked her fingers to feign her frustration. 'I have actually. It's the one thing I can't shake. It's what'll have me heading back into work on Monday morning.'

'Last chance then, Maddie. What is it?'

'Michelle Rice. She was talking about her daughter, about life after her dad's murder. She told me that for her daughter to have any hope, good had to win in the end. She said that people can accept that bad things happen, but good always has to win. She's right, Harry.'

'About her daughter?'

'About it all. Bad things do happen — they always will. But me and you . . . The reason we joined is because we believed we could be part of making sure that good wins, that we are the heroes who can do that. You're one of the heroes, Harry!'

The sound of a sneeze at the door dragged both of their attention towards it. Vince was rubbing his nose.

'Ducks do *not* like dog biscuits, and I reckon I might be allergic! To ducks! And with these muscles . . .' Vince pulled a small packet marked '*Dog treats*' from his pocket. 'Or maybe they can read and got offended. Mads, d'you reckon ducks can read?' Vince grinned and took his place back next to Harry to wrap his arm back round the inspector and grab him firmly. 'Do you wanna proper cuddle, boss? It's cold out there.'

Harry turned his attention away from Vince to fix on Maddie. 'Even him? The hero thing?'

'Yup.' Maddie giggled. 'Even him.'

THE END

Please join our mailing list for free Kindle crime thriller, detective, mystery, and romance books and new releases, as well as news on Charlie's next crime thriller!

www.joffebooks.com/contact

FROM CHARLIE GALLAGHER

Sign up at www.writercharliegallagher.com to be the first to find out about future releases and special offers.

And if you get a chance, please spend a few moments to leave your review on Amazon.

I'd also love to hear from you on social media:
Twitter — @Gloriouscharlie
Facebook — www.facebook.com/writercharliegallagher

Thanks so much for reading, Charlie.

Printed in Great Britain
by Amazon